Railsong

BY THE SAME AUTHOR

Pundits from Pakistan: On Tour with India
The Sly Company of People Who Care

Railsong

RAHUL BHATTACHARYA

BLOOMSBURY PUBLISHING
NEW YORK · LONDON · OXFORD · NEW DELHI · SYDNEY

BLOOMSBURY PUBLISHING
Bloomsbury Publishing Inc.
1359 Broadway, New York, NY 10018, USA
50 Bedford Square, London, WC1B 3DP, UK
Bloomsbury Publishing Ireland Limited
29 Earlsfort Terrace, Dublin 2, D02 AY28, Ireland

BLOOMSBURY, BLOOMSBURY PUBLISHING, and the Diana logo
are trademarks of Bloomsbury Publishing Plc

First published in 2026 in Great Britain
Published in the United States 2026

Copyright © Rahul Bhattacharya, 2026

Every reasonable effort has been made to trace copyright holders of material reproduced
in this book, but if any have been inadvertently overlooked the publishers would be glad
to hear from them. For legal purposes, the Acknowledgements on p. 403 constitute an
extension of this copyright page.

All rights reserved. No part of this publication may be: i) reproduced or transmitted in
any form, electronic or mechanical, including photocopying, recording, or by means of
any information storage or retrieval system without prior permission in writing from
the publishers; or ii) used or reproduced in any way for the training, development, or
operation of artificial intelligence (AI) technologies, including generative AI technologies.
The rights holders expressly reserve this publication from the text and data mining
exception as per Article 4(3) of the Digital Single Market Directive (EU) 2019/790.

ISBN: HB: 978-1-63973-622-5; EBOOK: 978-1-63973-623-2

Library of Congress Cataloging-in-Publication Data is available

2 4 6 8 10 9 7 5 3 1

Typeset by Integra Software Services Pvt. Ltd.
Printed in the United States by Lakeside Book Company

To find out more about our authors and books visit www.bloomsbury.com
and sign up for our newsletters

Bloomsbury books may be purchased for business or promotional use. For information
on bulk purchases please contact Macmillan Corporate and Premium Sales Department at
specialmarkets@macmillan.com.

For product safety–related questions contact productsafety@bloomsbury.com

P and B

May troubled wanderers who have lost their way
Meet with fellow travellers,
And without any fear of thieves and tigers,
May their going be easy without any fatigue.

                                                Shantideva

Contents

I: THESE GRIEVANCES ARE LEGITIMATE

1. Arrival 3
2. Dayin 8
3. Notun Dida 16
4. Aakaal 26
5. Mistake 34
6. Jigyasa 45
7. Ants 53
8. The struggle 63
9. One thousand women 75
10. The hamlet of the Asurs 88
11. Departure 96

II: SMART GIRLS REQUIRED

1. Kings & Queens 111
2. The Prasads 115
3. Digital time 121
4. Dhrubo comes to town 134
5. Shameless 143
6. Palti kar dene ka 154
7. Cosmetics 164
8. In the gully 170
9. Letters 174

| 10 | No objections are certified 187 |
| 11 | The wheels will turn 196 |

III: VACANCIES ARISE

1	In the P branch 207
2	Do you think I was doing nothing? 219
3	Impostrous day 223
4	The waiting 234
5	Booked speed 244
6	A short vacation 250
7	By the haemoglobin of the atmospheric pressure 260
8	Jackals 271
9	The Chitalias 281
10	A very important matter 288
11	The perfect day of marriage 296

IV: WELFARE INSPECTION

1	Beat 301
2	Eyes and ears 310
3	Wives 320
4	Missing person 346
5	Kamalpur 355
6	Census 373
7	Incompetence 382
8	Into the rain 387
9	Chitol's census 395

Acknowledgements 404

I

These Grievances Are Legitimate

I

Arrival

'I want to count people,' said Charu to her father.

'Your brother has started with buffaloes.'

'Let him count buffaloes,' she responded.

'All right,' he conceded. 'Do it from the window.'

'The door is bigger than the window,' she argued with a three-year-old's determination.

'Fine. Concentrate, don't miss any.'

She gripped his fingers tight and swayed by the train door, concentrating. He felt clever, even wise, for deflecting the coin crusade. It showed on his face as he waited for the bridge over the River Bhombal, and receded as he reacquainted himself with his worry: what if it got dark? Darkness, on top of the short halt, would make it hard to extricate the trunks and suitcases and all six family members – seven if you were to include the clothes horse in the brake van.

But everything went well for the Chitols. The infant slept at the breast in milky stupefaction; the children ran up competitive tallies and forgot to campaign for yet more new paise to fling into the water when they crossed the bridge – which arrived while it was still light, and so did their halt, where all the luggage and family members, including the clothes horse, successfully alighted.

Near-blemishless limewash coated the bricks at the railway station. Long fans hung off the iron beams, modern-sculptural in their repose. From the stationmaster's cabin protruded a sleek two-faced clock, bearing modern sans serif numbers, and the cabins too were marked in brisk lettering, of such gloss the paint still appeared wet. As before, they gave Chitol the feeling that here was potential, promise in the future.

Now too the modern feeling did not last, there being hardly any sign of modern life once they left the station. One-horse and two-horse carriages pucked and pocked on barely paved roads. Few electric lights came on to greet the evening. But it was invigorating, calling to mind the title of deceased eminence William 'Hilly Billy' Tomkin's booklet, which Chitol had taken care to peruse: *Observations, Records and Witterings from a Salubrious Railway Transhipment Point*. The mild altitude was perceptible; the air had a fine, calibrated nip. The beginning of spring was in the mauve and orange flowers where none were a week ago. Here and there great sal trees rose into the sky, and here and there, sure as fall and spring go hand in hand, their large yellowing leaves wavered towards the earth. A foresty fragrance accompanied the Chitols as they passed from the town into the township, under the curved iron banner that stated, incontrovertibly, 'Bhombalpur Railway Workshop, estd 1960'.

No sooner did they arrive than they were counted. It was February of a year ending in 1 and the decennial census was under way – the ninth general census, the second of independent India. This particular enumeration, the first of her life, Charu would retain no memory of. But she, too, was counted. Afterwards, the figures found her to be one of approximately 439 million in the country.

Of these fewer than ten thousand souls lived inside the nascent railway township of Bhombalpur, and no larger a number in the town outside. Chitol did not mind the absence of clamour. Mughalsarai had been busy enough for him. All he wanted, frankly, was to live in a cottage with its own garden, where he could drink tea, read and write among his family after a sincere day's work.

In Bhombalpur he got his cottage, of sorts. In the ascending township nomenclature theirs were C-type quarters. These comprised a small front and back yard, a little front and back veranda, three rooms and a kitchen. The quarters were of exposed brick painted a dull mustard yellow, theirs the last on the lane, their lane the last in the ward, facing on to the wild grass and bamboo-fenced backyards of the lane in front. The quarters formed half a bungalow; identical quarters the other. The Chitols quickly and crowdedly occupied their half, turning all rooms into some form of bedroom.

Their life in the township acquired the rhythm by which time moves along without being paid special attention. In the small front garden, where he set up two cane chairs, a cane table and a cane stool, Chitol spent his evenings amid growing plants and children. The backyard was wet, containing a bathroom, a separate Indian-style lavatory connected to a septic tank outside, an open cement tank to catch the water supplied in the mornings and evenings and a washing area on to which the kitchen activities spilled; there were no taps indoors.

Nistarini Debi controlled the back of the house. Although she had long surrendered to the requirements of widowhood, relinquished coloured saris and jewellery and meat, her zeal for daily living had barely diminished. She rose before dawn for a cold bath, collected whatever was blooming for the deities, and oversaw kitchen and religion in the home of her only living son, who had unaccountably married a woman outside community, caste and colour.

Towards the end of their second winter in the township, she, the wife, fell into a persistent fever.

At first it was thought to have something to do with the *jolo hawa* or wet breeze. But the fever stayed, intensified, brought headaches and bouts of shivering. A change in the weather, said the doctor at the health centre (a hospital was only yet a sanctioned project). Sudden drop in mercury, he pronounced with doctorly dispassion, may be a viral fever; she will be fine. She remained unresponsive to medicine, however, to bedrest, to Nistarini Debi's potions and prayers, to her husband's worries and compresses, to her own reassurances that it was mere exhaustion playing out. Then she started to develop grotesque symptoms. Her hands and feet bloated up oedemically; she suffered brief convulsions. There rose a ring of fever around her that those who came close felt on their skin, until one morning the children were no longer allowed into the room.

Charu, now five years old, prised apart the wooden windows to look inside. Her fingers sweated on the vertical iron bars, her round eyes marbled with tears.

All day she had noted the fretting around the word 'ambulance'. When at sunset it appeared, its siren was silent and the lights did not blink. Her father, his friend Pal, and the coughing, injection-poking doctor helped her mother into it. Before leaving, she pressed each of the children's hands and said with a tired smile, I'm coming back.

The words encouraged Charu. Her father was taking her mother to a big hospital, she understood. She watched the ambulance draw away, the neighbours spectating, her grandmother by the gate, the two boys standing by her. The older one, Dhrubo, now broke into a run behind the automobile. Their father sent him back. He returned to bang his head against a wall, and their grandmother hobbled towards him with the words, '*Na, na*, that is not to be done,' and he kept trying to break through her grasp and reach the wall with his head.

Charu rested her hand on her younger brother Anando, certain that although Dhrubo was the older he was not the wiser, at least not wiser than she. She led the boy away into the house.

From underneath an almirah she pulled out a pair of wooden dice, shook them about in a tumbler and released them over and over. Anando gurgled victoriously each time the dice rumbled out of captivity. They were foolish, all of them, she thought. Her mother had gone to a big hospital, where they know what is wrong and make it all right; a hospital, where people went in order *not* to die and fly to Thakur. Only those who did not go to hospital, *they* died and flied to Thakur. On closer examination, she could not tell if Anando was enjoying the game as much as usual. She leaned across to kiss him, lanced his madman hair with her bobby pin and recited him a recently learned verse. *Amader choto nodi, chole bake bake*. Our little river, curves this way and that …

But a bend in the river felt very far. It was not summer as in the poem. With neither parent around, and the skies opening weakly for yet another spatter of cold rain, an unbearable tension fell upon the house. Over the next two days, the messenger brought telegrams that were read aloud to their grandmother, being in English, by Dhrubo; the following evening, just as one telegram intimated, the slightly younger of their father's older sisters arrived with her husband.

Because Kolkata Pishi added immeasurably to the feeling of crisis, Charu began to resent her presence. In any case, she had noticed that Pishi could subdue her mother, sometimes into total silence, and in the past she had embarrassed both women by asking about it. For she knew that her mother was not quiet, she had her own way of making fun. Somehow her mother's silence – her absence – seemed connected to this arrival. Kolkata Pishi herself was not in usual form, not mock-scolding the boys at high volume, nor broadcasting her woes garrulously.

Charu felt a desperate need for her mother, in this fraught house with its prayer and dim lighting and cold air of catastrophe. She wanted her mother to tell Anando and Dhrubo what to do with themselves, and sing to her, just make her feel good. She felt indignant at the state of affairs that obtained, and went to bed in a blaze of confusion and tears, wishing Ma would come back and explain to everyone what a hospital was.

Instead, more relatives came the day after next, and more the day after.

When they were gone all that remained was the amazing absence of her mother.

2
Dayin

Nothing of their everyday was recognisable to Charu in the aftermath. Her mother had died and flied to heaven, this much she understood. But what about everybody else? When she went to hospital to become all right, they acted as if she had died to heaven and would *not* come back home. Now she had died and they behaved like she *would* come back. Her little brother had been told by so many people that Ma had gone to Thakur that he believed they too would visit heaven in an ambulance and return with her. But Charu knew her mother had been set on fire. She knew very well that when a thing is burned it is burned: it became a black powder and not even the magician who performed at the Institute gala could make it proper again.

Some days Dhrubo banged his head against the wall, as though their mother would come and give him her attention. That certainly was the case the day when the boys who walked together to school enquired whether she had become a witch.

'She has, hasn't she?'

'Lives in the empty quarters next door, we know.'

Those quarters were indeed empty, for it was a period in township development when housing was in excess of posts filled.

'Is it true, *motu*?'

'Ha ha. Isn't it, fatty?'

Dhrubo chubbied along vulnerably. They pushed his head up and he reacted with a violent swipe of the hand accompanied by a breathless sniffle.

'*Dayin! Dayin!*' the boys chanted in triumph.

'*Dayin! Dayin!* Ahh ha ha, *dayin!*'

Tushtu, the meekest, frailest of the chanters, trailing at the back, stopped to turn towards Charu with a sly grin. She pushed him. Dhrubo whirled around to look at her as if to say, 'What did you do that for?' The chants tapered off.

But Dhrubo knew they would come back with twice the energy and their reputation as children of a witch would only multiply.

Charu cried quietly, less for being taunted than the force of what she had done.

'Your mother is not a witch,' her friend Ranu consoled her. 'She has only died.'

'She has not,' replied Charu, not sure why.

She resumed walking with Ranu. Afterwards, she feared she would have dreams.

Anando had dreams. He was said to occasionally wake up screaming. But it was hard to tell with Anando nowadays. He was under the control of Thakuma and her perpetually cocked ear, and 'Why are you asking him that?' and 'Why are you telling him that?'

Instead she asked Dhrubo the next day.

'Do you have dreams?'

He still seemed annoyed with her.

'Everyone has dreams,' he told her, as if she was some kind of idiot.

'Does Ma come in them?'

Dhrubo did not answer the question. He pawed the mud near the chicken-wire gate to the house, as he often did for reasons best known to himself.

'When we give food to the crows,' he said, 'they take it to Ma in heaven.'

He leaned on the gate, continuing to paw the mud, concentrating on his footwork.

There were still seasons, birds and bees, and days and weeks in all their wretched assuredness. Roses took in the flower beds of the administrative gardens, their petals fell, gave up colour, dissolved into the eternity of cycles. Chitol brittled down, he cracked up, joined himself together again and again. In generations gone, he reminded himself, when every other child or mother died at birth, when the bloodline of every other family was shaped by tuberculosis, pox and plague, flood or drought, they carried on with strength and dignity.

Yet when he awoke before the first siren went off at five o'clock, he wished he could crumple up. He would look at Anando next to him, put his hand on the boy's forehead trying to divine whether he had had dreams. His own dreams he could not talk about, dreams that were hellish self-interrogations. Could you have done anything different? his voices tore away at him. Why didn't you? The last moments were seared into him, the first sight of his children afterwards. He marvelled at their fragility, their resilience, their trustingness. He brought himself to straighten up and face his days.

In the open backyard he applied tooth powder one tooth at a time, massaging the front and the back of each anticlockwise three times with his right index finger. Then he rinsed his mouth explosively three times. He received Shyamlal the milkman at the gate, walked to the ward market to buy vegetables from Hori. In his bath he attempted to feel, really feel, the freshness of the day as he ran the water over his body. If they were not already up, he woke the children by tickling the soles of their feet. In the garden or the front veranda, depending on the season, he had his tea and ruti or panta bhat. Before he left the house he wrapped around his neck, seasonally, a muffler or a thin cotton gamchha hung always on the left corner of the highest bar on the clothes horse. The entire point of routine is that its divisions are small and its aims achievable, defined to be so by the one who sets them. In getting from one thing to the other, merely that much, the chances of success are higher than failure, and in this way we generate the momentum for living.

Before the third siren at seven o'clock Chitol parked his bicycle alongside hundreds of others like it, his identified by a faded yellow piece of his wife's old sari around the handlebars, which doubled as a duster. She had tied it there. These objects of her memory he sought to apprehend with the same stoic acceptance he tried to apply to his predicament in general.

Mornings he spent on the floor of the Light Machine Shop. By designation, Chitol was Chargeman B, the intermediate grade among chargemen, reporting to a foreman, and himself in charge of about a dozen skilled artisans and mistries and half a dozen khalasis. In one set of shops, the Bhombalpur Railway Workshop turned around locomotives and coaches sent in for repair or periodical overhaul, while it aimed to become capable of assembling them; in another, it manufactured a variety of parts used in this railway workshop and others. In the workshop, surrounded by grinding and milling and sawing and drilling and lathe machines, amid sounds that tremored up towards the distant corrugated-iron roofs, in light that glinted off metal and grease and skin, it was almost possible to forget the hole inside him.

At the lunch siren he made for the subsidised canteen, for in his new situation he no longer carried a tiffin – his mother had quite enough to do with the children. After his meal he went into the grounds for a stroll and a cigarette, usually with his friend Pal from the Coppersmith Shop, who kept himself reliably up to date with gossip, riddles and jokes. Thereafter, to freshen up, he took mouri from his metal canister, scattering some of the fennel seeds for the birds and squirrels to experiment with.

Unless required on the floor, the afternoon he stayed in the cabin he shared with two others. Sitting there at his desk, his tumbler full of water again, covered by light lace, Chitol often mulled over the contradiction in his circumstances. In the older times of greater casual suffering there had always been a way. When the living was joint, the place of a mother could be taken by the house at large. Out in this railway township, where men were units producing units, families were units occupying units, he had nothing to fall back on.

There had been good reasons for coming here, he frequently reiterated to himself. The new works needed men; he considered it his national duty. With the move had come better prospects, and living quarters that were available as per pay-scale entitlement. He had not a permanent home. To the village left behind generations ago there were no ties any more; and now it stood in another country. Each generation and its movements, its itinerancies. His father had worked as a scribe, a schoolteacher, a clerk at a trading firm, a manager at a ferry service, in a swathe across northern-central-eastern India, living out of homes that were never self-owned. To be the first to occupy a house meant something.

Chitol retained the faith that the township was modern, progressive, with the tacit force of nation-building behind it, and likewise that he had taken modern, progressive steps with the tacit force of nation-building behind them. He had long been guided by these principles. A young man at Independence, he had partaken of its euphoria, shed the ancient conventions that had held the people back. He believed the caste system could be undermined by jettisoning caste titles; and rather than curtail his at the neutral but bland Kumar, he had adopted, first as pen name and then as surname, this delicate, delicious, absurd, oily fish, which, he reminded the baffled Chattopadhyays in his clan, was the very first avatar of Vishnu, thus terribly auspicious. He had married for love not society, and contrary to common recommendation did not wish to remarry from compulsion. Their children he had enrolled in school as soon as they became eligible in age, their girl too. No matter that the school was not the Jesuit or the Convent, beyond the means of a Chargeman B, the Bhombalpur Boys' and the Bhombalpur Girls' Railway School (English Medium), in whose hot queues he and his wife had waited by turns to secure first-come-first-serve seats, were superior to the state government schools, and almost on a par with the central government schools in the township, all for an annual fee of one rupee. In short, he had, he was, he would, he will, they will, we will, somehow we will...

Animesh Kumar Chitol, whose spectacles were thick, whose hair was jet black if thinning, his mouth sweet and gentle, eyes heavy-lidded, stooped over his desk in the manner of a calm babu tackling paperwork, did not readily give the impression of a mind consumed by worry, or the literary expression that was its subsequence.

He no longer wrote with any interest in publication. Unlike his children, his own schooling had begun at home, and Bangla remained his language of deepest articulation. What he wrote nowadays were not exactly stories, nor humorous sketches. They were pockets of prose influenced by his readings, high on poetic imagery that (it was his private opinion) surfaced like bubbles and left the juice of their burst on the page.

In one of them, a man is dreaming, and in that dream a man is dreaming of an enraptured conjugal relationship with every woman he has ever been attracted to, each of whom is herself dreaming rapturously of conjugal relationships with every man she is attracted to; the series of dreams erupt one by one like fireloom, and the original man is bedazzled, blinded, wishes to break out of the dream but cannot. In another, a man faces a wall in a hexagonal room. The man, named Bawrgiyo Jaw, is possessed of a tremendous mandible, and the black tips of his spectacles loop over the tops of ears that enclose a full head of black hair. He attempts to fill the wall with the Bangla alphabet, in a way that it includes every vowel and consonant, but no matter what he means to write they end up spelling the word Jigyasa, which is the name of the mother of the man's three children. There was nothing he could have done different. Could he?

As he embarked on another afternoon's routine, in front of Chitol manifested Charu. He studied the girl in her crumpled pinafore stitched by the railway wives of the Mahila Samiti and tried to ascertain where this piece of writing could go. A man works with machines, one day a machine spews out a fully-made version of his child, who creeps up on him when he isn't looking, and now the man must contend with the machine as well as the machine-made daughter. He wondered if it could be interpreted as anti-modern, or too modern. Then he heard Charu say 'Baba', and it hit him like cold water. He noted the collection of staff at his cabin door, the shop activity beyond, and right before him, in violation of all expectation and safety norms, his daughter.

'What has happened?' Chitol asked, jumping to life.

'Nothing,' she replied, as though weary of the question. But he could tell she was on edge.

He sprang up towards her, hoping the demonstration would scatter the audience. It also gave him the chance to close the door, although the top half of the wooden cabin was glass. In a minor slice of luck, neither Sahu nor Clemence was at his desk.

Charu looked around the cabin, so cramped compared to the huge shed with the highest roof she had ever seen. She wondered how anyone worked in this much noise. It was clear to her that she would have to answer. Yet, away from the house, where he seemed complicit in her grandmother's monitoring, she sensed her father was not so inclined to hold her to account.

She told him, therefore, without being further pressed, leaving him to visualise.

At the edge of their school ground, an old banyan tree. She and her friend Ranu, swinging from the hanging roots, which only the boys ever did, for the primary-school playground was shared, and if any girls did, it was when no boys were around. As she swung, her hands burning from gripping the roots, she saw a group of girls pointing at her and she already knew the things they might be saying about the daughter of a flying *dayin*, but it did not matter to her because she was flying and those girls they were not. Back on earth she decided she would not go back with the girls into the building. She stayed behind at the tree. Even Ranu left. She walked through the bushes near the periphery, which she had never done before. She saw broken bottles, torn shoes. Horrible smell. She entered a grove of trees dark as a jungle and she heard birds shrieking. Beyond the trees a fence of thorns. A section of the fence had fallen down, and she climbed over it and hurried down a path, her heart pulsing like a caught frog as she raced downslope – leaving her books, her bag, her brother, her entire school behind. Out in the full glare of the riverbank dogs were barking, clothes were drying on the ghat, little boys were playing with marbles, running about with strings, beating along old bicycle tyres with sticks. In the distance the shape of the workshop rose above the trees. She began to walk in that direction. It was much further than she thought, but the breeze that blew over the water filled her ears and she felt she could fly all over again, get knocked about in the air like a butterfly, and the fear left her heart. She kept going until she saw a path climbing up from the bank and towards the back of the workshop compound. And … is it true that Ma has become a *dayin*?

'No, it is not,' said her father, categorically.

'I knew it.'

Chitol considered the figure before him. For endangering herself on so many fronts she deserved a slap. For the sake of form he considered administering it. But he felt tears materialising. He hoped his spectacles concealed them, for were he to indulge himself, they would spill over and spread along the frame and smudge the glass and his cheeks transparently.

A peon came in and placed papers on the desk.

He is short, thought Charu, recently competitive about height; I can overtake him.

Her father gathered his things and put them into his cloth bag. 'Let's go home,' he said. At the time-office she was excited to see the time-keeper punch him out; and in the sea of bicycles she was excited to locate his by the yellow sari.

She helped herself on to the bar, as she had become proficient at doing, and he wheeled off slowly, his light-machine legs pumping away, up the long route that skirted the artificial lake and looped around the high-officers' mansions with their over-maintained gardens, through the residential ward of clerks people called Babupara, into their own ward, Gulab, their row of C-types, to their quarters with the precious flowering yard.

3
Notun Dida

Their quarters began to deteriorate. Nistarini Debi found it difficult to cope, even someone of her efficiency and energy. Without a daughter-in-law to command or condemn or commend, her very personality was dimmed. Unacknowledged by her, since she prided herself on cleanliness and purity, the house began to resemble what she would call in another a pigsty. Used utensils lay in heaps beneath the tap in the backyard; cats leapt over the fence and licked them out. The evening ritual of smoking out mosquitoes became irregular, so the Chitols were forever reaching irritably for their ankles after sundown. Too many meals for the children took the form of beaten rice with curd and jaggery. When anybody fell ill, the dread of another calamity overturned all flow and order.

It was natural, then, that she would enlist her granddaughter, for both their sakes. But unlike nature's beautiful vines for which the child was named, whose beauty derived in some measure from their tractability, Charulata proved training-resistant.

'Soak those pieces of cauliflower, won't you?' she would tell the girl, taking the trouble to explain why. 'How will the gas go out of them otherwise?' 'Will you burp less then?' Charu might answer with a seeming insolence that was, in fact, perfect innocence. Assigned the task of folding and returning the washed clothes to the correct places, she would, as if competing with the boys, make a great joke of it. 'Dhrubo, Anando, come arrange these clothes, *toh*,' she would imitate her grandmother's intonation, slapping her forehead: '*Ogo*, my hair will ripen because of these boys!' Then applying lime off the walls to her hair: 'See, it has ripened.' The three would roar monstrously.

Nistarini Debi's bones ached. She often thought to herself, 'I am not able any more.'

In a world that made any sense, which this strange township definitely did not, her son would have acquired a wife, not expanded the servant's remit.

But Chitol had succeeded in just that, by employing her own taunts against her: 'This is looking like a Kolkata house now' – a line Nistarini Debi used with an expatriate Bengali's smugness; and 'This is looking just like a Bihari's house' – which she uttered with special relish after the daughter-in-law entered the family.

The maid's duties were slowly extended within tolerable limits of touchability. Surji was to wash dirty vessels, but not arrange the clean ones in the kitchen, or even enter that room. She was to clean a soiled child but not feed a hungry one. She was to pick up a mess, but keep her hands off an extensive list of places. She was never to handle anything in the vicinity of the altar. Surji, a tall, gracefully angular woman, was the wife of Bidur Dusadh, a guard at the works.

Although her labour was badly needed, she served at Nistarini Debi's sufferance. She resented that, as if working two houses was not enough of a job, as though raising her four children, mending their clothes, keeping the earth of the hut cool or warm or dry depending on the season was not adequate utilisation of her time, now she had more to do, and for what – for her man to drink it away, and the humiliating superiority of the old crone?

Nistarini Debi could not bear to have the woman getting haughty and indispensable with her shoddy work – the look in her eye!

Eventually, she told her son that Notun Dida would be coming. He did not ask when or for how long.

When she acquired the name Notun Dida, she wasn't sure whether it was funny cruel, salt-in-the-wound cruel, matter-of-fact cruel or just a matter of fact. New Granny. A child had coined it, so nobody thought she would mind. In truth, like everyone else, she simply stopped noticing.

The events behind the name were as follows. When she was eleven or twelve years old, her father had firmed up her alliance with an excellent Gangopadhyay boy who worked in a white man's forest concession. Not long after the betrothal a rabid jackal sunk its teeth into the groom and condemned him to a ghastly death. Notun Dida was widely held accountable for the excellent young man's fate. She herself felt ashamed for being a transmitter of ill fortune, yet was relieved that efforts at finding her a next match ran aground because of it. If this was what marriage was like before marriage, what must it be like after?

Her family was not well off and under the circumstances let her out to whichever relative required her services. Put to use as a nanny while herself an adolescent, she gained, precociously, the skills of a grandmother – and the name. Through youth and middle age and menopause, through the tumultuous calls of her body, the acceptance of meals and shelter and saris, through the weakening but never-erased conviction that this life was better than that other one she had narrowly escaped, she fed, bathed, oiled, lullabied the children of others, tidied, minded, decorated their houses, planted saplings in their gardens, offered grain to their visiting birds. She had put in stints at her older cousin and milk sister Nistarini Debi's house before; indeed, had helped with raising Animesh. This house, Animesh's, would be a new one. Her sixteenth if her count was correct.

In due course Chitol received a postcard with the details of the arrival. Now that it was in writing, his governmental reflexes compelled him to evaluate it as imminent.

His mother was never quite at ease in the township. It was not that she was unaccustomed to change. But she always had society. Outside Mughalsarai, their last port, they had Banaras, where she had people, and Banaras kept her spiritually fulfilled. Here she had only Bhombal. It was well over a year since the tragedy. The short-term visits by relatives had dried up. It should not be surprising that she wanted Notun Dida. It did not feel to him a worse idea than instrumentally remarrying.

On the other hand, it was a reminder of how much his world had collapsed.

When Charu found out, she felt just as wronged.

'Why, why, why?' she harangued her father.

'Because you don't help me at all,' her grandmother intervened.

'I'll do it, I'll do whatever you want,' Charu replied, with a depth of feeling that surprised everyone.

But she did not protest very much, confusing as the development was. In any case, it was too late. She intuited that her punishment, and intimations of punishment would remain at her side, was to have someone she had never met as a partial replacement for her mother.

The morning Notun Dida was to arrive Charu awoke with a heavy feeling in her young heart.

'Which of you is coming?' she heard her father ask her brothers – because, she knew, the ekka he was going to hire on return permitted him to take just the one.

'I want to see a diesel locomotive,' Dhrubo staked his claim. Anando put in an identical one, and as a consequence of the sorry fight between them, the opportunity was offered instead to her. Although she bore a casual loathing for the locomotives that mindlessly excited her brothers, she *loved* going to the railway station.

She accepted, without disclosing her enthusiasm.

It was a fine day, requiring an umbrella for neither rain nor sun. They exited the colony from a side gate, coming on to a wide mud road that curved along ponds thick with water hyacinth. In between them a path cut away prettily towards a set of stone mansions older than the railway township. They belonged, her father remarked in some sahebi accent, to 'Calcayshians'. The two slowed their stride to catch a glimpse of the mansions, perhaps of the Kolkata sahebs and memsahebs themselves.

'Do you know what the vendors call them?' he said to her.

'What do they?'

'Damchi babu and damchi mem. They go to the bazaar and say, this is *damn cheap ya*, that is *damn cheap*!'

With this he began to laugh his particular laugh, through his nose, his eyes crinkled, his eyebrows raised. Charu could feel the humour and that it was directed at the airs of the mansion people. That, and her father's vibrating laugh, which she did not suspect he had enhanced for her benefit and his own, put her in a jolly mood too. They were still smiling as they got to a stall of ropes and baskets, woven by the Birhor tribe, her father educated her. 'So how are your damchi babu damchi mem?' he asked the vendor. 'All gone back, sahib. Why don't you take something?' Chitol briefly admired a coil of rope and moved along. Making their way through the market, a lively trading centre ever since the days of transhipment, she went over it with her father again and again – what do they call them, and why do they call them that, laughing fuller each time.

She knew they were near the station by the smell of horse droppings, and soon the horses themselves appeared with their thrilling trembling nostrils.

As they waited at a carefully selected spot on the platform, Charu asked:

'Baba, what is special about a diesel locomotive?'

'A good question, a *very* good question,' her father commended her. 'Now imagine the map of India in front of you. Let us say Bombay.'

He held his thumb at an imaginary shore.

The index finger of the other hand he raised to a point high above Bombay, waggling it. 'This finger is, let us say, Amritsar. If a steam train were going from Bombay to Amritsar, it may first go here. This is Bhusaval.'

He pinned Bhusaval to the air.

'Here the loco will be changed. A different loco will pull the train to, say, Jhansi. You know Jhansi? Where your Taga da lives.'

She watched his finger curl parabolically upwards from Jhansi.

'Another loco will take it here. What is the capital of our country?'

'New Delhi.'

'Good. Here maybe another loco change. That loco will take it to Amritsar.'

The finger completed its final leg.

'Now the reason the loco has to be changed is because it runs on coal. The coal burns out, *toh*. The engine has to be cleaned and checked, new coal has to be put in. With the diesel locos, one loco can take you from here to here –' he traced the conjectural arc from Bombay with a soothing *shhhh*, and let it drop off somewhere in middle-to-high India.

Charu stood hypnotised by the array of places hanging in the air before her.

'Baba, is Notun Dida coming because Ma has gone?' she asked after a while.

'Who told you that?'

'Nobody. I thought of it.'

'Your grandmother needs some help, that is all.' Her father looked sincere. But he did not deny it. 'She's getting old, *toh*.'

She nodded.

Belching coal smoke, the locomotive of felt green and black trundled in. Charu found herself yanked along in chase of a window.

Inside the coach she absorbed her. A slight woman, less substantial than her iron trunk, her mouth battered by paan, and when out on the platform Notun Dida enclosed her face, Charu registered the hands as more corrugated than Thakuma's.

'*Bah*, how beautiful. Her name is Charulata, is it not?'

She did not realise she was meant to answer until her father prompted her.

She nodded. Notun Dida's breath made her dizzy. She followed the trunk on the porter's head down the platform, walking beside a betel tang that for a long time she associated with diesel.

She looked out into the gloaming for her father. The lights in the house were down from the usual ration of three after 5 p.m. to zero. The lanterns and her father's late return were, as far as she could tell, the meaning of the war with Pakistan. After Notun Dida's settling in, and the new rhythms arising from that, the months had begun to roll by again, and each day presented less an individual challenge than before to the adults; the boys seemed not to care. As for Charu, if she sensed her father was taking advantage of the war, she was not entirely wrong.

For the first time since its inception a second shift was introduced at the Bhombalpur works, so that anything from screws to serviced bogies were ready should the war demand it. Like the majority of workers, Chitol continued on the regular shift and could have well returned home at the usual time. In a trenches spirit he started going along with colleagues to the Institute, where they untucked their shirts, smoked cigarettes, discussed the state of things, played Institute games: carrom and cards, boasts and brags and military strategy, until lights out and to the bleachers. The racing hours filled him with liberation and guilt. He admitted to himself that he felt out of his age group at home.

Fact is, he felt out of place at the Institute too. The men had wives to return to or stay away from; it anchored their behaviour. War talk wearied him; he found its bigotries reprehensible. He experienced no hot rush of conviviality standing around drinking in breach behind the bleachers. Still he senselessly lingered, dragging deep on his cigarette, as the earth grew sticky with spilled rum, as somebody broke down singing K. L. Saigal, as dragonflies fell asleep on wood and cooking fires dissipated into the enforced blackness of the railway colony above which no fighter planes jetted.

He will soon be here, thought Charu, her anticipation keener by the minute. She had not made headway with the task he had given her, teaching Anando. That was not her fault: the grandmothers did not give her a moment's peace.

Next to her Dhrubo lay flat on his back beside a hurricane lantern going black with soot, dramatically holding a textbook straight over his face, as if the wartime restrictions were formulated just to thwart him.

'Don't you think Thakuma started burping more after Dida came?' he asked suddenly.

'Yes,' Charu agreed.

'And Dida has started burping a lot, hasn't she?'

This matter was important to Charu, for in the latest permutation, she slept with Dida, on the floor beside her cot.

'I don't think Dida burps more than Thakuma,' she replied after due consideration, concluding that it was not the quantity of the output but the betel nut and the tobacco thing she put in her paan that made Dida's the more potent.

'That is because Thakuma started burping *more* than she used to after Dida came, didn't I say! You have the intelligence of a goat.'

'You just don't know anything,' said Charu, opting for superiority, and made as if to ignore his unfortunate existence.

Dhrubo adjusted his persecuted arms so that the light might hit the page at the sweet spot; he wobbled his chubby legs in concentration, determined to teach his tormentors in school a lesson through the sheer force of exam marks.

'*Khoka ... Ooo khokaaaa.*'

Charu called out to the little rascal in the style of her grandmother.

Anando emerged from the kitchen, Thakuma wiping his mouth with her sari as he did.

'What are you eating, *re*?' She knew very well it was leftover malpua.

'It's over,' he replied. Syrup bled out to the edge of his lips.

That Anando, then Dhrubo, would be the chosen beneficiaries of treats was not lost on her.

'Go quickly, get one for me,' she told him conspiratorially.

He applied a finger to the edge of his mouth and took it to his tongue. The finality with which he licked it suggested there would be no luck.

'Finished.'

'Come, let's see what is in this book,' she said, sour now at every member of her family.

Just then the call came.

'*Khuki … Ooo khukiii.* Come, girl, come. Come at once for *dhuna*.'

'I can't,' Charu called back.

'Why? You're just standing there. Doing nothing.'

'I am not!' she objected. This was the charge she hated most. 'Baba has told me to teach Anando.'

There was a brief silence.

Then the call repeated itself, sterner.

'Oh ho!' cried Charu. 'How can I teach him anything?'

She went in a huff to the kitchen.

Smoking out mosquitoes was an activity she used to enjoy, until it became a chore. She pounded frankincense the way she had been taught. Dida lit the husk. They went around room to room fanning the clay pot.

'*Eeesh*, how should I study in this smoke?' shouted Dhrubo, slamming his book against the floor.

'Not possible to learn anything in the smoke,' said Anando and skittered away.

Paying them no mind, Charu finished her task and returned the clay pot to the kitchen.

'Wait, where are you going,' her grandmother said. 'Give me that ginger Dida has ground.'

She did as asked.

'Did you touch the ginger with your fingers? Because –'

'Because if you touch your fingers to your face it will burn,' Charu completed the sentence with blatant impertinence and fled.

After a few minutes Thakuma came to observe her from the doorway, red with rage. She could not remember herself having a choice in matters. What she could remember was that at Charu's age, which is to say seven running eight, she was already suffused with habits. She could arrange the garments of twelve householders on a clothes horse in a way that the smallest child could pick out its own without trouble. She knew the phases of the moon, which auspicious day fell on which *tithi* of which *paksha*. Could even light the hearth. What was she to do with this girl? Mixed blood! Sometimes it was all she could do to hold herself back from expressing the sentiment. The streak of wildness. That incident of going to the workshop. Her son only made it harder. A few positives she could see in this task to tutor Anando. It was a caretaking duty, that was good. Education was no bad thing. But she had seen girls with BAs and BEds clueless in other affairs. Much had changed. Yet there were things that never did – the moon and its phases, habits and their value. Assessing her granddaughter, a great affection overcame her. She wanted to make of the girl something solid – make her invulnerable to the misfortunes of the past and any in the future. Never must she feel incapable.

Oblivious of the scrutiny, Charu sat on the floor with the books and the slate and attempted to do her best by herself, her brother, her father.

'Why is the swan's beak green, Didi?' Anando asked.

It was their only book in colour and it did not occur to Charu that the error might have been in the printing. She poured imaginative logic into the answer.

'Maybe because it has eaten those yam leaves growing on the bank? Yes, that is it!'

Anando was already making off, on all fours, driving along a marble with a piece of chalk like a hockey player. She dragged him back by his shorts.

'Which fruits and vegetables are in that man's basket, Didi?' he enquired.

She bent low over the book and tried to discern the elements. She took her doubts to Notun Dida, who, having started up the fire in the tin *unoon* with the mix of dry paddy and dry dung, sat laughing with a paan in her mouth as she watched the boy run rings around his sister.

Since she was only performing the duty given by her father, it did not occur to Charu that it was her sincerity being laughed at. Maybe there was something humorous in the illustrations. Seeking it, suspecting she had found it, she began to smile knowingly. Meanwhile Anando rolled along the floor like a log.

Notun Dida wheezed away with laughter. Charu stared in fascination at her mouth, which took on a childlike aspect, unclosing to expel diesel, the gaps in the teeth fluttering like bellows, the lips moving like red jelly, in a way that slowed down time and her childhood whenever she thought back to it.

4

Aakaal

Those who had chosen Bhombalpur as the site for the workshop, as those who did for their holiday homes, were taken by its exquisite natural balance. Set on a vast plateau, the ferocity of summer and the bitterness of winter were restrained by a play of altitude and latitude. The rains that fed forest, industry and the quick rivers flowing southeast fell in fair measure from July to September. When they erred, they did on the lower side, rather than in the floods that ravaged the plains to the north. Towards the end of the monsoon came the terrific cyclonic downpours of the *hathiya nakshatra* which matured the standing paddy and saturated the earth for the critical winter crop; a few months afterwards blew the short cold windy rains that were held responsible for the tragedy in the Chitol home.

The year before was a drought year. In 1966 the drought returned worse to southern Bihar. Midway in, the monsoon simply gave up. The hathiya rains never appeared. Grain withered on the stalk. Day by day, as fields cracked and died, the grief of wasted labour gave on to the terror of starvation. That great despair made its way into the railway colony.

Autumn turned to winter. An awful dry wind wafted across the landscape. The river kept dropping. One by one the steps down the river ghat became visible, then the margins of the bed, the ruins of the slipways used in the time of transhipment, the bases of pillars holding up the bridges, then so much silt and stone that the River Bhombal, which had sprung mythologically from nothing in order to nourish life, appeared in danger of reverting to its origins. Water plummeted in the two natural ponds and the one artificial lake. There was barely any to pump into the fifteen cement water tanks that towered over the colony like giant toadstools. Hours at the workshop grew shorter, so too at school.

In the residential wards, tankers showed up every day at the mouth of the lane to give a bucket of water or three, turning neighbours into haggling competitors, disadvantaging those who lived at the end of the street. The Chitol siblings, made to bathe twice daily, now merely sponged themselves with damp gamchhas. They heard that water dacoits were raiding what remained inside village wells, that water was being sold for as much as twenty-five paise a canister. Then the talk was no longer about water, it was about food.

At the rail-babu haat outside the southern gate beggars outnumbered customers. In the ward market Hori barely had any vegetables for his own children. Milk stopped. Shyamlal had run out of fodder for his cows, and so had the cow shelter. He stripped the nearby trees of leaves to feed them, then the straw from the stable roof. Soon he would have to go into his own roof. If it did rain again he would be in big trouble.

In the evenings Chitol's visitors railed against the government that did not care for irrigation, only elections, which were to go on regardless, and no government would declare a famine when there were elections, the only thing they cared about, not irrigation, not hunger. The words *aakaal, akaal, durbhikkho* carried a terrible spectre.

At night Notun Dida conjured the horrific times. The famines made by the white man had left people scavenging dead animals. So many vultures hovered in the sky they were like a black umbrella. The limbs of infants had shrunk to the width of a finger; there wasn't a mother who could squeeze more than two drops for her baby. She told the stories in the dark, lying on her cot, hoarsely whispering, the key that she tied to an end of her sari tinkling now and then to startle Charu.

Food stopped coming from the haat and stalls altogether, for there were no vegetables to be had. Hori sold his wife's silver. Shyamlal's roof went bare. He set one of his cows loose for he could not bear to sell her to the butcher. Realising his folly he went around looking for her in the night like a madman but she was nowhere to be found, and his defeat was carved on his gaunt tear-swelled face. Surji heard priceless cows were being sold for as little as eight rupees, so that was how reckless Shyamlal had been. It was heard also that the rich officers who ate meat were eating great amounts of it. Deep in a famine-struck village Bissesar the barber's great-niece came upon rotten food, or a poisonous berry, or diseased water, and it finished her. Not just cattle, said Surji, people were being sold.

Only grain and pulses entered the house. 'Remember, you have food to eat,' Chitol told his children. 'The children of poor people have nothing.'

For the first time in his working life he became involved in committee activity, even if the Workers' Food Security Committee was not exactly a committee but a large voluntary group. Among other things, its members inspected the railway station by turn to see the supplies weren't pilfered.

One such day of abrasive aridity, Charu, deprived, queasy in her stomach, the dry wind blowing about in her brain, at odds with her grandmother all morning, insisted on accompanying her father.

'Go, go, go,' her grandmother said, fed up with the girl. To keep the peace, Chitol agreed to take her.

At 'Carriage' Rangaswamy's quarters they found him seated cross-legged on an armless chair in the veranda, looking godly with three faint vertical lines on his forehead, listening to godly music. From inside his home blew the fragrance of incense sticks.

'Ah, Chitol, I thought you will come today,' he said. Every time somebody called her father by their surname it surprised Charu.

'How do you do, little girl?'

'I am fine. How do you do?'

Her father nudged her.

'Uncle,' she added.

'And what is your name, little girl?'

'Charulata, Uncle.'

Carriage Rangaswamy gruffly chuckled.

'Sweet girl. Fluffy girl.'

He screwed his eyes and pointed a finger at her.

'You are going to do the supervision?'

'Yes, Uncle. I will do it.'

He chuckled again.

'Fluffy sweety girl, brave girl.'

He turned to the father.

'They looted, you know, two vans of grain in Batidih off the highway, heard?'

'Is that so?' replied Chitol.

'Heard about the teachers?'

'What?'

'Relief milk powder from one foreign aid agency, got caught selling it.'

'Yes, heard about that.'

'Now, you know, the free kitchen has started. Be careful when you pass it. There may be rioting. Nobody will stop at anything. Dark times are here, Chitol. I hear they are going to cut off the noses of landlords.'

All of a sudden Chitol regretted he had brought his daughter.

Carriage Rangaswamy was holding up a key.

He was no longer the only scooter owner in the township but he still enjoyed a reputation of having been the first.

Chitol wheeled it outside. With a series of leg pumps he had it vibrate to life. Charu climbed on. He briefly considered dropping her home, but that would be a whole other riot.

He rode with the slow tension of a man on another's vehicle. He could not help but picture himself on it, wonder whether, in antithesis to its velocity, his hair flew about with flair, whether he looked dashing. Charu perched her feet on the engine casing so her bare legs didn't burn. The quarter-glass of water she had drunk before coming out sloshed about her stomach.

The colony looked wind-worn, ragged. Outside the gates, among the small clay idols and the debris of long-dried flowers, people sat around under the big banyan tree wrapped in strings tied by those asking God for a baby, Charu knew. They appeared as if they had been there for as long as everything else, families in tired sprawls, staring with dried-out eyes.

The town was unrecognisable. Nothing since the establishment of the workshop transformed Bhombalpur like the famine. Thousands of people from hundreds of villages came to the railway town looking for food, looking to be taken away somewhere, anywhere, for work and half a meal a day. Few carts and cycle rickshaws plied; horses, mules and humans alike were bereft of sustenance to carry themselves, let alone others. A lone cow with startling ribs snouted listlessly at the inedible. The unusual presence was the occasional jeep, sometimes with a shocking white person in it. Sullenness shrouded the market.

No traders called out in auctioneering voices, no vendors blared radio songs. The rumble of the jeeps broke the silence, and every now and then a shout or a wail pierced the air. Those were from the free kitchen at the single-gate government higher secondary.

Even the fights had a famished infirmity to them. People were disqualified for being neither children nor aged nor pregnant, for only starving. Some had blundered in carrying their red cards and so could not benefit by another programme even if they had not tasted rice in a month. Others charged the supervisor of favouring his village folk, his kinsmen, his caste brothers, of siphoning off grain to sell on the market.

At the far end their scooter came upon the physical training teacher at Dhrubo's school. He was volunteering with the state relief committee.

'What's happening?' asked Chitol.

'Supposed to feed five hundred. Supplies for fifty. Five thousand have come.'

Near them a man with a rather severe expression lay on the side of the road, propped weakly upon an elbow, being lavished with a great deal of attention.

'What happened to him?'

'Won't eat.'

'He is getting food and won't eat?'

'Refuses to be served from the common vessel. Says he is a Brahmin and would rather die.'

'Won't die, will he?'

'He will have his way. If the priest dies it will bring more bad luck and who wants to take that chance.'

Closer to the station, faces stained with dust cast exhausted glances at the scooter that put-putted through to an enclosure barricaded with bamboo and rope.

From here they could see the railway lines. Along the tracks: people and people. They weren't there last time, thought Chitol.

'Who are those people, Baba?' Charu asked.

'Poor people,' he muttered, aiming to be succinct.

He took her through a side gate on to the platforms and into the stationmaster's cabin. There, surrounded by people, a small quilly man, bristles bursting from his ears and eyelids, sat in a coat that struggled to shrink to his size. 'Babumoshai,' said stationmaster Dubey, who had a soft spot for Chitol ever since he had learned about his wife all those years ago. He waded his short fingers into the swollen pool of papers on his desk and began dinging a bell to summon a khalasi already in the room.

The khalasi solicitously led the Chitols out, whereupon they were accosted by a hollow-eyed woman carrying a bony child whose matchstick legs oozed with something that was not blood. 'Ooo, Babuji,' she started to say, but could go no further, for the khalasi crushed her with a shout. Turning to Chitol with a smile, he said, 'This way, sahib.' They walked down the slope at the end of the platform towards a shed.

Here a shunting engine and its small tender utilising precious water trembled with metallic heat.

Policemen squatted at the edge of the shed, leaning on their lathis.

'If you can do anything for our village, sahib,' the khalasi took his chance. 'Traders are hoarding grain to sell for the price of gold. People have eaten all there is. Eaten the bark of mahua, eaten the bark of tal, eaten grass. Finished the seeds they were meant to plant this season. If you can help in any way …'

'How is your family?' Chitol enquired.

'I have disowned my children, sahib.'

'Why!'

'Then they may be able to get a red card. If there is an earning member in the family we hear you cannot get one.'

Beside the lines, babies with extreme limbs and taut round stomachs lay on the stony ballast. Demonic dry rays arrowed down from a pure white sky. Charu watched. Her head hurt in the clean sun.

Reverberations approached them on the main line. The spent policemen stirred. Up and down the tracks rose the sounds of shooing and shouting, and muffled whumps of lathis on ballast, clangs upon metal rails, the odd crack against human bone, staving off the starvers and whatever their hunger was capable of. After a few minutes the meagre attack subsided.

In the ensuing flurry of activity, the shunting engine went back and forth, unloaded sacks were stacked up, horns and shouts sounded; a number of officials gave and took orders, exchanged papers, walked along the wagons decisively, Chitol among them.

Eventually, with a blast of the horn the grain train chugged away down the main line; the shunting engine loaded with ration trundled down the siding towards the workshop. From the margins people fell upon both lines, on their haunches, combing the permanent way. Nobody stopped them any more. Some had with them little cane baskets or sieves; a few women held open the pallu of their saris.

'What are they doing, Baba?'

'Looking for grain.'

A grain here, another there, a third and a fourth in a crack in the sleeper. A fifth and a sixth, maybe older, previously missed grains, hidden treasure-like behind a fastener.

The sharp wintry sun fell like swords, felt like it was cutting open her mind.

As they walked back towards the scooter, she felt she had swirled into one of Notun Dida's night-time stories. She looked up into the sky and her vision turned white pitted orange. Her father kicked the scooter awake once more and they were off. Again that sloshing feeling in her stomach. Now babies eating twigs, gravel, rat excrement and she could no longer tell what was real and what was a Dida-induced nightmare. She erupted into vomit, which flooded her eyes with yellow blobs, the blood vessels on her face burst with the fury of purgation until she was speckled purple. Noises and shadows bounced about her. Her back was warrantlessly thumped. Dead bees and seeds pouring out of her mouth. In another pit of her mind her mother flailed like a fish on a dry bed. A little water down her throat, warm sickly water that made her want to vomit again, Carriage Rangaswamy's scooter carefully wiped down, and then her father's striped kurta as her face lolled against it.

'Neither the oldest nor the youngest,' she was thinking in the post-delirium. 'Neither the first nor the last.' Thakuma and Dida were by her side. The winds in her mind began to blow, she wished to run past the two women and bolt into the open blue sky somewhere beyond right now, but fell limp into the bed as she tried to raise her head. Her grandmother's pale wrinkled fingers pressed on her forehead, crumbling like chalk as they did, her voice coming over from neverspace in neverland.

'Sleep, *khuki*, sleep. This is the time to sleep. The leopards have come down from the forest, there is no food for them to eat. The deer have come out of the jungle, there is no water to drink. The birds have left their trees, there are no berries left for them. At the river they saw a black panther looking at the children on the ghat.'

Charu felt another vomit coming on, and though it did not materialise, her bed, her body, felt drenched in it.

'Sleep, *khuki*, sleep. When will you sleep if not now? The world is turning upside down. When we saw the first train near our village we knew something was wrong. We were small then but we were not foolish. We are old now and still we are not foolish.'

The chalk powder of Thakuma's digits settled on her face, she felt it on her lips. Her mouth ached with its dryness.

'In the old aakaal so many people died it was like Kalinga. Mahadeb did not approve of what the white man was doing. Now he sees what we are doing even after the white man has gone. He has opened his third eye and the world has turned upside down. Upside down. *Ultapalta. Utpat.*'

The chalky fingers ran along her arms in the sweet sursuri of sleep-giving.

Ultapalta ultapalta ultapalta, utpat utpat utpat, the words rolled about her mouth, her insides, and plunged her into a gigantic sleep.

5

Mistake

When Charu awoke, for the purposes of our brief account, a year and a half had gone by. A wonderful spring was in place. The garden carried barely a trace of past privations. Once a week, Budhwa Asur, a casual worker in horticulture, tended to it freelance and his hand had helped the heal. The lime tree drooped with fruit, the spinach square was thick with green, the red hibiscus pistils flickered in the breeze. The entire township was proof of the resilience, the perpetuation of things. The winged seeds of sal helicoptered their way down with propagatory grace. Badminton bloomed, in trajectories that indicated whether adversarial or sororal. As the avenue of palash was lit up by coral ornamentation, so the avenue of silk cotton was carpet-bombed by crimson blossom, and she looked forward to the time around the corner when their grandmothers would send them out on missions to gather the fibre to restuff the pillows.

Standing before the mirror, Charu shook the tin furtively. Powder puffed out of the improperly punctured holes on to her palm. She daubed it across her cheeks and neck to overcome her brownness. She looked at herself again, could not bear further scrutiny and escaped outside. Exams were over and she was free.

Through the madhumalati pouring over the fence she peeped at the neighbour.

Pearl Flanger was her name. She was a teacher – at the convent, no less. It was said that her husband was the finest, fastest locomotive driver on this side of the Khyber, until he ended up in a ravine back in '56. She had brought a son. The boy had brown hair and dark eyes, light burnished skin, clavicles like polished bronze. He was tall and lean and performed push-ups and jumping jacks; he heard music of inexplicable kinds. Pearl Flanger was ruddy and handsome and unafraid to sit with her feet up on a stool in her garden with her big ankles and calves exposed beneath her floral dress, sometimes sat so even when the sun was up.

The sight of the widow with her large legs up like that, it was enough for Nistarini Debi to send the children off to the Bengali Literary Society. Her real grouse lay elsewhere. Those quarters, allotted briefly to the Sports Association, had again lain unoccupied and yielded the Chitols gourds and tomatoes the previous season. Then the administration, having got the Sisters of St Joseph to expand the convent into an institution worthy of officers' children, made available whatever accommodation it could for the teachers, disrupting the Chitols' fragile home economy. *Just our luck*, Nistarini Debi thought aloud with exaggerated prejudice, sharing our walls with cow-eating *tash* from Tomkin Compound.

Although, the Flangers were not from Tomkin's Compound, that small set of Anglo-Indian cottages dating back to a time before the workshop, before the bridge, before railway nationalisation, to the days of transhipment and the British. On either side of the River Bhombal had once run railways of unalike gauge. The two railways were owned and operated by different British companies, guaranteed different rates of profit by the Raj. From the riverbanks slipways declined towards the water, conveying metre-gauge railway wagons on to barges that transported them across the river to sheds, where labourers unloaded them and loaded on to broad-gauge wagons coal, grain, pig iron, ammunition, timber, leather, cloth, bones, stone, machine parts, animals, *misc.*, the exploitation of India. Tomkin's Compound was founded by none other than William 'Hilly Billy' Tomkin, a supervisor on those operations, which the vigorous annalist had memorialised in his booklet under the chapter 'The Formation of a Most Excellent Housing Compound'. It persisted in a vague reputation of sin, home to nearly all the very few Anglo-Indians of Bhombalpur.

Not to the Flangers, who had not set foot in these precincts until a few months ago.

Between the pink flowers on the madhumalati Charu spotted him. Daryll. Apprentice machinist. She moved herself at once, not wishing to be seen.

She dropped to the earth and pushed back against the fence. She fingered her neck where she felt perspiration, gaining for her troubles a talcum smear. She fretted, then went off running to the secret spot to meet Salima, who in moments of lucid sentimentality later in life she would think was the deepest friend she ever had.

Salima was already at the rocks. The spot was a depression between Gulab and Rajnigandha. Since right there between the wards, they believed it above suspicion. Yet when Salima first took her, leading her down by the hand under the shade of the tamarind trees, Charu's heart pounded with the power of the illicit.

Salima opened a knot in her dupatta. Today's offerings: small globes of firm white-green mahua, chunks of sugar cane, a picture of an infant they called the Chinese Baby.

Salima spread the picture on a rock.

'Hawww, hai, just look at its lips,' she said in their colony mix of Hindi and English.

'Like it has put on lipstick!'

'It's smiling!'

'It's happy here.'

'Why shouldn't it be, with us?'

They left it there to sun itself. They peeled back sections of the mahua, so waxy, so sweet, going through the whole lot in silence.

Salima picked up a dry pod of tamarind and bounced a seed on it. Then, bored by her mastery, she smacked it away into the trees, stretched out and scratched herself with the pod between her shoulder blades. Charu leaned back against a rock in order to look casual, but her eyes betrayed her admiration.

Salima was now cudding cane, working her jaws athletically.

'If you had chewed the tail of a goat when you were small those gums and those teeth would have become strong,' she remarked, watching Charu struggle.

'But doesn't the goat run away when you try to chew its tail?'

'Not when the goat is alive, madwoman!' Salima guffawed. 'What a madwoman!'

She loved when she made Salima laugh.

'I saw him right now,' Charu said when they had finished laughing. 'His elbows are like those round knobs on teacher's desk. I think he polishes them.'

'That means he must be a sportsman,' said Salima. 'I wonder what he plays.'

Salima was the best badminton player ever produced by the township, routinely 'doing us proud' with her trophies. Her father was the head keyman on the siding that joined the workshop to the main line. 'Mian Angrezi' they called Mansur Ali Khan, for he had started out in the white man's time, and gave perfect imitations of the white sahebs. The mimicry was one source of his popularity among officers. The other was his begum, called in as a special cook for parties, where she produced Lucknowi biryani, bringing back the unwanted parts – fat for frying, hooves for soup, tail for the gums of a teething child. Rashida Khatoon had no choice but to take her youngest with her while she cooked. Playing with the officers' children on the officers' lawns, Salima picked up badminton.

'Think he must be a football player,' Charu speculated, solely to keep the subject alive.

'Useless sport,' Salima yawned. 'Today I went for practice at five o'clock. My father is crack.'

'My grandmother says they came from Tomkin Compound.'

'Tomkin, Tom-*kin*. What a funny name. Tomm-kinnn, *Tomm*-kinnn.'

Charu giggled at the clown.

'Your grandmother is not telling your father to marry again?' Salima enquired for no apparent reason.

It took Charu aback. As far as she could remember she had never mentioned this, and now was no time to raise it. She felt exposed that Salima knew, but also a little proud.

'Sometimes. She tells him she is getting old and he should get a mother for us. As if we want that. Anyway, I know he won't.'

Salima could sense her friend's agitation.

'She has a screw loose,' she remarked to win her back.

'Who?'

'Your grandmother.'

'Oh!'

'Everybody is crack, that is the truth,' Salima now posited. She winched her index finger against her temple, drawing in her eyeballs towards her nose, dropping her tongue out of her mouth. The girls began to laugh once more, then shushed one another to maintain secrecy.

They sat around in happiness. Each knew the other was her best friend ever since they had floated a paper boat down a rainstream with their names on it. Other girls may have written their best friendships on their palms or carved it into trees, but none had set theirs sail.

'They are thinking about sending Dhrubo to Calcutta,' Charu said. 'For his studies. I don't think he should go. Anando is too small to understand. But he will miss him the most, the madman.'

'Don't worry, nobody goes anywhere,' Salima replied. 'My father has been trying to get my brother out of the house for years.'

Charu leaned back against the rock and sighed. Her small frame hugged the convex of the surface. Springshine bubbled down through the pinnate leaves into her eyes.

'Anyway, forget all that,' said Salima. 'Do you want to meet Jeetendra?'

She scraped the corns on her soles with a safety pin. Her nosering sparkled in the filtered sun.

Charu looked at her in astoundment. How could anybody be this much magic?

'I have an eagle's eye,' declared Nistarini Debi, a line she uttered whenever assailed by a sense of impending trouble.

Charu felt her hair stand to attention.

'I want to eat,' she stated. 'I want to go to sleep.'

She tried not to look at her grandmother, but the corner of her eye was full of her.

'Why? Are you unwell?'

Illness: a dangerous opening, with unpredictable consequences.

'No. We eat too late,' she said, training her focus on the ants in the cavity where the wall met the floor.

'*Tai?* We eat too late, is it? Are you hearing that?' her grandmother called out to Notun Dida. 'We eat too late it seems.'

'Is that right?' the junior grandmother obliged. 'She has not lived in Kolkata, *toh.*'

'She has not. Very fortunate,' judged the senior. She raked her old eyes over the children and went away.

Food was laid on the new phenomenon that was the dining table. Until its arrival the Chitols ate in the traditional fashion, cross-legged on the floor. 'Look, they have a dining table!' Charu had exclaimed when the furniture was brought into the Flanger home, prompting her father to splurge on the changing times. In Chitol's true conception of a modern world, a dining table was meaningless without a refrigerator. But a refrigerator was well beyond his means, and the women did not trust anything that encouraged staleness; they barely trusted the dining table. Besides, he had reasoned, what made the world modern was flexibility, a bit of this and a bit of that. The table came tightly wrapped in plastic, whose modernness, surpassing the table's own, was treasured by the householders. Two months in, it remained intact.

'Wash your hands with soap and come to the table,' Chitol announced, the latter part in English. The English was also new, part of the modern experience.

The children took their places.

Charu wiggled her little finger into a perforation in the plastic wrapping. The smooth Formica calmed her.

'Again!' Dhrubo shouted. She almost fell off her chair. 'You'll think I'm a liar! Again she is expanding the holes.'

She became tense again. Pecking at her food over dinner, she absorbed no conversation. Her grandmother made something of a scandal of her pickiness, as though she was too grand for cooked vegetable peels and tiny pond fish without a proper name.

She washed up and went to the lavatory.

'Again!'

Once more she jumped out of her skin.

This time it was her grandmother, and in the deep voice that conveyed displeasure. Charu, of course, knew why. She was not to use the latrine unless she wanted to defecate. To urinate she was to squat over the drain in the bathroom. Girls worked in the kitchen and therefore entering a lavatory required them to bathe immediately afterwards and become pure. She had not meant to defy; she had simply been preoccupied.

'I find it uncomfortable,' she defended herself. 'And the whole bathroom starts smelling of urine.'

'We can do it at our age and you feel uncomfortable?' said her grandmother. 'Now go take a bath.'

'I already took it before dinner,' Charu answered back. She looked towards her father for support.

'There is no need for this, Ma,' he said.

'Who will teach her? Am I nobody to teach her?'

'There are some things not worth teaching,' he replied.

'Is that so? Why do I open my mouth in this house? You will prepare her for life, won't you? You know a woman's responsibilities, *toh*.'

'Wash your feet very well,' Chitol sternly instructed Charu by way of compromise.

'I already have,' she said in a deliberately small voice.

'Then go prepare your bed.'

The last thing she had wanted on a night like this was a scene like this.

She quietly got on to her mattress, but the house stayed in motion. The frogs stopped singing, the jackals were yet to howl and Notun Dida did not retire for the night. Beams of moonlight fell through the grilles. In her hand she clutched a picture of the film star. 'Jeetendra smiles on Bombay's iconic Marine Drive.' She thought the caption as wonderful as the photo.

The light went out. Dida climbed into her cot.

Charu lay still and exhilarated, petrified to the bone.

At the first faint screech of an owl she moved. So did Notun Dida. Charu stopped dead. After a minute she arranged pillows to constitute a fake her and slipped out towards the back door. She felt a great urge to pee. Again she transgressed by using the latrine, emitting not the gush she had anticipated but a nervous spurt.

At the owl's next screech she went around to the front, undid the throw-over latch, refastened it without looking back at the house and walked down the path like a haunted doll. Her eyes saw nothing. A cold magnetic arrow in her gut directed her this way and that until she descended into the rocks.

An owl screeched again, softly this time, and then it laughed. Charu fell into Salima's arms, hushing her, breathing hard. Only then did she register the blunt pain in the soles of her feet. She had forgotten to put on slippers.

'Here, wear mine.' Salima took hers off. 'I like naked feet.'

She eased a long kurta and a loose salwar over Charu's nightie. They climbed out of the depression, walking under the trees to stay out of the baring moonlight. Pattering through the deserted ward market, heads and faces masked in dupattas, they entered a Rajnigandha B-type quarters as though to hold it up. Inside, two older girls in tight, coloured churidars and sequinned kurtas lined their eyes with kajal. One was a tall figure with long legs, long silken hair and dark brown eyes that danced over her pert nose; the other girl, muscular, with an administrative air, was Salima's *aapa*, part of the extended family, with whom Salima sometimes spent the night. Both girls were athletes employed on the sports quota, as it was hoped Salima would be one day.

'You people are *still* not ready,' Salima cried, looking around for footwear.

'Shh,' the cousin said, pointing at her room-mate, pursing her lips to secure upon them the majesty of scarlet. 'Even the great Jeetendra is powerless before Meena.'

Giggles twinkled about the chalky walls. A hustled silence. Lights out; latch latched; they departed with the soft shuffle of criminals. Charu's head buzzed. The gorgeous girl, who was Jeetendra's, this group, this night under the wild moonlight, these lanes she never knew in such dark. They crossed the siding that Salima's father kept in good shape, skirted the glimmer of the big pond and kept going towards the boundary. They scaled the brick parapet. Now they walked in pairs along the main road towards the district town. The looming shapes of unknown trees, each jangle of bangles, the insanity of this dacoity conduct, it was as if the world had moved on to the other side of secrets. She noted other figures walking in the dark. Perhaps they had been walking all along. It was the full-moon night of Chaitra and they were all going to see Jeetendra.

The trees thinned out and here came open fields just harvested. A large crowd was out. The girls held hands and advanced towards a stage lit by electric tubes attached to bamboo uprights powered by a tractor. Beside the tractor, in a kind of boudoir made by bedsheets and cushions, reclined Jeetendra. Warts on his neck, on his right cheek a triple-stitched scar, at the hands of a trespassing husband it was rumoured, in his eyes an elastic melancholy. The same lithe body as the film star, the same hero's quiff, the inoffensive young looks.

The utter fame of the moment was incapacitating. Never had Charu been so close to someone reproduced on posters, on cloth banners stretched across the biggest road in town, outside Lalji's Gramophone & Recordings, where the terse Hindi signs announced as if an essential service: 'Jeetendra's songs available here' and 'The modern songs of Jeetendra' – modern enough, certainly, to include the words 'Damchi mem'.

'Two of your young fans,' said the beautiful girl.

Jeetendra offered them a heavy-lidded smile and said in a heavy, breathy voice: *'Hai jawani khud jawani ka singar.'* He looked straight at Charu. She dug her nails into Salima's palms. He asked their names. They told him.

Then the sheets closed, Jeetendra disappeared, so did the beauty. The two young fans were left with Zareena *aapa*, discussing in detail that fleeting minute.

But Charu was speeding out of her daze. Now that she had viewed Jeetendra, it seemed the excitement was not about him at all. She had not really been crazy about his looks or his songs. It was about the stealing out; and here she was in the middle of a night-time field. Walking around the mela she saw Budhwa Asur. She spun round immediately. I cannot believe, she thought to herself, I cannot believe what I have done! How many informers here? Everywhere, among the drunken men, the groups of women, the courtships, appeared people who had spotted her under a moon so big not a star could be seen. Surely her absence had been discovered already? She hunted for the newspaper photograph she had clutched in her hand and could not find it; where would she have dropped the incriminating evidence? She went cold as ice.

'What has happened?' Salima asked her.

'Nothing,' Charu said purposefully. 'I want to do bathroom, but I will wait till home.'

'You have stopped enjoying,' Salima noted with reproach.

'Have you gone crack? I'm enjoying. I'm just controlling myself.'

By the time she returned home, creaking open the gate like a chastened ghost, she was in an awful way. She felt nauseous; her belly, her groin, were damp and miserable, her very body felt like someone else's. She went to the latrine to relieve herself and almost toppled into it in terror.

She dared to flick on the light for a moment. The interrogatory glare of the bulb revealed her condition. She was dying! Emitting crimson blood and globules and congealed dregs of everything inside her. There was no doubt about it: she was dying. She had been punished. She could not fathom the horrendous manner of her death. *Durga, Durga*, she started to mutter. She sought pardon for all her mistakes: overusing the talcum powder, peeping at Daryll Flanger, going out to the secret spot, peeling the plastic off the dining table, wantonly peeing in the latrine rather than the bathroom drain. And – please, please, never let anybody know – for sneaking out of the house tonight. *Durga, Durga; Durga, Durga.* As she beseeched the mother goddess thousands of her older mistakes flooded her with panic. No, not even Ma Durga could save her.

She cleaned herself sloppily and poured an entire bucket of water down the toilet to wash away her sins. Then she retreated indoors and lay down flat in her place. *A mistake I made, a mistake I made, a mistake I made.* Her mind burned with the words. Unable to contain herself, she shook Notun Dida awake.

'I have done something bad, Dida. Something very, very bad. And now blood is coming out of me. I am dying, Dida.'

Notun Dida's hair thinly wisped about in the moonlight. On examining the girl she, too, was taken by surprise. She had not expected it until the following year.

'It means you have become big,' she said in her hoarse whisper. 'You have become a woman.'

This hardly alleviated Charu's panic; rather, the grotesqueness of the transformation terrified her further. She dropped her face into her hands and hoped that sobbing with all her heart might stop her bleeding to death.

Dida rustled about in her trunk and came up with a sari. She ripped out strips from it and handed them to Charu. 'Wipe yourself clean.' Charu turned her back towards Dida, and felt as though she was ceremonially preparing herself for sacrifice, like a goat on Durga Ashtami. She began shedding fresh, slow, fearful tears.

'Shh. Go and wash your hands.'

When she returned Dida handed her a wad of folded sari and a strip of cloth.

'Wear this carefully. Tie it around your waist.'

She did as told and offered herself for adjustment.

'Now go to sleep. I will tell Thakuma. There is no need to tell anyone else.'

'I won't,' Charu promised. 'I won't. I'll never.'

Maybe that would save her. *Durga, Durga*, she mumbled. *Durga, Durga; Durga Durga*.

But her terror did not abate. She lay stiff with her arms stretched straight by her sides, her eyes wide open, waiting for her dying to resume.

6

Jigyasa

In the coming days her need for atonement grew stronger. Sometimes she raised herself on a cane stool to put herself face to face with her mother's photograph. It was an honest wall portrait, devoid of expression, as though anything else would be deceitful. The flat hair coired away to the back of the head; the eyes were flattened by the poverty of lighting; you hardly got a sense of the nose. Only the prominent cheekbones and lips, both detectable in the daughter, recalled the living face.

If nobody was around Charu might place her hands on her own face, pinch the bridge of her nose with her fingers, trace the width of her nostrils down to her mouth, span her fingers between her eyebrows and her hairline, check each of these proportions in turn against her mother's. From this close up she felt she was looking at a person she had never seen before. She would rub the glass; perhaps clearing away the dust would restore familiarity. But her mother remained that way, only the glass was smudged with fingerprints.

She wrote in her exercise book: 'What would you think if you knew?' At other times she wrote simple notes, like 'I miss you' and 'I am sorry'. Putting down the words she felt pressed into her mother's breast, a place where saline tears disappeared. Yet when she wrote, 'I have become a woman,' that felt false. She could not bring herself to trust this idea at all.

She was not sure whether Salima was a woman. Salima was a little older, so she might be. From what Charu understood it did not always work that way. She might have got around to asking – or she may not, since she bore some resentment towards Salima for tempting her into that night, tempered only by the insecurity that she would tell others. But Salima had gone away to her grandmother's house for the summer.

For a while she felt that they too might go somewhere. Instead she fell ill. At first the grandmothers contended it was to do with her womanhood. Then Dhrubo went down as soon as she recovered, and Anando as soon he did. The fever and weakness in each instance was more severe than the previous and raised the old alarms.

Eventually they made a short trip to their father's friend Paranjoy Ghosh, who worked at the steelworks in Burnpur, from where they went to view the great dam at Maithon. There they boated, watched the sun break into the water, encountered constant friction with the two Ghosh children.

Charu was very pleased to return home. It was the summer she became adept at spending time by herself, conscious of savouring it. She decided to attend to nobody's calls if she could help it, and with her grandmother's energy dwindling, it was easier to do than before.

The first half of summer was always pleasant. In a spot of shade in the garden she read her book, drew in her exercise book, traced the echoing ring of barbets. When a butterfly or a wasp died she interred it and bedecked the tomb with flowers. She lavished on the squirrel found drowned in their tank still more elaborate funerary rites. She stole peeks through the fence.

That was how she noticed that at some stage during the summer, three or four children, a little older than herself, had started visiting the Flanger quarters.

It did not seem to be a daily affair. She gauged the frequency to be two times a week. The children wore smart clothes, the girl especially. A proud girl. Her frocks boasted bows and sashes, and had likely been bought from stores, probably in the cities. Charu could not help but compare them to her own faded full-length dresses and salwar kameezes, stitched by her grandmothers, or handed down through improbable routes. It was less envy than inadequacy, which is a broader ailment, incognisant of such particular constraints as her father's (now) Chargeman A pay scale, Rs 335–425, responsible for six heads. She wondered if the girl had become a woman, for her frocks hung no longer than the knees. If she tied cloth around her waist it would have to be covered by panties. Then again, if she went to the convent – and the proud girl seemed like she definitely did – they wore classic-skirt uniforms, not salwar kameez, so she would be used to panties.

The children, Charu further noted, were accompanied by an attendant who carried their bags and water bottles. She deduced that they must be officers' children. Perhaps they had come for private tuitions. Pearl Flanger, as far as she knew, taught higher secondary classes, but naturally she would be capable of teaching the young. Yet if they were officers' children, surely the teacher would have gone to one of *their* bungalows? One reason this might not be the case, she reasoned, was that Pearl Flanger was fat. Then again, some officers had motor cars, so would not the driver be able to pick her up and drop her back? Most curious!

She anchored herself to a spot near the fence, in the arms of the madhumalati, where she could hear unseen the activity in the neighbour's living room. That confirmed it: the children were indeed there for English tuitions.

Not everything has to be *nice* or *very nice*, she heard Pearl Flanger say. Things could also be *excellent, delightful, marvellous*. Not 'he told this', 'he told that', she instructed them, he *said*. Not twel – twel*ve*. Not fie – fi*ve*. She took them through the mysteries of pronunciations. *Mirang. Scon. Clark*. She guided them in the art of composition. You don't always start at the beginning. You could also start with an *arresting* scene – but never a bad idea to start at the beginning.

How nice – how marvellous! – was the way English words tinkled out of Pearl Flanger's mouth. Sitting on the earth, leaning against the fence with a little stick in her hand, Charu whispered things back to herself. She was thrilled by the clarifications because they coincided with the period she became truly cognisant of the miracle of books. How fulfilling to jettison people for words! For in those words were people more real than real people. With them she could laugh and cry, at them she could stare, she could observe them without judgement or even comprehension. They expected nothing of her, yet they were always there for her, indeed gave her so much of themselves she felt accountable towards them.

She grew particularly devoted to a collection called *Thirty-One Great Stories From Around the World* purchased at the Institute book fair. The cover showed silhouettes of writers at work on their desks against a giant globe. The sedentary illustrations conjured up for her unparalleled foreignness; and yet when she opened the stories, the feeling of home was so strong it was an embrace. Having reread the book several times, she devised ways to surprise herself. She opened to a random page, until she became too familiar with which part of the book would open out to which story; she dropped a shred of grass on the contents page and went to wherever it fell. Some days she decided she would read the longest story, others the shortest; often she overruled the verdicts of these exercises and went to her favourites. Images from the stories filled up her mind like incidents from her past. *He saw that an old gentleman sitting in front of him in the first row of the stalls was carefully wiping his bald head and his neck with his glove and muttering something to himself.* She had so vivid a visualisation of this sentence in Anton Chekhov's 'The Death of a Government Clerk', she waited for it each time so she could transition from smile to laugh. *The light showed a pale, square-jawed face with keen eyes, and a little white scar near his right eyebrow.* She could not get past this sentence from O. Henry's 'After Twenty Years' without an unbearable knowingness.

There were phrases, passages and sometimes entire stories she could barely follow. The most baffling among them was called 'Why I Live at the P.O.' by Eudora Welty. For one, the English seemed faulty. In her mind's ear, she could hear Pearl Flanger's melodious correction: not *I says*, *I said*. The narrator was a young girl, she could tell that much. And she ended up leaving her house and family to live at the post office. It was possibly the best idea she had ever encountered.

No story moved her as profoundly as their very own Rabindranath Tagore's 'The Postmaster'. The story was contained in at least two Bangla volumes in the house, where it was entitled just 'Postmaster', but she had not gained sufficient proficiency in compound letters, and the vocabulary was difficult. Notun Dida read it out to her. They repeated the activity several times over the summer. So beautifully rendered was the relationship between the city man sent to a village and the orphan girl who looks after him that both the one reading and the one listening, over five decades separating them, had tears brim over their eyes each time.

Hai buddhiheen manabhridoy!

'The same hopes, the same delusions, that is the human heart, *khuki*,' said Notun Dida, echoing the sentiment at the end of the story. 'The human heart is a very big mystery. There is no bigger mystery in the whole world.'

Towards the end of the vacation a flurry of telegrams arrived from Kolkata Pishi. Dhrubo had gained admission into a school reputed for its academic achievers, prompting a great deal of discussion in the house. Deep down Charu believed the plan to send Dhrubo to Calcutta would not materialise.

Her grandmother, however, set about making preparations. Armed with a basket of white flowers and trident leaves of the bael, the family made a visit to the Shiva temple, where Dhrubo prostrated himself at the sanctum with his arms outstretched and his chest splattered on the cool stone. On a Thursday they performed an elaborate Lakshmi puja in the quarters. At various times of the day Dhrubo could be found chanting Charu's own favourite prayer, to Saraswati, the goddess of learning with the magnificent lotus eyes. *Saraswati mahabhage bidde kamalalochane bisharupey bishalakhi biddangdehi namastute, Saraswati mahabhage bidde kamalalochane ...*

He appeared serious, as well as a little nervous. She could not tell whether he wanted to go or not, but intuited that since it was for his betterment this was not a question to be entertained. In any case, she remained sceptical that he was going.

In spite of her doubts, the departure arrived. His grandmothers pressed rice grain into the wet vermilion on his forehead. He touched their feet; they blessed him with damp eyes; then he told his younger siblings to touch his feet, which they did with great smiling self-consciousness.

He climbed into a motor rickshaw with his father and, waving bye-bye down the road his mother had been taken one last time, Dhrubo, who had never stood first, second or third on any sports day, but with hard work and perseverance and if his exam marks and the lines on his palms were a reliable guide, he, the son of a diploma-holder, who might one day become a degree engineer, Dhrubo with his spiky hair was gone.

The void he left behind was unfamiliar. For the first time Charu sensed that the three siblings of the same house subject to the same misfortune might undergo radically different fates. Dhrubo was gone and she was a woman. If this could occur over a few months of a single summer, what about the future?

Some of the void she filled by advancing her epistolary efforts. She wrote Dhrubo a couple of letters, receiving no reply.

'Baba, what does it mean, *hai jawani khud jawani ka singar*?' she asked her father after he returned from Calcutta.

'The young do not need anything else – they are so beautiful they need no make-up, no fancy dress,' he started, gradually processing the query as admonishment for buying his children nothing beautiful. 'Why do you ask?'

'Nothing,' Charu said, and ran off, oblivious of his guilt, to complete the note in her exercise book.

'You are beautiful, you are marvellous. Forever young. You don't need make-up, you don't need anything at all. Your loving daughter.'

She decided, as well, to write to her mother's brother in Bombay. Quietly she helped herself to an inland letter card from her father's drawer.

First pressing the nib into her rough book to ensure no blotting on the inland card, she copied out the address from the diary on to the form. On the main page she proceeded to carefully inscribe her address on the top right corner, and the recipient's below it on the left. At this stage she saw that her block letters had caught a downward slope and taken up nearly half the page. Whatever came after that would have to be important. But there was nothing vital she could think of. All the things she considered writing were unconnected to one another. It would make for a very strange letter indeed!

Anando, whose confidence in percussive matters had grown since enrolling in tabla class at the Institute, was performing a feat of percussive choreography on upturned steel bowls.

'Didi, are you writing a letter to someone?' he startled her from over her shoulder.

She felt caught, annoyed. When she looked at his face, however, his black fringe and large inquisitive eyes, she was overcome with sisterly sympathy for the mere fact that he was younger.

'Even if I am writing a letter, what business is it of yours?'

'Let us write it together,' he proposed.

'No. That is not allowed.'

'And why is that? Are you writing a letter to Dada? I want to tell him sussur bissur mahisasur missur taboler hishur.'

'What is the meaning of that, fool?'

Anando began to laugh uproariously, demonishly, like they did in plays.

'It is not for you to understand, he will understand.'

'What is it, what is it, tell me again?'

'Sussur bissur mahisasur missur taboler hishur.'

Charu giggled.

'Say it again.'

Anando mounted a chair.

'Sussur bissur mahisasur missur taboler hishur.'

She put down the words. 'There. I have done it.'

She opened the bottle of glue, applied it with a matchstick to the edges, folded and sealed the letter.

'Do you know who this is going to, madman?'

Anando leapt off the chair, not bothering with the question.

'Not Dada, *Mama!*' she exclaimed. 'And look what you told him.'

Anando snatched the letter. Indeed it was so.

'Mama! *Shorbonash!* It's over!' He laughed the demon laugh again.

'Come, let's go post it,' said Charu, and hurried towards the gate.

They ran out barefooted and wild-haired like the motherless urchins certain ward members had begun to think them. Several wives in their row of quarters saw them. Surji, drying clothes in the Kumars' yard, saw them. They raced with manic breath past the ward market, where Hori saw them, a number of shopkeepers and their assistants saw them. Outside the post office they stopped. They had no need to enter it, since the inland letter card needed no stamp. But ever since 'Why I Live at the P. O.' and 'The Postmaster', she used any excuse to go inside. The postmaster saw them; the clerk behind the counter and those in the queues saw them.

Outside, she slid the letter up the incline of the mouth of the postbox.

'He has eaten it,' Anando said.

'He has eaten it,' Charu confirmed. 'Sussur bissur mahisasur missur taboler hishur.' She giggled uncontrollably.

At the ward market they asked the man selling nimbu-pani for two sips. Then they strolled back homewards happy in the heat in spite of their hot soles.

News of the vagrant behaviour reached the Chitol home even before they had returned. In their grandmother's telling of it to their father, Charu, the godforsaken girl, *lokhichada meye*, had forced Anando to go with her. Did the family no longer have a reputation worth preserving?

A punishment was necessary. It was decided that the children would not leave the house in the final week of the vacation. They would spend their time cleaning, sorting their things, organising their cupboards.

Charu, who was awakening to a thing in life called irony, marvelled that she who had spent half a night in faraway fields with no detection, had in fact begun that journey barefooted, was being made to scrub shelves and line them with fresh newspaper for going out barefoot merely till the ward market in broad daylight. No wonder a girl had to go live at the PO.

Her chores mounted, while Anando's restrictions were relaxed, and she was recruited into the grandmotherly kitchen work she thought she had successfully left behind. A more strenuous protest raged inside her. She felt terribly vindicated in her decision to run off at night; indeed, there were times it felt to her the most righteous thing she had ever done, the most befitting action for a woman to take. To prove it to herself, she snuck out of her bed half a dozen times in the near future, sometimes lingering outside the gate, at other times walking out all the way till the mouth of the lane, as if rehearsing for the unknown exigencies of womanhood.

She folded clothes with unsharp creases.

A. K. Chitol smoked cigarettes and felt their contamination on his organs.

The last days of summer passed in the warm gargle of barbets and the recurrence of sirens and the distant whistle of trains that did not halt at Bhombalpur.

7

Ants

'Good after*noon*, Mr Chitol,' said Pearl Flanger from over the fence, employing an emphasis habituated to errant schoolgirls.

'Good afternoon, Mrs Flanger. How do you do?'

'There is a matter I'd like to discuss with you, Mr Chitol.'

'Oh, certainly, certainly!' said Chitol, keen.

'There are ants in our house. Big black ones.'

'We are also facing this problem, Mrs Flanger. Rainy season, you see.'

'Well, Mr Chitol. I think they are coming into our quarters from yours.'

'Oh no, Mrs Flanger. There must be a misunderstanding. Black ants are everywhere in this season.'

'Last season they weren't here, Mr Chitol. They are coming through the holes in the wall. *Chota chota* black ants. Making me *pagal*. In the dark, *sur sur sur sur* they slither up one's legs.'

If her breaking into Hindi surprised him – it always did – the casual mention of her legs did more.

'It is not a biting insect, Mrs Flanger.'

'Frankly, Mr Chitol, I find them creepy.'

'It will become better after the rains, I am sure, Mrs Flanger.'

'Do you know the source, Mr Chitol? Where is their *ghar*? I do believe the source is in your quarters. That is where they come from.'

'Or maybe they are going *back* to the source, Mrs Flanger.'

'Well-nigh impossible, Mr Chitol. For weeks I have scanned the house end to end. The source is not here.'

'Nature shall take its course, Mrs Flanger, why worry?'

'She does not always take a favourable one, Mr Chitol, does She? I cannot find peace. I tell you, sometimes I have nightmares about these ants. I want to pull them out of my hair.'

'Oh no, Mrs Flanger.' Chitol let out an adult giggle. 'That will hurt.'

'Snakes, mongooses, toads, I can handle. We have hosted all manner of creatures on our postings. They tend to keep their distance. Now these ants. They run all over my food shelves, my canisters, my books. I watch them and I can feel them crawl all over my skin. I wonder, now that I say it, Mr Chitol, whether this is connected to the phrase *makes my skin crawl.*'

'A most interesting thought, Mrs Flanger. If you don't mind, I can make a suggestion. Take some neem leaves, soda bicarbonate, a few drops of eucalyptus oil or kerosene. Make it into a paste and apply. It may solve the problem.'

'Oh but where, Mr Chitol! I shall have to plaster the entire house. I am beyond remedies. I have tried them all. We must locate the source.'

'Let the rainy season pass, Mrs Flanger. It shall improve. I have no doubt.'

Charu could contain her curiosity no longer. She presented herself at the scene.

'Hullo, young lady,' Pearl Flanger greeted her in a somewhat intimidating manner.

'Hello, teacher,' Charu smiled shyly. Although Pearl Flanger was not, formally speaking, her teacher, she had continued to learn by eavesdropping. The private tuitions of the previous summer had resumed in the summer just gone. All of a sudden she felt mortified to be standing there, as though she had been found thieving. She could have heard this one too from out of sight.

'I invite you to have a look for yourself,' said Pearl Flanger. 'Come along, both of you, have a dekko.'

The two Chitols went out of their gate and in through Mrs Flanger's.

They stood on the veranda, peering into the house with unconcealed interest. Such well-dressed walls. A wooden Christ on a crucifix; paintings, of Madonna and Child, of the Sacred Heart, of the Himalayas; hanging knick-knacks – little bells, an ancient pistol; a great many framed photographs – couples in wedding clothes, sports teams in uniforms, generations of family in suits and dresses posing in formal rows, portraits of couples before studio backdrops of the

Big Ben and the famous tower of Pisa. On the bookshelf, beside a copy of *Principal Cities, Towns and Railway Stations of India, with Locations as on 15th August, 1947*, reclined a striking photograph of a man with a thick quiff posing with a locomotive. The locomotive Chitol could identify as a Baldwin 4-6-2, and the man was surely Ernest Flanger. A dynamic man – loco men were a dynamic breed, the vanguard of the railway workers' movement. The photographs made an impression on Chitol. They would have cost an amount of money, he thought, the commitment to document, the willingness to spend.

'Ants, ants, ants.' Pearl Flanger swept her hands with a flourish, interrupting his thoughts. 'Ants boring through the wall. Ants marching across the floor like troops, like Time itself.'

Charu was mesmerised once more by the tunefulness of Pearl Flanger's English.

'Oh no, Mrs Flanger. *Along* the wall. They are moving *along* the wall.'

'First they come *through*, Mr Chitol, only then do they move along. They come through from their source.'

'Actually, Mrs Flanger, there is no source as such.'

'Well, they don't just *materialise*, Mr Chitol.'

'That would be against the laws of physics, Mrs Flanger.'

'Or biology, for that matter, Mr Chitol.'

Something of a smile appeared on her face. A delicate aspect to Pearl Flanger revealed itself. You could see a hint of blue vein under her grey-violet eyes – indeed there was something of pearls about them.

'Let us say they are coming from no man's land, Mrs Flanger.' The edges of his nostrils blushed with wit. 'Ceasefire Line.'

Charu watched her father's grinning face. Why was he being this way? It disturbed her more than she knew. For without quite deciding to, she had taken two steps forward and stamped the ground beside the ants with her rubber slippers, sending off the insects in dizzy streaks.

Looking up, she saw the distress on her father's face and mild reproval on Pearl Flanger's.

'Nothing happens, teacher,' she said, gesturing harmlessness. Now she felt acutely embarrassed.

'Well, we should keep the *ladki* here as the ant guard,' said Mrs Flanger, attempting to restore levity.

Charu offered a smile. But her father's face continued to hold minor devastation.

All the action drew out the beanpole.

'Oh hi!' he said to Charu, in a thick, creamy voice.

She had heard him and peeped him, but these were the first words Daryll Flanger had ever spoken to her. He made a quick survey of the scene and loped back into the room.

'Oh hi!' Charu rehearsed to herself as they left the Flanger garden.

'Oh hi!' she told Salima at the rocks.

'Oh hi! Hai hai!' Salima laughed, cupping her hands over her mouth.

'He's just like a bamboo, long but strong,' Charu reported. 'I don't know how a fat person made such a thin person.'

'At least taking it out must have been easy,' conjectured Salima. 'Imagine when thin people make fat people.'

'Mrs Firangi.'

'Tommm-kinnn, Tommm-kinnn.'

'*Ladki* she called me. Bothered so much by ants and I am the girl? She must be *ladki*.'

The more Charu shifted things to Mrs Flanger the more she found herself thinking about Master Flanger. Ridiculing them did not work. That rubbing feeling between her legs; she couldn't bear for even Salima to know. Though Salima knew. Soon after Charu had discovered how to cross her thighs and let them rub for the feeling, Salima told her: 'I know what you are doing.' Charu had frozen. 'What?' she asked. 'I do it too,' Salima confessed. But Charu had not brought herself to. She pretended to locate the ant that had crawled into her salwar and caused her to squirm. Every rubbing feeling thereafter she generated with great care in solitude.

'Want to see something?' Salima said right then. Charu feared she had strayed.

Salima began to hitch up her trackpants. She stopped at the knee and turned, as if to model her calf.

Charu bent closer.

'Your brother.'

'With a skipping rope.' Salima ran her fingers over the weal.

'You should have shown him.'

'I could have shown him. Easily. But what would he do then? He'd cry.'

Charu had her own battle scars but they were never worse than scratches. And Salima's brother was twelve years older.

'Let him cry.'

'He is crack.'

When Salima said this about her brother she meant he was not crack in a way everybody is crack, but only some people are.

'My mother says if we throw him out people will eat him up like wild dogs. I can show him if I want to.'

'Just show him.'

'I'll show him. One day I'll show him.'

The girls, poised on the threshold of their teenage years, looked around at nothing much with disdain.

'Oh hi!' said Salima.

'Oh hi!' said Charu.

The little scenes above occurred towards the end of the monsoon of 1970. Not long afterwards, at the start of spring, the country held its fifth general election, where the prime minister strengthened her position handsomely. Immediately on its completion, being a year ending in 1, commenced that other gargantuan exercise, the general census, deferred from February to March on account of the election.

A designated man showed up at the Chitol quarters, a neat man with a preternaturally efficient way about him. The ease with which he put his papers on his lap without spilling any, took his finger to his tongue and flicked through the stack without creasing or smudging the edges, the clean hand in which he wrote out the answers without cancelling out anything, all suggested a genetic bounty in the matter of tidiness. Thakuma and Notun Dida were brought out for his benefit. They covered their heads for the stranger and cleared up a few things, mainly the year of Dida's birth, for which each woman provided an estimate of how old Dida would have been at Bengal's first partition.

'Who was that man, Baba?' asked Charu, who had set aside her studies to absorb these exchanges.

'He was the census enumerator, couldn't you tell?' her father replied.

'What did he come for?'

'They come to count all of us. Don't you remember the last time? How could you! You were so young.'

'Was Ma there?' Charu checked.

'Yes. We had just come here. She was there.'

'Was she counted?'

'She was counted.'

This appeared to establish something significant to Charu. She continued:

'He asked so many questions about us. What will he do with them?'

'They will be asked to every single person in the country.'

'Every *single* person in the country!'

'Every single person.'

'The same man!'

'*Dhut!* How can the same man ask the whole country?'

'He can. Why can't he?' she responded, enjoying her folly.

'It has to be completed in a month, for one thing. This time just twenty days.'

'Amazing!'

'Isn't it?' her father said. 'General election, census, railways. These things go across the full country. And the army.'

'What about post?'

'Hmm ... that too.'

'But why did he want to know so many things about us?'

'Imagine how much information we can get,' her father said expansively. 'The great thing about this country is that there are so many types of people. We will learn something about them all.'

'But why do we have to be some *type*?' she pressed him.

'You don't *have* to.' He seized the teachable moment. 'People may be of different types, the important thing is to treat everybody the same.'

'Everyone has to be something, *khuki*,' her grandmother came in. 'If you are not something, take it that you are nothing. We are Kulin Brahmin. There is no need to hide it.'

'The man didn't ask about that,' Charu pointed out.

'That is why I am telling you,' said her grandmother. 'What does that man know anyway? I remember they used to ask it.'

'So then?'

'Whether he writes it or not you are Kulin Brahmin, Kashyap gotra. Until marriage. And then, hopefully you will marry a Brahmin, and you will take the gotra of –'

'Ma,' her son remarked irritably.

'*Ki!* What did I say wrong? Do I have nothing of value to teach my grandsons-granddaughters? Should I never open my mouth in this house? Should I pack my bags?'

And as if to make good on her threat, Nistarini Debi prided off, although no further than the kitchen.

Quicker to melodrama than usual, Chitol observed.

Now he directed towards Charu the superficial show of strictness that was the usual compensation for his laxity in traditional matters.

'You have exams, don't you think you should spend some more time on studies?'

'Nothing is entering my head,' Charu replied, well aware that his recommendation at such times was taking a break.

In reward of her perception she gained an invitation to accompany him to the barber.

'Ma, we'll be back,' Chitol called out conciliatorily to his mother as they left, receiving no acknowledgement of his effort.

'You are big enough now to understand that your thakuma and your dida didn't get a chance to study – a lot of girls still don't,' he modernly lectured along the way. 'You have got the chance. You can become something.'

'Hmm,' Charu responded vaguely.

'There has to be an objective,' he continued, determined to be firm. 'And a strategy. I know you like reading, but you cannot just keep on reading stories. Weak subjects, target those first. Make your weakness into a strength. Maths, make it a daily habit. You will see for yourself how much you start enjoying it. Any doubts, you can come to me.'

'Ram Ram, Babuji, Ram Ram,' Bissesar nai greeted Chitol. 'I have been waiting for you.'

'Ram Ram,' he replied. 'Ram Ram.'

From the *chaupal* under the peepal, Charu watched the barber's implements dazzle in the sun. Soon her father enthroned himself on the wooden chair, tossing his head back as if for slaughter; Bissesar, his own nose sharp and curved as a sickle, draped him in a sheet. Light detonated off the blade, scraping flesh across the cheek, the chin, rounding the jawline, plunging towards the neck – 'Aah!' her father exclaimed as scarlet blood ballooned out of him. '*Maafi*,' Bissesar apologised, dabbing the nick with a piece of cloth.

The close shave seemed to restore her father's mood.

'In the villages here they call the barbers Thakur,' he told Charu as they walked away, 'because he has your life in his hands.'

His eyes crinkled in mirth.

'Baba, why did we change our name?' she queried him.

It caught him off guard.

'What is the big thing in that? You can always change it. You don't like it?'

'I do. It is like we made it. It is ours.'

He smiled. In fact, he was overcome with gratitude.

'Are we trying to hide that we are Brahmin?'

'Not exactly. Just that it is not necessary to show it.'

'What happens?'

'Nothing *happens*.' Recalling his rehearsal for the occasion, he added loftily, experiencing, however, a tremor of genuine emotion as he spoke: 'See the great teachers. Guru Nanak, Sant Kabir, Ramakrishna Thakur, Buddha Deb. They did not believe in caste and nobody looks at theirs.'

'Did Ma like it, the name?'

'She did,' he smiled. 'She liked it very much.'

'I like it very much also,' Charu concurred.

They walked along in camaraderie. She ran her eye over the wall of the football field.

'Why are there so many slogans on the walls, Baba?'

'When times are bad there are demands. When there are demands there are slogans. Don't worry, we will be fine. Isn't that red pretty?'

She thought so too.

As they approached their quarters, the dimming golden March light applied to their mustard-yellow cottages-of-sorts a touch of small melancholy heaven; in the Kumars' backyard at one end of the lane, where Anando watched the cat lick down her litter, among the bushes at the other end where Notun Dida tended to the inauspiciously perishing tulsi, gathered the precious weight of moments, like gently tumbling notes – life in *komal swar*, as it were.

'So in the end what happens, Baba?'

'End of what?'

'End of the census, the counting.'

'In the end there will be one number.'

'What will it be?'

'Maybe fifty to fifty-five crore,' he guessed, just within range it turned out. The number declared was near 548 million – a long way behind China, but nobody lost heart.

Charu sat down, once more, ostensibly to study. She grew fonder of her idea, the grandest idea she had known since the girl who went off to live in the PO, dispensing it liberally upon her notebook.

Mister Census climbed on his magic train called Bhombol and went everywhere at the speed of light counting every single person in the country. After each journey he patted it on its long chimney and said "Thank you, Bhombol Moshai"!! In his bag he had one lakh forms. Every form had one lakh questions. Whatever he wanted to know about a person he could find a question for it and ask them. Whatever was in their heart they would tell him. He would snap his fingers after each answer and laugh with knowledge. Sometimes the people became confused and asked what should I be, I don't know what to be!! Do not worry, does not matter, just tell me what is in your heart the census man would say, that is the biggest mystrey in the world. A young girl asked him, first of all I have a question for you Mister Census. "If something is in my heart why do you need to write it down"?? Very good, I will answer you, said Mr Census. If I write it down the biggest mystrey in the world will start getting solved. Now listen to my first question very carefully. Bhombol Moshai is going to start to blow his trumpet, he wants to take me to Kerala –

'Oh Ma!'
She leapt up at her father's cry.
Upon the kitchen floor lay her grandmother, still as the grinding stone beside her. Chitol fell down by the dignified figure whose open eyes imparted it a dull yet omniscient alertness. He shook it softly, as though not meaning to disturb it. Then he himself began to shake. 'Oh Ma, what have you done, my mother?' Noticing Charu behind him, he administered a more conscientious inspection, uttering the speculation, 'Heart, could be the heart.' Then he went quiet. His breath disappeared for seconds at a time, returning intermittently as short volcanic sighs. 'My mother. You too have left.' Charu had never seen him in this state of distress, the voice, the facial contortions. 'My

mother, my mother, my mother.' Soon, a patch of the widow's white sari was drenched in the tears of her only living son.

After the thirteen days of observances, during which the children nevertheless wrote their exams, while Dhrubo returned to Calcutta, Charu went with her father and Anando to Kanpur to see her grandmother's older sister, too infirm to have travelled for the *shraddh*.

Notun Dida stayed back alone. She considered it unwise to lock up a death house, just in case the soul had not been able to commence its journey. Nobody, anyhow, asked her to come. She lost track of time and duties. When the census enumerator came by for his revisional round, she failed to inform him of the death, upsetting the national count. Day upon day she consumed nothing except tobacco-stuffed paan, floating away into high fogs of rumination.

Who thought that she would be under one roof this long? Not she. She conceded that she had learned a lot in life from her milk sister. She missed her insults now, she yearned for them. Do you know what you told me once? You told me no matter how many homes I go to I will not bring good luck to any. I wished the earth would swallow me up then like it did Sita. Yet, I never understood, you brought me into the house of your only living son, why?

My name is Aparajita, did nobody hear me tell the census man? Listen to me, everyone: my name is Aparajita and I have not received the sympathy I deserved. Maybe you did not too. Worked your whole life for others. Lost a son when he was young, another when he was old, three children in your stomach, then the mother of your son's children. You had been through all that – so what was the need for you to go now? When Animesh's service is over, will he take me with him? Everywhere on these colony walls I see demands, demands. For my years of service, what are the benefits? My grievances are legitimate.

You would have taken me, said Notun Dida to her milk sister, feebler, higher each passing minute. I know you would. You would have insulted me but you would have taken me. So why didn't you just take me with you now? Ever since that insane jackal dug its *feu* teeth into the young Gangopadhyay, time listed and sank towards the bottom of the ocean. And, look, the moles from your insults have covered me like the march of ants.

8

The struggle

The figures on the garden patch were three, arrayed upon the ageing cane furniture, speculating about a fourth – a tall, bearded silhouette that emerged from the neighbour's gate and disappeared down the road.

'That is Vasudeva, isn't it?'

'Running Staff Vasudeva?' said Dulal Rahman.

'Yes, that's him. What was he doing there *re*, AK?' asked Pal.

'Who knows,' said Chitol, curious himself.

'Hmm … she lives alone, does she not?' Pal enquired.

'Yes,' said Chitol. 'The boy left the apprentice institute for the merchant navy.'

'Who could blame him?' remarked Dulal, although nobody had considered blaming Daryll Flanger. 'Long live locomotion. Too bad there isn't a merchant railway. Long live commotion!'

'Maybe he will have better luck than my son finding a job,' said Pal, blowing smoke. 'That man, Vasudeva, he is one good militant. From no cap on working hours, down to fourteen hours, and they would have won twelve if the federations had not gone behind their backs. And they are not finished. To hell with the federations. Strike and show your worth. I think now it is the only way. How else have they achieved what they have? Not with signature campaigns, *shala*.'

Pal was far too modest. As an office-bearer in the technical supervisors' association, one among scores of independent category unions that had mushroomed across the Indian Railways, his four-corners-of-the-country campaign had sent as many as twelve metres of signatures to parliament.

'Nor with your "people's stories" type ideas,' he added, looking at Chitol.

'Literature, like water, leaves its mark,' offered Chitol in his defence.

'This is hardly the time for literature – or signatures.'

'All I can say is that if non-militants like us sit around discussing direct action, there is something definitely the matter,' concluded Dulal. 'Give me a last cigarette, then I'm leaving.'

'You'll have to share it,' said Chitol.

'Don't have more?'

'Can't afford more.'

'One who has nothing will settle for half,' Dulal sighed.

'In the end, half of nothing is nothing.'

They finished up in a cloud of black humour and grey smoke.

After the men left Chitol remained in the garden.

His spirits were always good in the immediate aftermath, as the pebble slung flat frisks along the water before making its way down. They had been over the usual. Possible food shortage again, the wages at the Fertiliser Corporation of India, his friend Ghosh's salary at Indian Iron and Steel: these public sector undertakings that paid so much better than the Indian Railways, which provided the essential service without which the whole thing would collapse. The prime minister had lost all touch with reality.

While he did hand Dulal an entire cigarette, it was true that he calculated the cost of every cigarette he smoked, and not in terms of health alone. He watched how much mindless tea he drank. A year before he had gone from the ranks of the chargemen to the foremen. But no matter how many feeble interim-relief orders, no matter the Miabhoy Tribunal's nomenclatural alteration of Foreman B to Assistant Shop Superintendent, and the pay-scale revision to Rs 450–575, it was simply too distant a base from which to lasso this galloping inflation. His lenses were scratched well beyond transparency but he did not dare visit the optician. And this bicycle is really not so bad, he told himself; all it needed was a new chain and a new seat.

There were times Chitol thought it a miracle that his children and he had survived the tragedy that had marked their lives. He was certain that they'd never have times as difficult as those, and the certainty had helped him see any such through. The erosion under your feet you cannot always see. Bit by bit the earth slips.

It was about two years since his mother died. With her she took decades of household expertise, thrift, tradition, structure. His immediate anxieties material, Chitol contemplated spiritual faith, the security of its framework. He did not have belief, no, never really had belief. Yet, the expansiveness of the philosophies was even for sceptics, and some days early in the mornings here he was murmuring the Gayatri mantra, one, two, ten times, facing towards the rising sun, reaching for life force, concluding that the sun gave it irrespective.

A. K. Chitol looked a little worn, pressured, gently wrinkling. His hair had thinned at the dome and gone grey at the sides.

It was a cool night. The moon was strong and serene, hovering above the tree line. He glanced towards his neighbour's quarters, nearly hidden behind the madhumalati. From his low perch he could discern the dim illumination escaping the windows. A beautiful moon indeed, he thought, pouring light over dark, tugging the colossal waters in the oceans. No, the life force of moon and sun needed no validation, they generated their own metaphors. He picked up the pamphlet Pal had left him and squinted behind his thick scarred frames to read by the pearly moonlight.

'Food is ready.'

Charu said this much and retreated, not before taking note of the booklet her father held in front of his face. *Railwaymen and the Third Pay Commission: Will the Commission do Away with the Starvation Wages of Railway Employees?* A dismal, desperate title, like everything else nowadays.

She went about setting the table. The strength of the house had dwindled from six to four, and at the dining table four to two. As Thakuma and Dida used to serve and wait for the served to finish before themselves eating, Dida and Charu now did, on low stools at the mouth of the kitchen. It had pained her to watch Notun Dida eat alone this way; Dida had misinterpreted the act of sympathy turned compulsion as a mature embrace of womanhood.

Fine trick her mother had played on her, Charu sometimes thought. One woman of the house had left, then another. There was no more oppressing idea than that she too had become something like a woman of the house. For Notun Dida did not find it natural to assume the lead role: of no house herself, she did not ever develop the entitlement for it. The outcome was that she would need somebody at her side, and Charu would be that person. Although it was, in a manner, history repeating itself, the realisation dawned on Charu slowly, after circumstances had already put her in the position. This was the plight her father could not see. He was too frustrating for words – so why waste them?

She would have fared better if her pride let her put her plight into words. Her obstinacy in this regard allowed Chitol to get away thinking that if she had become withdrawn or sharp, it must be because girls undergo profound changes at a certain age, become women.

Anando breezed in, bringing his football muck.

'What's for food?'

'Dal, rice, cabbage.'

'Again? Eeesh!'

He breezed out.

'Tomato chutney,' she called out after him, herself disappointed in the staid offering.

A great irritation rose within her. The boy had no idea about the remarkable number of things that went into keeping a house on its feet. And what did he think, mutton grew on trees?

He was soon seated at the table, drumming his fingers impatiently on the plastic, preserved through the years. Now he dropped his head on the plate theatrically.

'The boy is tired,' observed Notun Dida with genuine concern. 'He gets *very* tired.'

As she put rice on Anando's plate, Charu flushed afresh. Table-setting was supposed to be his duty; he had simply given it up. Very tired, it seems. So he must always be the served and she the server? Why was it that he could go off to his tabla classes, whereas her drawing classes had stopped? And he could play all the football he liked, while she could not sink into her reading with similar abandon? And here came their blind father – how was she to find the time to conquer her weak subjects, as she had been advised in the past? It was not that she had an especial ache to become a ranker; it was the hypocrisy that enraged her. What could she ever achieve from these quarters, from this dismal township? Daryll Flanger had left for the merchant navy. Salima might become an all-India badminton player. She was only becoming the next Notun Dida.

Chitol took his seat and began to eat in a preoccupied fashion. Facts and figures about falling real income ran through his mind. The subheads of *Starvation Wages* rang out inside him like slogans. 'Railwaymen's Pay at Rock Bottom'. 'Plight of Contract and Casual Labour'. 'Refusal to Award Bonus'. 'What Should be the Principle for Wages?' 'How Workers in Other Industries Have Gained'. 'The Need of the Hour'.

He chewed on, busy in contemplation.

Charu averted her gaze from him in the way it was not possible to look a hypocrite in the eye. Neither had any idea whatsoever of the thoughts roiling the other.

When they finished, Chitol and son poured water from their tumblers and washed their hands over the plate, a habit from the floor-seating times that had persisted into the dining-table days. They rose from their chairs as though they had performed an important ritual. A few grains of rice and whole spices floated about in the steel plates they left behind.

Charu took them out to the tap in the backyard. Rather than scrub them with ash, she decided to rinse them clean and press them into service for herself and Dida.

The women took their positions on the stools.

There was barely any food on Dida's plate. She had grown ever more haphazard in her eating, preferring paan with tobacco for sustenance. Her consequent reminiscences were often unclear to Charu, involving people she had never met and places she had never been to.

'Do you know, *khuki*, I have lived in Alipurduar. I have told you that, haven't I?'

'Hmm,' said Charu, hoping she would not go on.

'Yes, I must have told you. I tell you everything, don't I, *khuki*? Was it just before I came here or earlier? Let me think now.'

She mumbled through names.

'Well, whatever it may be. Today is a full-moon night, *toh*, I had gone to Ma Lakshmi in the temple in the morning. That is how I thought of Komola di in Alipurduar. She told me she had a great desire to go to the Lakshmi Puja mela in Bijni. They would go there when she was a girl. Her heart told her she must go there again. Nobody else had the time, so she said let us go, just the two of us. We left very early in the morning by bus. On the way we stayed in someone's house in … what was the name of the place – *ki*-bari? Something *bari*, yes. But which one?'

Picking at her food, she muttered her way through place names.

'Well, whatever that place was. From there to Bijni the next morning. Do you know the Lakshmi Puja mela in Bijni, *khuki*? A very famous mela. We heard the Assamese women sing – how beautifully they sing! From far, far away people had come to set up their stalls. As we walked around, Komola di said when she was a girl she always wanted to shoot the arrow, but only the boys were allowed to. Now I am old, nobody can stop me – come, she said, when will we get the chance again? Everyone must have thought we had gone mad, two old ladies. People gathered around the stall. She picked up the bow. Janaki they called her! The man who ran the stall offered her free shots. Everybody clapped when she released the arrow. I did not do it. But I feel I should have. Today coming back from the Lakshmi temple I wished I could go back to Bijni and shoot the arrow.'

Charu smiled.

'You should have done it.'

'Komola di, she is no more. Now which year was it? Well, let me think. Anyhow, she was very fond of your mother, do you know that?'

'Was she? Why?'

'Called her brave. Married outside her community. Handled a strict mother-in-law. Was *very* fond of her. She used to say it was a pity that your father did not take better care of her.'

'What do you mean?' Charu paused on her bite.

'Her husband was a doctor, *toh*. He said, why was the fever allowed to go high? What was he doing? Why did he wait for so long? Well, what's done is done, *khuki*.'

Because of Dida's absent-minded delivery, as though Charu was not an affected party, she concealed her shock. She ate quietly. In a few moments, however, she felt devastated.

She finished up, went out to wash her hands and rinse her mouth.

Through the rear door she looked at the mess in the kitchen. When Thakuma was around, there used to not be this constant panic of things not getting done. She covered the rice and set it aside. A few utensils she rinsed lightly, stacked them on one another and then … let it be, just let this mess be.

She lingered amid the dark clotheslines. Her cardigan needed darning; Thakuma would have fixed it.

Through the hung clothes she could see the moonstruck cactus hedge Dida was attempting to grow to deter the interloping cats.

What a foolish idea, she thought to herself. What a dumb, foolish idea.

Perhaps it was true what her grandmother used to say, that Dida was a gossip at heart. But even gossips can carry truths. Tears rolled down her cheeks, almost unbeknown to her.

In the front garden Chitol allowed himself a final cigarette of the day.

These grievances are legitimate, he said to himself. These grievances *are* legitimate. The sentence repeated itself over and over in his mind. Was life about legitimising grievances or delegitimising them?

He started to hum a favourite Bangla song. *I left my address with the storm*, he began, *I cried, I laughed a lot, I floated on the tides of life*, and on and on until, carried away by the tide of words and life, he was singing with passion at a high volume, his voice carrying over the fence to his neighbour, and to his daughter in the backyard.

All year prices soared and workers struck. They struck in the newspapers, they struck in electricity, in the textile and jute mills they struck. They were striking in the tea gardens, they were striking in the docks, they were striking all over the railway lines. The loco men braved two strikes in three months in the cause of ten-hour workdays. They let steam out of the boilers, stopped locomotion. At some stage or other every division of the great network came to a standstill. That they bypassed the recognised federations to sit at the negotiating table was a source of fantastic excitement across the Indian Railways. If the loco men could, every category could.

As the year wore on a peculiar courage took over the township. The third pay commission's award, fourteen years since the last, was so paltry as to serve as provocation. Barely a week passed that did not bring some form of action. The technical supervisors organised a work-to-rule, observing each rule to the letter; the workshop slowed to inertia. The rank and file staged a walkout, the shops once more all but came to a halt. Ministerial staff put up a pen-down; hardly a paper moved in the administrative building. The switchmen, train lighting and headlighting staff called for mass absenteeism; canteen staff went go-slow; horticulture workers held a relay fast. One day everyone came together for a workshop-to-station march demanding foodgrain guarantees. They had put tools down, they had sat in, now thousands walked and chanted, raising their fists in unison and clapping their hands in harmony. Women led the march.

In retaliation, the administration enforced suspensions and pay cuts, inquiries and transfers, lathi charges, even dismissals and arrests. And in retaliation to the retaliation, gheraos – workers encircling a superior. In one such instance, the chief mechanical engineer haughtily permitted a leader to speak but one sentence. All right, said the talented leader, and crafted a single six-minute sentence ('Being that, yourself, the representative of the almighty administration, has granted a humble worker such as myself the permission to speak one sentence, let it be worth your while, so I say, sir, first of all, that it was once said that the law is an ass, and we may claim similarly that the administration ... and having gone through all these points, I can only request – raise your voices everyone – *meet our demands, meet them, meet them! meet our demands, meet them, meet them!*').

Other times the gheraos were not humorous. The fury in the eyes of the mob, the shaking fear in the eyes of the encircled. The foremen and chargemen trod a fine line between restive workers and overbearing officers. Officers could issue all the diktats they wanted but they were not on the floor, among the men, liable to be slapped with shoes or held up against a wall by the collar.

Chitol did not attempt to 'discipline' the workers under him, as the management would have him do. He did not join the technical supervisors' association. It became something of a running gag that Pal would try to shame him into it and he would in return make provocative observations about it. He had ended his subscription to a recognised union years ago, in consonance with the common disillusionment that they had turned into 'trading unions'. Supportive of the new independent category unions, he nonetheless held on to the instinct that groups curtailed one's capacity to think for oneself. He wondered whether there was a scepticism in his very appraisal of people's undertakings – and hoped that, on the contrary, his inclinations were in appreciation of man's spirit, to be guided by conscience, not affiliation.

There was no doubt that he felt the exhilaration. He contributed funds, participated in direct action. Direct action *was* a moral question, however. A work-to-rule was one thing. A strike, if it came to that, quite another. To take the position that I shall not do my duty unless ... the idea made him instinctively recoil, a violation of principle. They were not producing suitings-and-shirtings for some industrialist; they were the Indian Railways! In these contemplations he was frequently visited by tainted memories of the famine. For the first time in twenty years he turned to verse.

Grains of rice under the fishplates
How beautiful these pearls!
Who hid them there?
Did they know the value of pearls so well?
Or had they no idea at all
To stow them here like this under the fishplates?
We hear a train coming!
Rumbling like distant thunder
Maybe this one will leave us more.

It was, as it happened, a time for a little literature.

'Your Pearl Flanger,' said Pal to Chitol one day of these incipient struggles.

'What do you mean *your*?'

'All right, all right,' said Pal, with a dubious smirk. 'Your neighbour Pearl Flanger.'

'What about her?'

'She is not a radical or anything. I met Vasudeva at the station yesterday. Turns out he used to be a fireman for her husband. A good man, he said, carried his own line box, did not abuse the firemen, not like some other Anglos. Loved his locos. But more than Mr he praised Mrs Flanger.'

'Why?'

'Charitable soul. She would write out the notices and invitations in their church. Whenever he needed it, she helped him draft petitions for the union. He didn't know she was here till recently. So, how well do you know her?'

'Not very well. Why?'

'What we were discussing that day. I think she can help us draft.'

'I thought you dismissed that. What did you say, not the time for literature?'

'We have to do all we can,' said Pal, earnestly. 'If mainstream press will not support us we have to find ways.'

'I don't know what she'll say.'

'Vasudeva was sure she would agree.'

'A man like Vasudeva is always sure, that is his quality,' said Chitol.

Some days later, nevertheless, the pair showed up at her door.

'Ah, good evening, Mr Chitol,' Pearl Flanger greeted him, not in the least surprised.

'Good evening, Mrs Flanger. And this is Shubhendu Pal.'

'You must be the one Vasudeva told me about. You want me to write petitions, don't you, Mr Pal?'

'Messages travel like anything nowadays,' quipped Pal.

She seated them and returned presently with a pot of tea and biscuits.

'Oh, what was the need, Mrs Flanger?' said Chitol.

'There was no need at all,' Pal concurred.

'Do you know the amount of petitioning I had done by the time I was an adult? There, that should give you an idea.'

She pointed to a suitcase underneath the divan.

'When the system around status changed – who was European, who was Anglo-Indian, who was Indian Christian, they wanted documentary proof. I was a student, I had some spare time, so my family said off you go. We gave everything we could lay our hands on. Baptismal records, photographs, parish books. Mind you, Ernie made me write up a fair few petitions, too. Most of them about the state of the running rooms.'

She let out nostalgic laughter.

'Now, gentlemen, how may I be of help?'

Pal took her through an exuberantly verbose route down the history of the pay commissions, the shortcomings of the Das Commission in the matter of dearness allowance, the shamelessness of the Gajendragadkar Commission in that regard, the erosion of real wages, concluding with an illustration of how a sweeper in the Life Insurance Corporation fared better than a clerk in the Indian Railways.

'We want to give the situation a *human dimension*, you see,' said Chitol. 'Like Zola.'

Mrs Flanger nodded at him, seemingly impressed, as he wished she would be.

If they could compose short write-ups, explained Pal, showcasing workers, their importance to the nation, their grievances, and circulate these to 'all and sundry', there was bound to be public sympathy for the plight of the railwaymen.

'Does he mean pen portraits, Mr Chitol?'

'Yes,' replied Pal. 'Exactly.'

'Very well,' said Pearl Flanger after a little thought. 'Why not? That is something we can do. As long as it is nothing incendiary, and not *too* onerous in terms of time.'

'Very kind of you, Mrs Flanger,' said Chitol.

'Well, in times like these we must help our neighbours,' Mrs Flanger remarked, somewhat piously. 'And I know if he's looking down at us, Ernie would approve.'

First Chitol took Rampal.

Fireman Rampal's lungs are coated black with coal dust. He may look 70 but is a mere 44, in service for 25 years, starting as a loco cleaner. Through burning sun, pouring rain and chilly winds, through unimaginable hours of continuous work, Rampal has persevered in connecting this vast nation believed to be unconnectable. Colleagues will recall the time he stayed on a goods train for sixty hours, stranded by floods. By the time the waters receded the driver and his assistant had gone down with fever. Rampal piloted the train to the next station. For his troubles, this father of four, whose formal education may be low but whose practical knowledge is priceless, has been demoted to coal khalasi. The plans of training him for diesel traction lie unimplemented. Is he, like the steam engine, to be decommissioned altogether? Are his grievances not legitimate?

As Pearl Flanger read in her lovely cadence, Chitol felt a renewed surge of pride, almost ashamed that his role was not as heroic as Rampal's.

'I am Rampal and My Grievances are Legitimate' they titled it.

Every week over the next two months he took a subject. A fitter, a boilermaker, a casual porter. One day Surji's husband Bidur Dusadh. There was much Bidur wanted to talk about: the village lands that had been usurped for the railway township; the unpaid tasks they performed for officers; the prospect of losing the groom for his daughter since his applications for leave and advance had been rejected for merely participating in a peaceful protest after duty hours.

There was indeed much to say. Across ranks, across departments, across unions, for that matter castes and regions and religions, people were standing up, sometimes in the noblest way, via honest testimony and the written word: Chitol felt the warmth, the solidarity of struggle. Rice soared towards Rs 4 a kilo, wheat went over Rs 2, cooking oil Rs 14 a pack. Each petitioner felt inside him the inadequacy of things as they had turned out in independent India. Each knew he was marginal. But purpose was solace, purpose was the beginning of things.

'Goodnight, Mrs Flanger,' said Mr Chitol.

'Goodnight to you, Mr Chitol,' said Mrs Flanger.

Goodnight, heard Charu, goodnight.

9

One thousand women

Madhavi was the new girl admitted to the rocks. Square-faced, quick-eyed, shorter than Charu and Salima, better in studies than both. Her entry was hard won, a result of absolute persistence – so much tailing, so much chatter, so many unbidden favours that life became more unimaginable without her than with. And the truth was they needed a third.

'In life death is the only truth,' Madhavi said, apropos it was not clear what, but assertively, like she had been informed by an unimpeachable source.

'And how would you know?' asked Salima, carefully threading a long twig through the loops she had made of Madhavi's plaits.

'When life ends, the soul joins the Supreme Being, and the Supreme Being is the Truth,' Madhavi educated them.

'When life ends nobody joins anything, nobody becomes the truth and nobody becomes a *dayin*,' said Charu. 'Come back when you get some sense.'

Salima draped bits of leafy creepers over the twig, until a minor forest blossomed between Madhavi's plaits.

'Two of you, stop discussing nonsense,' said Salima, retreating from the forest. 'Abbu said there will be a strike like nobody has ever seen. The biggest strike in the world. The whole country will stop. A strike like never in history.'

'I hope it is after our matric exams,' Madhavi responded nervously. 'Otherwise we will get stuck very badly.'

Salima and Charu laughed at the depth of worry on her face, her swift return to worldly matters.

'You'll help us pass, won't you?'

'You people! Take nothing seriously. I have to go now. But what is this! Oh, aaooo!'

She pulled the creepers out of her hair.

'*Chee*, there will be ants in my hair now! You people!'

She stomped off with determination, turning back a few times in the futile hope that they would follow her. After a while, they left too.

A strike like never in history, Charu thought as she skipped along, her old shoes crackling under her like dry leaves. The biggest strike the world has ever seen!

Rail, rail everywhere – what a claustrophobia. Maths and the relative speeds of trains. History and George Stephenson, Father of the Railways. Science and the steam engine, conversion of energy. Geography and the linking of ports to rail lines for transport of such-and-such. English and *ever again, in the wink of an eye, painted stations whistle by…*

Meanwhile outside, Running Staff something something, something Mazdoor something, S&T something something, something India something Federation, something Association, something Pensioners, Bharat something something, Bhombalpur something or other.

Amid these distractions Charu wrote her matriculation exams in a spirit of near-indifference.

Its subsequent freedoms, however, were intense.

The girls went to two screenings of *Seeta aur Geeta* at the Institute. They played out its free-spirited songs. *Koi pass*, Salima pointed at Madhavi, *koi fail*, at herself; some are novices, at Madhavi, some are players, at self. They sucked on lurid ice lollies, pretending to be younger and freer of care than they were. They knew they were on the cusp of things. They had no false notions about how babies were made, knew the heights of the rubbing feeling. One thought herself too short, another was 'conscious' of her walk, another was crippled by cramp four days a month. They thought fuzzily of duties to come, things to pursue. Sari uniforms to be worn in inter college on the other side of this summer of endless twigs. There might be degrees, hostels. One day there might be marriage. And this place has nothing, Bhombalpur, this is no future. Get away from everything, make a life. They raced through a hundred skips of the rope. The crissing crossing shadows on the ground fluttered before their eyes. There is a moment where the going and the coming meet, shadow and light, but it barely lasts.

Even as all around her people demonstrated for their rights, she began to surrender her freedoms. Anando rid himself of the minor responsibilities he had temporarily acquired during her exams. Dida was keen to have her back by her side. Meanwhile her father drifted away, fiddling with his transistor radio, searching for the underground station, as he often did now. One evening a curious procession of words sounded off the transistor, like an oath, a threat.

Realise the strength which you possess. Seven days' strike of the Indian Railways – every thermal station in the country would close down. Ten days' strike of the Indian Railways – every steel mill would close down. Fifteen days' strike in the Indian Railways – the country will starve.

As a parade of voices pronounced these sentences, in English or Hindi, in a great variety of deliveries, she felt them stack up into something enormous and forbidding.

Setting aside her pride, Charu approached her father.

'What is that, Baba?'

'That? You know, the labour leader, the head of the federation. Fernandes.'

'Why wouldn't I know him? He came here.'

'That is from a speech he gave.'

'Who is speaking?'

'Workers. It is a relay reading.'

'When is the strike starting?'

'Eighth of May – oh six hundred hours,' replied her father, with military pretension. 'But it will happen only if there is no choice.'

'Who will decide?'

'Good question.' He leaned back in his chair and gazed up at the ceiling. 'What has happened is that more than one hundred unions have come together to form the Struggle committee. Fernandes, he is the head. But whether the strike will happen, how it will happen, nobody knows. The notice has been given.'

'I know that. They had the big demonstration that day.'

'Yes.'

'What exactly is it for?'

'Many things. Money. Food. Rest. Respect. Yes, I think I could put it like that.'

'Is it true that it will be the biggest strike in history?'

'It could be. Depending on how many participate. Seventeen lakh workers, if you include the casuals. It could be, yes. Charu, I wonder if you can tell me what is that number?'

She felt her excitement rising.

'One seven zero … zero zero zero … zero zero … *toh*? Will you do it?'

'Yes, I will.' He sighed. 'Oh, I don't know …'

'If you are going for a protest, I want to come too,' she stated plainly.

'No,' he replied, just as plainly.

'But why? I have seen girls in it. Even Salima has been.'

Chitol straightened himself.

'Absolutely not.'

'Why! Even my exams are over.'

'They can turn dangerous, haven't you seen? If there is a lathi charge what will you do? The question does not arise.'

'But why not?' she said, more forceful than either of them could imagine.

'Don't get these ideas into your head. This is not something for you to get involved with.'

'Do you think I'm a child? If I'm a child why am I given so much work in the house?'

'What is the connection?'

'I'm sure Ma would have let me go.'

Her father was unprepared for it.

'How do you know?'

'I just know. She wouldn't have let me rot like this,' Charu raised her voice, throwing her eyes wide open. 'Sometimes you want me to "become something". But you are just not bothered. You just want me to manage the house like Dida. You don't want me to see anything, do anything, be anything at all.'

He appeared stunned at her outburst.

'If you want to make something of yourself, this is not how to do it,' he said, not quite shouting, but getting there, in a quick, agitated tone. 'You will have to face your own struggles. Nobody else will be able to do it for you. You will have your own battles and you will have to fight them.'

'And I will, watch,' she said and stormed off.

Afterwards, by which we mean the long arc, Charu would come to experience this exchange as a kind of stimulating pain that re-alerted her, always a little differently, to some animating truth of her life, of life itself. But right then, rather than serve as a healthy outlet, it unvalved such reserves of repressed misery it seemed to cloud the very air. Her unhappiness felt as pervasive and incontestable as the conditions that could only be countered by strike. Once a thing was established, it was not generally in her nature to turn back.

He'll probably go write a poem now, she fumed to herself, uncharitably though not inaccurately.

Chitol's transistor kept pledging at him.

Realise your strength ... The country will starve ... Realise your strength ... The country will starve ... Realise your strength ... The country will starve.

Eventually, as forecast, he drafted a poem.

The man in the middle raises his voice.
A voice that screams,
But makes no noise.
Man in the middle, speak louder!
Shouts his voice at the man.
But that voice has drowned
In the middle of the man's own noise.

But his voice had not drowned. It did not shout, it reverberated clear as bell metal on a still night.

When the moment came, it came swiftly without warning. Early morning the night after May Day, with strike date a week off and negotiations in progress, police roused the leader of the Struggle from a railway retiring room. Across the country they began stuffing the jails, and across the country, in Poona and Bombay, in Ferozepur and Pathankot, in Gaya and Jhansi, in Allahabad and Hubli, railway employees responded with lightning strikes. In the Bhombalpur workshop they downed their tools; on the open line Vasudeva and his men struck, and soon afterwards the running staff of the entire division did. When the Territorial Army moved in to take charge of operations, their untrained men ran over a pointsman, crippling him. Protests rang like sirens over the township and beyond. Workers and in some cases their entire families came out to squat on the tracks, defying anybody to mow them down. The biggest strike the world had ever seen was well under way.

Nobody had expected the colour of their blood to be this iridescent. Crackdown was the word that went around. An Act for every end. By Defence of India Act, drafted for wartime, the strike made illegal. Under Maintenance of Internal Security, arrest without warrant. The Payment of Wages Act, on the other hand, suspended. Electricity, down to hours, to minutes. Water, to trickles, to drops. Telephone lines, cut; movement, curfewed; congregation, banned. Security forces flag-marched through the wards. Upon the bones of protesters police cracked their lathis. We'll see how you organise. Grievances like metal broaden out upon hammering. Bhombalpur organised, as Chittaranjan, Kharagpur, Golden Rocks organised, as Mughalsarai, Jamalpur, Perambur, Tughlaqabad organised, as Izatnagar, Amritsar, Ahmedabad, Gauhati, Secunderabad organised, as Bombay, Delhi, Calcutta, Madras organised.

The early days raged with face-offs. Then everybody backed off. Blood dried on the barricades. Electricity and water supply were fitfully restored. The strike remained resolute, breached only by the skeletal staff police locked into the workshop premises.

During this period Chitol received a mysterious visitor.

The man emanated on his veranda at dusk.

'You may not know me, but I know all about you,' he said.

Chitol tried to work out whether he was from the administration. Or an intelligence agency. Perhaps the ruling party?

'Who are you?' he asked.

'I am Sharma.'

'Sharma from?'

'New Delhi.'

The man wore a half-sleeve striped shirt tucked into grey trousers. His hair and moustache were unnaturally black. His eyes were opaque, something altogether unsettling about him.

'We have studied the membership lists of every union and association. You, Animesh Chitol, are not in any of them. We think you have the national spirit.'

'Yes,' replied Chitol, non-committally.

'I am sure you agree this strike is not in the national interest,' the man continued in his northern, metropolitan Hindi. 'Have they threatened you into joining? Have they scared you? Do not be scared. Do not doubt that we will finish them. Are you understanding what I am saying?'

'What choice was there but to strike?' said Chitol simply.

'Do you not know their intentions? Their plans of sabotage and derailments and bombs? Will prices fall because of the strike or will they rise? Does the common man deserve that?'

'Do workers deserve to be beaten and jailed for demanding the right to a decent life?'

'Traitors can think only of themselves. Does the prime minister think of herself? Does anything come before the country?'

'In this hot summer, do you know how difficult it was for babies, the sick, the aged?'

The man raised his eyebrows. Those, too, had a dyed blackness to them.

'I am surprised, Animesh Chitol. Maybe you do not understand the importance of loyalty in these times. We have studied your Service Record, your confidential reports. You deserve a promotion. You should be in better quarters. Are you understanding what I'm saying?'

'Very well,' he answered.

'I have no doubt you will show others the way.'

'I will do what my heart says.'

'Animesh Kumar Chitol.' The man said the full name. 'I have no doubt your heart will tell you what is good for the nation. Tomorrow I am confident you will be in the workshop. And you will bring your workers along.'

With that he was gone, as unobtrusively as he had come.

Curfew had begun, but Chitol crept out to see Pal. They stood inside his gate, talking in the low voice that is more conspicuous than the loud.

'Was he from the party?' Pal asked.

'May have been. He was purposely vague. Wanted to keep me guessing.'

'What did you tell him?'

'To get lost. Not exactly, but I think he understood what I meant.'

Pal scratched his cheekbone thoughtfully.

'They are going to start a Loyalty Drive,' he informed Chitol.

'Anything special?'

'The usual. Out-of-turn promotions, jobs for the children. Or suspension, termination, jail. A list is in circulation.'

'Is your name on it?'

'Not yet,' said Pal. 'First they are going after the, what was it, "militant anti-national elements". I hear they are acting on a, what was it, "not-too-early, not-too-late basis", *shala*.'

They were about to start evicting people from their quarters, Pal added; the listed were going underground, fanning out into the villages and quarries and jungles, taking shelter in temples, mosques, gurdwaras.

'What will you do?' Chitol asked.

'Watch how the game plays out, what else?'

Chitol stubbed out his cigarette and made to leave.

'Hear this one before you go,' Pal said to him. His jolly round eyes shone.

'What do you do to a Loyal worker?' he said in English.

'What?'

'Strike him.'

His friend's humour briefly lifted Chitol's mood, but he spent an uneasy night. There was no electricity for much of it. He sweated a river. He dreamed of the man Sharma. At an unearthly hour he got up with a twinge in his chest, convinced not only that his dream was a dream but that the man too had been one. He drank a tumbler of water, following the sound, the rise and fall of his Adam's apple, the heaviness in his belly. He became certain that he had not dreamed the man. We shall get through this too, he said to himself. My children shall be fine. He went to check on them, and was startled to see, as he turned, Charu staring at him in the dark.

'Go to sleep,' he told her.

The next day Surji brought news that the police had gone into the Dom hamlet to haul sanitation workers off to work. Cowards, the women called the policemen; here, wear our bangles, show the world what men you are. The police tried to grab and drag the women, and the women flung water at them. Things were going to get much worse, said Surji, and it was from her that Charu first heard something big was coming and it involved one thousand women.

One thousand women, Salima told Charu and Madhavi at their spot. One thousand women, and I am going.

'I will go too,' said Charu.

'Have you people thought about this properly?' said Madhavi. 'Just because matric is over doesn't mean you become crack.'

'They will enter our house, they will pull us by the hair. That is what my mother said. Yesterday she heard the officers say there will be no safe place. They will go to each house, house by house.'

'You people are crazy,' Madhavi said. 'They won't even let you leave the colony.'

'I'm coming,' Charu reaffirmed.

'We have to leave in two hours,' Salima said.

Things at this stage were not so secure between Charu and Salima. From the earliest Charu suspected she was transgressing. Nistarini Debi would not have encouraged this nature of friendship with a Muslim girl, the daughter of a keyman and a part-time cook; the girls rarely visited each other's quarters. With time the weight of their unshared circumstances began to feel as great as that of their shared. A constant subterranean game of who would yield first to the other's will went on. If Charu saw she no longer wished to be Salima, she recognised too that the things Salima did or said could rouse her into her best loyalty, her best self.

At the railway tracks at night, one thousand women would enclose the open saboteurs from all sides. The circle would not be broken. They would gather at the station before sundown. Together they would march the half-kilometre to the eastern cabin. Everything would be done in the open. That was the plan.

It was half an hour to curfew. The girls separated.

Consumed by thought, Charu took the normal, that is the wrong, route home. When she looked up, men with iron rods, others with cycle chains. Bloody, drunken eyes, from what she had heard of such eyes. They were the party goons. Probably from the youth wing – but not so young, quite old in fact.

'What do we have here?' said one paunch.

'A fresh mango.'

'A nice juicy Bhombalpuriya mango for the heat.'

They laughed, hovering around her, until she saw she was gheraoed.

'Is this one a traitor?'

'Why don't we check?'

'Come on, girl, say – Victory to the Prime Minister!'

She said nothing. She could feel their breath in her nostrils.

'What's happened? Are you dumb?'

'Say, Victory to the Prime Minister!'

'What's happened, you don't support the prime minister?'

'Come on, say after me – Strikers are Traitors!'

'What is the matter with this girl?'

'What's your name, girl?'

'Are you carrying messages?'

'Tell us, we know how to give messages.'

'Is your father a traitor?'

'Are you a good girl?'

'Come on, come on – Strikers are – Traitors!'

'Say, Prime Minister, Long Live!'

'Say, Strikers are – Traitors!'

Horrible eyes, scanning her body. She waited inside their circle, determined to say nothing. Her helplessness turned to humiliation. She wanted water, to be in her home – which they were now saying was not hers but the government's, did she understand this much?

Then she saw two uniformed men coming their way. Soldiers. Or were they police?

'Yes, big brother,' a hooligan greeted an armed man. 'Looks like we have a traitor here.'

'What is your name?' a soldier slash policeman asked her.

'Where do you live?' the other enquired.

'If your house is there, what are you doing here?'

She did not answer.

'She does not like to answer and she does not like to prove herself,' a hooligan intervened.

'Say, Strikers are – Traitors.'

She said nothing.

'Did you see that, big brother? Let us try again – Victory to the Prime Minister!'

'I think she needs our help.'

He tried to prise open her mouth with his hands. She bit down on the fingers in her mouth.

'Aaaah!' the man yelped.

A security man thrust himself in the middle, and it allowed her to flee.

The bitten man made to chase her. He was held back by the soldier slash policeman.

'Let her go, she is nothing,' he told his men. Watching her run down the path, he shouted: 'Anyway, we know where you live.'

Each step took her deeper into disorientation. Heat trampled across her face, and it was coldness she sought. She stopped against an electricity pole. *Thoo!* The feel of his flesh on her teeth, that salt on her tongue. *Thoo!* Think. What do you do now? What you do is join nine hundred and ninety-nine women. You yourself must be the thousandth. But how must I join them? What is the time? Why is the sun sinking so fast in these days of perpetual sun? And who is that man racing towards me? It is Budhwa da.

'They are looking for you, *mai*. We are all looking for you. We must leave at once.'

Now Anando was scampering towards her.

'Didi! Where did you go! Come, we have to go.'

'Where, madman, where do we have to go?' she said, reassembling herself.

'Underground.'

Struck by the glamour of the word, she followed Budhwa da and Anando. By the time they were in the quarters she was ruing her compliance.

Not their quarters – Pearl Flanger's. There she sat on the upholstered sofa, and Shubhendhu Pal, and in the throes of some great drama her father in a pyjama and kurta. It seemed their names were on a list. Shri A. K. Chitol, Smt Pearl Flanger: Propaganda, Explosive Literature, Anti-National Activity.

Shri A. K. Chitol, Smt Pearl Flanger – coupled together like that! It was enough to make her want to tear up that piece of paper.

'Disaster.' Chitol acted out the word by holding his head in his hands.

'Why on earth should my name be on this?' Pearl Flanger said, in a pitch that suggested it was not the first time she had done so.

'She is not even a railway employee,' Chitol argued.

'Somebody must have seen those pen portraits and been unhappy,' explained Pal swiftly. 'If you are going underground, go fast. There is no time to lose.'

'I think it is that man Sharma.'

'Who on earth is Sharma?' said Pearl Flanger.

'Does not matter,' said Pal. 'There is no time to sit and think.'

'It is very strange, why is our name on the list?' Chitol said. 'Why is your name not on the list?'

He had started rhetorically but as he asked it, looking his friend and senior in the eye, he wondered if he knew precisely why. He could barely acknowledge it to himself, let alone say it aloud.

'You have two choices,' Pal advised them. 'Approach them and pledge loyalty. Or leave at once, before they get you. Nobody can save you later.'

With that Pal hurried out.

So they were to leave. They were going, in fact, just like family, Charu and Anando, their father and Pearl Flanger. Budhwa would take them. Notun Dida would not be able to handle the journey.

'Wait,' Charu declared at their gate. 'I cannot come.'

'What does that mean?' asked her father.

'I am not coming. That is all.'

'Charu, come *at once*.' From her father's gritted teeth, from the impatient eyes of the others, in the face of adult decision-making, she knew she was not going to be the thousandth.

Dusk slinked towards night as they lined away like ants out of Gulab, wide-berthing the market, into an unknown cut through the field of fern and lantana earmarked for a driving range at the persistence of the chief workshop manager. After a while, without so much as scaling a parapet, they had come clear of the township. Hills were visible on two sides. Sparse sal towered above them. They were moving parallel to the river, beyond the line of the impassable bridge manned by the forces. Well past the *kheyaghat* the children had been taken years ago to observe the beauty of tied boats, they descended to an indent in the bank, where a boatman agreed to paddle them for triple the usual. As they crossed the river with secretive splashes, the details clarified themselves to Chitol – that Pal, with only two years of service left, had not jeopardised his pension, indeed might well move up a grade 'as reward for specially meritorious work'; that his unemployed son would not for long be so; that he had chosen to risk a thrashing or face-blackening or whatever else strikers might do to loyals for the sake of this future, perhaps even given up his friend and yet come to help him – and it was all so sordid he never ever wanted to discuss it with anyone.

On the other side they climbed to higher ground. Pearl Flanger stumbled and slumped against trees, crying God Almighty, scratching at her skin as if to peel it clean off the muscle. The climb eased off. They walked into a faint dry breeze, until, at lamps flickering in a settlement, the line came to a halt and the guests, as they were, had their feet washed for them.

Meanwhile, near but so far, the numbers dwindled down from a thousand. Women were thwarted by the police, the army, by hooligans, by husbands beaten or bribed into loyalty, by common obstacles or their own better instincts, so that in the end about two hundred of them shepherded the saboteurs, artists of the permanent way, who undid the fish bolts like shoelaces. They bore lathis, bayonets, blows, slashes, the tugging of their hair and the ripping of their blouses, but, amid chants of 'we are one', the symbolic sabotage of four thirteen-metre lengths of rail amounting to fifty two metres of track – that much they could do.

10

The hamlet of the Asurs

All night in the hamlet of the Asurs she wept. She felt useless for ditching Salima in the enterprise she could not talk about. When her tears dried out she lay on her palm mat on the earth floor staring at the straw above. Until she relived the invasion on her tongue and in her nerves. And here came morning through a crack in the door.

Anando's voice called from near her.

'Didi?'

'Hmm?'

'Are you sleeping?'

'No.'

'Didi.'

'Hmm.'

'Want to shit.'

She let out a lifeless laugh.

'You?'

'No.'

'I think you're sleeping.'

Their father sat at the back of an adjacent shack, his thin hair violently heatswept. Something big had happened last night. Budhwa had got the news from the boatman. Hundreds of women tried to lay down their lives on the track, that is what he had heard.

'Sahib,' Budhwa cautioned Chitol, 'everyone has to be careful. We must be quiet. We are only a few, that is our advantage. That is also our disadvantage. Nobody must see you. Do not go anywhere alone and do not be all together. The girl can be with the girls, the boy can be with the boys. The village is over the fields that way. People don't come this side. But if you are seen who knows who will carry what to whom.'

Fresh out of betrayal, Chitol instinctively tested for loyalty.

'What do people here think of the strike? Do they support the demands?'

'Sahib, only those who have jobs can have demands.'

Chitol nodded in embarrassment.

'What happened to the girls, Budhwa da?' Charu asked.

The men turned round.

'What girls, *mai*?'

'The girls on the tracks.'

Budhwa Asur sensed at once that she had intended to be there. Ever since he had spotted her in the fields on the full-moon night of Chaitra all those years ago he knew she had a different kind of daring.

'I heard they were beaten, *mai*,' he said.

Feeling she may have given away too much, she began to walk back.

'Go inside, Charu,' her father called out for good measure, deepening his voice the way her grandmother used to. One of the things she still remembered about her mother was her scurrying across from wherever she was to ask, 'What has happened?'

'Nothing,' Charu found herself muttering.

A little later she was taken to be with the girls, as Budhwa had suggested.

Days and nights they stayed in the hamlet of the Asurs.

Chitol spent as much time as possible inside the home of Soma Asur. The smell of the smoked maize sheaves hung above the hearth did not agree with him; the dark began to take its toll.

His spirit responded to the outdoors. Before and after the bleach of day he watched the colours in the sky. The strike and its problems felt at a remove, the demands that filled up his last year not so pressing. Out in the wilderness, where no day brought a guarantee except that it did begin and it would finish, he grew a new appreciation of their securities. To be sure it was hard how his family had landed up here, but he reminded himself how Budhwa's had: down from the *paats* via a labour contractor in whose debt they remained for years.

Contrary to advice, he began to show up at the mud *chaupal* beneath the mahua tree, where the men, taut of body, would sit after catching wage work in town or preparing little patches of land for the rains. There he was treated like a revered dignitary. He demonstrated he was a man of the people by taking puffs from communal bidis; soon he became adept at constructing one himself, and kept it tucked behind his ear. He asked the men about bird calls, flowers, fruits, to tell him in their language. He queried them about their traditional craft of smelting iron in earthen furnaces, no longer practised, or making the *lattha* from dried mahua flowers and tamarind seeds that he ate in the mornings, which cooled the stomach so well. For his part, he employed a Hindi dialect he considered 'tribal', throwing into a Nagpuri lilt a mix of Santhali and Asuri words, a vocabulary which grew to two dozen. There were moments Chitol was so positively enthralled by the learning opportunity that had come their way he remarked to his children: 'You may never get a chance to go underground again.'

Some men remained in awe of the babu; for them all, he was a curiosity, perhaps even a bit of a fool. Chitol noted their respect for him ebb away. He saw that Budhwa Asur assumed a body language that he would not have in the township and certainly not in his garden. To counterbalance his obligation, he remembered the time his mother wanted to sack an inebriated Budhwa and he had stepped in. He recalled the advance payments he routinely extended, as well as his intentions to compensate now. How petty, he observed, our need to assess everything for the balance of power. Not even gratitude is exempt.

Eventually he could not help but fall back into his circumstances. Pal had left a stain on his mind. He found himself justifying to his wife. Dragging their children out into the jungle – better this than to flee alone, as other men had, leaving them to face the authorities. Over the years, in flailing moments his wife's death was something he held against her. He stored it like a trump card if they were ever to argue: 'But you died.' And a full-body shudder when he heard Jigyasa's comeback. 'But you let me.'

To have somebody by one's side, the need that is never entirely erased. He wished he could go over to Pearl Flanger's hut, talk to her, lay down beside her, and – that is all.

Pearl Flanger, lying like a fugitive among the weevils in the fifty-third year of her life, closed her eyes and whispered to herself, 'Father, give me strength.' Her calves and forearms were covered with rashes, to which Karmi Asurin applied pastes.

She watched the labours of the Asurin with guilt. From the break of day to when the lanterns fell asleep they swept and cleaned, fetched pots of water from the weak stream, sieved rice or pounded millet with babies upon their backs, went into the jungle for firewood and roots, some of which they took to the stream to neutralise their bitterness, cooked meals; there was no wage work to be had in the railway township or in the fields, where it was not the season. Her appetite was shot. Once a day she ate gondali porridge without chillies on a plate of sal leaves. The austerity of the gruel comforted her. She felt the strength of the fibre, though not enough, she hoped, to compel her to go in the open.

She sang the babies English lullabies passed down to her through generations, and it soothed her more than it did them. For the older children she lined up twigs and seeds to demonstrate numbers and their unlimited potential. She watched them create stick figures and drawings and felt afresh the miracle that was the mind of a child, some alive as the bees, others listless, anaemic and eczemic. She did not want any news from the township, or from out in the divisions, workshops, town and cities – nothing except for when this strike and strife was going to be over and done with.

She took stock of the decisions that had led to this moment of her life. Petitioning to stay on in those quarters after she had been offered accommodation near the school. Drafting for the struggle. Coming underground when she could have cleared herself by petitioning the officers whose children she had tutored. There were reasons, yes, there were. All happens for a reason. We are not to only repent; we are to grasp the message.

She thought of the last time she had made the journey out to Ernie's grave, washed and decorated it, as the grave of a loved one ought to be. That was two years ago, on his anniversary of passing. The coming All Souls' Day she resolved to make the trip across the country to Velankanni with Joy and pray for him.

She fortified herself with old family prayers. For any missteps or misthoughts she wished to be forgiven. She wished to be of use. Before her eyes she summoned the Sacred Heart. The people around her could be helped. In the way she herself could be helped.

Your mother, one of the girls told Charu, while looking at the other girl. She doesn't look like you.

Charu maintained patience. She is not my mother.

The girls smiled. They said something to each other and returned to weaving palm-leaf mats to be sold at the haat. They liked the haat, she learned that much. They made themselves look nice for it, met people, sometimes drank *hanriya* or mahua and sang and danced. The girls wore flowers in their oiled hair, coiled into a huge bun, a set of rings at the top of each ear, and another set across their toes. Through their earlobes they had pierced a roll of the same palm leaf they were weaving into mats. Charu grew to admire the accoutrements. She felt bare. She hated hair oil. But never was her hair so beautifully oiled. Never had she put a flower in her hair but for a joke.

The girls had taken her in with mixed feelings. But they noticed her township superiority strip away. They were curious about this unadorned one; they sensed vulnerability, which was a good start for companionship. The girls were interested in talking about love. They instructed her never to plant banana or bamboo, which bore fruit and flower but once in their lives and so would the girl who planted them. They tried to probe her about strategies of love; she had none. Under pressure she offered up a Dhirendra from the boys' secondary. It is true that she found him attractive, but also true she had never had rubbing thoughts about him, except perhaps in dreams where the rail gates of the mind upped themselves and any crazy thing rushed through. Now that she had allowed Dhiru into this space she felt neither alarm nor shame. Her mind went to Daryll Flanger. She wondered whether they wore uniforms in the merchant navy. Then she became repulsed by the thought because of its proximity to Pearl Flanger.

The girls called each other Kachnar. One Kachnar had fallen for a Basdeo Asur who worked in a mine. He had fallen for her too, but they were from the same *killi*, and their marriage was not permitted. They planned to run away to the tea gardens of Bengal–Assam where they could work and live as they wanted.

The other Kachnar had a problem of plenty – she had suitors everywhere, at the haat, back in the *paat*, but she was not interested, she would leave them all behind. She would run away to Hazaribagh or Ranchi. A girl she knew had done it, and she could do it also.

With each of these revelations Charu felt herself useless in the matter of love and escape. Still, she finely detailed for the Kachnars a picture of Dhirendra so persuasive she almost began to love him. I too might run away, she said, just like you.

The Kachnars laughed. They told her their given names, Sukhmaniya and Phulmanti. Since they had vowed friendship by exchanging the kachnar flower, they were to call each other by that name alone. They invited Charu into their eternal friendship, for soon they would all be in different places but they could still be connected. One Kachnar exchanged a pink-and-white kachnar with Charu five times, then the other Kachnar did. They placed the flowers behind their ears. *When do the kachnar trees flower, so the entire forest is ablaze?* sang one Kachnar. *At midnight do the kachnar trees flower, and the entire forest is ablaze*, sang back the second. They sang in beautiful spirals and the newest Kachnar began to cry, she knew not for whom or what, she could not help herself. She felt she was crying all the time. Her cheeks were hot, hot was the air that blew upon them.

The boys told Anando they could cure the strike: the spirit that had entered the train would have to be driven away.

They sat at work under a tree, crafting bits of wood, metal and wire into a credible wagon and locomotive. Over this they ceremonially shredded a train ticket. They led away the contraption with a string, each one taking turns to pull it in a direction opposite to the railway township and therefore the strike, while the others beat it along with sticks. At a suitable distance they abandoned the train. At this stage they were to sacrifice a white chicken. This the boys did not have. Instead, in a shady grove of sal trees, a proxy for the sacred grove back home, they split open a gourd with an axe. They drank a little rice *hanriya*. With this they declared the strike finished.

From the township news came that it had been broken more or less. In places across the country it had long ceased; in others it was only now coming into its own, or finding a second wind. In Bhombalpur, which struck early and held strong, enough workers had been lured, starved, threatened back into the shops; the longer the rest stayed away the greater the punishment.

'We did what we had to, Mr Chitol.'

'Not just us, Mrs Flanger. Lakhs of others.'

'Well, Mr Chitol, *we* indicates any number of persons greater than one. Unless we are Her Majesty.'

They broke into slightly aged smiles. How long could they stay anyway? Chitol perceived a strain of resentment among some of their hosts. At the time of departure he declared, a little grandiosely, whatever it was that he could do for them, they only had to ask.

'I will tell you, Babuji, because he will not,' said Karmi Asurin, gesturing to her husband Budhwa.

'Babuji, when the world was young the Asur were its first people. We are people of iron. We knew how to make iron from rock. Our iron was purer than anything you could buy in the market. We are not allowed to any more. They said we burned too many trees. But we know how to look after the forest. When the *dikus* came to dig their mines what did they do, they destroyed all our trees. They told us those lands were not ours but theirs. How many trees cut for the rail colony? We know what happened to the eight Santhal villages when they made the rail colony in Chittaranjan. Their bows and arrows were not enough against the guns of the police. This Asur *tola* is the only one around here. Who knows how long it will last. Sometimes the villagers there, whose fields we work for grain and who take firewood from us, threaten to drive us away. Sometimes we hear the forest department will come after us. We hear they will give it to a contractor. It seems the forest is only for those who don't know how to live with it. People think we are demons. They do not know that we are people of iron, that before there was Tata, we were Tata. Every single person here has worked in the rail colony or on the rail line. Supervisor had told us he would get us jobs. When you go back, Babuji, get us rail jobs.'

During the strike when every willing worker was precious as gold, they could have risked the wrath of strikers and got what they wanted. Chitol wondered if it had occurred to them. Her words went to the heart of the modern enterprise, meant for contemplation another time. He comforted himself, therefore, with the idea of going back and rescuing with railway jobs the tribe that had rescued them, as Pearl Flanger did with the thought of rescuing through service them who had rescued her.

Of course, Chitol barely had a job himself, and in the coming days would be drafting reply upon reply to chargesheets, showing cause upon cause, complying with the imposition of 'I will not indulge in Anti-National Activity' five hundred times on ruled sheets of paper, and facing with stoicism the break in service by which he lost all accrued benefits – but keeping his employment, an act of survivalism that diminished and strengthened him for years afterwards. And Pearl Flanger, all out of petitioning stamina, would relinquish her job, her quarters and the township, and move into the Catholic mission on the far side of Bhombalpur station (not so far, in fact, from Tomkin's Compound), where she would teach, administer, surrender herself to the greater work, and at teatime at least one Sunday a month receive a visitor from the railway colony. 'Good afternoon, Mrs Flanger.'

As the hideouters walked away from the hamlet of the Asurs down towards the wan river and the tiny twinkling stars pushed with all their might against the leaf-blackened evening, Charu's mood began to transition. At the tender farewell she had shed more tears. Now she felt sourness, and readiness. Her mouth was dry, her jaw was set. Coming into the township by the fern and lantana route, she could not bear the thought of further life in it.

At home the lights were out and there was nobody inside. 'You are the mother of a traitor,' Notun Dida had been told by the police who threatened to evict her. When Surji took her away to her own home, the old woman thought of Nistarini Debi and chuckled: her son and grandchildren living with Asurs, her milk sister living with a Dusadh, her son mistaken for mine, I don't know what is worst for her and I am glad she did not live to see this day.

11

Departure

The three days she struggled to get the house back on its feet clarified her grievances with extraordinary lucidity. Then she was overtaken by clinical fervour. Unrest ceased. The game of life was of daring and the daring was of the self. Going underground had made her very confident. She oiled her hair and washed it clean, copied out the information from the black diary, scrutinised the contents of her newspaper-lined shelves.

At the morning hour when her father had cycled off to work, Notun Dida was in the bath and Anando asleep, she slung her duffel bag on her shoulder, briefly met eyes with the framed photograph on the wall and with a murmured *Durga, Durga*, pushed open the chicken-wire gate.

The path was strewn with the stones of her childhood; she felt their edges and rounds upon her soles. Morning had outright escaped the clutches of yesterday. From its ribboned orange and lavender emerged the shape of athletes in the football ground. The sight of a bouncing ponytail lapping it boosted her. She glanced down Salima's lane towards Salima's quarters, where there was no Mian Angrezi, no Rashida Khatoon and no Salima – only the brother, bruised and beaten, who had warned her, do not try to contact Salima. The checkpost of her molestation was down to a single sentry slumped wearily upon a chair. He blinked at Charu with gallows eyes and she gave nothing away. As she forged through the township that she could not wait to leave, she became admiring of its half-kempt order. The earthen streets, the fading mustard-brick homes, the cane fences of uniform height, the wild grass and bush erupting from the margins, the great trees that lined the metalled avenues, each lined by a different variety of tree, trees that had grown with her. At a medial roundabout she stopped to study the giant map, its 2956 acres and 6111 residential quarters broken down into component elements, as though to memorise it forever. She moved along, leaving behind the colonnaded officer bungalows, the hospital campus, the officers' club, its hedges, the chirping birds, and ultimately the main gate bearing the curved banner for the Bhombalpur Railway Workshop.

Everything outside the gates seemed unclad, unformed. Although a large number of workers in Bhombalpur had been beaten back into the shops and although the biggest strike the world had seen was in its last flutters of resistance, it was not yet called off, and in fact throve in certain pockets among certain categories. The streets were littered with the debris of protest and crackdown. Across the main intersection in the market lay fallen a giant cut-out of the prime minister. She stepped over the woman she had come to hate and made with propulsive freedom towards the railway station, the bag on her flank beating time. There she was assailed by an undefendable stink, and she learned from the chatter that the sanitation workers were still striking.

After the desolation of the streets, she had not anticipated the crowds here. People had postponed their journeys by days, by weeks, she heard them say, and even now there was no certainty whether this was the day it would begin. As it was her first attempt she felt no reason to be apprehensive. When she reached the ticket counter, the booking clerk, with the harassed air of booking clerks, told her before she could speak that nothing was going east and if anything was it was liable to be stopped along the way. He then replied to her query, in the secret-information manner of booking clerks, yes, there was a Mail going west meant to come through at night which did not ordinarily halt here but, he had received the message, would do so in these circumstances. 'Bombay,' she said, a little amazed at herself as she did. 'Bombay VT,' he said, leaving her further amazed that he was prepared to simply sell it to her. She paid up and placed the precious piece of cardboard inside her purse fat with coins from years of festive occasions.

On the platform she fought the urge to look around and see if anyone had come searching for her. Sitting on the corner of a red concrete bench in a cloud of excretic decompositions, she instead bolstered herself with metamorphic homilies. 'I, too, can become something.' 'To become an extraordinary person, you have to do just one extraordinary thing.' The crowd built, and built. Over an hour passed. Two trains went by; neither stopped. Then an unmistakable buzz went about the platform. At the distant clattering of the metal caterpillar her heart leapt. From the odour of stagnation, she would climb into one that moved.

The coaches were choked past capacity. Men stuffed their children and their bags through the grille-less unreserved windows and thereafter attempted to fold themselves through. The unsuccessful and the women pushed, pulled, yanked their way through the door. She did so too, as if her very survival depended on it, grabbing a woman by her plait to keep her balance, receiving a retaliatory backhand slap. Both women were a little abashed for their overwrought manoeuvres. But both were securely aboard. And the bell did ring, and the train did move.

She submitted herself to the gridlock near the door. People, people, people. What was one to do? What, indeed, had one just done! Frozen in the jam, the one manoeuvre she nevertheless managed to execute was remove her money purse from her bag and ease it to her chest, keeping an arm barred across it. Over time, like melting ice cubes, people lost volume, wriggling their way into improbable openings. Imperceptibly the gridlock began to resolve itself.

She melted her way up to the second compartment, leaning against hot metal. They were in a sitting coach, and people sat unreservedly – on the floor, up on the luggage racks. Down the corridor she could see men, men, men. She stayed where she was, a family spot of women and children. When at a significant halt came the churn she claimed a sitting spot. Her tenancy was secure, even if on half a buttock.

Here she was befriended by a middle-aged woman laden with gentle brown warts.

'First time travelling alone?' the woman asked in a crisp mix of Hindi and English.

'Ji, aunty.'

'I could read your face. How old?'

'Sixteen.'

'Running or complete?'

'Complete, aunty.'

'Just gave your matric?'
She nodded.
'Your name is Charu, isn't it?'
'Yes.'
'See, I knew it.' The woman smiled mischievously. She pointed to the notebook sticking out of a pocket in Charu's bag. Charu knew, but smiled nonetheless.
'Full name?'
'Charulata.'
'Very nice. I mean, Charulata, after that?'
'Chitol.'
'Chitol?'
'Chitol.'
'Bengali? Bihari?'
'Both, you might say.'
The woman looked doubtful.
'It is a caste name?'
'We are Chitols.'
'Chitols? Meaning it is … Is it a gotra or something?'
'We are Chitols.'
'So that means you are …'
'Chitols.'
'Oh, Chitols,' said the woman.
'Chitol,' said Charu.

If you repeated it enough times, her father had told her, they would either be convinced or give up.

Over the next half-hour, sinking into an expansive conversational style, so that the old man between them swapped positions, the woman extracted a family history and a summary of circumstances.

'And so where is your mother now?'
'Gopalganj. Got stuck because of the strike.'
'These railway people made such a nuisance for everyone,' said the woman. 'There are good people everywhere,' she clarified. 'Your father must have had no choice, no?'
'No, aunty.'
'Anti-social elements must have forced him. I was *wondering* why a girl like you is travelling alone. From the moment I saw you standing over there. It is for your future, after all, your studies. I would not

have myself travelled like this. There was no choice. Family needs me. Have you packed food?'

Charu bobbled no.

'Because your mother wasn't there? But mothers can't always be there for everything. You have to do some things yourself. Come, have this, I got extra anyway.'

The woman displayed alu paratha and lemon pickle in her steel tiffin box.

'I knew it would be crowded so I didn't bring plates,' she said, again with the mischievous smile. 'See how to do it. First wipe your hands on this napkin.'

She plopped pickle along the centre of the paratha and rolled it up. She handed one to Charu and started to eat one herself, laughing at their recklessness.

Once they had finished she leaned towards Charu. 'The best way to keep from using the toilet on the train is to only drink when you are thirsty and only eat when you are hungry. Eat only a little and drink only a little. People keep eating and drinking to pass the time and that's what causes trouble. Avoid tea.'

Then they sat as committed companions in a heat that enlivened the odours from toilets already run dry.

'Every two minutes stoppage, what is this?' the woman grumbled.

Charu, eager to earn her paratha, made enquiries of those standing in the aisle, as if they would know better from being on their feet. Some speculations had workers squatting on the tracks, some had them sabotaging signals. Other conjectures were benign, to do with the chaos of having so many services back on the tracks. One passenger asserted that the train was changing routes in order to proceed, a point she was unable to assess, since ignorant of the original route. 'Timetables have gone for a sixer, aunty,' she summarised. In longer lulls someone or other declared that everyone had to get off right here in the middle of nowhere. The unscheduled stops did not cease. Yet each time the train recovered from the rumours and continued to stutter across the humongous country.

As evening commenced the woman became confessional with Charu. Her son had disappointed her. He had married without listening to or even consulting anyone, and they were all paying the price now. She wanted Charu not to make this mistake. Moreover, she wanted her to be sure that the boy she married did not defy his family.

'Promise me that much,' she said.

'Why, aunty?'

'There is no bigger heartbreak for a family than to lose their son.' The woman soothed herself by running a hand over a forearm.

'Imagine if he had not liked the match made for him. That would have been even more heartbreaking. Especially for the girl.'

'Some things you will understand only when you grow older,' explained the woman. 'As one progresses in life, one understands how much wisdom there is in traditions. People have thought about these matters over thousands of years. So traditions, you can say, are the perfection of thinking.'

'But at what stage does one know that it has become perfect? What if there is still time to go?'

'Perfection was achieved a long time ago,' replied the woman. She sounded regretful that they had missed it.

'That is the other problem,' countered Charu amiably. 'If you have gone past the time of perfection, then? If something is cooked too long –'

'Does not matter,' the woman came in. 'It still saves us from our mistakes. The young must realise they do not have experience.'

She put down her glasses to press her eyes.

'Sometimes the young are misled by the old. See my nephew. He joined this JP agitation against the government. He got suspended from his college. What is his future now? When I was young I supported JP, but that was in the British time. His relief work during the famine, that was helping the people. Now he is simply instigating the young.'

'But fighting against corruption is a good thing,' posited Charu.

'What will happen to this country if people only agitate? There is JP, there is Railways. These Naxalites. Then those Dalit Panther people.'

Charu did not advertise her excitement at the thought of so many upheavals.

The woman came back to her son.

'When he was small, he used to tug my hair so hard, so hard I cannot tell you, it would come right out of my head. And in some patches the hair never grew back.'

She lowered her head to exhibit those bittersweet reminders.

'His father was not firm enough,' she reflected, biting her lips.

'It will be fine, aunty,' Charu said.

Dusk had smokily fallen. They now had the window. The woman's stop was to have come, but there were still hours to go. She said, with her clever smile, that she had anticipated these delays and packed extra food. Once more she offered Charu paratha, who, from embarrassment, took just the half, although she was hungry enough for a whole.

After dinner the woman folded her spectacles, held them in her clasped hand, which she nestled in the pleats of her sari, and closed her eyes with the words: 'I am not sleeping, just resting for some time.'

'I am also not sleeping, aunty,' Charu stated.

Soon they were lolling against one another.

At a deep hour of the night the woman shook Charu awake.

She handed her a slip of paper with her address.

'If you ever need any help in life, you can contact me.'

'Wait, aunty,' said Charu, dazed. 'Where will you go at this time?'

'My husband must be there. He keeps phoning the station for updates.'

'Okay, thank you, aunty. You helped me so much.'

'Be careful of this window.'

Charu stared at the woman in the dark and felt a stab of shame.

'Actually, aunty, my mother is dead.'

The woman thought her in a nightmare. She slapped Charu rapidly all along her jawline to bring her out of it, then ran her hand tenderly over her forehead.

'Nothing like that has happened,' the woman told her. 'Be very careful. Now I am not there.'

As soon as she left, Charu felt bereft. She slid towards the vacated window seat. The metal covers were drawn. She rechecked the fasteners. No thieving hands could come through these shutters, only slatted sweeps of warm dust. Although what might dacoits benefit from this coach? She rested her head on the shutter, letting it rattle against her temple. She had had no choice but to lie, she justified to herself. To declare oneself a motherless runaway was one step away from being reported to the police. Besides, motherlessness was a condition best endured in secrecy. She pulled her bag out from under the seat and placed it on her lap, feeling for the shapes of her things to confirm they were still there. She removed her flask of water and took a strategically small sip.

Her compartment was occupied by parts of two or three families, spread across the seats, the luggage rack and the floor. The families were poor and her interactions with them had been minimal. She had, however, developed an unspoken yet true rapport with some of the women and children, the truest with the one lying across from her, curled into half the length of the bench, a fat highway of sindoor glowing from the parting in her hair, covering her spooned child's head with the pallu of her sari. Charu found them comforting to look at. Her own berth she shared with an old lady who sat cross-legged throughout the journey, and a recent wife, judging by the bangles ringing her forearms, the brightness of her sari and sindoor. Her sleep was gone. She had brought, in another unethical act, the novel *To Kill a Mockingbird* from the Institute library. But it was too dark to read. All she could do was sit tight in the crowded night and face the bald fact that she was a runaway.

By morning her bum ached on the hard bench. At some important station, the men of the families got off and returned with jerry cans of water. The woman who had been curled around the boy went with him to the lavatory. When she came back, she told Charu: 'You can go if you want to.' An offer, in effect, to watch over her bag and keep her seat. Charu accepted. She had forgotten to bring a lota or a mug; she took her flask. The state of the lavatory compelled her to limit her ambitions; besides, she needed to ration her drinking water. While brushing her teeth she noted cloth bags hanging from nails and deduced that people must have spent the night here.

Even if it was crowded, she used the opportunity to stand near the door of the coach. A pool of urine sloshed about in the vestibule. Flecks of excreta rode on it, like dead petals upon waves.

At the next station she was joined there by the recent wife, looking outside tensely for her husband. She was very pretty.

Although they must have not been more than a year apart, the gulf seemed enormous to Charu.

'How long will the train be here?' the newly-wed asked tentatively.

'I don't know,' smiled Charu.

'Have you been to Bombay before?'

'When I was small,' Charu said.

'Is it safe? I heard him tell someone there is a lot of sin, but no matter how much the sin more is the virtue.'

'Haan,' Charu responded, awkwardly. The comment made her nervous; she had not considered her destination in such terms.

'I forgot the lota,' the girl now confessed, and the congruence had the effect of bringing her closer to Charu's age.

'So did I.'

'It was right there,' she said anxiously. 'I don't know how it got left behind. He is very angry.'

'He could have remembered too,' Charu said.

'Does not seem to be that kind of person,' the wife observed.

Charu registered the reply with a touch of amusement, but it left a deep impression on her. In her train life to come, positioned at a door just as she was now, passing women, bent double in a saturated paddy field, stoking fires in trackside shacks, releasing a hand from a scooter handlebar to adjust a lab coat, hurrying a child along a trail below a sweltering sky, reposing on haunches under a mighty tree by a great river, she would often find herself thinking back to it and the young wife.

At the opposite door a mixed group of boys and girls, probably college students, chatted relentlessly, taunting one another, discussing democracy and the nuclear blast called Smiling Buddha. They passed around a cigarette, then *saunf*, which came around to Charu too. She was honoured to have been offered, and accepted with a reserved smile. The freshness in her mouth consolidated the feeling of a new day. She felt too shy to stick around.

Slowly, feverishly the heat rose again. All morning a carnivalesque movement rumbled across the coach. Farmers with white turbans, grey moustaches and brown sacks shouted in guttural voices. Men bearing chickens fluttering in cloth bags cackled. An admirably built young soldier came on, announcing, as though for public service, that it was mother-swear forty-seven degrees outside and a few weeks ago he was in mother-swear minus temperature; he cracked sugar cane with his teeth, locating gaps between people to project the cud out of the window. By afternoon a group of pilgrims registered their presence via singing, sometimes to wide participation. The main singer had a loose, flowing way with melody. Under his leadership the popular 'Raghupati Raghav Raja Ram', which had a dirge-like quality when sung in school, stirred Charu. A little later she noticed that he was blind. Long after the pilgrims alighted, he left behind the sung words in her soul.

She became less conservative with her consumption, purchasing through the grille-free windows that made vending easy two ladoos, one samosa, two bananas, a green mango with chilli and salt, even a cup of tea. One ladoo she handed to the child, who had started to wail in the heat. He liked that, and so did she.

In time, three men in their twenties and thirties, travelling separately, pitched themselves in her compartment. The youngest wore a wide virginal moustache and the mien of someone whose every problem is intractable. He was on his way to accept the position of a watchman in a cotton mill – even though he was a full-fledged graduate in chemistry. The two older men were divided in their opinion of his decision. One believed something worthy of his qualifications would emerge and he must not short-change himself; the other thought he was only being realistic in this jobs crisis.

'A man may well want to eat biryani,' the latter declaimed, looking around, reiterating it as though a famous couplet – 'A man may well want to eat biryani, but if he is hungry he will settle for boiled rice.'

'He will be lucky to even get that,' the first responded. 'She can explode an atom bomb but she cannot give a hungry man rice.'

A lot of people came to participate in the young man's dilemma. As the conversation grew outwards to the state of the country, such a veteran of the compartment did Charu feel that when the subject turned to the railway strike she defended it. Because of her quietness thus far, and the fact that she looked like she was English-medium – indeed, some of her co-travellers had seen an English book in her bag – her words were accorded consideration. The man who had delivered the biryani couplet, it turned out, was a peon in a central government office and had participated in the massive one-day strike in solidarity with the railwaymen. 'Future generations will thank these workers,' he said volubly and emphatically enough for nobody to challenge it.

The tension between being at once in this tightly enclosed space and the great wide world was so great Charu felt she might burst from it. When she next went to the door, it was to the far end of the coach. On the way she spotted a young girl, petite and bespectacled, who appeared to be travelling alone. She wondered whether the girl, too, had run away. She entertained the possibility that many travellers in the train had left home without notice. She was not sure, for example, if the confused young man had declared his intentions before departing, or all of the college youth of the morning had. She was confident that the two Kachnars would perpetrate their escape competently when the moment came, and so, one day, would Salima.

From the door she watched the country, brown and busy, busy yet passive. She fell back on the childhood technique her father had taught her. She counted dogs, goats, a certain kind of tree. Counted buffaloes. Briefly counted people. As the sun began to dip, she felt herself lowering into crisis. A great amount of time had passed since her departure and she was a very long way from home. She could think about nothing other than when they would have discovered her absence. Would they have found her note? What would they have made of it? After all, it only said, *Do not be worried. I will contact you soon. Charu.* They would have hunted the entire colony and gone desperate to the police, sick with worry. She felt shot in the heart. She was a traitor.

At the next halt she contemplated going to the stationmaster to contact her father in Bhombalpur. But watching the decisive movements of passengers, their passionate struggle to embark on journeys or terminate them, she understood that it was not a time for halfway measures. She rehearsed her reasons, exaggerated them. Her grievances were legitimate. Yes they were. By God they were! They asserted themselves with such energy that she felt like going back and escaping all over again. She bolstered herself once more with self-made adages. 'The same railways that bounds one in takes one away!' 'What a strange and unpredictable journey life is!' She wished to write these down. That being impossible, she simply thought them.

Another night crept in; once more she barely ate, consuming the second of her bananas and a handful of muri she had brought with her. The slats were rolled over the windows and latched into place; the floor became full once more with prone passengers. Again the sight of the woman with the sindoor highway and her cuddled child gifted her a sense of security. Her body was hot; she was running a temperature.

Dust and sweat caked her. When she rubbed her skin, thick dark grey strings peeled off it like eraser shavings. She felt enormously tired and was likely dehydrated. She drowsed in and out of dreams. The last name she heard on her second night of crouched vigil was a place called Jalgaon.

Through the inky heart of 1974 the caterpillar crawled on.

In the perspirational morning a man who had yesterday been a few compartments down the corridor and reminded her of Mian Angrezi held court in her aisle. The mood felt fantastically different. He shushed everybody to calculate the speed from the frequency of clicks on the track and announced the result:

'Once you take into account other stoppages, at the current rate we will reach in ... another six and a half days!'

People laughed with abandon. Some had been on the train for over seventy hours. Maybe the journey was indeed coming to an end. Tropicality steamed in through the windows, the feeling of coast, then the commute-stricken conurbations, then more and more and more of everything. One stop they made in the anarchy of a city station. As the city injected itself into her bloodstream she felt knocked out. Soundclouds, peopleswarms like she had never heard or seen. No next step could be devised in the face of an arbitrariness so large. She felt slayed by the gigantry of her folly.

The stunned rake inched into the terminus. The thousands of inhabitants emptied out like a plagued village. Migrants, runaways, their boxes, bedding rolls, slippers, infants, ambitions, compulsions pouring out on to the platform underneath a tremendous roof of steel and light. Whereupon they resumed on foot like an ancient caravan.

At the concourse the caravan was fissioned into infinity by countless commuters. These vigorous city commuters were kineticised by a hissing in-breath-out-breath *ssssss* that appeared to be a form of commuting release. Now she was distracted by a different nature of mouth-sound, pucker-lipped *pchew-pchews* and close-toothed ones that went *chhh-chhh* or *ttss-ttss*. She realised they were meant for her to move aside. She did, on unsteady legs folded too long. Drawn into successively parallel streams of human movement, she strayed into an area built like a cathedral. Marvellous pillars, *marvellous* golden stars above – but here were mere ticket counters, above them stained glass, behind them the water containers sleek modern cylinders not plump claypots. She was at the exit.

Edging past the threshold of inside and outside, in the heat of her unbelievable folly, under pigeons hustling and hurrying as though themselves late for a next train, one alighted on a beastly projection in the facade and emptied itself on her head.

'*Vanda nai*, it is good luck,' a man said brushing past her, without glancing at her, and pointillated away into the crowd. She shifted out of the stream. So many women: smokeresses, workers, idlers, women who looked like machines, like mannequins, like ragamuffins, groups of marching women beating rolling pins on steel plates demanding the end of price rise. Wiping the pigeon shit with her mother's monogrammed handkerchief that had served her well over the past two days, exhaling a deep breath that collapsed in a puddle on her toes, determined to make enquiries at the stop where the decked red buses wheezed and resumed with great asthmatic roars, into the city of Bombay stepped Miss Chitol.

II

Smart Girls Required

I
Kings & Queens

The loneliness at the centre of a person never disappears, it only changes shape. Sometimes no lonelinesses lock into place. At other times they fit snug, and the lonely hearts sing together like the song of rain, indifferent to the loneliness that created the song.

People, people, people. Rain, rain, rain. People like raindrops, too many to count.

Musing so, Miss Chitol, poetically inclined, twenty years old, looked out through the glass.

The shop smelled of Rexine and cardboard and leather, and so did she, Rexine and cardboard and leather and the unwashable attitude of certain customers who came into Kings & Queens expecting to be treated exactly as such. Not all, she conceded. Most came and went without seeing or saying or buying much, masked in a preoccupation she too had cultivated to keep in step with the city.

She lowered her gaze towards the feet falling on the footpath glittering with grey water. Nobody bothered to hitch up their saris or trousers over puddles, the time for that had passed. Quick-dry terrycot saris, terrycot trousers, invincible rubber soles. She never thought she would come to this city to shod it.

She glanced at her wristwatch. An hour left on duty. Mr Chheda had gone; his son was at the counter, smirking at nothing. They spoke in Kutchi to the boys, who climbed into the mezzanine loft and pelted cardboard boxes of this style or that size at the salespeople on the shop floor. It was not Miss Chitol's duty to slip shoes on to unappetising feet, nor her colleague Nalini Pingle's. Three times over the last week, upon indication from the junior sheth, she had got down on her haunches to help customers into their footwear.

She tried not to fall into the despondency trap. Despondency only made her core cramp harder.

At last it was time. The girls could leave. The boys would pack up and pull down the shutters, junior sheth would turn the key in the big lock.

'Let's eat pattice today,' said Miss Chitol, feeling a brief expansiveness within. Nalini assented, tentatively, but once she did the girls hit a fast, unhesitant stride towards their usual New Deluxe Cafe and Restaurant.

'Two chai, two veg pattice,' they said in unison to the waiter who hurried over as they sat down on the bench.

The tea arrived in an instant.

'I don't like it, Nalli,' said Miss Chitol, sipping it. 'I don't like what they are doing at all. We should complain.'

'Cartoon you are,' Nalini laughed. 'Complain to? Senior sheth? He will say: leave. He anyway thinks this was a bad idea.'

'Do you remember what junior said. He said, your duties will be to welcome customers, talk to them about their needs, guide them through the range, help them make a choice. The boys will put the shoes on. What did the advertisement say?'

Smart girls required. That, in fact, was all the advertisement had said.

'Life is not like that, missis,' said Nalini. 'If you want a job you have to be flexible. He pays on time, lets us go home on time.'

'Those feet stink. Especially in the rains, they smell like gutters.'

'Arre, how many times have you had to do it? You have to be a little clever. Just pretend to be busy till a boy comes to do it. Go into the back room for a few minutes.'

The waiter plonked down steel quarter plates with the pattices and a steel bowl of pumpkin ketchup.

Miss Chitol brooded.

'There is another thing,' she said. 'That advice you gave me. It's not working.'

'Monthlies?'

'Hmm. First of all, in that full building there is only that one dirty latrine. Then the bulb is gone, so it's dark. Cramps in your stomach, the toilet stinks, you are trying to change it and someone keeps trying to open the door without knocking. The cotton balls were fully soaked. I can't manage.'

'You have to layer it properly. Are you doing it properly? Try double cloth.'

'I have.'

'Double layer of cotton balls also?'

'I'm thinking I'll buy disposables,' said Miss Chitol.

'You have too much money looks like,' Nalini taunted her. 'Do you have anybody who will ask for it? You will have to go and ask the man yourself.'

'So what? I will ask.'

'See, Charu. Life is like a weighing scale. Before every decision you have to put plus points on one side, minus points on the other side and see where the needle stops. You are younger to me so I can tell you. Sometimes you think too rashly.'

Miss Chitol fell silent. She watched the dry remnants of her pattice tremble under the wall fan. She fingered the flakes. Those which stuck she brought to her mouth. The flakes were the best part.

'Maybe you are right,' she said.

The waiter slapped down the bill. The women went into the money zips of their handbags. Coins tinkled on the table.

Observing the shortfall of fifty paise, she looked at Nalini.

'Bus that day. Forgot?'

'Oh! Yes,' said Miss Chitol, and reached into her zip for extra.

'Cartoon you are. Joker.'

Nalini ran off towards Victoria Terminus in a bid for the 7:21 slow. In the wind-brushed arcade Miss Chitol sought shelter from the ceaselessness of the city. Final hustles at the stalls. No, she wanted no alarm clock with radium display, nor an electric parrot, and she had nothing to give the girl with an infant slung across her chest. High up on the great terminus she perceived the terrifying gargoyles, off which the pigeon had spattered her with welcome, spouting angry rain.

Onward to the chemist, she decided. Pushing the square button on her umbrella she prepared to enter the rain. It bloomed open and kept going with the gushing wind, past perpendicular, until convex. One by one the octants of black cloth tore free from their spokes, leaving her much like the Lady of Progress atop the Victoria Terminus and no more protected from the rain. She carried on with the crowd, pretending this had not happened, that her umbrella was quite intact. Water fell like the eternity of automobile horns, the wind gasped at her. She mentally calculated the expense. Passing a heap of rubbish she flung her umbrella on it. The second one this season.

The cramps in her abdomen settled into a tight knot. Raindrops and possibly tears, yes certainly tears, streamed down her cheek, smudging them with kajal. She felt let down by the compliance of the eyes with the temporary disappointment of the heart. She would stain; that tension now overcame her. But perhaps not all the way out till her kurta. Stopping under an overhang she looped her ponytail into a bun. She sought refuge in practicality, never mind if the price was ridiculousness. From her handbag she fished out a translucent plastic packet and looped the handles over her ears, as she had seen some Bombay men do. She tried to adjust the bag in a way that the handles could not be detected – why, may even pass for a shower cap or a scrub cap. Maybe I look like an intern at the hospital, she bucked herself up. But nobody really cared how Miss Chitol looked with her plastic bag on her head.

At the chemist, she put down exact change on the counter in order to keep conversation to a minimum. 'Stayfree.' The man, serving three simultaneously, gave her the disposables in a brown paper bag, while looking at no customer. No, nobody cared at all.

Having put away her purchase safely, she took the wind in her face and considered ways and means to get home.

2

The Prasads

Her uncle had a reputation for joviality. Before others he bared his hilariously crooked teeth on every other statement, some of which were truly funny and some convincing counterfeits. His eyebrows were shaped like arrowheads, although with off-centre tips, and they shot up at the slightest excuse. His nostrils were long and curvaceous and proved themselves to be flexible and humorous. He kept his moustache to the exact width of his nose, also the exact width of his mouth and his square chin, giving his lower face an altogether contrary symmetry. This too seemed a joke. His major skill was mimicking the accents, languages, intonations and gestures of peoples across the country, so he could befriend virtually any Indian, who received the jesting as flattery. He had perhaps once been fat, or was simply putting to use a gift, for his belt wound around him one and a half times, fastened through one of the extra holes the cobbler had punched in.

Miss Chitol knew the belt well. It was the same belt, she was sure, he had employed on his wife during a fight. She found herself staring at it whenever she saw it hanging on the hook, as though it was the belt and not her uncle that was out of its mind.

She felt then that her uncle maintained the joviality for the reputation. He was as jokeless as that piece of leather. Until then she had not noted how strangely glum was his face, how fallen his eyes beneath those arrowheads, how loose and haggard his cheeks, how frustrated the stoop of his posture, a man who could not keep himself straight. Yet her mami pretended nobody knew. In the aftermath there prevailed a household rhythm that felt not abnormal in the least, so that Miss Chitol asked herself if there had ever been a beating. She wondered if she had dreamed it, much in the way she sometimes wondered whether she was dreaming living here in this house.

All night it rained and all morning too. There had been no chance of getting to work. The tracks were under water, said the radio, trees had crashed across roads, vehicles were submerged. Mudslides had taken the huts on the hills down with them.

Evening now, ensconced in her converted balcony room, Miss Chitol idled her way through the week's newspapers, when she was startled to see her father staring at her with fingers raised in the air. '5 reasons why businessmen like me choose – *India's first* – Neoprene© Jacket.' A young version of him, with a larger mouth, smugger eyes, a blander smile. Maybe not like her father at all. Absurd! She mocked herself for her mistake, as though Dhrubo or Anando were around to have seen her think it.

The languidity of rain crept over her. *Ogo*, I am tired, she thought to herself in a theatrical quavering Bangla, O let me become a little horizontal, extinguish a little my eyes. Before she could stretch out her aunt called, herself affecting a dramatic style – in the aunt's case, although she was born and raised in Bombay, a rustic Bihari that intimated to Miss Chitol that there would now be demands.

'Charu ... *O Charuwa* ... Ei niece of Jagdish.'

She grimaced and pulled herself together. Using short shuffling steps to better convey her labour, she arrived at the bedroom. A mild sting in her eyes alerted her that it was an Iodex call.

'Mami?' she said, with the bright curiosity that was an important part of earning her keep.

Bhagmati Prasad, always a little younger than Miss Chitol's image of her, was positioned on her cushioned chair, her feet resting on the bed. Beside her lay open the tub of Iodex, whose very scent had started to soothe her weary ankles. It was Miss Chitol's view that her aunt had a misguided belief in the utility of the ointment, as well as ankles.

'O Charuwa, there you are ... I can't explain it. My ankles, they are feeling so weak today, God knows why. They are really troubling me.'

'You must be working hard, Mami. And in this rainy season.'

'Hmm ... I was thinking the same thing. In this season everything just swells up. If one does too much work ... but then if hard work is written into one's fate? I think this Iodex will make me feel better. Charu, can you …?'

'But of course, Mami, is that even a thing to ask?'

Miss Chitol accepted the tub like the beneficiary of a surprise gift. Settling on the floor, she studied her aunt's cracked soles and wondered whether in her own fate was merely the feet of others. She began applying the ointment with something like malice. Her aunt moaned; her nostrils fluttered with pleasure. Miss Chitol experimented with over-liberal use of the ointment. As usual, rather than burn it only produced greater satisfaction in the recipient, and as usual her malice began to ebb away, her intentions graduated to noble, and she gave and sought in the task sincere therapy. They took me in. They gave me a roof. And how good that I am able to help her stand comfortably on her feet. She felt her aunt's leg twitch, looked up at her face in the throes of ankular rejuvenation, and knew that she would now speak.

'Our Biru is coming over the weekend,' she announced. 'Poor boy does not get to study at all at home.'

Birendra, the only son of the Prasads' only daughter, had been Miss Chitol's best companion in her first months here. Then she sensed his mother discouraged the closeness. Meanwhile his grandmother moulded him into a sly tyrant whose demands and machinations it was Miss Chitol's duty to accommodate.

'That Biju, you know, is studying for Competition.'

Bijendra was Birendra's older cousin who had gone to live in that house to prepare for a future as an administrator.

'Biju locks the room and studies inside. Where will our boy go? He is young, but he also …'

'Has to study,' Miss Chitol said.

'That is what. Does the whole world stop because of Competition?'

Miss Chitol understood the implications. She was to hang around on the weekend, keep the youngster hydrated with lime juice, help in the kitchen with the special items made in his honour.

'Truly, nobody thinks about that,' reiterated Bhagmati Prasad, whose ankles had become blue. 'This boy also has to study.'

If Bhagmati Prasad was not especially concerned about her niece's studies, neither, to be fair, was Miss Chitol. Her education never really took off. Owing to the different education systems in the two states, and deadlines and original marksheets and transfer certificates, she could not get admitted into inter the year she came. She sat at home, at her aunt's disposal. The following year the state of Maharashtra introduced the new two-plus-three system, and she enrolled in junior college, in the Arts stream. By the monsoon of 1978, the time of our present narration, having commenced her second year of senior college, Miss Chitol stopped attending it (although she intended on writing the exams). This was, of course, a secret. She could not possibly reveal that she had taken up a job at a shoe shop, or anywhere at all.

Hosting Biru meant missing at least half a day's work. As Miss Chitol fretted, the main door opened. In walked her mother's only brother, Jagdish Chandra Prasad – JCP to friends – looking as though he had been roaming about viceing.

'*Jai Bajrang Bali!*' he said, noting his wife's Iodex-coated feet sticking out of her petticoat and, she could not help herself, it made Miss Chitol laugh.

They watched him wander about the little living room, shedding his shoes, socks, his printed shirt with collars the size of airplane wings, drop into a chair in his sleeveless white vest and conical grey trousers held up by the oversize belt, and fall asleep.

'Look at him,' said Bhagmati Prasad, that and no more.

For the first half-minute he did not recognise her. He pretended to nevertheless and welcomed her because she carried physical traces of family. On touching his feet she used the word 'mama' and only then he knew. She sat reluctantly on the sofa, for the stench of the country was all over her. She looked up for air, and two tiny fans whirled in her eyes. Two little ceiling fans for this room. Astonishing city.

There was an extreme enervated intensity to the guest. Without putting to her lips the glass of water given her she leaned forward and said, in near delirium –

'I have come to learn about my mother.'

'What do you want to know?' He was not sure whether he was humouring her or negotiating with her.

'Tell me everything.' Now she took a sip of water in a way that felt threatening, requiring tact.

'She was my younger sister. She was naughty, then she became quiet. Jigyasa. She was named correctly. Curiosity was her nature. A determined person. She loved her children, you all, more than anything. You must be knowing that.'

'Tell me things I don't know.'

He could not tell why but this seemed a necessary interview, for him more than for her. He obeyed.

'The month was Magh when your mother was born. Babuji worked for Post and Telegraph. The British ruled us then. They were the masters. He felt he was treated like an untouchable. What did we know? I understood all this much later. Babuji didn't like talking much, not to us at least. We were scared of him. There was reason to be. Maybe I am saying too much.'

Jagdish Chandra Prasad's eyes reflected the deranged intensity in the pair before him.

'A cold month. Ma went to our nani's house for the birth and she took me with her. In the yard they built a small hut for her. I was not allowed inside. If they wanted something I gave it at the door. I stood outside and looked at her. She asked me questions: have you eaten, did you take bath, how cold was the water. I knew a baby was going to be born. I was seven years old. Between me and your mother one baby lost its life in our mother's stomach and one after it came out. So everyone told me I had to behave well, do all my tasks, she should not have any worries because of me.'

His speech got slower, his Hindi stricter.

'Your mother was born in broad daylight. I remember running off with Lalchan to call the *dai* in the morning. From outside the hut I heard everything. I had heard goats and dogs give birth but this was different. I was scared. When I heard your mother crying I closed my ears in fear, but they told me everything was fine. Everything was fine, everything would be fine. Babuji saw the baby one month later. He was unhappy because of the astrological charts. But he was usually unhappy. The baby was here, she was crying with life, everything was fine, everything would be fine, everything ...'

Tears were flowing freely down his cheeks but his interlocutor had passed out. He stood over her, amazed at himself, and the one who sometimes sent him nonsensical letters. He looked on in kinship. Like this waif he had come to the city, what, three decades ago, like her he had passed out, when a stranger had come to his rescue, and here he was still, all its sins and virtues were his and his its.

Tears dried in the crevices of his neck. He vowed never to expose himself in this way again, not so easily.

The key turned in the door. Bhagmati Prasad entered huffing and puffing with a grandchild squirming in her arms. She put him down, and all three stood staring at what the wind had blown in.

3
Digital time

According to Miss Chitol's calculations, freedom could be hers in three months. By then, the envelope in her enamel box would have swollen to the thickness of Paying Guest rent, inclusive of security and advance. These forecasts did not account for the increasing frequency of evening pattice, or the eleven birthday rupees she intended to send Anando, whom she considered a theatre artiste in need of support.

Guilt played a part, no doubt. The guilt was an awkward leftover because, now, four years since her escape, nobody thought of her as having run away, not even she. In an unspoken, concerted effort to deshame the move, it became that completing her education in Bombay had been the considered plan, just as Dhrubo's going to Calcutta had. Her father sent money to this brother-in-law's household in Bombay in the way he had done to that brother-in-law's in Calcutta for Dhrubo. If in the process Miss Chitol never entirely contended with the drama of her deed, neither did her father, who had settled at a philosophy for the matter. Perhaps, he told himself, in order to regularise his hurt as much as her flight, she had acted in compulsion – compulsions being as indiscriminate as the weather, landing on whomever, however.

In Bombay, Miss Chitol knew that she had reduced the spend on the servant as well as the housewife's labours. If she could liberate herself from this house, she could also liberate her father from his remittances to it. But she was stuck in the pretence. She had manoeuvred herself back into a Notun Dida life. She had been outwitted by society. In the city she saw possibilities – if only she could give herself a chance in it!

To persuade her calculations into real life she needed cool, passionless discipline. But here she was, 5:31 a.m., mind racing since 4:11. And now she must open the taps to catch the municipal water in buckets, take yesterday's milk bottles down to the booth and return with new ones, bottles whose silver caps, when you pulled them the right way, could make a delicious sound, *sllrr-puck* – a sound like success.

City time was digital. Each minute was dynamite. She wanted definition, non-negotiable values, not sweeping arms that turned time elastic. On her wrist blinked a brandless watch she had bought from a cart outside the station. At the press of a tiny button beeped a tinny alarm; at the press of another glowed a tiny light; beneath the day and date and month, between the hours and minutes, blipped a colon to mark every escalating second – definition all the way.

At 6:00 the milk booth was to open, but not before 6:10 did the young squint they candidly called Kania get it going. Nevertheless, to secure a top-three spot it took a 6:03 arrival. By 6:15 – 6:20 *max* – she must purchase the pouch of flowers for Bhagmati Prasad's altar from Kashibai, who sold out fast and entertained no laggards, and a ladi or two of pao from Kadarbhai outside the recycler, who sold used books by the rupee and bought them by the kilo. Back up the four storeys of Jhunjhunwala Building amid the melodrama of Juna Tanki crows; milk to be boiled, tea to be concocted, and time, fleeing away in domestic assistantship – kneading, peeling, julienning, to the sounds of Vividh Bharati – only seized back in the separate privacies of the lavatory and the bathroom, where she speed-washed her undergarments. Swallowing a breakfast of pao-butter-jam or pao-fry-egg, packing her tiffin of two parathas and pickle, by 8:05 – 8:10 *last to last* – she embarked on the fraudulent journey to college.

Down the staircase descended Miss Chitol, digital seconds detonating on her wrist. She had acquired a final height of five feet, two and a quarter inches – was keen on the quarter-inch, maintained a 'ramrod-straight' spine for it. In her eye, beneath an occasionally furrowed brow, flickered a hopeful if strained tenacity. Everything there for the taking. The numbers on her wrist determined whether she would part the crowd or march in sync with it. Between 8:11 and 8:20 her bus appeared at the stop. If the bus arrived towards early and she arrived towards late, which was often, then, armed with her second-class season pass, she beat on past the garbage-filled reservoir said to be the titular tank of Juna Tanki, to the railway station, and surged into a rush-hour ladies second-class – moving in a direction one hundred per cent opposite from college.

Not in her experience was the ladies coach a space of women singing songs while stitching embroidery, as she had read in a women's magazine – not at morning rush hour. Pea-shelling, methi-plucking in the evening, yes. The mornings held latency, carefully guarded before the day manifested; things not yet done that must be done; worries, worries. Women in a variety of saris worn in a variety of styles, in jeans, nightgowns, in tent-like T-shirts over tights, high-waisted trousers that flared for days, in mangalsutras, shakha pola, lipstick, sunglasses, ceramic bangles, lapis pendants, each woman doused in her perspiration.

At Churchgate they expelled themselves on double-discharge platforms susurrating with commuting whistle-exhales. Office women shuffled with rapid office steps, looking downward to efficiently avoid the feet of others. College girls ambled, deluded, as though life was one long stroll, unless alone – in which case they might walk as fast as the office-goers, guarding their chests with books or folders. Miss Chitol was between one thing and the other and emerged in the halfway spirit into that great downtown thrum of maidan, sweat, basalt, breeze.

Regardless of her transport, her ambition, and it had become something as big as ambition, was to be seated in the David Sassoon Library and Reading Room in Kalaghoda before the 9:00 siren soared over the metropolis, as if this too was a workshop town, which in a manner it was. For defrauding herself of an education, she had directed from her monthly salary of Rs 225, Rs 15 towards the library as quarterly subscription fee, and an equal amount as a one-time 'entrance fee'.

That hour it was modestly inhabited. The students who threw themselves into studies with ferocious muttering concentration shamed her; then she would look towards the odd retiree who seemed to be reading for pure pleasure. A few black-and-white advocates of the nearby courts rifled through their case papers, pausing to lasso with their pens a crucial clause that would leave milord no choice but to yield to it. Newspaper readers perused affairs of the day in one of five languages. On a planter's chair on the balcony, always, with a stack of periodicals balanced on its arms, reclined an elderly man she took for a Parsi but afterwards heard was a Jew from Baghdad, related in some fashion to the founding Sassoon. Watching the movement on the thoroughfare from that balcony of pointed arches, sitting at the magnanimous teak tables inside, granted Miss Chitol a belonging to the city, even the world.

Reading in this marvellous building of this fine institution, she felt her way into her young republic's history. *Please do not destroy the foundations that the Fathers of the Nation, including your noble father, had laid down. There is nothing but strife and suffering along the path you have taken*, she read in JP's letter to the prime minister. *A people who fought British imperialism and humbled it cannot accept indefinitely the indignity and shame of totalitarianism. The spirit of man can never be vanquished, no matter how deeply suppressed.* These words in *Prison Diary* from her present vantage, a year after Emergency was lifted, JP no longer in prison, the prime minister no longer in power, returned her viscerally to the beating down of the railway strike, which should have made Emergency no surprise.

By contrast, her attempts to tend to her studies were marred by superficiality. She found it too easy to cold-shoulder her own socio-anthro primers, prizing the livelier range of literatures winking behind the glass in the cupboards. There were times she barely touched a book. She cogitated on matters from two hours ago or from her past life in Bhombalpur; she assessed her behaviour in particular situations, sought to recreate, without meaning to, the precise texture or mood of a conversation or a scene. From benign reflection she could work herself up into little pace-abouts in the balcony or the garden of red mud downstairs, sometimes catching herself talking aloud. Life was a strange and unpredictable journey indeed, but what exactly was she doing with hers?

In these ways the ninety minutes set aside for her education sped by.

The Kings & Queens Shoe Emporium upped its shutters at 10 a.m. The first thirty minutes were devoted to spiritual and commercial rituals. Mr Chheda prayed for unobstructed prosperity to Ganesh and Lakshmi, rotating clockwise on his axis with folded hands as he did, thereafter swirling incense sticks around the idols, the registers and the cash box. The boys, led by their manager Hasmukhbhai, took stock of inventory in a rapid symphony of trade code. The smart girls were not required here. If the girls arrived by 10:40–10:45, up to 10:55 *final*, the sheth did not mind; he nodded a smile when they entered. Any later, he did not so much as look at them. The old man knew better than to relay his point with drama. He was a survivor of the Partition, but regained much in Bombay by his pragmatism. He stocked the Batas and Coronas, but believed the margins lay in the footwear coming out of Dharavi and Thakkar Bappa Nagar, and his son's hi-fi ideas, such as the smart girls, he indulged solely in order that he might learn his lessons.

Miss Chitol was never late. It was a matter of undeclared competition between the smart girls as to which one arrived first. The competition extended undeclared into other aspects of the job. Miss Chitol knew her English and Hindi were smarter than Nalini Pingle's. But Nalini had the advantage of Marathi, even if they were downtown in Fort where it mattered less. To Miss Chitol's annoyance, Nalini had a habit of intruding upon her conversations with customers. She had been a working woman for a little longer, and was a little older, and therefore, believed Miss Chitol, assumed seniority even though each was a smart girl of equal rank and wage.

At regular intervals in the afternoon, when colleges, schools and offices let out, bursts of customers came through, sometimes so many that a girl, if she was not smart, needed to slip shoes on to feet. Miss Chitol dreaded them – calloused soles, malodorous toes, rat-bitten toenails – never suspecting that something of her grandmother's caste sensitivities had seeped into her. Of the rare beautiful foot, arched and curved, the kind that might be represented artistically as paisleys, the kind she would die to possess, she was appreciative. Indeed, she spent a great deal of energy dividing the world into two types of customers. Those with beautiful feet and the rest. Those shopping for themselves and those for others. Those dying to spend and those who would kill not to. Those who wanted to buy for a season, those for life. In such taxonomical exertions amid the performative duties of a smart girl ('always smile'; 'make each one feel special') the workday progressed towards 18:30, when, barring a customer hold-up, the girls could leave, a little ahead of shutters-down.

By the time they got off, the unspoken competitiveness of the morning had evolved into bonhomie, even fierce intimacy. They came away from the shop like athletes whose peculiarities and vulnerabilities could be understood by nobody but the other, their most equal opponent. In the heat of after-competition they too often went to take tea, plus or minus pattice, or sometimes simply walked at high pace. Adrenaline coursed through their blood, lactic acid lulled their muscles, freedom sang from their hearts, heaviness weighed upon their souls. Their chatter reflected these states, which rarely lasted beyond twenty or thirty minutes, and as they returned to equilibrium they considered one another barely more than bustling strangers. They were smart girls, working girls in their prime. Move along, breathe that commuter exhale, look at the exact time – and bloody shit! the light in the watch is conked again, that scoundrel!

'You were in Sheetal's group, na?' said a voice to her in the garden one day.

She turned to look at it.

'I came over to your college sometimes. I knew that group.'

Skinny boy, fingers like noodles; pleasant demeanour, unthreatening.

'Sheetal the boy or Sheetal the girl?' she replied.

'Sheets. Sheetal Kedia. That guy is mad! You were in his group, na?'

'I was. For some time. But more in Sheetal the girl's group.'

'Ya, that was also a good group.' He broke out in a smile. 'But Kedia's group is solid. *Dhamaal!*'

'I don't like groups,' Miss Chitol stated.

It may have come across as a cut. But it was a confession on her part. Groups were what she found hardest about college life, while she still had one. She was a rank outsider, without the permission to spend the kind of time outside that group-going demanded, or the funds for the casual drip of expenses to sustain it. Whenever she did find herself in a group, she registered in it an acute lack of friendship – of the type that had existed between herself and Salima and Madhavi, that tightness.

The boy did not take it as a cut. He was waiting, in fact, for her to elaborate, which Miss Chitol duly did.

'Actually, Sheetal the boy's group was started by Sheetal the girl. Then the group split. For some time there were people who were part of both groups. Then Sheetal the boy did big drama and people had to choose their group.'

'So you joined Sheetal the girl's group?' he asked, discerning in her an enjoyment of groups.

'I was already in Sheetal the girl's group, which was also Sheetal the boy's group for some time.'

'And now you are in just Sheetal the girl's group?'

'No. I told you, I don't like groups.'

'Arre, don't feel bad' – both ironic and sincere.

'I'm not.' She smiled defensively.

They moved into the shade of the mango tree.

'Do you come here often?' asked the boy, before deciding to take the question himself. 'I come sometimes. I like to read humorous books, funny books. If we are not laughing we are wasting our life. You have heard that saying?'

'No.'

'It's mine.' He had a cheery grin on. 'The other side is important too. I like poetry. I love lyrics, sad songs. The great lyricists, they turned themselves inside out for us, just to tell us how we feel. I prefer listening to reading. You like reading? I have concentration problems.'

'Who doesn't?' Miss Chitol offered in consolation. 'It used to not be like that for me. I could read for hours at a stretch.'

'If you were in Sheetal the girl's batch you must not have passed out, right?'

'Still in SY. But I don't attend any more.'

The boy received this news not only with total understanding but extreme glee, as if he had plotted it with her.

'Ha ha, very good! I passed out. Started work also. There is hardly any work to be done. Bore, yaar! Should I go in for MCom or not, that was the question. Then I thought, let me try this. It is a textile trading company, someone known to us. I joined for free. They said they wanted some young blood. I thought it would be good for the experience. Total time-pass.'

'I started work also,' Miss Chitol said.

'Where?'

'Not so far from here. Actually, I have to leave now or I'll be late.'

'*Chal*, let's go.' He blew his floppy hair out of his eyes with a dexterous realignment of the lower lip – truly were Bombayites masters of exhalation! – and with his chowmein fingers helped some of it behind his ear.

She found she did not mind.

They were soon on their way, he with his loping limby gait, full of ramble, drift, carelessness, take me as I come (she liked his height); hers taut, quick, one step after another a mission makes, with a slight sway at her love handles (which caught his attention).

They walked at a brisk clip.

'You're a socialist or what?' he asked jauntily.

'Me? Why?'

'You were reading the JP book, na?'

'Yes,' said Miss Chitol. She didn't realise he had been up there. She liked that he had noticed.

'They pardoned the railway workers for the strike, they suffered enough,' Miss Chitol said, without giving away anything further.

'Anyway, what difference, she *toh* made us socialist and secular before she went.'

'And what is wrong with that?'

'Nothing wrong,' he laughed. 'Some secularists, I feel they have a great attachment to all religions except their own.'

'Are you a Sanghi?' she asked. 'Anyway, what difference? Socialists and Sanghis are hand in hand now.'

'Ha ha,' he laughed open-heartedly. She saw that he had a large mouth and face, which sat generously on his thin frame.

She found herself smiling along.

In the past few minutes she had recalibrated her opinion of him as a group gallivanter to somebody who knew a thing or two.

When they arrived at the crossing near the store, she said: 'There, that is where I work. At that shop.'

Having made N the first person whom she told the facts about her employment, she crossed over to her workplace.

Nalini had won today. She was busy touching up the display window, but not so busy that she didn't notice the boy, and wasted no time in asking about him, what was his history-geography.

'Just someone I know from college,' said Miss Chitol coolly.

'I think you might get late sometimes now,' said Nalini. There was triumph in her tease, but also a pursed-lips-something Miss Chitol did not enjoy. Added Nalini: 'Who knows, maybe soon you won't need a job.'

'What is your view on fried idli?' asked N the next day.
'Why not eat medu vada if you want something fried? That is my view.'
'You can't have medu vada with ketchup.'
'You can eat ketchup with anything.'
'Say frankly. You have not tried it, na?'
She laughed.
'Na?'
'Have not.'
'Want to try?' he put it to her. 'We can split.'
'Where?'
'Satkar.'
'I just came from Churchgate!'
'So what?'
'I'll get late for my job. Won't you?'
'Arre chal, na, if we keep talking here we both will.'
As they cut through the Oval he annotated the maidan for her: the pitches on which, if you were lucky, you could watch India-level cricketers in action; the part of the bedraggled wire fence where the brown-sugar sellers stalked the night; the part behind the coconut trees where men did it with *laundas*, by which he meant cross-dressers or eunuchs she wasn't sure; the patch where old men scouted in the dark for young naval boys from the Sailors' Home.

'This is what people don't realise,' said Miss Chitol enthusiastically. 'All places are secret places.'
'Meaning?'
'That only. The more public a place is the less we know what all happens. Na? I wish I could know the life of every person passing by right now.'

N nodded and lengthened his loping stride and she quickened her step.

'How do you like it?' he checked at Satkar, about the fried idli.
'Hmm ... nice,' she answered, in a tone and expression of profound sincerity – such sincerity they both began giggling.

'Hmm ... *nice*,' he said, adding a tweak. 'I have an important question for you.'

'Ask,' she said.

'*Amar Akbar Anthony* or *Sholay*?'

'*Amar Akbar Anthony* or *Seeta Aur Geeta*, I can understand. But *Sholay*? People keep saying *Sholay* is *Sholay*. Really! What else can it be?'

'I can tell you what it can be. The Japani movie it is copied from. I have studied movies closely since Amitabh. *AAA* is a full original. It is the masterpiece of our country. Three giving their blood to the same mother Bharati. Ai hai!'

'And just yesterday you were making fun of secularists.'

When they came out they were still discussing *AAA*. And now he was letting rip word for word Amitabh's exuberant verbosities, doffing an imaginary top hat in the zu-zu-zu-zu-zu-zu-zu-zu dance. She was in splits.

Every day except Sunday for the next eleven days Miss Chitol met him where he had never before been seen. They started off separately in the reading room, soon descended to the garden for a chat, and were invariably out through the doors and into the streets for a short roam before work, giggling at commonplace things. He revealed his nativeness companionably, in a way that did not annoy her at all. They went to his top tea shop, his favoured sugar-cane juice stalls, the sandwich wala with the most unfathomably successful combinations. His knowledge spanned the city; he knew faraway roads and routes, knew where to get things. In his opinion excellent footwear was coming out of Dharavi.

The source of at least some of his information, it became clear to her, was drives. N did not own a car; he did drives in the sense that he was available for them. One previous night his friend Parag had to pick up someone from the airport, so he went along for the drive. One night Shendi wanted a paan, so he went along for paan – and a drive. Another night, Shendi, who clearly had oil to burn, wanted to take a drive just for the drive – so they set out and ended up – guess where? – Khopoli. Miss Chitol took a keen interest in the drives. She marvelled at the fact of them: to drive the dark streetlit city and understand it. No need to confront the endless jigsaw by sun. No *gardi, garmi, ghai*. Let the day cease and knowledge will be yours by night.

On the twelfth day when N did not come Miss Chitol was concerned. She stared at her textbook, and suffered whenever she looked up. As the moment of his arrival kept not coming, she got up to leave before her usual time. Despite her efforts she could not defeat her heavy tread.

The following few days N did not come again. The strange thing, she considered, was that she did not feel any of this intensity while N was with her, so she had no idea why his absence should escalate things this much. Or not – no escalation, what kind of foolishness was this? It was only that she felt easy in his presence, she reasoned, natural, no strain. He did not judge her job, or her.

Even so, she stood before the mirror more than usual, scrutinising herself for blemish, adipose, plainness. She held her eyes so that they twinkled, her mouth so that her lips looked sensual. But there was too much Miss Chitol could do nothing about. The straightness and slight squatness of her legs, above feet that resembled wooden slippers really; or these recurring patches on her face for which she incurred expenses in the form of calcium tablets; or the fact that some girls were tall and fair and glorious, and had the time for aerobics, with fragrance drizzling off their hair not perspiration. She vaulted between worrying for N and for herself, battling an aloneness that crept in soft-footed and established silent residence. She dealt purely with the feeling, not him, so that she could put it in its place.

Soon she restored her balance, but a new balance.

She did not see N again.

Because a thing had happened to Miss Chitol where she felt unaccountably heartbroken. She became severely cognisant of it, and even ventured to wonder, 'I think I am in love,' and asked herself, 'Is this what love is?' Yet, unaccountable, because she concluded that she had not fallen in love, and had never ever fallen in love. She investigated whether *that* on the contrary could be the cause of a broken heart. She knew the symptoms, she had seen it happen, in movies and books, to girls in college who wept themselves out. She had participated with little success in counselling one such – from Sheetal the girl's group as a matter of fact. She knew it hit like a devastating ailment and dropped you into a night without stars. The stomach heaved, the breast sobbed in silence, the mind spun in spirals, limbs felt unequal to their functions. She knew the mystery of mending a heart was the search of the ages. Could it be the search for the break rather than the mend which afflicted her?

At night, when the exhaustion drained out of her into the mattress, she endured thirst, pain, desolation. She buckled upwards, juddering at her groin, recoiled with stabs of abandonment in her chest. The fan tore like a blizzard above her. Her sweat did not cool. Her wants did not flee. She had florid dreams, drenched in the colour and scent of the forests around Bhombalpur that she had barely got to know, trees shaking with birds, birds shaking with song, and she dreamed of wonderful inexplicable rubbing love. The more sensual the dream, the greater the absence within herself, the bigger the break of the heart – which, of course, she knew even in the 2:53 a.m. turmoil, was not broken. What kind of carelessness of the heart was this?

In the balcony below hers the man with the kidney stones moaned; on the streets the mongrels of Juna Tanki howled at automobiles rattling past like toolboxes. The sounds made vivid distortions of her vacantness. When at the point of the morning she ordinarily waked to practical calculations, she surfaced to her senses like a ghost resigned to the material world. She felt like something had happened, something to be got over. It filled her with longing or its absence – purely emptily filled her.

She submerged herself in the poems of Faiz obtained from the recycler, and the heart attacks of the words kept repeating themselves inside her. It became as though all her pain derived from them, as though if they did not exist neither would her pain. Unbidden they shot arrows into her. An ache to set every vein aquake, as the poet had it. Or was it the other way round? If she did not feel this ceaseless pain, would the words exist? Her brokenness was the poet's opportunity, her downfall his triumph. Her spirit flew away into nothing, like the last orchestra, like the withered flowers, like the lightless lamp, the shattered mirror of a poem. Collapsed like the tent pitched in the desert places of her body, of another.

She steeled herself in the face of this new companion, heartbreak, figuring she could defeat the poet. She made sure nobody got wind of her prevailing condition, dissipating herself through carefully cheerful letters, countering the poet's connivance with clarity – leaking out, however, a great lonesomeness. Her smile at customers became strained, yet it was always there, and could be easily mistaken for a charming reserve unexpected from a salesperson – so unexpected that the sheth embarrassed her by remarking to Hasmukhbhai, in Hindi, not Kutchi, for her benefit: 'Looks like she has become a guest in her own house.'

In the house of the Prasads she bore her aunt's irritation over her delayed returns. All girls want to do nowadays, remarked Bhagmati Prasad with suspicious emphasis, is hang around in *college*. Miss Chitol deflected the comments by pretending they were jokes.

But when her quarterly subscription at the David Sassoon Library and Reading Room ran out, she did not renew. She did not wish to go there any more; and saving fifteen rupees a quarter would not hurt her. By this move, furnishing to her aunt the near truth that her first lecture was invariably cancelled owing to classroom unavailability, she could depart later in the mornings and pull her weight at home. She set about pulling it. She cooked dal and parwal, washed utensils, picked up the clothes, dusted and tidied up, stitched poorly pillow covers, went down for groceries, stood in the ration queue on her day off, washed everybody's clothes when the dhobi did not show up. Three months since her last calculation for independence, an independence where she could wallow when required, dream loudly when necessary, where unrequited passion could express itself as wholly as nothingness could – those three months, on a fresh review of her finances, began to look like another three months away, or four, or, considering the matter in the aching clarity of 3:19 a.m., let's face it …

4
Dhrubo comes to town

In the midst of these urgencies her elder brother came to Bombay. For reasons never discussed, Dhrubo considered himself from the father's side of the family. Until Miss Chitol reclaimed the mother's side, this may have been true for all three siblings, as those ties slowly wore off after her death. But it was felt to be true of Dhrubo even while she was alive. He did not so much as ask to stay with his maternal uncle.

Miss Chitol took a half-day at work to meet him at Supreme Restaurant for a late lunch.

'So you will wait on the road?' she had asked him on the phone.

'No, I'll be hanging from the trees.'

It made her laugh at the time but she was less amused while waiting on the road for thirty minutes, elegantly dabbing her face with a handkerchief.

'Hi, idiot,' Dhrubo said from behind her.

It was about a year since she saw him, when they both went home at Pujo. He had evolved significantly since. He looked fatter, thus shorter; his eyes had grown puffy; his hair had thinned out of its spikiness altogether, so that limp strands blew about exposingly in the afternoon breeze.

'What a city, I say!' remarked Dhrubo as they settled into a tight alcove beside the washbasin. All the good seats were taken, and it had taken her special pleading with the waiter to save them the famed keema. 'People talk like clattering utensils. No matter what language they are speaking in.'

'At least there are jobs,' she replied. 'How did the interview go?'

'I have bad eyes.'

'They *have* become a little swollen.' She peered at them through his thick glasses. 'But not as much as your backside.' It was comforting, after her recent moods, to fall back into Bangla sibling jousting.

'It's hard to see *your* backside,' Dhrubo responded. 'Don't they give you any food in the *mamabari*?'

'What do eyes matter? It's a tailor's job, *na ki*?'

'Eyes have points. Everything has points. They have made a chart. Production line, *toh*. This is what another fellow waiting for the interview told me. Said he has given twenty-six interviews so far.'

'So now?'

'So now – my backside. Came second-class, return third-class.'

'Third-class has gone, Dada.'

'I know, idiot. That is why I said it. You have turned into a special kind of idiot over here.'

'Did you get padding on your seats?' Miss Chitol enquired.

'Got it. It's actually quite good.'

'Though with a backside like that you don't really need it.'

Dhrubo grunted. His face reddened a touch.

'Don't lose heart,' she said, adjusting. 'You may still get the job. Wait till they declare the results.'

'Oh, the question is not that. Question is do I want it over here?' he pronounced grandly, then turned the tables on her. 'Wait till *your* results are declared. I hope you know Pishi has been hunting. She'll soon be here with five grooms in her trunk.'

'Whole or cut up?'

'However she likes them.'

'But *five*? Am I Panchali?'

'She wants everything to be fixed and settled by the time your degree is done. BA to *biye*, understood? It won't do to become a part of the furniture in the *mamabari*.'

This made Miss Chitol feel uneasy. She did whenever anyone raised her BA, or marriage. But it was not only that. It was the last part. It came from Dhrubo like a reprimand.

The keema arrived with its sensational aroma, green with dill and chilli. They squeezed lime, plunged pao into it. It pleased her to watch Dhrubo's relish. The heat of the dish did not permit them to speak. Pao, pao, cold drink!

When they finished the waiter brought them a golden-brown plateau of caramel custard shivering in a pool of syrup, this too a fruit of her advance plea. As always, Dhrubo was quicker on the draw. The first bites sweetened their mouths, cooled them.

'When I think of Bhombalpur, do you know what I remember?' said Dhrubo eventually. 'I think of the walls of our quarters. I used to lick them when nobody was looking. Nobody knew. Except Ma, she caught me doing it. When I left, that taste of chalk was so strong in my mouth. Whenever I think of Bhombalpur, I can taste it again.'

'Calcium deficiency,' said Miss Chitol, feeling herself an expert in this matter. But she was moved by the confession. 'When I think of Bhombalpur I think of wasp stings at the start of summer and applying onions on the bites. What a funny thing.'

'It was a funny place,' said Dhrubo. 'We hardly knew what was going on in the world outside. Yet when I went to Calcutta I missed the taste of that chalk.'

'You could have licked walls there,' she suggested.

'The weather is very different.'

She appeared to appreciate the merits of this argument.

When the bill came she insisted on paying it, countering his vociferous claim to seniority with hers of local hospitality. The circumstances were undoubtedly peculiar – him jobless and trying not to show it, her employed and lying about it. There was a moment of hesitation in which she saw his pride weaken. 'All right, all right,' he said, persuaded quite easily in the end, she noted. 'Better not go around telling the *mamabari*,' he joked. But she could see he meant it. It embarrassed her to be told to keep his honour. It did him too, for almost at once he removed from his bag a gift. She unwrapped the layers of newspaper and twine to unearth a small terracotta figure.

'Because you like locos so much.'

Despite her feelings for locomotives, and the crudeness of the work, she was touched. She smelled in it the earth, not of Bankura, from where he had got it, but of Bhombalpur: some synthesis of the emotional, artisanal, industrial.

'It's not so bad,' she said. 'You could have done worse.'

She had not told her aunt and uncle about Dhrubo. It was her calculation that she could surprise them at tea. Dhrubo, too, knew a visit was unavoidable.

They walked over, sluggish after lunch.

Coming up the building, they ran into Biru, standing around in the stairwell the way Bombay children did. The boy's waterfall of hair dropped straight to his eyes of tutored insolence.

'My name is Dhrubo and I am *your* mama,' said this young uncle, a little intimidatingly. The boy bent his lips into a nervous smile. His teeth were like the city's pavement skirtings. On the exposure of such indentations there was all to love about him. Miss Chitol pulled his cheeks.

The door was open. Jagdish Chandra Prasad was reclined to near horizontal, hands clasped behind his head, staring at the blisters that were the souvenirs of so many monsoons. He noted the girl had brought home a boy and briefly wondered whether it was to be accompanied by an announcement. Bhagmati Prasad, less dull than men in these matters, recognised Dhrubo at once, even though she last met him a decade and a half ago. She raced into the kitchen to get the tea going.

Soon the room was lively with chatter. Yet there was something false and strange in the air. Between the Prasads and the Chitols existed a chasm and stretched across the chasm was Miss Chitol. Dhrubo behaved, in his sister's view, in an obnoxious manner. He touched the elders' feet in a palpably perfunctory way. Then, perhaps taking his cue from his uncle's jocularity, he threw himself into sibling like banter with him. He mimicked Biharis speaking Bangla, Biharis speaking English, Biharis speaking Hindi. His uncle surpassed him by producing superior imitations of Bengalis speaking Hindi, speaking English, speaking Bambaiya, and mimed a certain kind of ineffectual *bhadralok* who carried a precautionary umbrella as a walking stick, scrunched up his nose and raised his hand to draw his wife's attention and, having failed, let it drop to his head to scratch his scalp. The boy Biru laughed. Dhrubo felt insulted, immaturely, since he himself was not unfond of mocking, with the bachelor's disdain, the same kind of middle-aged henpecked husband.

What sort of one-upmanship is this? Miss Chitol wondered, alarmed at each man's disregard for the other's age. She watched Dhrubo's efforts to reposition his job quest as a recce trip, and in turn ask his uncle, as if this was now a conversation between professionals, what he did.

As far as Miss Chitol could tell, her uncle did whatever was desired of him by Kevalchand Jhunjhunwala – the son of a prior Jhunjhunwala, possibly Balchand, a son of possibly Ishwarchand, the Jhunjhunwala who built this five-storey Jhunjhunwala Building. There was a hardware store, a plastic goods store, a tents-for-hire service, a money-lending agency, a chit fund, the last two of which were connected, there was the landlordship; he was influential enough to have arranged a telephone connection for her uncle. If pushed, Jagdish Chandra Prasad sometimes used the word Distribution, sometimes Collection, sometimes Manager. All were probably true and he employed all three now.

An hour passed, with Dhrubo registering needless failures in the competition. A second hour moved towards a finish, in which their aunt, by her chatty, unthreatening way of questioning, had all but established that he was struggling for a job, leading her to express sympathy for strugglers in a general way, and then it was time to leave.

As they walked into the lane, the effects of the visit weighed on them both.

She showed him where she got the pao and the flowers in the morning, the waste-paper merchant from whom she bought books.

'I don't know how you live with these people,' he said at last.

'What does that mean?' she replied.

He said nothing, but in a bristling kind of way.

When the bus approached, she instructed him once more on what to tell the conductor. They bade each other a subdued farewell. Off he went towards the railway station, where he would unchain his suitcase from the retiring-dormitory bedpost and return to the east.

Feeling brittle and traitorous, she watched the back of the bus merge into the traffic, the taste of chalk from their childhood walls drying on her tongue. He should have said a better goodbye. But she supposed it was okay to have gone away thus from her who had gone away worse.

Not long afterwards, Miss Chitol got a letter from Smt Deboshree Chakrabatty. It was the first she had received from Kolkata Pishi in adulthood. It took her a while to get through, since written in Bangla, running to six pages in a meticulous hand very different from Pishi's personality.

The letter began pleasantly, providing information about everybody's slightly poor health, in particular her granddaughter Toomki's, and a few connected lines about the weather in Calcutta, where autumn had set in. Then, as Dhrubo had warned during his little visit, it approached the main topic, but in a roundabout way: by recalling Miss Chitol's parents' wedding. As perhaps the children knew, wrote Pishi, there had been some resistance to a union with a non-Bengali, and from a different caste too. Some family members had boycotted the wedding for that reason. She herself did not attend at her husband's instruction; he believed it would send out a wrong message. That was something she always regretted. Since she had not attended her own brother's wedding, she was taking it upon herself to at least help his daughter find a good match. After all, he would not have confidence to organise a match for her, as by going away from home Charu had broken his heart.

This sentence stunned Miss Chitol. So accustomed had she become to the idea that she had come away consensually for the sake of her education that she had forgotten that her deed could be activated against her.

She continued reading.

Pishi wanted a few things of Charu. She needed copies of a good photograph. It was worth taking the effort, she advised, to locate a studio known for these kinds of portraits. She recommended making the minimum number of prints at first; if the photograph did not turn out well, one could always try another studio. If it met her expectations, she should store the negative carefully. Here her aunt hoped that Charu had been taking care of her skin and not been spending time in the sun. You may think it won't show, she wrote, but it will.

Next, Pishi wanted a copy of the horoscope. While her father may not believe in horoscopes, she remembered clearly that Thakuma had got a *thikuji* made for each of the children. The horoscope was still, in all likelihood, stored in Bhombalpur. Pishi could ask for it, but it would be much better if Charu was to. It would signal to her father that this was something she was interested in.

The point she was about to mention next was, Pishi admitted, not easy. She believed it was worth reverting to the original name. It was a complicated matter, no doubt. But it was a fact that a name like Chitol confused everybody. It was a fact, too, that they were nothing less than Chattopadhyays. Those not acquainted with the family would find it difficult to believe that they were indeed Kulin Brahmin. Her father must have had his own reasons to change the name, but surely he did not mean to disadvantage his children when it came to marriage. He would have documents with the original name. And it was easy enough to place a notice in the newspapers. If they were ever to spread the word in a wider way, the name change would be of benefit. This, too, was something she should discuss with her father. But if embarrassed, Pishi would gladly talk to him on her behalf.

Before she signed off, Pishi hoped that Charu was satisfied with these suggestions. Not only would it help her find a beautiful path in life, a betrothal would bring good luck to the family. Perhaps Dhrubo would find an excellent job and himself find a bride! It was her great desire to see all three children well settled, nothing really would make her happier.

Miss Chitol folded the letter and put it away, seething.

She continued to seethe over the coming days.

The hypocrisy! Wishing to arrange a match in her father's name, but wishing to change his very name! Wishing, in fact, to enforce everything he stood against. She had not properly considered these matters before. Doing so now made her feel more closely allied to her father than ever, and them together in solid opposition to this onslaught of orthodoxy.

Then, implicit in the letter was that Pishi would disregard completely her life in Bombay. As far as she knew, Pishi had few or no connections in Bombay, and had certainly made no mention of them in the letter. Where a match was found, there she would be expected to go.

Finally, the presumptuousness. Pishi had not bothered to so much as consult her. She had simply sent her a list of instructions.

Raring as she was to get all this off her chest, Miss Chitol was too exercised to begin her letter. She waited so that she might be temperate in her response, savouring her indignation in the meantime.

When she did eventually get round to it, she found herself struggling. Part of it was the writing in Bangla, which she decided to do even though she knew she could have used the English script. She threw herself into the process, approaching it with almost calligraphic intent. The script, its accompanying cultural associations, made Pishi's suggestions seem not so outrageous, perhaps even natural.

She composed what she believed was a clear and firm reply. She was not thinking about marriage right now, she wrote. By today's standards she was still young, still contemplating her options for the future. Lots of girls in Bombay found themselves in extremely interesting fields and were doing very well for themselves. By the time she finished, Miss Chitol had even come round to thanking Pishi profusely for thinking about her.

The letter was neither as firm nor as clear as she had imagined.

For a few weeks later she received another missive from Smt Deboshree Chakrabatty.

Kolkata Pishi sensed from Charu's response that she was feeling shy, as she had always known her niece to be. She understood this perfectly well. She too had been extremely shy on the matter of marriage. When she was a girl, she would run away into another room if the topic was even mentioned by anyone! But she was secretly excited while the arrangements were being made. She guessed Charu might be feeling something similar. After all, it was a time of uncertainty in a woman's life.

To make things easier, she was attaching a Mukherjee boy's photograph. The boy was the son of a friend of their friends, whom they had visited in Bhilai. There was too much in common to ignore. His mother too had been Kayastha (although Bengali Kulin Kayastha), his father too had worked in the Railways, and this family too had been *probashi* for several generations! As for the boy himself, he worked in a refrigeration company, and was now pursuing a higher degree sponsored by the company. By the time Miss Chitol completed her BA, he would be working again in an excellent position. So the timing would be perfect. Of course, nothing had been discussed in any detail, but she was taking the liberty of sending a photograph since the family had themselves sounded enthusiastic and Pishi knew her niece was shy. Here she praised Charu's handwriting and noted that artistic abilities are always appreciated in a bride. She had no doubt that her shy niece could create wonderful *alpanas* and such, which would not only add lustre to any house she went to but those talents be passed down to her children too.

Miss Chitol's tore open the enclosed envelope to look at the picture. *Eesh!* She felt more insulted than she could say. The boy sat on a sofa, flanked by his parents. The parents looked very pleased; he was the one not smiling – indeed looked incapable of it. His chin was large with a pointed tip to one side, just like a pairi mango. His eyes were droopy, absolutely bereft of life. She pictured sharing a life with such a dullard. It horrified her. Was this her level? She had not dwelled on her level before. If this was the truth, it was undoubtedly a bitter one.

The more she thought about this entire affair, the more Miss Chitol's precarious self-esteem slid, and each time rank irritation hauled her out of it. She believed she had done very well by coming away to Bombay. She cursed Dhrubo. He must have gone back to Kolkata and carried stories of what awful people she was living with, supplying her aunt the impetus she needed. She detected in the developments a father's-side versus mother's-side tug, Bengali versus non-Bengali, Brahmin versus Kayastha, as though she was to be rescued, like a girl who had strayed.

She decided to not reply to Pishi at all. If that was received as a snub, or put her in an awkward position with the refrigeration dullard's family, well, all the better.

A few weeks later, instead, she wrote to Dhrubo. She mentioned, curtly, that Pishi had no need to get into all this *ghotkali*, she was not interested in matches. She knew Dhrubo was not much of a writer and would not reply but he would convey the message to Pishi. They could discuss it to their hearts' content, jobless people.

By the end of these correspondences, however, Miss Chitol believed she was cured of her unaccountable heartbreak.

5

Shameless

For a customer S was oversolicitous towards the shop assistant it was plain to see. But there was something factual about it, and Miss Chitol had come to appreciate the facts of life. For example, if interested, *be* interested. Praise for the shop assistant's eyes while listening to the merits of tapered-toe semi-formals was no doubt shameless. Remarking on the embarrassed smile that followed was double shamelessness almost cancelling the first. She was grateful that Nalini had to leave early. She would have caught this in no time.

Afterwards, she found him waiting in the arcade, holding a bouquet of rajnigandha.

'These flowers have your name on them,' he said mellifluously.

My God, shamelessness personified, thought Miss Chitol. But a frisson of wrong sensations ran through her.

'Won't you have a cup of tea with me? If you say no, say it gently.' He contracted his smile into a play of words. 'I don't want a taste of shoes. I have just bought a pair from your shop.'

She smiled.

Cafe Shalimar. He leaned forward all the time. He likened her eyes to fireflies in the dark, whose light, however, does not die, to glimmering lakes in the mountain, upon which, however, the moonlight vanishes not. Heights of shamelessness, she thought, but went a little red. As for your fragrance, it is intoxicating like the rajnigandha, whose night does not end.

'Is all of me for the night?' she said.

His shameless eyes turned sincere.

'Can I tell you something? I don't know why, when I saw you in that shop, I felt I knew you. I had no intention of entering that shop or buying shoes. But I could not stop myself. You must be meeting so many customers every day, and I pass by shops every day. Have I ever had tea with a person like this? Have you? We must be connected to each other in some way.'

She thought him charismatic. Radiant skin and eyes; long curls of dark brown hair; a classical delivery, a smooth, flattering voice. Let him talk. No doubt he is shameless (but her heart was beating quick).

S talked. He took the initiative of pushing his knees out so that they might touch hers. Shamelessness, fact of life; on contact she negotiated both sensations; she withdrew her knees, and hooked her feet to the crossbeam of her chair.

Why should we not watch the sea? said S, with a flamboyant smile, increasing his handsomeness; let us, you and I, go and sit by the waters. But I must go home, she replied. Back and forth they went, and she permitted him to drop her home by taxi. In the smell of tide receding over detritus and excretus, the back of an evening taxi was a piece of private garden. Decadent was the scent of the rajnigandha she placed between them.

An auspicious date. They were caught behind wedding processions. Everything looked in splendour, the revellers in their finery, the dressed-up mares, the dark red of the buses, the yellow tops of the taxis under the darkening violet sky. The traffic opened up. S talked, but she could not keep track. Neither could she keep track of what she said, though she too was forming sentences and giving them breath. Occasionally she watched his mouth and when she felt shy she zoomed out to take in his entire face, his locks of hair, now ruffled, until she was at a remove again. His focus on her was tight, she could feel it, he was intending it. And what was it they spoke about that made her smile and in turn him?

Oh yes. He had a company job but wanted to become a pilot. He was going to begin training. What? She had never been in an aeroplane? When the clouds are below and heaven is above, that place in between, that is the place he wanted to be, and he wanted her to be in it too. I will take you, he said, to fly beside me.

Till you haven't seen the sun rise from behind the Kanchenjunga you haven't understood what the sun is and what a mountain is, she replied, so it must be that until you have been above the clouds, you don't know what the sky is and what the earth is. (But how unhappy she had been on that trip to Darjeeling, how resistant to rise at that dark hour, to watch day leap over the great mountain.)

When she instructed the driver to make the next left, S lifted the flowers between them. He drew closer. When he drew too close she angled her elbow out, as against grazers in the bus. He attempted to take her hand. She did not think she liked that. She closed it into a fist. He draped his fingers over it. There she allowed it to rest. His palm and the back of hers breathed in harmony. This much was fine, this much was nice.

Then he tried to kiss her and she did not like it one bit. She turned her head away. He pretended that was from coyness, and reached out further towards her neck. This time she allowed her elbow to poke him.

From that *naka*, yes, turn, she told the driver.

S laughed softly, as though being challenged was part of his charm. He stroked her hand, traced his finger up to her elbow. He moved across once more to kiss her. She pushed him back from the chest.

'Stop it, just stop!' she said, louder than either of them foresaw. The driver braked. Then realising it was not him being addressed he drove calmly on.

'Are you mad?' S said, a flash of anger before retrieving his mask. 'I want to show you how much I care for you.'

He made another foray towards her lips. She shoved his face back, feeling the abrasion of his nascent stubble as she did. He looked, suddenly, large and formidable to her. Her heart was galloping.

'Stop it,' she said again. 'Here.' The taxi chugged on. 'I'm telling *you*,' she slapped the driver on his shoulder. He braked.

'You are shameless,' she told S, flinging open the door. He held her hand, and she broke free. 'Shameless.'

'Who do you think you are?' S called out from the window. 'Have you even seen yourself?'

He lingered inside the vehicle, then paid up. The taxi-time and taxi-money were worthless, the flowers were not. Extracting himself from the back seat, he sidled off with his tuberoses and his new shoes.

She should have flung the fare into the taxi, she thought, hurrying up the lane. In calculations that she did not mean to perform she concluded she could not have – not the entire fare at any rate.

Two coins on his face, that would have shown him. I should have shown him.

Shameless. But the girl has daring. No doubt – daring is there, said Bhagmati Prasad to herself, watching from the terrace of Jhunjhunwala Building. She had gone up to bring down the clothes – another task that was to be the girl's. So that is where she is all day, doing *tafrih* with boys. Just as I thought. Daring. And clever, very clever. Will not bring the flowers home. Will not give away anything. Her mother was like that.

Bhagmati Prasad was in her nightie. She had been in her nightie all day. She hated being in her nightie all day but today was not an ordinary day. And besides there were things she hated more. She hated Juna Tanki and dreamed of living in Walkeshwar, under the gulmohar blooms overlooking the sea. She hated having been married off at seventeen to a man nine years older because he too was Kayastha from Bihar, and as loyal as her father to Jhunjhunwala, who liked to say fortunate is the merchant who has a Kayastha for a manager. She hated having been told by anyone with a working tongue that she was not a woman when in truth the man's bow was so weak it took six years for an arrow to reach its mark. She hated not being able to recite the Hanuman Chalisa every day, and hated more the fact that she had no time for it because certain people were not doing their part. Most of all she hated being made a fool.

Shameless. It was like the Hitopdesha fable of the mouse and the sage. You shelter a mouse, give it all it needs to survive in the world. To protect the mouse from the cat you turn it into a cat. To save the cat from the dog you turn it into a dog. To keep the dog from being eaten by the tiger you turn it into a tiger. And then the tiger wants to eat you. As the sage did, we will have to turn the tiger back into a mouse. And a mouse has no place in anybody's home.

I am in my nightie and I want to be. To feel unbathed and angry. Ever since that phone call in the morning my whole body has felt hot with anger. I don't want to cool down. I want to tell the woman on the phone again I am not Mrs Chitol and if she is not in college and will not be allowed to sit the exams, it is not my problem. Did the girl know to even tie a sari when she came here? Could not cook a simple *chokha* till I taught her. Oh I took her to cinemas, made her festivals bright, what have I not done for her? But if my house burns today she will warm her hands on the fire. Chitragupta is recording every single deed, whether she knows or not.

As Bhagmati Prasad climbed down the stairs from the terrace, Miss Chitol climbed up to the house, working on her game face. Neither woman looked at each other as they approached the door.

Jagdish Chandra Prasad was on the sofa. His hands were clasped together in front of his chin, where his index fingers met each other in rhythmic taps, a man about to consider something, exercise power, take decisions that, even if injudicious, were for the best, for upon men fell a responsibility. Benevolence was not out of the question. The fingers tapped, in the fingers were nerves, nerves were connected to the brain; the tapping male fingers would provide the solution. The brow must play its part, creased to a vertical line in between intellectual flexion and moral outrage. The lower half of the face must be relaxed, easing the intake of oxygen that aided clear male thinking.

'So, where are you coming from?' he asked.

'Me?'

'Yes, you. Mami is coming from the terrace, I know that.'

'Library, where else? After the lectures …' She had too much adrenaline to say any more. She let the sentence trail off, slid her sandals under the junk cabinet.

'Achha, library?'

Something has happened, she knew; something has happened.

Bhagmati Prasad could not bear her man's detective-in-a-movie impersonation.

'Enough! Enough! Enough! How much will you let the girl lie? Aren't you sick of her lies? And you, missis, are lying. You are lying and you are a liar. Roaming around with boys, do you think I haven't seen him with his flowers? Don't you *dare* lie any more.'

'You calm down, I will handle this,' snapped Jagdish Chandra Prasad.

His wife ignored him. 'There was a phone call from your college today. Your attendance is zero. So what do you do all day, let us hear.'

They were taking attendance now? And nobody was proxying for her? It had been so long since she had checked in at college she knew nothing. Her adrenaline drained out. She felt supremely, lactically, vanquished. She was beaten. And yet she needed to find energy, energy for tremendous, Ashwatthama-sized lies.

'Let us hear,' repeated Bhagmati Prasad.

To tell a lie, Miss Chitol knew you needed the conviction of its emotional rather than its literal truth.

'Mama, Mami, please don't shout at me,' she remarked with genuine weariness. 'Yes, it is true I have not been going to college. A waste of time. Even the teachers are not interested. If you see the state of our library. So I started going to a library in Kala—'

'*Wah ji*,' interjected Bhagmati Prasad with belligerent sarcasm. 'A library where they keep flowers instead of books. Romeos instead of students.'

'Mami, you must be angry right now but there is nothing like that. We have a group in the library. That person you saw he had to come this side today. *Bas*, that is all.'

'And all this time why did we never hear about this library, this library group? If I was your mama, I would have thrown you out of the house. Sent you straight back. Are you listening – Oh are you listening?'

Jagdish Chandra Prasad was listening. In order to demonstrate control, however, he chose not to respond.

'But, Mami, he doesn't need to send me anywhere,' said Miss Chitol. 'I am already leaving. In one week's time I will leave the house.'

'Yes, yes, leave, go, go, leave,' shouted her mami, calling out her big talk. 'Leave and go where, let us hear. Where do you think you will go! And what shall we tell your father?'

She used the word *baap* rather than baba, which offended Miss Chitol immensely.

'I have already told him,' she retorted.

There was silence.

'I don't want to be a burden on you any more.'

Silence again.

'Who do you think you are?' Jagdish Chandra Prasad now roared.

She could not bear to hear that question so soon again.

'Let her go, let her go,' said Bhagmati Prasad. 'Clearly she has a lot of plans. Just remember it the next time she comes running and lying to us.'

And before she could finish, Miss Chitol did indeed go. First, to the toilet, where she passed a prodigious quantity of urine. Then into the kitchen, where she began washing the afternoon utensils.

'Look how hard our girl is working,' her aunt shouted from the living room. 'Oh what a hard-working girl! We are so fortunate! Every house should be blessed with a girl like this!'

She needed to stay on the firm ground between the quicksands of guilt and panic. She kept on with physical tasks, mopping the kitchen platform to a shine.

To broadcast his displeasure, Jagdish Chandra Prasad went out the door and slammed it on Miss Chitol and her lies and Bhagmati Prasad and her nightie. A minute later they could hear his noisy scooter with side-car wake up.

What a family, Bhagmati Prasad remarked to herself on the blood that joined the kitchen-cleaner and the house-fleer. Then she went into the kitchen and said: 'Get out.'

Miss Chitol obeyed.

It was late and nobody had eaten. The appropriate form for an occasion like this was to not eat, in fact to out-not-eat the other. To Bhagmati Prasad's surprise, Miss Chitol went and helped herself to a roti and a spoonful of bhindi, over which she ladled thick arhar dal that she had prepared in the morning. Then Bhagmati Prasad served herself. Eating brought the women relief; doing it in silence cemented the tragedy.

When the girl had first come, Bhagmati Prasad was amazed to realise how much she missed having someone in the house after her daughter had gone. And although it was true that her presence lightened domestic duties, reduced the reliance on maids who overcharged and underworked and thieved besides, the girl had gained much more than she had given. The wretch. What Bhagmati Prasad failed to see was the girl too had begun to feel herself thought a servant.

Meanwhile, Miss Chitol, incensed again at her mami's crude term for her father, the *way* she said it more than the word, began to clear up with a vengeance. Once more she was told to get out of the kitchen, and this time she strode out.

Out in her balcony room, her limbs felt like anchor weights. She felt exhausted out of all thought. No strength to roll out the mattress and lay the bedsheet and wash her feet and wipe her armpits and change her clothes. She wanted to slump down right there on the floor. Become a little horizontal. Extinguish a little her eyes. Which were burning with the jack-in-the-boxness of tears. She dropped into a deep slumber. When she woke up and looked at her watch twelve minutes had passed. The sensation of the taxi violation was still on her. The exams situation was serious. Would she indeed be barred from them? And what about her father? She was perspiring fervently.

The facts and fictions of life tugged away at Miss Chitol, left her twisted like a dupatta wrung to dry. She felt she must write to her father confessing everything, but found herself instead drafting a letter to Salima, living at her grandparents' in Gorakhpur – not that she had an address. She ripped it up into four pieces, crumpled it into a ball and held it tight in her fist. Now she grappled with the thing still withheld – that she was a working woman. Her game was up. She had been shameless. She lay back down and stared at the ceiling with the gaze of a repentant liar. *Durga, Durga*. She closed her eyes and chanted to herself, *Durga, Durga*.

At some stage she noted that her uncle returned home and had a blazing row with her aunt, and she was the subject, each blaming the other for the very existence of her in their life.

In the morning Miss Chitol was less certain of the facts of life than ever before. She fulfilled her morning responsibilities with silent efficiency. She decided to dress well, pairing her current favourite kurta, a Madhubani print on mellow yellow, with Kolhapuri slippers enlivened by a silver band on the strap, a ceramic bracelet and a bindi. She brushed her hair and left it daringly open. To taunts from Bhagmati Prasad about *guldaste wale* gents, the men with bouquets, she left the house early.

Immediately she was directionless. She strolled about a while, watching the world. Eventually she wound up at the bus stop. There she studied the board carefully. She got herself a sing-chana mix and waited for a bus that would take her to another bus, which took the finest route. At the second bus stop she engaged in a short friendship with an office-going lady about bus timings and the effects the millworker protests had on them. When they parted, she told the lady, 'I felt really good meeting you.' 'Me too,' the lady smiled back.

It was a sparkling morning on the 123. Boarding at the first stop from the originating depot, she was able to get a seat on the top deck, all the way up at the front window, although on the off side of the aisle and, nothing could be done about this, on their side of the road, further from the sea. The wind blasted her. The conductor came by with his handsome leather satchel, clicking away with his puncher, his metal ticket box stacked with little paper tickets bearing numbers in tiny squares from which he alone knew what to punch out; he alone knew the code to your future. She waited for the moment they would sweep into the thrilling arc of Marine Drive and the glint off the Arabian Sea would tantalise her, at which point she would open up her paper cornet. Each of these things occurred as per desire, but she found the pleasure had been in the anticipation.

'I am a liar,' she got busy admitting. 'Yes, I am a liar and I am trapped.' Yet, as she justified her impulses, she edged towards the conclusion that truth was the greater trap. There would be reproach, there might be forgiveness via an improvement programme, by which there would be greater domesticity, leading one day to matrimonials. After all, one aunt had already perpetrated her schemes. She could not stand the prospect of another swinging into action, although she might not do so while Miss Chitol was still useful to her. Her announcement about leaving the house had been instinctive, but surely she must have been spurred by these reasons?

She climbed off at Fountain and began walking in preoccupation. Entering the warren of Fort, she stopped to seize her racing mind at Borabazaar Tea House. Here she ordered a giant French Heart, coated with fungus-like sugar, and a Special Tea, served her by a short man with a flaming orange moustache. She took the glass and noticed that it was chipped along the lip.

'What is this?' she grumbled.

'*Palti kar dene ka*,' replied the man in a problem-solving Bombay way, gesturing at the empty cups on the table. *Palti kar dene ka.* Just upturn it. She did, from one into another. The tea did not spill. She drank it in satisfying slurps. She placed her coins on the table and left.

A special tea indeed. Fresh wind in her sails. She had made mistakes but mistakes could set her free. *Palti kar dene ka!* Turn it upside down, turn it right around. She was at this moment on the threshold not of prison but the world. Same threshold, looking the wrong side.

It was not easy to sustain the flighty stride. She worried again that her uncle would contact her father, even if she suspected he would not deign to. She must reach him before they did. Thank God he did not have a phone! She threw herself into her next construction.

Baba, I have taken a job – no.
Baba, I have taken a house – ridiculous!
Baba, I have found a place to stay – but why?
Baba, I will be moving – oddly formal.
Baba. Have started working alongside studies. Will shift. Everything fine. Love Charu.

Those words, finally, Miss Chitol handed on a chit to the operator at the Central Telegraph Office, and experienced a flitting relief, as though the chit had been the problem. The parcel was in someone else's hands and if the music stopped no eyes would point at her. She made for work, preparing for a conscientious day. A kind of PO escape-memory stayed on her, the time she had written a line of gibberish with Anando to send their mama in Bombay and been punished for her urchin ways. There really was no choice but to leave.

Miss Chitol soon untruthed her way out of the Prasad household.

She did not mention her job. She did, however, slip in a sentence about looking for work experience so she could stand on her own feet. She said she would move into her friend Nalini's house. This was true.

If her aunt reined in her tongue it was because she intuited there was something bigger going on that she had still not worked out. And she was in no mood to shelter a problem she could not put a finger on.

As Miss Chitol had anticipated, her father made a trunk call from the post office. As she had hoped, it was at that hour of the morning she was still in the house and could intercept it. It was the norm in long-distance calls to talk loudly while reassuring the other party that all was well, since anything less than birth, death or at the very least a heart attack did not merit the expense. This she did, and so did her uncle, in lower key. It seemed a continuation of the old face-saving play. There was much one could get away with in the name of shame: one just had to hold one's nerve.

Eventually it became clear to the Prasads that Miss Chitol would indeed be leaving. On her final evening, her uncle, who was not without sympathy for anyone who had wanted to escape first Animesh Chitol and then Bhagmati Prasad, handed her a few envelopes.

'Here,' he said. 'You had once asked.'

They were her mother's letters. Miss Chitol was surprised by the gesture. Her hands felt clammy as she took them; she could not afford to sink into whatever feelings they would provoke. Her uncle noticed. 'Keep them with you,' he told her.

One last night she enclosed herself in the converted balcony in Juna Tanki, under the whirring fan, reading from the Mahabharata, purchased at the recycler's, where they landed up because of their reputation for starting feuds in the homes they were kept. Like Anando, like everybody else, she too had a soft spot for Karna, born in an armour and destined for tragedy.

Ours is a lost cause. But, Krishna, unsuccessful life, like love unreturned, has its own rainbow. You cannot have a rainbow in life unless there are tears to be lit up by the setting sun.

We are all born with armours, she told herself, and steeled herself to sleep.

6

Palti kar dene ka

Over the next eighteen months, Miss Chitol became the temporary occupant of half a dozen accommodations, starting with Nalini Pingle's, from where she pored over 'Paying Guest – Bachelor Girls' advertisements, only to keep falling, alas, at preliminary hurdles.

The Hindu South Indian landlady, Miss Chitol could not discover from where – the name seemed generic to her eye – who conducted a detailed interrogation, down to what marks she had scored in her board exams, left her feeling that, never mind that she did not have the right culture to boost her case, with a few more percentage points she might well have sneaked through. A Jain landlord wanted vegetarians only – perplexing, since there was to be no access to the kitchen and no outside food allowed in. She reconciled herself to the taint of her impure breath. One landlady was put off enough by her shoe-store job to terminate the interview right there. A Mrs Sanyal gave the impression that she favoured Bengalis, and from the enquiries that followed, preferred them of the suitable castes. Here Miss Chitol's hopes were raised. '*Chitol?*' Mrs Sanyal twitched her nose. 'Chitol, Chitol, Chitol … *adbhut.* Like the fish? … *Peti ba gada?*' She emitted a stern giggle. Failing to convince the landlady that she was nothing but a specimen of Chatterjee, Miss Chitol acknowledged Pishi's retribution, grimaced and moved on.

But her stay in the Pingle home became increasingly fraught. She had enough Marathi to understand that the inconvenience was a matter of daily discussion. Nalini put to her, a little impatiently, that she needed to expand her range. Could she even afford the places she was trying over and over only to be rejected? See, life was like a weighing scale and you had to …

Miss Chitol took the advice on board. She went to look up a Govandi room of one Mrs Konshekar. Not a question asked except: 'From when?'; and a palm proffered for a mere month's advance. Miss Chitol placed currency on it, almost euphorically. But Konshe Maushi, as everyone called her, just didn't care.

The house was run in a way that conformed to no preconception Miss Chitol harboured of paying-guest accommodation. She had imagined that for a friendly price she would become a friendly guest to a friendly family while maintaining a friendly distance. Konshe Maushi's place was a cluster of tiny rooms with quick turnovers, Maushi herself lodged in the living-and-dining. Cockroaches, shrews, moss and rust throve. The entire neighbourhood reeked of garbage. In the middle distance the great dumping ground was identifiable by the pariah kites wheeling above it.

While here, Miss Chitol was constantly exhausted, down with low-grade fever or on the verge of it. Forced to acknowledge that squalor was deleterious to mind and body, she felt utterly downtrodden. The food was meagre and soon intolerable – the same dry roti or bhakar with chutney and a watery potato dish, at breakfast as well as dinner. The Govandi railway station was a first-class-first, gold medallist in filth. Its special claim to notoriety was that every morning very young rowdies flung a packet of faeces at a ladies compartment as the train left the platform.

But she stayed on. Against expectation, the college had accepted her written apologies: she was allowed to sit her exams. She obtained grudging leave from work. Perpetually sneezing on her dust-sodden bed, she attempted to cram for short-term success.

These experiences left her yearning for home. She left the day her exams finished, taking along a bush-shirt for her father, a Hero fountain pen for Anando and a wooden comb for Notun Dida. The visit was so short she spent nearly as much time on the trains as in Bhombalpur, yet it was fruitful in ways she could never have anticipated.

It so happened that the Chitols were hosting a relative at the time, something of a legend in family circles. He had broken every rule: travelled across the seas without a care for caste loss, hitchhiked across borders, sustained himself on these expeditions by performing all manner of menial jobs – cleaning dishes, clearing leaves, shining shoes – all while barely in possession of any language other than

Bangla. His education he had acquired by travel; he remained a bachelor. His presence in the house had a cheering effect on everybody. Notun Dida was laughing all the time, not least because he repeatedly proposed marriage to her; Anando chased him for one adventure after another. Her father, who was an old favourite of Jajabor Jethu, as they called this wandering uncle, was in convivial mood, and to see him like this, a man entirely at ease, without the anxiety of raising children, singing songs, absolutely *cracking* jokes, made her happy. It made her feel forgiven. In fact, forgiveness did not much come into it. It was just that, in one of those complex transactions of the heart, he had accepted what he could barely admit to himself: that having thus taken her life into her own hands, she *had* relieved him.

In such an atmosphere, nevertheless, Miss Chitol felt liberated to inform her family, without delving into too many details, that her studies were proceeding all right, paint a carefree sketch of her accommodation, as well as her assistant's job in a footwear store. Jajabor Jethu applauded her. He recalled that when he first went to Europe he was amazed to see so many young working women, students who supported themselves through college in this way: what spirit, that is the spirit! Her father did not express disapproval. Perhaps, she hoped, he was a little proud. He did not broach the topic of marriage.

She returned to Bombay buoyed. She told her landlady she would be leaving, and to that end forfeited ten days of rent and ten days of squalor. Konshe Maushi accepted the departure with as little perturbation as she had the arrival. On her way out Miss Chitol encountered the drunk on the abandoned chair she suspected was Konshe Maushi's good-for-nothing son, since Maushi referred to him as *halkat* with a hateful intimacy and he her as *haurat* likewise. As she hauled her bags past him, he threw pucker-lipped *pchew-pchews* her way, shouted 'Hello missis how do you do?' after her, and, eliciting no response, followed up with a '*Chal, vatak, vatak!*' Soon after, it struck Miss Chitol that he had been shaking away, and a moment later she arrived at the unfortunate but accurate conclusion that the convulsions were masturbatory.

From here commenced the periodic relocations of Miss Chitol. She became adept at presenting herself as a most desirable paying guest, perfectly suited to the host. But once in she wanted out. She left the home of a Kannadiga couple in the Dadar Hindu Colony because – Nalini Pingle and her weighing scale did not lie – non-squalor extracted a commensurate price; besides, the old man seemed a little too eager on friendship whenever his missis was out. To the operation of a Goan Catholic retired-teacher couple in Mazgaon she bade farewell after the ceiling collapsed on her bed (she was not in it). Pity, because that joint was not joyless, especially the fiery mackerel on offer. She briefly established herself in the home of a Punjabi family, in a room devoid of a window, or a ceiling fan, uninstalled as a measure against suicide. The pedestal fan was not so bad if you sat up bolt upright two feet in front of it, but she found it an inconvenient posture for a full night's sleep. She left in perspiration.

From the premises of a strict Marwari widow and her two aged female assistants she withdrew on account of an overpious roommate. Piousness was well and good in the elderly, but trying in one so young. When not reading out from the scriptures to the landlady, the girl, Sirisha, read them aloud in the room, chain-lit incenses, and observed a stupendous number of fasts and abstinences. Miss Chitol sensed Sirisha disapproved of her under-participation in these matters. At her prodding, Miss Chitol joined her a few times in prayer, but found Sirisha's presence inimical to spiritual endeavour. The girl's conversation was laced with snide bigotry; her laughter felt fake. With grim territorial ambition she had captured much of the shared space in the room for an ever-expanding altar and associated articles of faith.

'Don't you believe in *anything*?' Sirisha asked her pointedly one day.

'I believe we should think of others,' Miss Chitol rejoined with a sharper point still.

A crashing silence followed.

Sirisha stepped up her campaign.

Some days later, the landlady elliptically conveyed to Miss Chitol that she might do well to start looking for another place. Asking no questions, that is what she did.

In the course of her peregrinations, she suffered crises of direction. In particular, the education matter oppressed her. She had cleared the majority of her papers; for those she had not she was Allowed To Keep Terms. She thus progressed into her third and final year of graduation as a Bachelor of Arts. But the search for housing, the moving, the settling in, the exiting, the keeping up with her job – at any given point these felt more urgent than studies. Regrettably, attendance-taking at college did not lapse back into its old derelictions; the teachers not only took roll-calls, they looked at each student who answered, to guard against proxies. It became evident to her that she could not cope with the final-year syllabus, alongside the backlog of ATKTs from the previous year, and a full-time job. Out of helplessness she let it go, and made a self-promise to get herself together the following year. Perhaps she could complete her BA by correspondence. In today's day and age such things were easy to do and, who knew, may be the more exciting.

As soon as she loosened her grip on her degree, Miss Chitol felt incredibly free. She embraced her adventures, she thought of Jajabor Jethu, hummed the jajabor song. *The world has made me its own, I have forgotten my home!*

There were days she felt on the edge of her finances. Her severe day-twos drained her of energy. She had put up in so many parts of the monstrous city, got lost so often, she wished to walk around with a sign for help hanging on her neck. Yet, bit by bit, the Western, Central and Harbour were laying down their tracks across her mind; the tangles of bus routes were lodging themselves like nerves; neighbourhoods were mapping themselves on to her brain. She was inching her way up to the city's eyes to meet them as an equal.

One day, while still serving out the Marwari widow's notice, she shared a bus ride with a girl, bug-eyed, pinched-faced and diminutive, perhaps the quietly competitive kind but with a teamwork bent of mind, who was as invested in accommodation as she. The girl was more expert in the matter. She admirably enumerated the benefits of working women's hostels over every other form of accommodation. By the end of their time together, she had taken Miss Chitol through a list of working women's hostels and given her a good idea of their requirements. Miss Chitol never asked her name, and often thought of her afterwards – very sentimentally so the day she was accepted into the Lalita Devi Hindu Stree Samaj Working Women's Hostel, close enough to the Vile Parle railway station.

The hostel was low on paperwork, as the girl on the bus had indicated. It did not need a local guardian. A character certificate was compulsory, yes, but just the single one, and not necessarily from a 'prominent citizen'. Miss Chitol nonetheless supplied a double certificate, from the Goan teachers whose ceiling had collapsed, and who in support of her character made a special note of how helpful she had been during that unfortunate episode.

The difficult piece of documentation was the employment letter, detailing emoluments. The sheth was not a man who liked to commit things to paper; any transaction that valued paper over the given word felt to him *khottu*, false. But the younger sheth relented, as Miss Chitol had hoped. The emoluments were of procedural significance, since the hostel fees were calculated at seven and a half per cent of the pay. There were three types of room: two-, three- and four-seaters. The working women themselves were categorised into five: Unmarried, Married, Divorced, Deserted, Widow. Together, Miss Chitol and her three room-mates covered the first four.

Rules of admission may have been few, but once inside there was no shortage of them.

On her first day the matron asked Miss Chitol to read the rule sheet and return a signed copy. Alcohol, Tobacco and Narcotics were prohibited. So were Pets and Males. Chatting with Males near the Compound Wall was banned. In-Time was 9 p.m., Late-Night Leave until 11 p.m. could be sanctioned two times a month, Night-Out once a month. Each strictly against Prior Written Permission. Participation in Monthly Community Evening and Annual Picnic were Compulsory. Exemption by Prior Written Permission only. Ironing was banned except in the Ironing Room. Open Hair was forbidden in the Dining Room and the Recreation Room. Extra Friendship with staff was not allowed. Dress code was Decent. Rooms could be searched at any time. Breaking rules could lead to Expulsion with 24-hour notice. Suicide was banned.

Watching her scrutinise the rule sheet, the desertee called Vimla laughed. 'Don't look at it so much or you'll think you are in jail. Just do what everyone else does.'

Miss Chitol smiled along but thought, this is not very different from my life so far.

The game of rules she knew; it was the proximity of her room-mates she had to adjust to.

The oldest was Rajashree the divorcee from Karwar, thirty-plus, Miss Chitol estimated, and she was not at all discouraging of divorce with Sujatha the married from Ernakulam, whose husband worked in Kuwait, although Sujatha's trouble was not so much with her man as her in-laws. Vimla the desertee from Neemuch was the youngest, and she damn-cared whether married, unmarried, divorced, deserted, so long as there was no bloody-fool man controlling them. Living among the married, divorced and deserted, Miss Chitol felt secretive about her virginity, even ashamed of it. She had barely lived.

Rajashree the divorcee, whose manner was confident and elevated, worked in sales at Balmer Lawrie, draped her masculine meets voluptuous figure in coloured cotton or georgette saris, pairing them with matching petticoats and contrast blouses, tamed her hair, wrinkly when loose, in a chopsticked bun, painted her thin and broad lips neutral shades, left early and returned late, never spent Sundays in the hostel and generally struck Miss Chitol as a success; they said she had affairs. Sujatha the married, who had a waxy sheen to her mouth and plaited hair, as well as her dark dimples and intelligent eyes and scrawny arms, worked on the reception at a private hospital dressed in solid blue salwar kurta and white dupatta sets they provided, polished her bitten nails crimson, read serialised novels in Malayalam magazines, complained about the monthlies-hygiene of room-mates to other room-mates, and played carom in the recreational room with enough purpose to have won the hostel competition multiple times. Vimla the desertee, who was granted the licence of a young rebel, who nonetheless balanced her frank tongue by such marks of respect as suffixing *di* to every older inmate's name, administered manicure-pedicure-waxing-bleaching at a beauty parlour but wanted to work with animals really, used a variety of pins, clips, bands and partings to keep her shoulder-length hair off her face and thus prove herself ruly to hostel authorities, even if her oxidised-silver anklets jangled beneath her loose salwars with transgressive melody as she lounged on her cot, raised upon bricks to accommodate her steel trunk, listening to two main cassettes, *Romance with Rishi* and ABBA's *Voulez-Vous*, on a two-in-one that she often took up to the prohibited building terrace, where she maintained a prohibited cat and might drink prohibited rum between legitimate water tanks.

Sometimes Miss Chitol slunk upstairs with Vimla, who never spoke about her desertion, so that after some time Miss Chitol could not remember how it was that she had first learned of it, and whether

Vimla was indeed deserter or desertee. And although she took rum only once, then twice, then three or four times, which each time hit her like a truck with headlights blazing and horns blasting, afterwards Miss Chitol's principal nostalgia for those days was the immense mood of damn-care drunkenness on that terrace, beneath the fuzzy stars, among the leaking tanks, amid the turbulence rising from the city, stray lines from the two cassettes braiding themselves into her memory like Facts of Life. Us four women – when would we meet again?

Of course, the present is more prosaic than nostalgia, and for the greater part Miss Chitol merely coped as the others coped. In real-time life, she discovered Rajashree had a way of issuing minor snubs, Sujatha's sneaky streak was rather broader than a streak, and Vimla could be temperamental – 'she has psychology', the matron's assistant Vatsala Tai put it. As for Miss Chitol, once she saw these facets in clear light, she unconsciously carried the air of a woman put upon by some girl she had met on a bus. Her room-mates picked up on it, and relished getting irritated by it.

There was plenty to cope with: the fight for barracks-style bathing cubicles, of which there were five for thirty inmates on the floor; the four Indian-style toilets that required one to perfect the art of respiring through the mouth and disabused Miss Chitol of the notion that girls did it more fragrant; the perpetual competition for the mirror in the room, its corners reserved for each one's special cards, photos and bindis. The debilitating suspicion that another's work was more fulfilling than her own consumed Miss Chitol, so that she began to feel embarrassed about her job. That persisted right until the moment she was sacked.

There was nothing wrong with Miss Chitol's performance. It was just that the senior sheth had been proved right: there really was no need for the smart girls. Their departure from Kings & Queens was not bitter or dramatic. Simply the smart girls were let go, and simply they went. Their attempts to rouse themselves to indignation felt untrue and tapered off into garden-variety grousing. There was no farewell party. They were given a choice between two weeks off and two weeks' bonus. Both chose the latter. On their last day they were each gifted a pair of sandals. Hasmukhbhai said with a valedictory grin: 'Come back as customer.' Miss Chitol appreciated the words, and the sandals.

The smart girls left early that evening, and walked towards New Deluxe for an extended session of tea and pattice. There they sat chatting in melancholy fashion. They had worked here for two years – where had the time gone! Each conceded, tentatively, that she was relieved that this phase, which was meant to be a short little stage of her life, was finally over and now she was free to pursue the things that *really* interested her, such as homeopathy, in the case of Nalini. 'Maybe this is good for us,' she said. Miss Chitol nodded. Outside they embraced long and hard and made promises to keep meeting, remain solid friends. On the way back, she felt very low. Lying in bed that night she could hardly believe she was not to return.

The next day raised her spirits.

It was the February of a year ending in 1 – 1981 to be absolutely precise – and the fourth census of independent India was under way. A census enumerator visited the hostel, at an hour that the great majority of the women were away. Not Miss Chitol, who was scanning the felt board in the recreation room for notices, as her room-mates had advised her to do. There she was unexpectedly enumerated.

The enumerator, Fatima Memon, who taught in a government school, seemed to enjoy Miss Chitol's slightly younger company, such company carrying the element of makeshiftness one still clearly recognises. Miss Chitol found herself providing humorous answers. For 'Description of Work' under 'Main Activity Last Year', she answered: 'Observing people's feet.' For 'Attending School/College': 'Debatable.' Sex: 'High time, ma'am!'

Through the laughter, they got down census-friendly answers. The enumerator left the form as a sample with the matron, guiding her on how to compile them for the other members of the Institutional Household, as the hostel was categorised.

'I really wish *I* could have done it, ma'am,' Miss Chitol told the enumerator, seeing her off, although she was careful not to express the desire before the matron and expose herself as a non-working woman. Near the Compound Wall, she detained Fatima Memon, since she was not Male, for further chat. She told her how clearly she remembered the last time she was counted. It was the day her grandmother had died. She remembered wondering afterwards that since her grandmother had been counted, whether somebody would have been born to cancel out the death and automatically resolve the total. An amazing exercise indeed!

Thinking back to the current exercise afterwards, however, she harboured more than a lingering dissatisfaction. She had been unfaithfully represented, like a parallel version, a refraction of herself. Her birthplace – Varanasi, from the Mughalsarai years – always surprised her for not being Bhombalpur. Her reason for migration, Education, was disingenuous. Her mother tongue she returned as Bengali; upon learning that the mother tongue was not the father tongue, as was normally understood, but the language the mother had spoken to the child in childhood, Miss Chitol did not revise it, unsure as she was about the answer, or at least the one single answer. That she had just become unemployed went ignored; in collusion with Fatima Memon, she provided her work details as though she had not just been fired. The privilege of her caste going unrecorded did not strike her at all.

She wondered whether she was improperly formed censally. In between languages and places and studies and employment, in between the mother's side and father's side, in between inner truths and outer facts. But then are most lives not so? Could it be that there were people whose everything is so neat and clean and stable so as to be tabular? If not, perhaps the enumerator will make them so. One could only know from the other side.

When the provisional population was declared, Miss Chitol found she was one of about 685 million in the country. The figure included a projected number for Assam, where the census could not be conducted because of the Foreigners issue.

7
Cosmetics

In the fortnight after her sacking Miss Chitol experienced a life of great happiness. She began her days reading. She took her bath when there was no pressure on the bathrooms. Then she resumed reading. Once a day she embarked on a long, leisurely stroll and experimented with street food. She discovered the best snacks mart and the best cheap fish-plate going. At night she read. In a short time she made her way through *The Story of My Experiments with Truth*, *Atlas Shrugged* and much of the *Women's Era* collection in the recreation room. She luxuriated in time, sweet time, as if soaking in a hot spring of the kind she read existed in the Himalayas. She oiled her hair and constructed plaits. She catnapped. Her face looked well rested and so did her feet. Money worries did not hound her. She saw that others in the hostel were worse off; she was still far from the borrowing stage. Then money worries resurfaced and with it all other worries. She was in breach of a cardinal rule: non-working women were prohibited in the working women's hostel.

To maintain the semblance of a working life, and in the process become eligible for a different category of job, she admitted herself into a heavily discounted Basic+Intermediate typing course at Ribbonwala Typing Institute in King's Circle. The course was intensive. Accounting for the commute, with some strategic gallivanting added in, she could be out for more or less the entire working day.

The atmosphere at Ribbonwala was more purposeful than it had ever been at her college. Ninety per cent of the class were girls and several were driven enough to surpass the prescribed words-per-minute goals. Miss Chitol understood early on that she was not one of them. She fell into an effortless friendship with a Parsi girl called

Beneifer, whom she found most gay and who seemed to hold a similar view of typing as herself. Beneifer lived in the nearby Parsi Colony, and sometimes invited Miss Chitol home for a glass of lemonade and spicy wafers in the recessed balcony. The house seemed to be occupied by the very young and the very old. One of the latter was a keyboard tutor, whom she could hear supervise iterations of 'Congratulations and Celebrations' and 'She'll be Coming Down the Mountain When She Comes' from behind a wall, breaking out every so often into tetchy interjections that could well have applied to her in typing class: 'Xerxes, what did God give you two ring fingers for?'

At the end of the course, Beneifer told her about openings at Hariani Trading in Nariman Point. This company was out to recruit a large number of typists. Miss Chitol showed up for the walk-in interview. There wasn't one, as such. A man, supari stuffed in his right cheek, had a quick look at her typing certificate.

'Tomorrow you can start?' he said, straining to push the words past the supari.

'Tomorrow? Yes, sir.'

'Then start.'

'Sir?'

'Then start.'

'Definitely, sir.'

'Probation,' the man said, rounding his lower lip to contain spill, and gestured to the next girl in queue to come forward.

'Thank you, sir,' said Miss Chitol and fled before he changed his mind.

Day after day she was to pound out forms and letters concerning imports, exports, customs and clearances. The stipend was negligible, barely enough to cover travel and a rice plate for lunch on the street below. But there was the glamour of working in Nariman Point, in a skyscraper close to the sea. Every day she shared the elevator with attractive boys; and the elevator with its automatic doors – although operated by a liftman – itself felt like progress.

She did not cope. She was too raw as a typist. She had no experience on any machine but the World War era Underwoods at Ribbonwala and struggled to adjust to the Godrej Primos at Hariani. Her spellings were good, but the vocabulary was unfamiliar; nothing moved automatic to her fingers. The typing hours were about twice as many as at

Ribbonwala. She lacked stamina, and consequently speed, which fell away drastically as she went on. Her fingers ached; she became cognisant of metacarpals, phalanges and webbings in a revelatory manner. She sometimes saw the supari man nod pityingly at her. She was not confirmed.

At this stage, Miss Chitol began to rue everything. She rued tossing aside a college degree for a shoewoman's job. She rued that her inclinations were towards the arts rather than commerce, for what could have been more sensible than a BCom in this city of accounts clerks? She upbraided herself for not enrolling in the advanced course at Ribbonwala, even if she knew that a career in typing would be the heights of misery; Beneifer had, despite her feelings. She regretted that she was not married, divorced or deserted, for such experiences generated their own propulsion. She had come to a standstill: a working woman who was not a working woman, and soon to be out of a working women's hostel accommodation.

Hereabouts she partook in a colossal night by the tanks, listening to a cassette of English hits Vimla had compiled. She was amazed at Vimla's appetite for English songs, much as Vimla was by hers for English books, for Miss Chitol had lately been lugging around a copy of *Doctor Zhivago*. 'I have to read it in English, I can't read it in Russian,' protested Miss Chitol. 'Why don't you watch the movie? There are groups who screen these old-type films,' said Vimla. 'There is only one word for that,' replied Miss Chitol. 'Cheating.'

That night the girls got drunk.

A song called 'We Don't Need No Education' Vimla kept rewinding, without even pressing Stop – rewinding with the reckless screeching sound. *The dogs are gathered in the classroom!* Perhaps this tuneless wonder was meant to make her feel better.

'I'm a fraud,' announced Miss Chitol.

'The world is a fraud,' declared Vimla.

'Oh I am a bigger fraud. When I was a working woman I pretended I wasn't one. Now I'm not a working woman and I'm pretending to be one. I am a joker. I am a cheater. A fraud I am, a fraud I am.'

She stopped the tape and sang Geeta Dutt at a dangerous volume, worrying the cats. Vimla shushed her on the way back down. Miss Chitol held the railing tight and vowed to improve herself as a human being.

The following morning she scrutinised the felt board more penitentially than ever before. She spotted a notice for a 'fantabulous opportunity' in market research. Everybody knew that market research was an up-and-coming field, and Miss Chitol was all open to fantabulous opportunities.

At the agency office she learned that the opportunity was not a job, but an assignment for a company – 'a *giant*, trust us' – whose name was withheld.

She was placed in a room with other candidates, who were instructed to 'interact freely' with one another. Perhaps her shop-assistant experience had held her in good stead after all, since she was an early pick.

The assignment was to quiz working women about their cosmetic desires. On the back of their half-day of training, she went forth and executed with fervour.

She did not cheat in the least. She created no fictional respondents, and made up no answers for the real ones. She conducted only a few interviews with hostel inmates, and then went wider, gaining access to their workplaces, as the agency had wanted. The interviews were designed for fifteen to twenty minutes – but under her careful shepherding could last twice that long. Lack of application from the women annoyed her; cooperation made her profoundly grateful. Suppose an interview got stuck needlessly in the shallows – let us say to the question 'Do you own a TV?' the respondent replied, 'Here, or in my native place?' and the answer to either was 'No' – Miss Chitol did not lose her patience. Rather she saw it as commitment.

'What do the following words mean to you: glossy, earthy, silky, smoky?' she asked the women, some of whom did not have much English and cackled with laughter.

'Do skin pores bother you?' she queried them.

'Do you know your hair type?'

'How much of your income do you spend on looks?'

'How often do you visit a beauty parlour?'

The surveying prompted her to reckon with her own habits. Many women had a strong idea of exactly what they wanted – which is to say they had a very sure sense of themselves. They had established routines, no matter the budget. Her own habits were limited to, if energy permitted, washing her face with soap at night, and if time did, applying cold cream on her face and arms after bath – in a city that was never ever cold, not even once by mistake. Why had she never tried vanishing cream? Why not massage coconut oil into her limbs, as waxy Sujatha did? How about soaking her feet in hot water before bed? Why did she never glug down a litre of water first thing in the morning and watch her skin turn translucent? Why had she never trusted haldi and instead wasted money on all those useless calcium tablets? Her special move was kajal, but she had never experimented with eyeliner or mascara. Nail polish she wore in old-fashioned reds and maroons, not the new 'coppers' that Vimla was trying to paint on her. Perhaps she was true to herself, she postulated, and cosmetics were about presenting oneself as true to who one was, only achieving that through untrue means. Regardless, maybe she would do well to consider the matter of routines. Who did not want to routinely look nice?

By the deadline, she managed to collect ninety-seven interrogations with working women between the ages of twenty and forty from the appropriate socio-economic strata. She found the exercise, she told Vimla, 'highly interesting'. According to her analysis, unmarried women did not want anything '*jhataak*' or flashy; rather, they preferred something that suggested authority. On the other hand, married women wanted something that suggested youth and in keeping with the times, yet not something their in-laws or husbands would fight about. Both the married and the unmarried had similar concerns. They feared that heavy make-up, especially rouge and lipstick, would suggest they were loose of character. Bad skin was a universal worry; they had seen that modern cosmetics left behind craters in the cheeks. Everybody wanted fairer skin. Vimla, who worked in a beauty parlour, dismissively said she could have told her all this and more in a single chat.

Nevertheless, these thoughts Miss Chitol wrote down in the Extra Notes segment in the individual forms. And in order not to deprive the agency of her insight into the overall patterns, she crafted a covering letter. This was, she was told at the agency office, 'well received'.

The agency docked her pay by Rs 7.50 for the shortfall of three interviews. The fulfilment of the Rs 242.50 due to her required two follow-up trips to Mr Monteiro, an executive who streamed a long ponytail beneath a bald patch, addressed his male colleague as 'cats' and his female colleagues as 'kittens' and splashed around phrases like 'Mother of God!' and 'Have a heart, man!' Tilting back on his chair, an unlit cigarette between his lips, Monteiro told her through his barely opened mouth to report the coming Monday to 'pick up another assignment, yah', leaving little doubt that he rated her highly.

When she went to get her pay the accountant handed her a cheque. Her expression must have given her away because he told her she needn't worry if she did not have an account: since it was a bearer cheque, she could cash it at the bank. This convinced her, however, that she must get a bank account and when she went to take her money she initiated the process.

She waited eagerly to meet Monteiro the coming Monday. In the intervening nights, she found herself recalling the faces, dress, voices, turns of speech, confessions and evasions of the women she had interviewed, and wondered what the new assignment might bring. On the Sunday evening she applied nail polish and hair oil, wrapping an old dupatta around her head overnight so that she didn't catch a head cold at a critical time. On Monday morning she shampooed it off and painted on kajal before setting out for the agency office.

Monteiro was busy. When she vied for his attention he seemed not to recognise her. On being reminded, he released the words 'no go', gliding past her with his ponytail in pursuit. While gliding back a few minutes later he repeated the words, accompanying them with twiddly gestures of his thumbs, in case she had not understood.

She returned empty-handed.

She could not tell whether the project had been cancelled or whether she had not made the cut. Maybe, she thought afterwards, she had failed badly by coming in three interviews short; if only she had spent a little less time on each! Maybe it was that her observations were found to be wrong. Maybe it was because Monteiro was a cat, and she was just Miss Chitol – whose English was perfectly good, just not like a cat's, or a kitten's.

8

In the gully

'Tis a fact of life that sunrises seen,
make more misery than those unseen.
The missed sunrise causes no suffering,
for there would be other such.
The seen sunrise finds no such luck,
for there cannot be another such!

Thus surveying daybreak, Miss Chitol, the sporadic veteran of as many as two market surveys, mentally composed another poem she would not write, aboard her Annual Picnic bus groaning up the western shoreline on this the second Saturday of the month.

At the same time, in the evanescence of Calcutta dreams out east, securely employed Dhrubo, who cherished morning sleep – not to mention afternoon and night sleep – snoozed on until he could no longer delay the factory visit at his diversifying Marwari conglomerate. And in the railway township of Bhombalpur in the heart of the country, Anando, his spectacle frames too large for his sweet beakish face, shared another cigarette at the apprentices' hostel, debating wanton industrialisation, balletic footballers and the formation of a new theatre group called Rakht.

In that same stagnational railway township – but so recent! so full of national hope! – Animesh Kumar Chitol, Shop Superintendent, erstwhile known as Foreman A, of the Inspection Shop, picked his muffler off the clothes horse, wrapped it around his neck and set out on his bicycle by the long route towards the workshop in this, his last fortnight of service.

It was the month of Kartik. He felt the bite of the latening mornings. From a patch of grass the moonshine of kash waved at him. From above him the leftover night scents of chatim fell like scrapings of cardamom. Two nights before there had been a magnificent storm, when sparkling silver lightning raised divots from the startled red earth. The fresh air cooled Chitol's cheeks; he thought he saw a hare prancing across his path.

His mind was on the future. He had some time. He could, on payment of 'normal rent', retain these quarters a little longer. Then he would rent beside his friend Dulal Rahman in the Railway Retirees Colony on the outskirts of the expanding town. He would buy that scooter after all. Maybe, in time, even build a little house, for the realisation had crept up on him that Bhombalpur was home.

He cycled on. His breath was laboured, his circulation dull. In a stretch between the new pumping station at the lake and the bungalow of the chief workshop manager, towards whose daughter's wedding he had steadfastly declined to make a 'donation', he felt a storm breaking out in his chest. His body shuddered, his bicycle wobbled. Still seated, he tottered into the broad rain gully on the margin. In the gully, under the linear metallic crush of his bicycle, which felt like a rebuke, he endured a spate of intergalactic attacks through which he felt dead and never more alive. He battled and befriended pain of a nature he had not imagined let alone experienced, and a similarly frazzled intensity of thought and feeling. He watched himself dead from a state of life and living from a state past death.

It was so early. The route was not a busy one, used mainly by officers in their vehicles. Occasionally he was aware of men walking or a bicycle scissoring by. He had not the physical capacity to call out. All went past him. His presence there in the gully and their obliviousness to it struck him as absurd. Another pocket of unsubmitted, unpublished prose. Strange was this detachment from life and death, a detachment that was nevertheless fevered. In any case, which was the wiser way to have lived or died? Detached and wise or attached and terribly alive? Impossible question – and look at this handlebar here on my intercostals.

Explosions of night and sun burst before Chitol's eyes. His left arm felt like lead, his chest simply unable. He lay there thrombosed, incapacitated, erratically lucid, surrendered. Since he had surrendered, time seemed to spread out before him. There was enough of it for judgements and exonerations. A light perspiration lit up his forehead. He wished he could loosen his muffler. *Chitol* – that was a good one! He recalled the formula hp=2plan/33k, watched chattering squirrels on a tree, remembered how the American in the famine time of the strange red PL480 wheat called them chipmunks. Into his ears Madhuri Chattopadhyay sang like a blessing, *there on the bend in the small river, there lives my beloved.* He felt this life was nothing but an *ashadher golpo*, one fantastic tale, and concluded that his entire existence had nothing but a horse's egg. He began to weep through crinkled eyes at the impending sadness of things and the incalculable fear of any moment now.

When sadness came it came like a barrage-breaking flood, making difficult breath impossible. He had done so little for the family he raised. My wife, I love you like anything, I will meet you on the bend, I shall swim to you, I am coming. In a hopeless distortion of fact, he felt sickened to have married and sired children with Mrs Flanger of the tinkling English while Jigyasa his real wife slaved in the kitchen. His insides heaved and squirmed. Occasionally he was washed over by lulls of comfort. Every so often somebody reached out into his heart and applied a brutal little twist as though to a radio knob. He saw the faces of his children from a distant past when their new eyes were so full of sparkle, their laughs so pure, their cheeks so soft, and he felt a love so spiritual he was maybe already on the other side, unlimited love that he would carry through the stars and ice and fire. Given you nothing, I am sorry, my children, my Charu, my Dhrubo, my Anando, please forgive me, my Anando Dhrubo Charu my children. *But I am in harness*, he smiled, with ultimate love, I am in harness, smiled like he had pulled another fast one. And there he still kept lying and lying, thrombosed and coronaried, and still the universe knew nothing and nothing.

In time Mr Chitol was so dead the animals and insects became curious and took their chances. It was the crows who alerted the humans.

Vatsala Tai, the assistant matron, alerted Miss Chitol. She said there was a telephone call. A telephone call in this dharamshala near the beach town of Bordi? There was a near drowning earlier in the day, conjectured to be an aborted suicide attempt, by one of her own room-mates, Sujatha the married. For a moment she thought the phone call concerned this, and then, no, what sense did that make, and then she knew exactly what. The physical details of that room would stay with her forever. The Gandhis, Mohandas and Kasturba, hanging from the pale blue walls painted that colour till three-quarters up, the plump cream fans whingeing from the ceiling, the window grilles shaped like the sun and its rays, the window frames so swollen by sea they needed fastening with coir ropes. She took a long time to leave the room and walk to the telephone. She felt seasick, her legs felt gone. She could use the back seat of a bicycle but the rider was ... she knew exactly what.

Afterwards, she took the first plane ride of her life.

9

Letters

From a very tender age the Chitol children suspected they deserved death, that somehow, unspokenly, they caused it. When the three orphans convened at the morgue in the Bhombalpur Railway Hospital, they eyed each other a little shiftily, as though to conceal and also confess their role in the occurrence. Miss Chitol had little doubt of her own culpability. She had abandoned him. Perhaps her aunt had been right: she had broken his heart. Weakened it certainly.

When the coroner was not looking, she placed her hand on his cold white forehead. She resisted the urge to put her head against his chest. Instead, she prodded him to see if he might respond. He did not. She saw that the coroner had been looking.

Chitol was brought home. Friends and neighbours and colleagues converged at the quarters; the small garden became packed with people, offering flowers and prayers at his feet, his big toes tied together with red thread, turning him, reverentially if chaotically, into a minor public spectacle quite in contrast to his living personality. Then commenced the long procession to the cremation ground near the riverbank, Dhrubo and Anando and other men holding the bier upon their shoulders, chanting 'Hari Bol' as they went along.

In contravention of tradition, Miss Chitol accompanied it. At the ghat, watching the pyre blaze up towards the sky, as her elder brother circumambulated the crackling flames, it was necessary to hold on to the idea of the soul, for a burning of this kind seemed too harsh, too spectacular; there could be no reason to so severely finish what was finished if not release.

Her attendance at the cremation, as she anticipated, was not met with universal approval. Yet she appreciated that Dhrubo had not stood in opposition, and that Kolkata Pishe and Pishi had been restrained in expressing their misgivings. It was her other pishi who gave her trouble.

Foreign Pishi, as they called the slightly older of her father's elder sisters, lived in the Middle East after marriage. Despite having crossed the waters, she had not only successfully retained caste and associated custom, she had become stricter about them. In the country at the time of the death, she arrived in Bhombalpur the evening after the cremation. 'What you did was very wrong,' she told her niece after they had cried together. It was not necessary to specify the what.

'He was my father too,' Miss Chitol stated in her defence. She found support from Notun Dida, who deemed the practice *lokachar* rather than *shastrachar*. There was no such prohibition in the scriptures; it was simply to account for a woman's incapacity to bear tragedy. This, Dida opined, they could do better than men.

Both pishis agreed, however, that rules must now be followed well. Miss Chitol suggested her father did not particularly believe in such, mainly participated in them for the sake of those who did. That being the case, the aunts said, since the family believed in them, of course they must be observed. Besides, her father was more of a believer than she gave him credit for. They reminded her of the thread ceremonies for her brothers, further back the handwriting ceremony for them all on Saraswati Puja, further back still, the *annaprashan* ceremonies for their first morsels of food – all of which, Miss Chitol remarked, would have been her grandmother's doing, and where it came to the sacred thread, her father himself did not wear it.

Don't forget, said Kolkata Pishi, that he observed the rules after your grandmother went. All three of us wrote examinations during that time, countered Miss Chitol, and he too had to step out of the house to take care of this or that. I remember him saying, not all duty is written in the scriptures and not everything in the scriptures is our duty.

And do you know that it was on the advice of a Banarasi astrologer that he had changed the name? insisted Foreign Pishi. If it was for any other reason, would he have not kept it at Kumar? That is what Uttam and Kishore did, she said, trotting out a famous Chattopadhyay and a famous Gangopadhyay.

Not Amitabh's father, Miss Chitol pointed out, remembering that N, the reading-room boy, had told her how the poet had taken his pen name, Bachchan, as the family title.

But they had digressed strenuously, comically, and everybody smiled.

She did not have the conviction to argue further. She could not be as firm about his scepticism as they were about their belief. Nor did she have a better alternative to propose. She had wished to exist in a state truer to her father, but she was moved by the emotion of her aunts, who had both begun to cry while making their case. She had to admit that there was a comfort in knowing that things were supposed to be a certain way, no matter the obfuscations, that in this hour of altered reality one could get busy organising and surrendering, which they did in the manner the clan was always said to.

Dhrubo and Anando stayed largely confined to a room. They wore unstitched garments, did not shave, and slept on blankets on the floor. Miss Chitol, unmarried and thereby belonging to her father, had her observances run the full ten days. She did not use soap or hair oil or trim her nails. Were the floor not so cold, all she would have liked to do is sleep and sleep, sleep through to the other side of grief.

Every day Dhrubo, who had lit the pyre, lit the wood fire on which the *habishya* meal was cooked in the backyard – ghee, rice, raw banana, devoid of salt or spices. This everybody ate once a day on banana leaves, even those in the house to whom the restrictions did not apply, such as Notun Dida, or the married pishis, who could have limited themselves to three days.

As a result of the austerities and confinements the mood in the house became prickly. The fare left Dhrubo hungry, and he could find little peace. Neither could Anando, distracted by his brother's flatulence. He developed a mild rash on the skin where his shawl made direct contact. Foreign Pishe found it difficult to navigate the township and expressed his frustrations in surprisingly ripe language, while concealing his legitimate indulgence of deep-fried snacks and tea at the market; everyone suspected him for a quarter-bottle of whisky spotted over the cactus hedge. Miss Chitol once overheard the women discussing her mother's complexion and her own, which deeply upset her. She caught a cold. Every day Foreign Pishi read from the Gita; she did not have a harmonious rendition. Every day the purohit came for a *pind-daan* puja, instead of employing the common provision of performing them all together on the tenth day. Here Miss Chitol and Anando felt things going too far, but they recognised it would not be easy to stand between Foreign Pishi and her control over the priest, and vice versa, underwritten as the relationship was by foreign currency. Everybody acknowledged, too, that it had to do with the fact that she had not been able to come home when her mother had died. In death, thus, A. K. Chitol, received, Brahminically, every chance of success at liberation from cyclical existence.

On the tenth day the brothers were tonsured on the riverbank and had their nails cut.

On the eleventh day, everybody wore new clothes for the *shraddh*, which was completed with the donation of bed, footwear, umbrella – each of the sixteen items to equip the soul on its passage from the earthly world.

Afterwards, they hosted a meal in the community hall; these expenses the children insisted they would bear themselves. A few relations and friends made a journey for the *shraddh*, and some stayed on a night or two. Their mama attended, coming from Patna, where he had been with relatives, and left the same evening. Jajabor Jethu made it. Their father's old friends were there, people she hadn't seen in a long time. Shubhendu Pal; Paranjoy Ghosh and his wife; Foundry Rangaswamy. Pearl Flanger came. Miss Chitol found she was not upset by her. Rather it triggered an old nervousness, which soon subsided, noting how fragile she looked, attended upon by a young Adivasi girl who wore the rosary. Although it was a working day, there was a reasonable turnout of colleagues, with whom, across shifts and seasons, Chitol had kept some national wheel turning. One or two members of the artisanal staff remembered how in the days of the great strike he had pacified as well as motivated them, later helped them write petitions, loaned them money and never asked when it would be returned. They held her brothers' hands and wept. Some spoke of Chitol's artistic spirit; a few praised his subtle humour or the quiet courage with which he had raised his three children.

On the thirteenth day the family broke the observances with the *matsyamukhi* meal featuring fish.

By evening, back in the quarters, Miss Chitol had not a particle of social energy left, especially as Jajabor Jethu had made everybody positively rambunctious. She had negotiated far too many questions about her life in Bombay over the past days; thankfully, on an occasion like this talk of marriage was inappropriate.

At dusk she noticed Anando steal away. She found him under a tree at the end of a parallel lane. As soon as he spotted her he tucked his cigarette behind his back.

'Give me one,' she told him.

'Didi.'

'Didi what?'

'Actually, I don't have another one.'

'At least take that one out of your backside.'

She took it between her fingers, lightly tossed back her head and put it to her lips, as she had seen Bombay smokeresses do. The terrible taste entered her mouth, but she kept herself from coughing.

'Eesh! Which brand is this?'

'Charminar.'

'Terrible.'

'Your first time?'

She shot him a convincing glare.

'Does Dada know this … ?'

'He does not have to know anything.'

They passed the cigarette back and forth. She felt it an appropriate tribute to her father.

'What days,' she exhaled.

'By the end I thought Foreign Pishe and the purohit were going to come to blows.'

'And the pishis each other.'

'And what about Dada just farting and burping and shouting?'

'Despite everything, it was good everyone stayed together.'

'I'm not sure anyone can take a day more.'

'Everyone has to. Just as well you've got used to sleeping on the blanket. You can take the garden.'

'To shit I'll definitely have to go out to the trees. Waiting list is too long. But after all the ghee, it comes out very smooth, doesn't it, Didi?'

'*Chee!*' she said, confidently ashing now. 'It went well today, didn't it? I am glad we were able to get chitol, even if it was expensive.'

Anando smiled, running his hand over his shaved head.

She touched the hairline above his temple, as if to determine whether the recession was that severe.

'Football,' he said. 'When you play in the rain, going for headers. Hair falls like leaves.'

'Your brains are falling out, madman. Have you seen Socrates? I don't think his hair is falling like leaves.'

'He does not use his head so much, *toh*.'

'He uses his brains.'

'Name is Socrates.'

'One person I did not see is Budhwa da.'

'Budhwa da? He is dead, Didi.'

'What! When? How?'

'Maybe six months ago? He had malaria. Even we found out a few weeks after he was gone.'

'I can't believe it. Why did nobody tell me?'

Anando said nothing.

'Tell me, Anando, why did nobody tell me?'

'Didi. The way you went away … ' he trailed off. 'It is not possible to keep telling everybody everything.'

She thought she was up to date. She knew that the Asur *tola* was no longer there, and when the evicted families had returned home, Budhwa Asur had stayed on, making a wage as a cart-puller in town.

'I thought, if you didn't want it, we could ask whether he wanted Baba's cycle,' she said, her voice trembling a little.

'You know he had decided to buy a scooter?' Anando said. 'This time really.'

'Sometimes I get so angry with that cycle.'

She did not wish their spirits to slide. She took a deep drag, and allowed herself the explosive cough she felt coming.

'Eeesh, *beeshri*! Charminar.'

'First time!' said Anando.

'And let's go, people will ask one thousand questions. You have *mouri, toh*?'

They walked quietly back, chomping on the evidence-erasing fennel.

'Baba was right,' said Anando to her as they got to the gate. 'Why, after all, should one wear a caste thread?'

A few days later, once everybody had left, he buried his in the garden, under the tulsi.

Bhombalpur had stood a distant last. To what it did not matter. It could barely see the finish line while others had collected their medals and loped off the podium. She heard talk that the workshop was to be downsized, tardy as it had been in the transition from steam. In the proliferating bush, in clumps of unplanned trees, one could detect nature's fightback, alert to the opportunities in technological obsolescence and the shrinking horticultural budget that left no room for Budhwa Asur.

In the mornings she went on long walks. Cold was creeping in by the day. The winter birds had arrived. Brahminy ducks, geese, ibis, gadwalls, pochards. If she went early enough the ponds were orchestral with bird call; a little later the vegetation was aflutter with kingfishers, rollers, orioles, barbets, wagtails, grey hornbills. Some birds she could identify in one language or another; others, if she could summon the concentration, she looked up in her father's Salim Ali.

The book told her birds had air sacs in their bones, which helped them breathe and fly. The birds gave her life breeze. Otherwise she felt wingless. For much of the time she felt she was moving through cotton, which blinded vision, stuck in the throat, retarded movement.

She resorted to old habits but in excess, wetting glucose biscuits with water just long enough for them to acquire a texture that was neither crunchy nor mulchy. And that was all she wished to eat. The biscuits sat in her stomach like cardboard in rain.

Dhrubo had gone back to his job in Calcutta, returning once to put his signature on documents and chide the others into action. Anando re-immersed himself into the apprentice life he had barely begun. As for Notun Dida, she looked a hundred years old. With ten working teeth and no dentures, a tongue as bloodshot as Ma Kali's, skin that had turned into a crepe of mole and vein, she went about keeping the quarters operational in the final days, as she had done for the better part of two decades. Miss Chitol would catch a glimpse of her and her own resolve would fall crashing down. While they had lost a father she had lost something like a son, and would soon lose the only house that had become anything like her home. The thought oppressed Miss Chitol. We are all of us cursed with the capacity to see the pain of others and repurpose it into our own. The dispossessed one becomes an item in the schedule of pity, which is but the finer side of contempt.

While cleaning out her father's almirah she encountered decades of life stuffed into envelopes and folders. In some of these she found heaps of Bangla prose and poems in his tiny, restless handwriting. She was able to make out the odd phrase and sentence, and with patience might have been able to decipher all of it.

One envelope contained a number of fine sketches, including a detailed pencil illustration of 'Jagannath', the first locomotive assembled at the Bhombalpur workshop.

Another was wrapped in cloth – a piece of red sari, secured with a thread, so that it appeared to house scriptures. She opened out a folded page to find a drawing of her mother. She stared at it for a few seconds, and folded it back. She felt she had trespassed. The envelope contained their correspondences.

A sheaf of papers inside a Railways folder she worked out were drafts of the pen portraits from the time of the strike. This made her stop – these proofs of his guilt he had preserved.

Next she came upon a heap of carbon copies, and these slayed her.

Dear Sir ... I humbly submit that due action has been taken against me in the form of loss of seniority and accumulated benefits ... I plead, therefore, that I am not dismissed from service ...

Respected Sir ... I may have committed a grave error, however not a sin ... It was not my intention to create trouble against the administration but to help create conditions by which workers may be able to perform their service to best ability ...

Esteemed Sir ... Please find enclosed my response, in which I have clarified some charges against me ... At the very end, it may be noted that I am a father of three children who were deprived of their mother who died when they were very young. If I am dismissed from service, Sir, their sole source of support in life will be cut off ...

Honourable Prime Minister. We, the undersigned, humbly request your kind intervention in the unparalleled victimisation of railwaymen ... Thousands of our colleagues are in jail, while others amongst us, especially those in the lower grades, are struggling to cope with the harsh disciplinary actions, including dismissal ... Our motive has always been to be part of a strong workforce that is able to rise to the challenges before the country ... We appeal humbly, therefore, that the jailed workers be released and disciplinary actions be dropped ... We remain, sincerely, servants of the Indian Railways and servants of India ...

I will not indulge in Anti-National Activity. I will not indulge in Anti-National Activity. I will not indulge in Anti-National Activity. I will not indulge in Anti-National Activity. I will not indulge in Anti-National Activity. I will not indulge in Anti-National Activity. I will not indulge in Anti-National Activity. I will not indulge in Anti-National Activity. I will not indulge in Anti-National Activity. I will not ...

She needed to lie down. She did so right where she was and closed her eyes. A familiar ghost hand stroked her face. She welcomed it, waxy and corrugated as a used candle. Stroke, stroke, stroke, stroke, overpowering breath. The hands of time swept across her forehead down to her cheek, making everything a little better.

'Nobody has given you the sympathy you deserved, *khuki*,' the voice said, employing the English word.

'What do I need sympathy for?' said Miss Chitol, her eyes still closed. 'Am I Dhrubo?'

Then she slowly took Notun Dida's hand off her face. After a few minutes she left the house.

As she walked up the street her face began to contract in a manner a fun-making bystander might perceive as hilarious. She went out to the spot she frequented with Salima – not seen or spoken to since the day of the thousand women. In her old sanctuary, which in adulthood proved to be not exactly a depression, barely a dip, she could no longer lean on the rocks; they were too short. She sat upon one. She wished to bawl like a madwoman but only managed to dry-retch her insides from time to time.

The retches did contain unreceived sympathies, and she did want to receive them. The thought of her father writing up these petitions at the time she left his side made her desperate. She felt such pain at his humiliation she felt she understood nobody in the world better, and at this moment his love for her and hers for him seemed infinite.

Hopeless was the non-crying of Miss Chitol. She wished to be done with it but grief was so disobedient. She wished to flee back into life, but life was too damn difficult.

At night, like an addict aware that another hit could be worse but worse could be better, she ventured into her parents' correspondence.

She was surprised that these were in Hindi. Her mother's clean writing, the words as she heard them, evoked a blurry ancestral memory. As sentence upon sentence materialised before her the barely remembered voice sank into oblivion. A whole new woman, or women, rose from them.

One of her was very funny, chronicling everyday events with the easy wit and sarcasm of a *hasya-vyangya* writer, addressing her correspondent as Shriman Chitol, Mahashay Chitol, Chitol Babu. Here she made an astonishing discovery. These appeared to be the very first times the name had been used. The rapture with which the man had described the qualities of this species of fish had apparently led the woman to address him so.

Miss Chitol was jolted out of her mood. The archives were incomplete. The letters were loosely arranged by chronology. But the individual envelopes had not been preserved, and not every letter was dated, so it was not possible to know from where and when each originated. The jumps in the correspondences left unclear how much happened in the interim or what each reference stood for.

In one letter, inferior in language to the woman's, not, however, without a certain literary vim, the man let her know that he had decided to identify himself by other than a caste name. This was something they seemed to have discussed before. Its genesis appeared to be an incident that the man referred to here with the words, *I felt a shame I could not wash away.* So, for his pen name he had chosen the unsurpassable Chitol. Chitol Babu he would indeed be.

This exchange, she surmised, would have been from soon after her parents had spent some months as visiting neighbours in Kanpur. She knew this much about how they had met, and that it had been a long time between it and marriage. When marriage did come into the correspondences, another woman rose, fluent in her indignation.

For you, from a position of highness, to consider yourself against highness and lowness may be admirable, she wrote. *But to the one considered low – nimn the word she used – lowness pierces in a different way. It is all very well to talk about the Hindu Marriage Validity Act, as though I will mark those clauses upon my head rather than the sindoor. You may think these things ridiculous but it is hardly amusing for me to know that your family does not think the scriptures have provisions for asavarna weddings, even less that they think according to scriptures there are no provisions for Kayasthas to wear the sacred thread. I can only say that our family and many others believe that the Kayasthas are their own community, not a component of any varna (some do indeed perform the thread ceremony at marriage), and as you know, a highly literate and literary community they are. The president of our country! But he too went and washed the feet of Brahmins of Banaras so what am I to say. I am angry with myself to have written these words. Within my own family I fight and I tell them, why do you think the Chitraguptavanshi Kayastha is so special, so delicate, that if a girl marries outside you shall be ruined? All of this has made me very upset and I think I shall go up to the terrace and walk where nobody can see me. I wish I could spend the night there by myself without anyone calling my name. I cannot bear the idea of being thought low in the house I may become a part of. Nobody is low.*

Perhaps the man had explained, assuaged, apologised, won her over, for in a subsequent letter another shade of the woman expressed itself.

I am thinking fondly of you, she wrote. *I am telling myself that whatever this does to my spirit it is not worse than being shown to men who are complete strangers, towards whom one has no affection. I have told you already about Babuji's position. He is orthodox but because of that has a weakness for Brahmins, much like the president! He is keen to fulfil his responsibilities, especially after Ma went, and so may not stand in the way in the end. It is nice to hear that you think your side will accept the union (did they say so clearly?) and that you are confident things will be fine in time. It is a good thing that I have a natural pull towards the Bengali language, a beautiful language indeed, I hope that will help matters. How and what form a wedding will take, how many people will openly support it, I do not know. Maybe it is for the good. Think of how much money people squander on weddings. I will be happy to spare my father that. Whether society will consider me as Brahmin or you as no longer one is for it to deal with. I think ourselves fortunate we have the name Chitol to remind ourselves that there is life outside restrictions, but I advise you please not to disclose the source to your family. That will only make it harder for me. It is true that the matsya avatar is my favourite, and yes, it does sound pretty, and is a cheering thought and I smile as I write these words.*

It was getting to the coldest hour of the day. Miss Chitol wrapped her shawl tightly around herself. She turned to look at the garlanded portraits hanging side by side, asymmetrical in dimension. The letters were they, and they were her parents, the same she had known a few hours ago.

Her mind was on fire. Now it was her mother's humiliations that coursed through her. Although her mama and mami had mentioned the difficulties – the opposition to the marriage, certain elders refusing food served by her – she had taken them as charming tales of valour against the old ways. Perhaps she had wished to preserve her mother's happiness.

She burned with questions. There were many more letters by her than him. Was that because she was the more prolific correspondent? Or had she destroyed his for the fear of being discovered? What was the incident that prompted him to reconsider the caste name? Could it be that he had envisaged this inter-caste union, and that was what ultimately fixed the decision – was it love that did it? A name she had coined, for him, and now them, and she too smiled, resembling as she did the woman in the letters more than she could ever know.

She dove into the pile again, going over things she had missed the first time, averting her eyes when the contents were too tender. All of a sudden she felt the force of her violation. Mindless was this trespassing. She stopped. After a while she returned the letters to their envelope, wrapped it back in the piece of sari and tied the string. She brought the bundle to her lips, then lightly touched it to her forehead. She told herself never to read them again. She was not sure how much of them she ought to even retain.

She was very tired and wide awake. At the start of the night, a long time ago, she had played Lata and Mukesh on the two-in-one and they had left their notes on all objects in the room. Day would break soon.

She got up and brought out the letters she had legitimately got from her uncle, letters she had carried around in her bag like a talisman but never opened. It had never felt the right time.

Now she read the words of a woman with a life too full to commit to correspondence. She brought greetings of a season, gestured at by morning dew or the basanta's bird call, told of progress with her children, a school admission gained, a hornet sting endured bravely, discussed the possibility of visits, asked for news in brisk fashion. She gave out her heart only in one instance. If I too could do a job and contribute, wouldn't I feel better? wrote the woman in the letter. *Tumhari Jigyasa*, she signed off, a dot under her name. All three letters Miss Chitol had been given finished thus.

10
No objections are certified

A. K. Chitol had died, as he noted in his final throes, 'in harness'. When a government employee dies in his last days of service an amount of suspicion attaches itself to the death. The railway administration had seen cases where a father had sacrificed himself, or a wife a husband, to secure the son a job on compassionate grounds.

Chitol's death was swiftly certified as natural by the chief medical officer of the Bhombalpur Railway Hospital, and the administration moved quickly on the report. There should be no excuse for survivors to invoke the Workmen's Compensation Act, since the deceased did not suffer an accident and was certainly not on duty. Yet, ever since a zealous young personnel officer on the Northeast Frontier Railway had argued 'notional extension of duty' for a pump operator trampled to death by an elephant while returning from the site after his shift had ended, nobody wanted to take any chances.

A. K. Chitol *had* died in harness, however, and his survivors were entitled to the appropriate death benefits. Fortunately for them, as earlier observed, the short-lived government after the Emergency had revoked the punishments meted out in the great railway strike, even granting the bonus the railwaymen had fought for. The calculation of the death gratuity, of which Miss Chitol was to receive a third share, took in his entire length of service. She was to gain a similar third of the provident fund and leave encashment dues. These, together with her share of their father's savings, and the fixed deposits that he had for each of the children, amounted to a sum that made her almost nervous to be in charge of. She resolved to put it away where she could not see it. There was no property, no investments to speak of; jewellery was scant.

Since Dhrubo was already an earner, she was now first in line for the family pension. For the same reason she was first in line for the compassionate grounds appointment – unless Dhrubo were to shed his job and claim it. Having trained at a private engineering college, found employment at a private metropolitan company, Dhrubo had cultivated a disdain for government service and the static provincialism it conjured. So had, if she was perfectly honest, Miss Chitol.

But as she gave herself over to the bureaucracy of death with the numb focus of a chain stitcher, needling her way through forms and certificates, letters and applications, originals and duplicates, goading the thread towards completion, the thought of railway employment did not seem outrageous after all. She saw the signs, the reparative logic. A job her father had saved by humiliating himself, now made another available to his children. A job the likes of which her mother never got a chance at. She considered her circumstances, the unreliability of assignments, her breach of the working women's hostel rules.

When there remained no doubts in her mind she wrote to Dhrubo in Calcutta to say she had decided to claim the job. He should inform her if he had any objections, else send a no-objection certificate. As for the family pension, she had worked out a plan for that. Anando was eligible for it until he got employed – by the Railways, she hoped, since apprentices were usually absorbed. He would keep a half-share to bolster his stipend, and send a half-share to Notun Dida, who was left with nothing. She had already discussed this with Anando, whom she had also helped open a bank account. If Dhrubo had any objections, he should tell her, else send a no-objection certificate.

Dhrubo did not like the letter. He felt he had been comprehensively superseded. But he knew he had exercised the option of getting away, leaving her to clear up. Miss Chitol knew this too, of course, and also that because of it the papers would arrive.

As soon as they did, she went to look up the welfare inspector in the administrative building. There she learned he had gone away on extraordinary leave. The clerks who heard her request laughed her out of the room. Because what Miss Chitol wanted could not so easily be got. No way she was going to take an appointment in Bhombalpur, no way in these death quarters: she wished to be posted in Bombay.

The clerks were right.

For when she apprised assistant welfare officer P. K. Mishra of her wish he reshaped his forehead into a stern frown of administrative unfeasibility.

'*Aisa hai*, it's like this,' he began. 'It is no use, what you are asking for. We can forward this, no problem. But there is no guarantee. They may ignore. They may reject. They will have their own lists, quotas, their own requirements. So you can forget about it.'

The a.w.o. reached for his comb to direct a displaced bridge of hair from a parting near the top of his right ear towards the distant shore of the left, and in the same effortless motion returned the comb to his coat pocket. Its hole rose like a periscope above the pocket line.

'Sir, I have to be in Bombay at any cost,' Miss Chitol pleaded.

'Is there some close relative in Bombay?' he enquired, patting down the hair above the ears. 'If you ask me, for a young girl, this is a safe, comfortable place. Your brother is here. What is the big thing in Bombay?'

'Actually, sir, I have settled there.'

Wrong word.

'Settled? It says here you are unmarried! Married daughter we cannot grant compassionate appointment just like that, we will need special approval.'

The agitation displaced his bridge all over again.

'Unmarried, sir,' Miss Chitol hastily clarified. 'My meaning is I live there now.'

'With whom?'

'In a hostel.'

'Anyway, it may be only for a little time,' judged a.w.o. P. K. Mishra. 'You start here. After one year you will be able to marry.'

'Meaning?' asked Miss Chitol, then understood. He was referring to the eligibility of tradition, the period after her father's death.

Just then a peon arrived bearing a summons from the workshop personnel officer. Miss Chitol was asked to think on the matter and, as ever, come back tomorrow morning.

Several mornings later, the assistant welfare officer took her to the larger office of the workshop personnel officer, P. K. Mittal.

Perhaps a decade lay between a.w.o. P. K. Mishra and w.p.o. P. K. Mittal. Featuristically speaking, they looked nothing like each other. But each maintained a trim, slate moustache; each was fond of starting his sentences with '*Aisa hai*' and each dug his chin into his neck gravely, gaseously as he did. Each parted his hair off the same far-right position, with the comb similarly accessible in the front pocket.

Miss Chitol watched with stupefaction a conversation between the combholes. There were long-standing indents for junior ministerial staff in Stores where she could be compassionately appointed at once. They asked for her papers; she compliantly handed them over to the inferior combhole, who produced the relevant ones for the superior, and her future was all but sealed before she remembered to intervene.

'No, sir.'

The men did not pay her any mind.

'I have brought the letter, sir,' pulling it out of her folder.

They looked perplexed.

The letter was a result of her conversations with young B, a clerk in the welfare section. 'A transfer will be more difficult than joining,' young B had advised her. 'Remember, in a compassionate appointment, the pressure is on the administration to accommodate. Don't lose the advantage.' Then, as though in a show of marksmanship, he had resumed flicking the edge of his handkerchief against a glass paperweight.

Consequently, Miss Chitol prepared a missive, affecting a contrite tone that might have been the influence of her father's entreaties, wherein she humbly requested that she be granted a Compassionate Grounds Appointment in Bombay, where she had been pursuing her education, and intended to continue in evening college after taking up the aforementioned appointment. As such, she needed to remain in Bombay to maintain continuity in her life, and yet she needed the job after the untimely demise of her father. Wordily did Miss Chitol leave no doubt that her request be kindly considered, and hence workshop personnel officer P. K. Mittal and therefore assistant welfare officer P. K. Mishra did.

'We can put up the papers,' a peeved a.w.o. P. K. Mishra said to Miss Chitol in the larger office of w.p.o. P. K. Mittal, this time more ominously. 'But we cannot guarantee. We cannot do it directly from here. We have to go via the channels. Ninety-nine point nine nine per cent nothing will happen.'

'Hundred point nine nine,' w.p.o. P. K. Mittal corrected his inferior.

And with that he dinged a steel bell, indicating to Miss Chitol that she should take her leave.

As she walked out of the administrative block, through the avenue of upright ashoka trees, their trunks painted white and terracotta till the specified height, she was satisfied that she had made progress.

It was only as the days dragged by that she understood she had tossed herself afloat on the shoreless sea of bureaucracy.

Every day she made the long walk to the administrative block, for some clerky wit or other to remark: 'Apply, apply, no reply.'

She began to go at different times of the day to see if her luck would change. One day she learned that Western Railway had replied with a rejection. No reply still from Central.

Here, young B, the handkerchief-flicking clerk, asked Miss Chitol whether her father had been a member of a recognised union. Was he close to any high-ranking officers? Did she know anybody at Central Railway who could push her case? Did she have anybody in Bombay who could 'arrange' something? At last he said: 'Then what are you doing here, why are you not in Bombay?'

Young B offered this with a winning smile. He then quickly asked, for nobody was in listening distance: 'Will you eat ice cream with me?'

This was well known in Bhombalpur as the most forward thing a boy could ask a girl.

Miss Chitol agreed at once.

Young B encouraged Miss Chitol to choose an elaborate ice cream like Tooty Frooty. She opted for a Mango Duet stick, he a Vanilla cup. Although B felt young to her in that room of clerks, he did not among the winter romancers in the ice-cream part of the lake.

'You must have heard a lot of things about the welfare department,' he said, straightening his geometrical-design sweater as they settled down. 'How they take advantage of women in compassionate cases.'

She had not heard such things.

'But did I ask you anything for my help?' the clerk continued. 'No, I am not like that.'

It turned out young B was not averse to assessing himself. He was full of talents and his life was full of broken trajectories. 'When I was small,' he told her, 'I used to play karate. All through school I took classes. I was very good. My plan was I would become a sensei.

Then I stopped.' He did not say why exactly, although it sounded like misfortune. He told her similarly that he used to paint in watercolours, sunsets like this over the lake; people would get emotional looking at them. He believed he could have become a big-name painter had financial needs not got in the way.

After she finished her ice cream Miss Chitol sucked on her stick. Young B licked his wooden spoon clean and gently masticated it.

The first time they met they sat face to face across the single table by the ice-cream stall. The second they were side by side on the backless cement bench by the water, watching the sun scatter into the kind of colours young B's brushes once recreated. Here he spoke Miss Chitol's date of birth.

'Did you see it on the form?' she asked.

'Won't you ask me what day it was?'

'The day that you saw it?'

'The day of your birth. Ask me.'

'What day was it?' asked Miss Chitol.

'The day was a Saturday,' answered young B.

'It was,' she confirmed.

'Ask me any date and I'll tell you the day.'

'But how will I know if you are right?'

'Think, think. You must be knowing the day of some special dates.'

She knew them for her brothers' birthdays. She asked. He was right both times.

'How do I know you didn't see their dates also on the forms?'

'Even if I saw the dates, I would not have gone and checked what day it was, would I?'

'It is not out of the question.'

'For your brothers, no. I could imagine doing it for you.'

He wriggled his finger under her palm. She was startled, thinking for a moment it was a creepy-crawly. She allowed it to remain.

The third time, young B, reversing his initial advice, made a case for Miss Chitol to stay on in Bhombalpur. She made as if to be upset by his backtracking, but rested her head against his shoulder.

The fourth time, some ten days after the first, they took no ice cream and descended to the rocks among the bush where mosquitoes and couples from the inter college were the price. They spoke whisperingly into each other's faces. Here before the water lilies and weeds

Miss Chitol informed young B that since there was still no reply she had decided to leave for Bombay the following week.

'Is it because of my community?' B asked her.

'What kind of things are you saying?' she replied. 'It is just that if I do not leave now, I will never be able to, my life will never find its path.' Young B was torn between offendedness and maintaining his position of the strategic man. 'What you had advised me to do made a lot of sense,' she said, as if to comfort him.

At the end of the conversation he asked for a goodbye present. She gifted them a sitting embrace and felt a tremble shoot through her body. Through their layers of clothing, the innumerable sensitivities of her bosom expressed themselves to her, her full lips grazed his half-day stubble, her fingers wrapped themselves on his karate shoulders. They were pecking, pressing against and then purely kissing each other. At this stage young B overplayed his hand and attempted to recline her into a horizontal embrace. She stood up. In a breathy manner that aroused young B further she said she must go. He claimed a final, vertical embrace, a very long one; the sun subsided, the lilies went dark, the crickets shrilly chirped, the frogs started up, when at last against the heaty instinct of her groin Miss Chitol unstuck herself. They kissed again, and again, and she left young B with the drama of hands sliding over one another until their fingers untouched.

Her departing words were: 'Please don't come to the station.'

Over the next few days the surviving residents of A. K. Chitol's C-type quarters emptied out. The two siblings saw off Notun Dida at the railway station where many years ago Miss Chitol had received her. She could remember much of that occasion: the walk with her father, their laughter about the damchi babus and damchi mems, the great map he had conjured out of the air as they had waited, even the queasiness she had felt about this new entry into their lives – but she had no visual memory of meeting Notun Dida, or of the train that brought her and where from.

Dida was now being put on a train to Calcutta with her big iron trunk. Among its contents were the first instalments of her share of the family pension, knotted into a handkerchief; folded into another garment one month's basic pay, Rs 880, due to the family for resettlement to a place farther than twenty kilometres; a set of Bangla books;

idols from the altar swaddled in cloth; wrapped in thick paper framed photographs of the deceased Chitols, for Dhrubo; and the meagre collection of plain saris she had been gifted over the years. Ageing, shrinking, curving, low-utility, no home seemed to have a permanent space for her. Pishi was to host her at first, and there was talk of putting her then in an – respectable was the epithet used – old-age home.

When they touched her feet in farewell, Notun Dida began to cry, and could barely say the words, 'Stay well.' Then she on the Mail tapered away, as futures do.

The following afternoon Miss Chitol was herself gone, leaving Anando the last standing Chitol in the railway township of Bhombalpur. He returned to the near-vacant quarters, hung his muffler dutifully on his bar of the clothes horse and started to leadenly organise his things in order to move into the apprentice hostel, whose conviviality he had always sought. Suddenly he stopped, sat down and wept. He underwent an attack of severe desolation. The stream of life was dry; he was writhing about in the stones and sand. Cuts and burns. Nobody to call out to. But was he not supposed to have become a man already?

Meanwhile drongos dropping their forked tails off the telegraph wires as Miss Chitol chugged onomatopoeically away from Bhombalpur, along with suitcasefuls of her father's papers and books, her mother's saris and their letters – but alas not the clothes horse – once more towards the distant city of Bombay. They were gone; she was gone; everything was gone. Even so, she was overfull. Indeed, having known her a while now, we can say that never before had she contended with these many competing sensations of this much strength. Some of her was so profoundly jittery she was unable to identify it as a form of grief. Some of her dazzled with the audacity of her liaison, which dazzle obscured the tarnish of shamelessness she knew she had tempted. Some of her darkened with the incurable guilt of abandonment – though what more, she asked herself, what more could she do for Anando or Dida? *Be with them, take care of them*, another part answered, *in the way you never did your father.* But why only me? What about Dhrubo, given away like a bride with no remaining responsibility to the house from which he came? What about Anando with his head in the clouds? *Is that their fault, that one was sent off to become an engineer, that the other is young and sensitive? What kind of sister is so harsh on her brothers?* And, stop, stop, stop. She cooled her eyes on the evening orchards. The endless dust of the country settling, smoke rising, this coach, this rake, these rails, so much passenging, the sweet rhythm, chuggedy-didit, chuggedy-didit. Some of her sweated at the fact of her unemployment. Some of her thrilled at the idea that she who hated locomotives was in a trick of destiny being taken along on the great railway system whose railsong plucks at our souls no less musically than sitar string.

11
The wheels will turn

But the city will test you, it will flick its fingernails against you and listen for the sound. Real and counterfeit will both be admitted but it can tell them apart and it will let you know.

At the end of her journey Miss Chitol discovered that for being away (far) longer than thirty days she had lost her place in the hostel. Her things had been put inside the storeroom, among disused drapes, broken furniture and a three-limbed mannequin. She made an emotional appeal to the assistant matron, Vatsala Tai, and in turn heard her frustrations. Would it have been so difficult to make a phone call or send a letter? Nobody even knew how to reach her. Had she, Vatsala Tai, ever failed to help? What if she were to lose her job trying to help an inmate? Especially when it seemed that there were some people in the working women's hostel who were not working. Did they think her job was easy? And now there was no choice, the matron would have to expel Miss Chitol. She used the English word, waving the rule sheet.

Miss Chitol went away in a panic. After a while she returned with a packet each of bakarwadi and potato chivda from Hulyalkar snacks mart. It was accepted without acknowledgement. 'I spoke to the matron,' Vatsala Tai said. 'You will have to register again. We will have to see what room. For a few nights why don't you ask to share your old room? Did you see a mattress in the storeroom?'

Every working morning thereafter she set out for the Central Railway headquarters at Victoria Terminus.

It was important to show one's face. If she had learned anything about the way of things, it was that you had to turn up. It was necessary to face down rejections with uncomprehending stares, defeat evasions by the adhesive force of sticking around. Showing up meant enduring the indignity of being seen an irritant and coming out on the other side to familiarity, so that one day Vithoba the zonal peon might ask: 'You did not come yesterday?'

She trained herself in the art of not taking the message, not getting the point.

'You are wasting your time,' a taciturn office superintendent in the personnel department at the headquarters told her. 'And our time.' *Time passes, and then times change*, she averred.

'We cannot accommodate you at present,' remarked (politely but unequivocally) Shri P. C. Sinha, the deputy chief personnel officer of the Central Zone, once she had worked her way up to him. *At present*, she contended, *meaning it is a phase*.

From the chatter in the zonal office she picked up that while the zone would have to process this unprocessable request, the vacancy itself would have to come from the division.

It had taken her many visits to gain this crucial insight.

She shifted base from the great old building to the annexe that housed the Bombay Division offices. In the personnel room bursting with clerks in tumultuous conversation her uncertainty caught the interest of a head clerk who sat near the door.

'Good job is difficult in this day and age,' said Mrs Ghorpade once she had heard the matter. 'Means, government job is not *halwa*.'

Miss Chitol was relieved; she was not fond of *halwa*.

Another day Mrs Ghorpade made it known that she was not enamoured with compassionately appointed widows.

'Means, they are not doing the work properly, but they want suitors. Ward appointment is quite okay, but widows, you can say they spoil industrial relations.'

This left Miss Chitol glad she was an orphan not a widow, and more optimistic about her chances than before.

'Compassionate, compassionate, compassionate,' mused aloud harried assistant personnel officer (labour & welfare) Noble Pereira. 'Some females are desperate like anything.'

Notwithstanding her doubts over whether this was an arbitrary observation, a systemic critique or a direct proposition, Miss Chitol looked at him with such blank prolongation that it was he who broke eye contact and returned to his eight thousand one hundred files.

'It is not that I do not want to help,' divisional personnel officer Arun Sonawane clarified. 'But I will be retiring soon. And the correct person is the labour & welfare in-charge. You will have to persist with Pereira.' Miss Chitol was pleased to learn that there not only existed a correct person to deal with a case just like hers, but that she had already established contact with him.

'Today suppose we can give you a Group D appointment, will you take that?' a.p.o. (l&w) Pereira warned her many days later. 'Will you become a sweeper or a peon? You are matriculate, no? Higher Secondary pass, no? Going for the degree, hmm?'

She made it a point to slip into future petitions, which she sent all and sundry, right up to the divisional railway manager – even to the general manager, truth be told – the critical words: 'Group C appointment'.

'Indian Railways is bound to give you the appointment, Miss uhh Chetan,' stated in his overcrowded room balding Shri Tapan Borthakur, an absent-minded technical genius she had been given to understand, climbing up the administrative ranks, currently in the shape of the senior divisional personnel officer. 'We have our conventions. You see, Miss Jindol, first of all, pressure is there from our own Bombay Division and within the Central Railway. Then, preference is given to cases of on-duty accidental death, followed by off-duty accidental death, followed by natural death. So the best decision, Miss umm Veedol, is you return to Bhombalpur and take up an appointment there.'

And Miss Chitol smiled inwardly at the innocence of the man who would try to send her back.

Meanwhile, Ganpat the divisional peon who sported the long pinkie nail began to tell her: '*Ho jayega*, it will get done.' And Namdeo, who brought around the divisional tea said: 'Arre, madam, you are already a person of this office. If I am giving you tea means you are here.' And yet, '*Aali, aali,* she has come,' the two sniggered to one another when the lunatic was sighted once more in the corridor.

One day she saw a woman in knee-length nauvari sari go around with sweets. Beaming, the woman pressed one into Miss Chitol's hand, saying her village was famous for these pedas and this was a happy occasion. That was Sunita bai, Miss Chitol found out, a casual cleaner at the officers' transit flats. When her services were terminated, she told nobody, kept showing up for work *for no pay*, in the belief that if she held on something would happen. And now, fourteen months down the line, it had. A woman officer staying at the transit flats had taken up her cause, helped her become a temporary employee; even arrears were promised.

Whenever her morale sagged, Miss Chitol turned to Sunita bai's story. If she could keep going and have this happen, she thought, I can. If only I too could already be at work and prove myself.

It was Mrs Ghorpade who gave her the first inkling.

In the past, Miss Chitol learned, personnel officers were drawn from across various railway cadres. A dedicated cadre, the Indian Railway Personnel Service, had only just come up. Now that the first batches of officers had trained and joined service, the department was set to expand.

'Means,' spelt out Mrs Ghorpade, 'you have come at the right time.'

'Really?'

Mrs Ghorpade lowered her voice to high-confidential.

'You can get appointed to this room.'

Miss Chitol surreptitiously looked around for clues. She found none.

For days and weeks nothing happened. Everybody stonewalled or sidestepped her.

One day a.p.o. (l&w) Noble Pereira sent her to the zonal office.

There the taciturn office superintendent asked her personal details, made jottings on a file, and sent her right back with the words: 'Don't open it.' She did not.

A.p.o. (l&w) Pereira received the file, gave her a date for a written exam by tapping on his desk, leaving her to work out which of the two hundred and twenty overlapping circulars the glass pressed down upon pertained to her, while he returned to one of his ten thousand nine hundred files, muttering 'crazy fellows' and 'mad fellows' and 'gonecase bloody fellows', and 'insane female' and 'conked female' ... prompting Miss Chitol to make off, just in case it was her he meant.

'For compassionate appointment, written exam is very easy,' Mrs Ghorpade counselled her. 'Means, it is to make sure you are not a mentally retarded person. In the upper storey, everything is fit and fine. I have seen you, you will manage. Main thing is, in the joining interview don't cry. These widows specially they just start crying, they cannot speak one word.'

The written exam was indeed very easy. The arithmetic questions did not stretch her who was said to have a 'phobia' about maths. The general knowledge questions were so straightforward she became complacent and put down Jammu as the capital of Jammu and Kashmir.

For the short essay, she chose 'A Happy Outing'.

She wrote out the topic in capital letters, underlined it with dots. The words 'marvellous sky' came to her unbidden. She and her mother had won a competition, and as victors were to go parachuting at Chowpatty. She had indeed read of such a prize in the afternoon newspapers, and she poured her heart into the fiction.

> *It was as if our very souls were leaving our bodies and reaching towards the heavens, if there be such things as the soul and the heavens ... We inscribed circles in the marvellous sky ... the whooshing wind ... the blast of air in our ears, the giddiness in our stomachs ... Birds have special bones and special air sacs that help them fly, but we humans had just this colourful fabric ... my mother's colourful pallu ... The city stopped to look ... Even the sea seemed amazed that we were flying over it ... We were laughing and crying at the same time ... alert and frightened ... Fear, we must remember, is a type of magic ... Magical, we told the people when we came down, magical and marvellous ... They all wanted to know what it was like ... they all wanted to magically fly ...*

She was never sure when exactly she was appointed. She did not have the opportunity to not-cry at the joining interview because there wasn't one. More than one person remarked it was because nobody could bear to talk to her again about the appointment.

She suspected she had made it through when the lower rungs began advising her to pay her respects to higher rungs.

Mrs Ghorpade instructed her to thank a.p.o. (l&w) Pereira. A.p.o. Pereira nodded, and asked her to pay her respects to s.d.p.o. Borthakur. 'Congratulations, mmm, Miss Chintan,' said the s.d.p.o., and suggested she pay her respects to the divisional railway manager, whom she could never meet.

In the zonal office, the taciturn office superintendent, quarter-smiling at her for the first time in their history, told her to thank deputy c.p.o. P. C. Sinha, who had been on her examiners' panel.

Dy.c.p.o. Sinha turned out to be in charge of the zonal literary quarterly. 'It seems you have a flair for writing,' he remarked. 'You may contribute to our magazine.' He told her she may wish to pay her respects to the chief personnel officer and the general manager.

She waited outside the office of the general manager, Shri K. T. R. Muthiah, for two hours and five minutes. Officers, dignitaries, peons with important files busily went in and out, while she stood outside with a growing set of audience seekers. Some of them were from the railway Scouts and Guides; another lot were in their last days of service. Several other stricken men and women gave the benches a public hospital feel. At last, one minute before lunchtime, they were ushered together into the mighty office. Miss Chitol alone neither touched the general manager's feet, nor handed him a bouquet, nor requested a photograph for some internal purpose. She had only her thanks to offer, which she did with her palms pressed tight and a bow of her head, and the general manager, dressed in a steel-grey safari suit, took them briskly, without finding out why. Then he dismissed the congregation with a buzzer and a fluttering of the left eye, a condition of the nervous system perhaps, which made him appear all the more powerful.

Miss Chitol felt it had not gone as it was meant to. She had been expecting more than a mere flutter of an eye from the general manager, she had been expecting words – had, in fact, prepared herself to remember them, and regretted not having said or done anything to elicit them.

The chief personnel officer, Shri Harsharan Singh Bedi, however, did have words for her.

'*Shabash*, keep it up,' he said as Miss Chitol entered his cabin.

His eyes were shut, but he could not have been sleeping since he had spoken to her – and now continued to, in slow, expository fashion.

'You see, I am a very fortunate man. I have been with the Indian Railways for three decades. Started in traffic, and here I am in personnel. I am a fortunate person, and so are you. Because it is the Indian Railways that makes India. Consider the following. Every day we carry ten million passengers and half a million tonnes of goods, on a network of seven thousand stations, using eleven thousand locomotives. Our fares are among the lowest in the world, four paise per kilometre per passenger. Every day we face tremendous challenges. Seven hundred cases of alarm-chain pulling daily. Thirty lakh ticketless passengers annually. Tremendous challenges that we overcome. Indian Railways does not see difficult or easy. Indian Railways does not see religion, caste, language, state boundaries, summer, winter, rain. We have to meet the challenges because without Indian Railways this country will not be India.'

The chief personnel officer sported a net around his beard. His shirt was the identical shade of sky blue as his turban. As he relaxed his face further the skin between his eyes and beard fell in drapes. His eyes remained closed. His chest vibrated a little. He continued as mesmerically as before.

'It is the job of personnel to manage the seventeen lakh people that manage the Indian Railways. Every department in the Railways needs some other department to work with – but all departments need the personnel department. Consider the following. In 1947 the highest man in the Railways was paid forty times more than the lowest man. Today the differential is twelve, and it will grow smaller. The highest man and the lowest man will shop in the same market. Schools, hospitals, sports facilities, the recruiting of sportsmen and sportswomen, recreational opportunities, cultural associations, vocational centres, eye-testing and blood-sugar camps, a thoroughly excellent range of welfare schemes – you can say we provide a whole way of life. That is the enlightenment of the Indian Railways.'

At this stage, a stronger vibratory effect overcame the chief personnel officer. He shook the drapes on his face as though to dust them off. Shifting sounds escaped from beneath him. A dwarf, a midget rather, emanated from under the desk. The c.p.o. and him nodded courteously at each other, the former's eyes still closed. The midget walked out with a tiny cloth bag in his small hands. Miss Chitol inferred, since inference was necessary, that the chief personnel officer had received a foot massage. The midget's departure had not the least interrupting effect on the c.p.o.

'In Central Railway we have a legacy. You see, in India we started right here with the Great Indian Peninsular Railway, from Boribunder to Thane. Now if you turn round, not that way, the other way, you will see a piece of historic paper framed on the wall.'

Here the c.p.o.'s voice assumed a quivering, punctuatory grace, and his lips trembled in high-pitched elocution:

'The Railways are and will continue to be our *greatest* national undertaking. They deal *intimately* with scores of millions of people in the country and have to look after their comfort and convenience. They deal also with a *very large number of employees* whose welfare should *always* be their concern.'

He reverted smoothly to his regular manner.

'That, as you can see, is a message our first prime minister sent when the Central Railway was formed. Today Central is one of nine zones. Our seven divisions stretch *right* across the torso of this country. Behind you, not that side, the other side, there is a map. From Bombay via Bhusaval and Itarsi, all the way up to the outer signal of Delhi. From Itarsi via Jabalpur all the way up to the outer signal of Kanpur. From Bhusaval to Nagpur. From Bombay to Pune, to Solapur, all the way down to Wadi. Neral to Matheran; Daund to Baramati; Manmad to Daund. The old narrow gauge Pachora–Jamner Railway, that is PJ Railway, which the Marathis jokingly call *Pai Ja Railway* – meaning the same speed as going by foot, ha ha. Every day there are tremendous challenges, but the wheels must turn. And the wheels *will* turn, because of all the people who make them turn, without whom there will be no India. You see, in personnel we do not look after the locomotives or the rolling stock or the permanent way. We look after the people themselves. *Shabash*, keep it up.'

The chief personnel officer's eyes stayed shut, but he ceased to speak. He breathed heavily through his mouth, generating wafts Miss Chitol suspected contained clove, possibly to alleviate tooth pain. She surmised she was dismissed.

Just to be sure, she said her thanks and shuffled backwards and sideways towards the door, like a bearer of yore, and as the c.p.o. did not intervene in her retreat, she turned round and emerged from the office with a twitching, insuppressible smile, skipped down the magnificent staircase tingling with a sense of mission, and on a bobbing, beating heart strove towards the annexe, where she would play her part in the lives of forty-five thousand something employees as junior clerk in the personnel branch of the Bombay Division in the Central Zone of the Indian Railways.

She was to begin in the Rs 260–400 scale; upon that dearness allowances and house rent allowance and city allowance, which might double her pay or more. A bit of her was dissatisfied that she who deserved much got *bas* this much; much of her was astounded that she who deserved nothing had got *sab*, all this.

III

Vacancies Arise

I

In the P branch

The universe begins again for Miss Chitol. She has lost her parents, her home, the pale shadow of her childhood, her wayward quest for an education, all the work she ever found, but she has unearthed from the cosmic debris this job. She must not let go of it. At night she grinds her teeth unaware, in waking hours her oblivious fists clench. She makes it a point to start over by arriving early. As a junior clerk her task is to learn, and in before time allows her to miss nothing.

'Better to come early and wait than come late and wait,' chuckles Shankar Bagul, who too has arrived well early. He looks up at the long fan and releases a prolonged post-post-commute exhale. Shankar Bagul is an Anti-Malaria khalasi of many years who, finding the spray detrimental to his health, wishes to put in a transfer application for Mechanical khalasi at a workshop in Western Railway. To the P branch he has come to ask whether he can keep his lien and seniority.

Miss Chitol learns lien. She learns the consequences of administrative transfer, own-request transfer, mutual transfer.

Some afternoons later she finds two compassionate-appointment candidates taking the psychological test to qualify as assistant stationmasters. Senior clerk Digambar Bharti comments that one of the candidates will *purposely* fail. The candidate will not want the post because of the stress, which killed his stationmaster father, and will claim a non-safety category post instead. From her gestures, it is clear that white-haired head clerk Sandhya Nair, impaired of speech, disagrees.

Miss Chitol learns safety-category posts and non-safety-category posts. She learns selection posts and non-selection posts. The candidate does fail the psychological test. She does not think it deliberate. She does not learn cynicism. She learns about Rulemaster Chitnis.

He has seen deep into the soul of every rule and sub-rule, has Rulemaster Chitnis, and the P branch is nothing if not rules, sub-rules and their souls. Within his five-foot one-inch frame he holds every syllable of the Indian Railways Establishment Manual and the Indian Railways Establishment Code, their correction slips and concordance lists, every Master Circular on every topic devised and those still to be conceived. Versed as a great pandit is he in the clauses of the Factories Act and the Workmen's Compensation Act; in his human form dwell the infinities of the State Railway Provident Fund Rules, the Railway Services (Liberalised Leave) Rules, the Railway Services (Conduct) Rules, the Railway Servants (Discipline & Appeal) Rules. He positions himself before his volumes with a calm intensity, like a highly realised master. Miss Chitol discreetly watches him whenever she can.

She develops a horrible fascination for the Establishment Manual and the Establishment Code. She returns to them again and again, attempting to divine in the pages the meaning of life, or at the very least that of advance recovery, which is currently much of her life. Office superintendent Kapadia observes the tendency. '*Ghadi ghadi*, what is there to keep looking at it?' he asks her, a little annoyed.

1102. Purposes for which Advance can be sanctioned.
(iii) For purchase of table fan, Miss Chitol learns.

She counts about four hundred clerks in the P branch, sectioned by cadre, such as loco, electrical, health, civil, accounts, et cetera, and some non-cadre sections, such as bills and settlements, pass, welfare, et cetera. Most clerks, herself included, sit on the ground floor, the rest are up on the second. The six officers in charge – one senior divisional personnel officer, two divisional personnel officers, three assistant personnel officers – are in possession of cabins. The clerical ranks sit in columns. At the head of the columns the office superintendents face the clerks from behind large desks, like teachers in a classroom. The junior clerks, such as herself, are moved from section to section, as the need arises.

She does not have a desk. She is not disheartened in the least: she has a chair. She carries it like an appendage around the ministerial room, as the room of clerks is called, and places it beside the desk of whomever she is to be learning from. At other times she presses it against an empty space by one of the pillars that hold up the hall or jams it between the racks at the periphery. On occasion she is sent to somebody important with a file; on such occasions she does not carry her chair with her.

The first time she is sent to divisional personnel officer Chaturvedi, she waits cautiously outside before entering. The phone trings. 'I am Chaturvedi,' she hears, issued like a warning. Once inside, she finds office superintendent Kulkarni seated across the table from him. There is a third man, shaking his legs incessantly, so that even his collars flutter, like a butterfly, bearing upon its wings, however, a human head – of a union secretary, she gleans. The union man complains: 'My nephew's name was missing from the list.' 'Which list?' enquires d.p.o. Indra Mohan Chaturvedi with interest. 'The training course,' says the union man. 'Achha? I will make sure he is in the next batch,' d.p.o. Chaturvedi assures him. When the man is gone, smirks divisional personnel officer Chaturvedi to office superintendent Kulkarni: 'I purposely left his nephew's name off so he would have to come to me.' 'He will remember the favour,' replies o.s. Kulkarni with a deferentially appreciative smile. 'The man must have not done a day of regular duty in the last two years, but you know how much he is worth?' asks the d.p.o. He raises one mystifying finger in front of him. 'That nephew has even gone abroad, the no-objection-certificate application had come,' remarks o.s. Kulkarni. D.p.o. Chaturvedi, who is a wee bit, maybe five to ten per cent squint, receives the message and the file from Miss Chitol and signs papers on the left side while an eye stares at the papers on the right. She leaves with the file, wondering whether she has heard things she was not meant to.

Every day she helps someone fill out some kind of form. For the unlettered, she writes. Often she does not know what these forms are, and it makes her insecure. Other days she feels secure and works out that for the secure feeling you must stay within the boundaries of what you are required to know. To know the boundaries you must know the rules. But the rail and its ways are too big, too bewildering. Read the manuals and codes, she tells herself, become Rulemistress Chitol.

Old men, loose-skinned, frail, bespectacled, sometimes touch the feet of those much younger than themselves in thanks or supplication. Not Hemubhai. Hemubhai is ancient. He was a railway employee in 1947. As a Group D worker from before Independence he can never, ever be asked to retire, even if he lives to be a hundred. He is already sixty-seven, and that is, frankly speaking, a high age for a sanitation worker, posits Rulemaster Chitnis. Rulemaster Chitnis may not shake Hemubhai's hand but nonetheless goes for a '*Kem chho*, Hemubhai?' in Gujarati, with a smile that suggests that although he may not be touchable, he with his eternal job symbolises good luck as well as good rules.

Miss Chitol observes that Ganpat the peon is no longer growing his pinkie nail. She observes that a stenographer is. Remarkably, even though it is half a foot long, and on the right hand, with which he shorthands, it does not seem to get in his way. Then she notices one on the left hand too! Miss Chitol wonders: in the toilet it gets in the way, does it?

Two women in the typing department, she notes, are growing their nails, despite the intolerance of typewriters towards them. The one with the bright polish is Krunalini Patel. Miss Chitol tells her about her short-lived typing career. 'The important thing is to keep your mind blank, nails don't matter,' laughs vivacious Krunalini Patel. They become friendly and start visiting the canteen together.

It has been some time coming. Mrs Ghorpade wants Miss Chitol back under her wing. She begins to warn Miss Chitol about people, specifically that Yogesh Ambolkar resents her. Miss Chitol does not know Yogesh Ambolkar. 'Think about it,' suggests Mrs Ghorpade.

After days of fruitless thinking, Mrs Ghorpade reveals that Yogesh Ambolkar is one of the compassionate candidates appointed at the same time as her. 'But what have I done to him?' asks Miss Chitol. 'Think about it,' says Mrs Ghorpade, somewhat irritated.

Upon investigating, Miss Chitol learns that Yogesh Ambolkar has been appointed to the leave reserve office clerkage. He is sent wherever required, depots and offices and sheds and workshops all over Bombay Division. Say a clerk is on maternity leave, Yogesh Ambolkar goes to take her place. 'What is my fault in that?' says Miss Chitol. Mrs Ghorpade can hardly bring herself to ask Miss Chitol to think about it. But she does.

The moment of full disclosure arrives. Yogesh Ambolkar believes he should have been appointed to Miss Chitol's position in the divisional office, says Mrs Ghorpade. He was shunted to a leave reserve position only because Miss Chitol is a woman. And an outsider, that too, adds Mrs Ghorpade, presenting Yogesh Ambolkar's case rather persuasively. Miss Chitol protests: 'I am a Bombayite also.' Mrs Ghorpade does not volunteer her support. 'Means, outsider issue is definitely there,' she remarks instead. A loaded silence passes between the women. Says Mrs Ghorpade eventually: 'These people don't want ladies to get anything.' Miss Chitol takes it up: 'That's what. What is he talking about?' Adds Mrs Ghorpade: 'Also, he is getting the benefit of travel allowance, so he should thrive. Grateless boy.'

1107. (2) An advance for the purchase of bicycle should not ordinarily be granted within three years of a previous advance unless satisfactory evidence is produced by the railway servant concerned to the effort that the bicycle purchased with the help of the earlier advance has been lost or has become unserviceable.

A commotion erupts in the office when members of the Scheduled Castes and Scheduled Tribes Association raise slogans outside d.p.o. Chaturvedi's cabin. It is his new cabin, infinitesimally larger than the previous. When the d.p.o. opens the door, a sloganeer rushes in and brings out something from behind a cupboard. It is a framed wall calendar, now cracked, with a picture of Babasaheb Ambedkar. D.p.o. Chaturvedi, it is alleged, trashed the calendar. Further, it is alleged that after taking possession of the cabin from the recently retired d.p.o. Arun Sonawane, he conducted a purification ceremony. D.p.o. Chaturvedi denies the charges. The puja was nothing but a *griha pravesh* ceremony for the new cabin, he argues; as for the calendar, that must have been done by workmen before he moved in. Indeed, he summons two peons and shouts with such ferocity with his divergent eyes they appear almost contrite; placatorily he dusts the calendar with his own handkerchief. In the subsequent inquiry, d.p.o. Chaturvedi is acquitted. The sloganeers receive an official censure. The d.p.o. is not a man to lose property disputes. Where hung Dr Ambedkar now hangs Lord Ram.

1127. The orders regarding the grant of the advances on festivals will remain in force till further orders.

Digambar Bharti stands humming in the corridor, his hip thrust sideways, doggedly fingering a spot near his anus. A bush-shirted man hastening by, chewing on paan masala, drops a spit bomb, red and granular, almost on Miss Chitol's feet. 'Do that in your house!' cries Miss Chitol. Digambar Bharti freezes. He turns stealthily to check whether it is him being spoken to. Miss Chitol proceeds inside. Relieved, Digambar Bharti resumes humming, but ceases to dig his bum.

While she waits in d.p.o. Chaturvedi's cabin, the telephone rings like a fire alarm. 'I am Chaturvedi,' the d.p.o. answers with a penetrative frown that resolves into a grin. The joke strikes Miss Chitol like lightning: I. M. Chaturvedi for Indra Mohan, what a prankster! 'Achha?' continues the d.p.o. on the phone, 'Is that so? Is that right! Very interesting. Listen to this.' The d.p.o. glances over the table at the railway doctor awaiting paperwork for his specialisation course. 'There used to be a Ghanshyam Pandey of Vigilance,' says the d.p.o., addressing the cabin as much as the phone. 'Pandeyji classified three types of corruption. *Jabrana*: sit on file, don't move till the reward comes. *Nazrana*: receive regular gifts, do the needful when the time is right. *Shukrana*: accept a thank-you for job done!' The doctor laughs participatively. D.p.o. Chaturvedi looks at him, expecting him to go on longer, or perhaps at Miss Chitol. She wishes his squint were more extreme so one could read it better. She does not like to smile for him. 'About my missis' cholestrol, Doctor ... ' says the d.p.o., plonking down the receiver.

One fine morning a tall woman in an emerald sari and a whisper of sophisticated perfume is welcomed into the office. People clear the path so she may walk unhindered. Others look on from the sidelines. That, Miss Chitol learns, is assistant personnel officer Gitanjali Rao. Direct recruit from the Indian Railway Personnel Services. Her father is Secretary to the Government of India. A proud girl. Reasonably young. But exudes power. She takes possession of d.p.o. Chaturvedi's old cabin. Strings of marigold welcome her from the door frames; her name on the brass plate carries the suffix IRPS. Inside, an air conditioner is soon installed.

Table Fan Advance Recovery Register
Bicycle Advance Recovery Register
Motor Scooter Advance Recovery Register
Provident Fund Advance Recovery Register
House Allowance Advance Recovery Register
Overdrawn Wages Recovery Register
Electricity Charge Recovery Register
General Insurance Recovery Register
Festival Advance Recovery Register
Court Attachment Recovery Register
Employee Cooperative Society Recovery Register
Warm Wear Advance Recovery Register
...
Total no. of Liability Registers to maintain = 34, Miss Chitol tots up

As always, two people are inside d.p.o. Chaturvedi's cabin. He is screening a bungalow peon – for 'absorption', is the term she learns. The dour, nervous youth cannot tell his interrogator the name of the school given on his record. 'These johnnies are brought on as personal servants by officers,' says the d.p.o. after he has had his fun. Perhaps he is addressing Miss Chitol, since the other person left in the cabin is a timid young girl, younger than Miss Chitol, whose purpose she has not yet established. D.p.o. Chaturvedi turns towards the timid girl and asks, 'How did your father die?' 'He used to drink too much,' the girl replies. The d.p.o. adds to his previous thought. 'The officer gobbles up the bungalow peon's salary because one day the johnny will be rewarded with a regular post.' He asks the timid girl again: 'How did your father die?' 'He used to drink too much,' the girl replies. The d.p.o. adds to his corollary. 'Out in the divisions it is much worse. The johnny's wife or sister will also get exploited.' He turns towards the timid girl. 'Haan, how did your father die?' 'He used to drink too much,' the girl replies.

1129. Advance for purchase of warm clothing to railway servants transferred from the plains to hill station – Group 'C' and 'D' railway servants posted at hill stations whether on first appointment or on transfer from the plains to a hill station on a permanent or long term basis (i.e. for a period of not less than 12 months) may be sanctioned advances for the purchase of warm clothing irrespective of the fact whether they belong to hill tracts or not, subject to the following conditions:–

A man, not so young and not so old, centre-parted, pear-shaped, comes into the P branch to invite d.p.o. Chaturvedi to a Promotees function. He asks Miss Chitol, seated upon her chair wedged between two slotted-angle racks, to point the way. She stands up to do so, graciously. The man invites her to the function. She blushes. 'I am just a junior clerk.' 'Don't worry about that,' he tells her with a plasticine smile. After a few moments, he is still standing before her, watching her face, maybe her neck, her chest. She wishes to withdraw her graciousness. 'There, the cabin from which the peon came out,' she says.

There *is* a function she enthusiastically attends: the final of the annual Bombay Division singing competition. For two hours she listens and hums along in a cool room up in a building close to the platforms, generous in her applause, forgiving in her judgements. The ladies' competition is won by fingerprint examiner Reena Kadam, whose voice is likened by the compère to a lonely koel in a mango tree at the start of summer. The gentlemen's is taken, for the second time running, by hours-of-employment-regulation inspector Abdul Irfan Rasool, of whom it is held that Rafi does not sound so Rafi as this skilled note-taker of an employee's minute-by-minute activities. The duet champions are Digambar Bharti and Deepanjali Ghose for their dramicomic rendition of 'Uth Sajani Khol Kiwade', which defeats – unfairly, in popular opinion – Abdul Irfan Rasool and Mahek Saini's 'Yeh Hai Bombay Meri Jaan', which barely qualifies as a duet, but has the entire auditorium singing, laughing, swaying, screeching, croaking, weeping in their seats. At the end, her erstwhile head of department Shri Tapan Borthakur, who has advanced to additional divisional railway manager but receded in hairline, delivers a fine speech. 'I come from a small village in Assam and today I am here in this honoured position. Fellow railwaymen' – *What about the women, sir?* the women sitting in front of Miss Chitol and Krunalini Patel shout, and the two join in. '*Baap re baap*, you have to be careful, ladies have become too much demanding nowadays! Fellow railway-men and railway*women*' – claps and laughs – 'I am basically a positive person. As an engineer I say nothing is impossible. Archimedes had said, Give me a place to stand and a pole long enough and I can move the earth. No place in the world has crush load like Bombay suburban, three to four thousand per train meant for nine hundred sitting, eight hundred standing. Such load that the chassis becomes concave. But still we do a jolly good job, we are Bombay Division!' Huge applause and cheers, and the impromptu singing of 'Yeh Hai Bombay Meri Jaan'.

Afterwards, reflects Miss Chitol, the one who sang Yesudas should have won the gentlemen's. Voice like honey, dripping still, dripping sweet.

1129. Notes: 1. To obviate the risk of the advance being paid again during the stipulated period mentioned above to a railway servant who has drawn the advance and fully refunded it, with interest, if any, prior to his transfer from one establishment to another and happens to apply to the latter for the grant of second advance, the railway servant should be required to furnish in his application for the advance a certificate to the effect that he had not drawn the advance applied for prior to his transfer within the stipulated period mentioned above. This certificate may be test checked if considered necessary.

Miss Chitol believes a.d.r.m. Borthakur when he declares he is a positive person. She discerns two types of railway employees: those who declare themselves to be a 'positive person' and those who declare themselves to be a 'negative person'. Employees frequently make these self-attestations. Welfare inspector Kshitij Deshmukh tells her, 'I am basically a positive person. I have an itch to help, you can say.' Kshitij Deshmukh's sincerity may be in doubt, she senses, but as to his positivity there is none.

Rulemaster Chitnis comes out to Miss Chitol: 'I am a negative person.' One might surmise that is so because as the repository of every employee rule ever made and those still to be made, he ought to be designated nothing less than Rulemaster, Railway Board, on a par with Chairman, Railway Board, and here he is stuck on chief clerk and may not get to office superintendent before his time is done. But that is not the reason. 'I am basically negative,' says Rulemaster Chitnis, 'because I have seen too much in service. In the P branch you can make life hell like anything for an employee. Lose a document, tear up a file. Our rules are very good. Negative comes why? Not because of rules, negative comes because of people.'

1129. Notes: 2. (iv) The authority competent to sanction the advance will be the Head of Department or the Divisional Railway Manager. He should certify in each case that the advance is in respect of a railway servant who is likely to stay at the hill station for the entire period of repayment of the advance and that the members of his family are residing with him at the hill station.

Passing I Am Chaturvedi's cabin, Miss Chitol hears him chortling: 'Pandeyji of Vigilance used to ask, if you want to clean a dirty room, do you start from the ceiling or the floor? Achha, any update on the air conditioner?'

1129. Notes: 2. (vi) In deciding whether a place should be treated as a hill station for the purpose of the advance, the classification made by the State Government concerned should generally be followed.

Sadness occasionally visits the ministerial room. Francis the motorman, who was in a few months ago to complain about his running-kilometre allowance, is back, this time without legs. Sometimes news of an on-duty death filters through the clerical ranks. '*Deva, deva,*' say some; '*Arra ra ra,*' say others. Still others, accustomed to death and its paperwork, when asked if they had heard about so-and-so, simply remark: 'Yes, he has gone off.' After a death, head clerk Sandhya Nair lights a diya and places it beside a Ganesh idol on a shelf in a corner of the room. A death leaves Miss Chitol a little desperate, as though there are no good outcomes to living after all. When the family members of a deceased employee visit, even if they appear composed she detects in them a jitteriness, that they are not really seeing what they are seeing or listening to whom they are hearing. She wonders if her own condition had been so transparent.

She notices that people often stop doing the usual when something sad happens. After his mother expires, Digambar Bharti does not perform his favourite time-pass of spinning a register on the tip of his ring finger. She is not sure exactly when it is that head clerk Ajmal Chopdiwala's wife suffers a stroke, but it may well have been the time he stopped propping up his transistor atop a heap of registers to broadcast cricket commentary for the benefit of all. Still, there is something in that room. Sadness falls upon it, dissipates into registers, into problems small, tiny, insolubly minute. The ministerial room is like a sanctuary. You could take refuge in the room of personnel clerks, which compassionately appoints the distressed, itself accommodates those who cannot be taken in elsewhere. Children of the dead in harness, of the missing, the medically incapacitated, the underqualified, the deaf, the one-armed.

The room with its wooden-top metal-frame desks, its S-chairs of metal frames and plastic netting, its filing cabinets arranged around the load-bearing pillars and its slotted-angle racks pressed two- or three-deep against the perimeter, marked by algebraic acronyms in dusty white paint. The handsome transom windows at the entrance, the long white fans dangling from the ceiling off five-foot stems, swirling the perspiring air into eddies. Two-foot by one-foot tubelight cages suspended from cables the same length as the fan stems. So much metal, cool to the touch. Punching machines, staplers, paper pins, paper clips, rulers. Double-sided files that open the other way, as though Arabic or Japanese, soft pink cardboard files with their Noting side and Correspondence side, their edges and binding of coarse indigo cloth, secured by white twine pinched into cool metallic tips. The room that half an hour before closing time starts to empty out as Namdeo comes around a final time and employees make a reckless show of buying each other a last cutting of chai and delay departure by critical train-minutes.

And do you think I was just standing around, doing nothing?

2

Do you think I was doing nothing?

Everyone has to start somewhere, and I started right here at Victoria Terminus. A terminus may be an ending point but things begin for me here. Here the train left me eight years ago, close to here I became a working woman, at Kings & Queens Shoe Emporium. Here I am again at Victoria Terminus.

It happens that people can forget where they are. When I come to VT I am reminded of the city I am in. I know these streets. I know where to get the best kothimbir vadi, brun-maska, cheese-chilli-capsicum dosa, where to find inexpensive letter paper, replacement nibs, satin ribbons that last. I like this city. Every person is staking a second, third, fourth, up to a ninth life. Some days the coconut fronds rustle and sway to just the right degree and you can walk under them feeling marvellous and unbeatable.

Therefore when Mrs Ghorpade told me about Yogesh Ambolkar I was taken aback.

That was, I remember, a puranpoli day. We had a code for such days. 'PP,' Mrs Ghorpade whispered to me, since the demand for them was too much. Once everybody was busy with their lunch we started. She took ghee out of her small box and smeared it on the puranpolis with her mini spoon. Mrs Ghorpade was very particular about not applying the ghee in advance. A lovely balance of jaggery and cardamom in her *puran*, delicate, papery *poli*. I was enjoying it wholeheartedly, but just as we were finishing, she mentioned Yogesh Ambolkar's grievance against me. 'You are an outsider, no?' she then added. She licked her lips clean and poured water into her mouth, gargling it around so no morsels remained stuck between her teeth.

I argued a lot with Yogesh. This is a city for everyone, I told him, a country for everyone. Without the Indian Railways there is no India. The officers are drawn from all over the country, trained in Pune, Secunderabad, Jamalpur, Baroda, posted anywhere. Candidates from anywhere appear for railway recruitment exams anywhere. The locomotives are manufactured in Chittaranjan and Varanasi, the coaches in Kapurthala and Perambur, the wheels and axles in Yelahanka, minor parts even in Bhombalpur, and the trains so constituted run across the length and breadth of the country, without care for state boundaries, without care for religion, caste, language.

I have never met Yogesh. These were arguments with myself.

And if I am to be honest, I *do* sometimes feel an outsider. To the city, to the railways, to my family, even to my own self. Did Yogesh Ambolkar know this about me? Did he find my secret vulnerability? It is my desire to be able to take things for granted. I have a right as much as him.

Sometimes I am surprised that I am here in this office. I am shocked when I think of the years I spent not learning anything, not dedicating myself to anything, a little ashamed that it took till Baba's – responsible, I want to be responsible.

Here in the P branch we are responsible for thousands of employees. Ours is minor work, but it is important work. Without it the house of files will collapse. We help maintain Service Records, which is the entire Ramayana of an employee's career: the letter of appointment, the letters of recommendation, awards and disciplinary actions, increments, major advances drawn. We maintain the Index Register. This gives us, at a glance, the essential details for an employee, so that each time someone needs the information they need not go into the SRs. It is us who manage the liability registers. When we are asked to carry a file to an officer with a message or a query, I like that. It makes me feel that I am not failing in my responsibility.

As a general rule, we junior clerks are sent to only certain officers, such as a.p.o. Pereira or d.p.o. Chaturvedi, whereas to others the office superintendents go themselves. It took me some time to understand the reason. The former were Promotees, while the latter were Group A officers, recruited directly from the Union Public Service Commission. That is why I was sent just once to a.p.o. Gitanjali Rao.

I remember that occasion clearly.

It was shortly after lunchtime – but certainly *after* lunch hours – that I knocked on her door. No response. I knocked again. 'Hmm ... yes,' I heard a reply. The door was shut firmly and I had to push hard to enter. A.p.o. Rao did not acknowledge me. On her clean desk lay a stainless-steel bowl filled with black grapes. She lifted a grape and slowly placed it in her mouth without looking at it. Then another, and another, engrossed all the while in a P. G. Wodehouse novel. On her ears she shone diamond studs set in gold. She was wearing a beautiful peacock-colour sari with a golden elephant-pattern border. The air conditioning in her cabin worked so beautifully that she was not sweating even though she was in silk. I stood in front of the desk for one, two entire minutes, while her eyes remained fixed on the book and her hand conveyed grapes to her mouth. Maybe she was coming to the end of a chapter. I, too, hate to be disturbed at such times. Waiting there, however, I could not control myself any longer. 'Ma'am,' I said. Then louder: 'Ma'am.' She finally turned her face up at me. Her eyes were full of laughter from the book. I showed her the file. 'This is for me, is it?' she asked. 'Yes, ma'am,' I said, and gave her the message. She glanced at the file. 'Has the d.r.m.'s office seen this?' 'I think that is where it has come from, ma'am,' I replied, surprised. What sort of question was that? How could she not know this? 'Where are the notations?' she asked. I pointed them out. 'This makes no sense. I will discuss it with s.d.p.o.' Then she returned to her book and her face was full of pleasure once more.

As soon as I came out it hit me how different the worlds inside and outside her cabin were. I found out a.p.o. Rao's exact age. She was three and a half years older than me. Multiple-degree holder. A gazetted officer, appointed by the President of India. She could sit in her cabin and say: I will discuss it with s.d.p.o. For the rest of that day I could not concentrate on my work.

In the end I believe I can learn the department better than her. From her height, everyone must be looking like an ant. She seems bored of the view. In fact, the work is really interesting. It takes us right to the heart of people.

I often think of the day I was told to carry a file to dy.c.p.o. Sinha in the zonal headquarters. I loved going to the historical building, as we called it. Amazing creatures were sculpted into each nook and cranny.

Elephants, crocodiles, lions, owls, peacocks, flying foxes. 'Gargoyles and griffins', I learned from an issue of the magazine that dy.c.p.o. Sinha oversaw. As you climbed up the massive floating staircase towards the light filtering through the stained glass near the dome you thought, so majestic that, yes, not for kings and queens, this must be for something as grand as the railways.

The day, I remember clearly, was so humid that even the file I was carrying turned soggy. It reminded me of my grandmother's line about Calcutta: 'A bath there has no meaning.' Standing outside his cabin, soaked in sweat, it occurred to me that since I had been sent here, he must be a Promotee. That gave me hope, to see he could rise all the way up to deputy chief personnel officer.

When I entered, dy.c.p.o. Sinha was leaning back in his chair with his hands clasped behind his head, dictating to the stenographer.

When one makes a complaint about a caste certificate comma one has to state specifically that the certificate is either forged or fabricated comma based on adequate and reliable information stop Shri Walawalkar cannot command the administration to investigate any matter stop The decision to investigate rests solely with the administration stop

Once he had finished, dy.c.p.o. Sinha said with a sigh: 'Each person, on average, has five to seven grievances at any given point of time. This means, in the entire Central Railway, at any given point of time I have nine lakh to thirteen lakh grievances to deal with.'

This statement left an impression on me. I would examine the registers and the Service Records I was in charge of and think to myself: 'What could be his or her five to seven grievances?' Similarly, when somebody walked into the P branch, I found myself asking: 'What might be his or her five to seven grievances?'

Grievances are at the heart of a person. They are at the heart of the P branch too. Sometimes the burden does weigh heavy, the number too large. Every day requires bravery or we are finished. City is like a rocket. Inside here we must persist. Things do not always happen fast in the P branch, but they happen every day. Sometimes the fans turn slowly. A drop of sweat falls upon a page in the register. I press my handkerchief on it and it is mine again.

Anyway, I did not want you to think that I was just standing around, watching others.

3
Impostrous day

Certain days the fronds rustle and sway to just the right degree and you can step through the swishing chiaroscuro marvellous and free. A mutiny in every heart. If the card players in the maidan are losing and laughing too early in the morning, good for them. If girlfriends are squealing with entwined pinkies, it is what the day asked. Slow your step, become a little late. Find your coins, take the kanda-bhajji-pao extra dry chutney, savour its fire and crunch.

The merriness in some eyes was from the landslide election victory for the prime minister's son on the weekend. Two months to the day and Miss Chitol still found her assassination hard to believe. Her first instinct had been to ring her father, who did not have a telephone even while alive. His life, and hers, were playthings in the hands of the giantess. The bareness she felt, it was as though somebody had come onstage and removed the backdrop.

But with every step from Churchgate to VT the year was going, a year of pogrom and poison. Bye-bye,'84; bye-bye, doom and gloom. The burn on her tongue was sweet, and the whistles around her were not lascivious, they were freedom. She felt young again.

At the office the mutinous spirit was evident in the attendance, so much so that it was her, a junior clerk, that office superintendent Kapadia asked to draft a letter.

'*You, you, you* everywhere,' he considered her work with distaste. 'To senior officer you will write *you*? Make it *your office*.'

'No problem, sir, I will do it right away. But only he can do something about the matter, his office is getting renovated again.'

And o.s. Kapadia, world-famous for never smiling, spread his lips in enjoyment, revealing the tops of turmeric incisors.

At lunchtime she left the premises without a plan for lunch. She paused conjecturally at Raufbhai, rising from his circle of customers, peeling and slicing boiled eggs, placing them on newspaper squares, sprinkling them with masala, five seconds flat.

Here a man smiled at her.

'Egg?'

'I'm thinking,' she smiled back.

She recognised him instantly.

'You sang Yesudas in the competition, no?'

The twitching pride in his moustache indicated yes before he did.

'You sound a lot like him,' she said.

'That I can never, that I can never!' J protested. 'No matter how much I try.'

'But you do!' she exclaimed with temperate exuberance.

'What can I say.' He glanced up at the sky. 'KJY is like God to me.'

'I think the reason you did not win is that it was an upbeat song,' she proposed. 'Judges are like that. They think sadness is more important than happiness.'

The singer looked flattered.

'The instrumentation may have been a reason too,' she continued. 'Had you rehearsed together?'

'You are *dead* right,' responded J, discernibly impressed. 'I missed one session. We could not get the alignment right.' He drummed his fingers in the air arrhythmically.

How talented, she thought, to be able to demonstrate musical dissonance without sound.

Now he surprised her. 'I have seen you in the HQ. You used to come there, no?'

That might have been, she worked out to herself, from the time she was cutting rounds of the historical building for her appointment. The thought of it being witnessed embarrassed her. But she, too, was flattered.

They began to walk together. He clerked in general administration. They asked about the set-ups of each other's departments and commented on the eccentricities of their own. She sensed they had in common a departmental pride that non-technical departments like theirs were not thought to possess.

'We are definitely more efficient than operating,' she remarked with comradely spirit. 'You saw the parliamentary report?'

He was aware of it, public grievances being a matter his department dealt with, but he hardly needed to read a report to know that punctuality on Central suburban fell short of seventy per cent – he knew it from bitter daily experience. What about her?

'Western,' she replied, trying not to sound superior now that they had unfortunately been split into competitors.

'Ninety-five per cent punctuality, no?' he said.

'That is what the report says.' She made her excuses. 'I only read it because, one, I can read anything and everything. And two, we have a Rulemaster Chitnis who gets every report that was ever commissioned. Sometimes I think he commissions them himself.'

As she spoke, she put on the bright in her eyes, the bright that made another feel: wish I could laugh with that girl. And J did.

So pleasant was their stroll, so fine the day, she didn't think about where to, turning off into the streets until they slowed to a halt at the entrance of a dilapidated Fort building.

'Here,' said J.

It seemed his friend supplied shops and stalls in the area, items from Ray-Ban sunglasses which she heard as zenglasses to Yardley Lavender. The friend was in the Gulf, he kept a room here for his men and material.

'He is contacting me to make sure everything is okay,' said J.

'Oh,' said Miss Chitol, realising she was in the way.

'You want to come up?' he offered genially.

'I think you have the wrong idea about me.' She started as a joke, but by the time she finished it had an edge.

J looked troubled, even ashamed.

'I think you have the wrong idea about *me*.'

At once she felt uncharitable, too prim. Was she no better than the no-risk types in the hostel? To hell with no-risk, nothing sublime or ridiculous ever came out of no risks.

Up a flight of stairs steep and narrow as a ladder they went. At each landing J turned subtly and solicitously, she felt his glance grazing her wrist. On the highest floor, he pushed open a narrow double-hinged door.

Inside, the man sprawled beside a mound of coconuts sprang up. The two men began to speak and she could only discern repeated use of the English word 'corporation'.

There was a raid by the municipal corporation on the pavement vendors in the morning, J translated for her. The coconuts they were able to save were brought up. Upon instruction, the man lopped off the heads of two, offering them with straws and left.

'Fresh,' J said.

All around them were cartons, flattened cardboard boxes, coir ropes, tape. On the walls clothes hung on a row of bare nails. In one corner a washbasin.

She became intensely aware of their aloneness, conscious of his physicality. She had thought him old-fashioned-handsome at the competition, and if his speaking voice did not drip like honey it still recalled the sweetness of the singing. His eyes held chivalry, his hair was dense and virile, lush was his mouth and his moustache, perhaps too lush, a moustache that might be oiled. Tall, taut, a flat chest and stomach, tensile hairy forearms.

Looking around the room, holding her coconut with both hands, she said: 'Are you a smuggler?' and she could tell from his response that he found her delightful.

Miss Chitol had an invitation for the night and she did not like parties. She felt no compunction in staying in reading on a New Year's Eve. Far from suffering loneliness, she savoured the companionship of a book, nice and cosy as the fireworks went off. Yet such was the day she found herself positively excited about going out.

She made an extravagant visit to the beauty parlour, crowded with girls on account of all the parties to be attended. She had decided to wear a sleeveless blouse. That too was not something she usually did. She had never developed a routine for the maintenance work, and because she rarely wore them, it felt a bold decision each time she did. The beauty parlour was Vimla the desertee's. Vimla no longer worked there, and she had long left the working women's hostel. It was her party Miss Chitol was going to.

Running late after waxing and threading, and a fruity facial, she raced to get dressed. Against her off-white sleeveless blouse that mercifully – the thought had been gnawing away at her in the beauty parlour! –

– still fitted her right, she matched a flowery burgundy chiffon handed down by Rajashree the divorcee, and her mother's string of pearls, kajal, a conical black bindi that tapered like the culmination of her nasal bone; she kept her washed hair loose. Leaving the hostel dressed so bold, she decided she must take a taxi. A costly evening.

Inside the taxi she felt glamorous. Night released a stickiness the day lacked, developing its mood. Cigarettes and bangles stuck out of the black-and-yellows, diamond red lights tailing them, whispers falling on any girl's cheek who dreamed it, maybe every girl's. A day seductive enough for rotten decisions, loose enough for inspired ones, impostrous enough to not know which is which.

As she arrived at her destination she felt her reserve clicking back into place. Vimla tenanted a one-bedroom-hall-kitchen flat with friends. She was into jewellery in some way – perhaps she made it, or assembled it, or had it made and sold it, maybe all of these, Miss Chitol was not sure. Who could keep up with Vimla and her ideas?

They greeted each other like forever friends. 'How *elegant* you are looking, yaar,' she said to Miss Chitol, adding in a lower voice, 'and *sexy*.'

One was a railway clerk, teetotal except in the company of Vimla, when she could sometimes get totalled, who didn't cut her hair, had never raised a pet, could not swim, drowned herself in books – was in outward terms the exact opposite of the other. Yet they were alike in fundamental ways. In the working women's hostel they had helped each other get over something; they never talked about what, it was understood.

Vimla led her by the hand into a room full of people, feeling sisterhood. Both men and women, Miss Chitol observed, were dressed in Vimla's baggy, free style. Some were jewellery types, one worked in a travel agency, another was on her way to becoming an air hostess. One boy did theatre, another pursued higher studies in psychology. A few had the louche ease of the occupationless, like the cats who revealed themselves in unexpected spots around the room. None was a government servant. The flat was cluttered with rum, vodka, an icebox, improvised ashtrays, floor cushions, wafers, pop music – Vimla and her English music! Outside a rotting window coconut fronds swished in the sticky moonlight as excellently as they had done by day.

Vimla poured a massive Old Monk and Thums Up for Miss Chitol, who wandered about between the bedroom, hall and kitchen, feeling her way around, shedding party dread. What remained was under the surface. To maintain the right surface was half the art.

In jeans and a sober non-baggy shirt, perhaps implying that dressing up and dressing down were equally pretentious, the terse-eyed psychology boy stood smoking with his back to the rotting window. He looked the thoughtful, perhaps the brooding, kind. He had set himself apart, but seemed aware that a presence like his was essential to the scene.

He acknowledged Miss Chitol with a withdrawn quarter-smile, accompanied by the merest nod. She responded in kind.

'I don't drink,' he said, a touch presumptuously, as if being offered. 'And, anyway, what's there to celebrate?'

His note of quiet irony put Miss Chitol at ease.

A year this awful had made her contemplate her political positions. The various religious riots, in particular, had led her to consolidate on her father's secular beliefs, and in the process she subconsciously attributed a greater idealism than existed to the railway colony in which she grew up.

It was as if the psychology boy had discerned her concerns.

They entered a conversation, at first exploratory, assessing the other's views.

'Delhi was nothing short of a genocide.'

'At least with his mother you could say she had the heart to keep Sikh bodyguards.'

'She was no Mother Teresa.'

'Definitely not.'

'What a year. Amritsar. Delhi. Bhopal.'

'What about Bhiwandi?'

'Why so far as Bhiwandi? What about Govandi, Bandra, Pydhonie?'

'Did you see the posters: us two, our two children; them five, their twenty-five?'

'We heard rumours that Muslim bakeries were poisoning their bread.'

'But somehow *only* for Hindu customers, not anyone else.'

'I think sometimes, how are we to become a modern country?'

'Or even a decent one.'

At some point in the conversation, P said to her: 'You are hiding something.'

'I haven't understood your meaning,' replied Miss Chitol, thrown.

The psychology boy bore into her with his thoughtful coal-black eyes. He held her gaze just long enough to bother her and interest her. Presumptuous thing to have said, no doubt. A little unnerved, she left for the kitchen to get another drink. There she got involved in fixing a raita for the biryani. She intended to return to the boy, who had settled in her mind as her party companion. About then, in an unforeseen development, his 'girlfriend' arrived. People said 'girlfriend' with an odd inflection, indicating that perhaps she was not a girlfriend, or much more than a girlfriend.

She was now at the rotting window where Miss Chitol had been with the psychology boy not so long ago. A proud girl, Miss Chitol gauged. Fair and tubby, with the airs of a budding memsahib. The pair spoke with an expanding range of gestures. Against the escalating music, events played out as if by mime. First the boy walked out. The girl remained, staring out of the window, tossing her hair and turning back occasionally in a way Miss Chitol judged was designed to draw attention. Then the psychology boy returned, and the girl left, her hair flowing behind her, clearly wanting him to follow. He did not. In a few minutes she came to fetch him with a somewhat motherly blaze in her eyes.

Typical, those two, someone remarked. Miss Chitol pretended to laugh along. She had not-watched watched the drama with growing unease. What was her role in this – and why on earth should she have a role! She became royally annoyed with herself. She thought of J from the afternoon, whose eyes teemed with enthusiasm, unlike this psychology boy's, which were dark as a tunnel.

But the party appeared unconcerned about Miss Chitol's inner life. The icebox was melting and emptying, the ashtrays were filling and spilling, and people were dancing – more than dancing, dancing *away*. Shaking, twisting, hooting, vibrating their limbs, puckering their mouths into uncommon shapes and just dancing away.

Come a come a come a come a come a chameleon

A tremendous song. She tapped her feet, poured herself a third rum. The notion of a chameleon who came and went was a fascinating one.

At this point the psychology boy came back. The night felt suddenly overloaded. She wished she had stayed in the hostel reading and dozing, the sweetest of life's pleasures, why oh why did she succumb to the lure of this party? She zoomed through her third rum and told Vimla that she must go. Vimla would have none of it, but knew her friend was the firmer in her resolve.

Against the run of things, the psychology boy offered to drop her back. And Vimla seemed to be encouraging it, in a teasing way that embarrassed Miss Chitol.

Afterwards she could never remember Vimla's exact words, but maybe they were: 'Hai, so cute!' What did she mean, cute? Did she mean here was a possible pair? Or was it cute because they were so obviously *not* a pair? Was she too governmental, was that it?

She refused the offer. Yet she could not, under the circumstances, resist too hard and thereby indicate that she had been affected. Unlike these relaxers I have a job to concentrate on, she told herself, and bade farewell.

The psychology boy accompanied her downstairs. By the time they reached the street she felt thoroughly offended. A strange passion developed between the two, as though it was they and not he and the fair girl, or rather the fat memsahib as Miss Chitol was mentally referring to her, who were squabbling lovers – if that, in fact, is what the psychology boy and the memsahib were. She told him she did not wish to trouble him, and there, down the road she could see a taxi with its For Hire meter standing up.

Here he played a wild card. What he really wanted was a choffee at Dadar station, he said.

He seemed to always speak with the quality of intellectual enquiry, which required participation from an interlocutor.

Choffee? Was that chocolate and coffee? she asked.

Chai plus coffee, said P. You must try it, it opens up one's thoughts to oneself.

She agreed, she realised, perhaps a little quicker than proper.

The mount was a distress-look scooter, except the distress was authentic. Soon they were clattering down the night. The psychology boy sat erect, leaning back ever so little towards her. She gripped the rod behind her and kept herself from leaning forward into him. Wind blew into her eyes, through the freedom of her unsleeved armpits, billowed her pallu like a sail; she ran her fingers over her pearls, checked the clasp. She was smiling, soft at first, then harder and harder. This was the wildest thing Miss Chitol, twenty-six years old, had ever done in her life in Bombay, whereas, funny to think, in Bhombalpur she had been too wild. If a dog barks louder in its own street … did it mean she was at heart a Bhombalpuriya not a Bombayite? Should Yogesh Ambolkar be taking note? They were hammering through the smells of sewage, entrails, fried everything, through heart-shaped balloons and soap bubbles, past footpath séances and lines of the faithful, and chawls and their railings, children dangling their legs through the balustrades screaming and shouting, for here it came, with the unsynchronised detonation of firecrackers, the end of one numbered year and the start of another, conferring upon the moments the irrational significance that is the special requirement of the human species. 'Happy New Year,' P shouted, not without that note of irony. 'Same to you,' shouted Miss Chitol. They could see each other's laugh, the thrill. She was tight; it had been a long time since she'd had three rums. Now they were by the tracks, alongside trains rattling past like the starts of stories. At the flower market the sellers were gone. Those who remained offered cut-price dahlias, gladioli, rose, rose, rose. At a spot that he would have to yield to baskets of marigold come 4 a.m. stood Murgesh the choffee man with his kerosene stove.

'*Kya*, Murgesh, Happy New Year,' P said.

'Happy New Year, brother,' Murgesh replied in English.

'Two special,' said P.

The concoction was the kind of pure Bombay mix she was partial to and only added to her intoxication. Was she, therefore, at heart a Bombayite after all? Note to Yogesh Ambolkar.

'The thing is,' P was saying, sipping his choffee contemplatively, 'when one hides something, one is being honest. With oneself. Yet dishonest with the world. That is the clash. That is the turmoil.'

'Why do you think I'm hiding something?' she asked.

'I can sense the honesty inside you, it is very obvious,' he replied. 'When you are dishonest, it troubles you.'

This did not answer Miss Chitol's question, but it satisfied her in a deeper way. To be thought of as honest was fulfilling. Was she indeed honest? she asked herself. She believed she was. While working she saw that there was a certain kick in honesty that nothing could match.

But was she really? So many lies she had told in her life. Did notions about oneself ever hold up? When she was younger she used to think she was brave. Years later she learned that she would wake up in the middle of the night, go to the window below which her mother had lain dying, hold the grilles and speak in a language nobody understood. When she found out, she felt like an imposter. The notion that she was brave took a pounding. She would have to give up that person, or try all over again to be brave.

'At my age my mother had already had me,' she said to P.

Why she had to declare this, she didn't know, maybe some form of honesty. She was hot with confessional feeling, like I owe you nothing but the truth. Nothing but the truth, yet not the whole truth. She did not say her mother had had her and was soon to go. Anyhow, the psychology boy was supposed to know, intuit, whatever it was that he was doing.

He said nothing and looked into her. She understood what gave his eyes the special penetration. Set close together, not much white around the iris, thick long black lashes framing them, no inconsequential blinking or fluttering.

'Why did you fight with your friend?' she enquired, since they were being honest.

'Yaar,' said P, pausing a beat to gather his thoughts. 'It is all about control. There was a time we were close. Her funda is, if I am something to her, then I should be everything to her. She wanted me to go to some other party. There is not a single person I could have talked to there.'

This admission made her Miss Chitol feel awfully chosen.

The song kept playing in her head. A song that couldn't be shook off, the mouth organ, the flat foot-tapping voice.

Tama tama tama tama tama Tamilian

P asked: 'Was she ill, your mother?'

Miss Chitol looked at him in astonishment. What a psychology boy this boy was!

'It was probably encephalitis, we never got to know hundred per cent,' she said. 'How did you know?'

'Just the way you spoke about it. Are you around that age now?'

Waste flowers were strewn about all around them. When crushed they seemed to release fragrances. Certain walkers tried not to trample them out of piety. Her grandmother had told her, don't pluck flowers off the plants for the altar, pick up the fallen flowers. In her mind fallen flowers were devotional with no equal. Tamilians come and gooo, just come and goooo-oh-ooohhh.

Yes, she conceded to self, she was tight tight tight, tun tun tun. At the end of certain days and years you want to lie sleeveless among the cut-price petals in praise and pity of the world and appreciate the nature of your new troubles.

4

The waiting

And love may be short, as the poet wrote, forgetting long, but why did he omit the waiting, the waiting is so strong. Paddling in the tranquil waters of friendship, Miss Chitol waited for the great waves gathering on the foam-flecked horizon.

Every other day J showed up at her office in the annexe. She waited for it. Then, feeling exposed before her colleagues, she pre-empted his visits by showing up instead at the zonal office in the historical building. That exposure, too, troubled her.

'I think we should meet near the gate,' she told him. 'People will talk.'

'So what, let them talk,' said J. 'People will always talk when there is friendship between a man and a woman.'

'It is different for the woman,' she replied tentatively.

She noted that he had emphasised the word friendship.

Whenever they met, she felt that J knew the real her, the daily her who worked as a personnel clerk in the Bombay Division of the Central Railway, whom he advised on such matters as how to take advantage of leave entitlements – the her who liked so well the kinds of songs he sang, even if he had never sung for her in private.

One day, a day she had waited for, over fresh-lime water and pattice at her old haunt, New Deluxe Cafe and Restaurant, he laid down the condition that she join him. Together, coyly, they did a little of KJY and Asha's 'Jaaneman Jaaneman'. So effortless was their alignment in the harmonies! She carried the melody, that alignment, back with her to the ministerial room, all the way on the train back.

When she reached the hostel that evening, she saw P on his scooter across the road. She had waited for him every day since he had told her he would come. And now on this same day of the singing? Must the alignment between these two men always be so?

She felt embarrassed to be seen in that state: grimy after the commute, bereft of kajal, in a plain cotton sari and quietly expanding maps of sweat on her blouse. What a letdown she must be! As she put herself together and approached him she saw that he, too, was different from the man in her mind's eye. He seemed littler, and his sparse facial hair lent him a slight inadequacy. Nonetheless his long-lashed eyes were as intense as she remembered. His lips were finely shaped, with a distinct outline, and his hair fell thick on either side of his off-centre parting. Even if in an inadequate way, he was striking, beautiful you could say.

'I told you I would come,' he said.

'Talking to boys near the compound is not allowed,' she replied. The bright in her eyes was on.

They convened at a milk booth two corners away. There they each sipped a pineapple Energee and discussed what P called the psychology of difficult circumstances. It was not clear to Miss Chitol whether by this he was referring to himself, or to her, or the truly unfortunate, or the world at large. The suppression involved in difficult circumstances was very great, he said. Circumstances were like gravity, one needed a tremendous amount of energy to escape them, and one could, but the generation of such momentum left one depleted. Boys seem to have a different understanding about this, she responded, not exactly disagreeing. To boys, difficult circumstances appeared to be events, hurdles that might challenge them. Whenever she read an autobiography or a profile of a successful man, she was struck by this. For girls, circumstances were continuous. This is why generating energy was not easy, for there was not always a defined hurdle that you could build up speed towards and jump over. Where was the space? Sometimes you were not even aware of circumstances, you only had a general recognition, a haze, a fog, and you wondered if it was just the climate.

The psychology boy appeared to take mild umbrage, not because of the challenge to his point, which he seemed to welcome, but perhaps because it implicated him too. Although he tried not to let on, Miss Chitol did discern it, and he was aware that she did. As a result their parting was a touch heavy. She regretted this, and while returning to the hostel she hoped she could make up for it the next time.

Later that night, lying in her bed, her mind too busy for sleep, she reflected that they had stood for over an hour talking by the milk booth. Their conversation needed no context at all. Yes, J knew the daily her, but P seemed to access a deeper her.

And her waiting went on. She met J several times a week. She registered the days they did not meet.

P sometimes phoned and said he would come and did not show; at other times he showed up without intimation.

If Miss Chitol were a man she would not have informed one of the other's existence. She was not; besides, she was honest. She mentioned each to the other in casual ways, while recounting something calculatedly trivial.

She became certain that J liked her. She suspected P wanted her to fall for him but she could not be sure if he liked her.

On the parapet along the Gateway of India she got to know the feeling of J's hand in hers, the firmness of his arm around her shoulders, got to know J's kisses as they watched boats and rubbish bob about in the grey-brown harbour. There must be clerks along this row, she thought, but I hope none from the Central Railway. Although she had committed waterfront love in Bhombalpur, she felt conscious of doing so here in Bombay. She had seen the sight so frequently it was part of the landscape; she had not thought she herself would be one of those forming the landscape for others. Now that she was, she felt her life was truer to what life was supposed to be.

She would have preferred if it did not have to be so, if passion were the propulsion, but he was right, a little preparation would help. From the Family Planning stall near the station superintendent's office he had picked up the needful. It was arranged for a late morning. They set out separately from Victoria Terminus, linking arms once they crossed over into Borabazaar. She felt an inelegance accompany them, as though she had been sent by higher authorities to an ethically compromised appointment.

The stairs were narrower and steeper than she remembered. On the first landing, an old woman with scraggly white hair opened the door and stared contemptuously, muttering insults until they had climbed out of view. At the top Miss Chitol felt short of breath. J struggled to find the key. Once he had it, he grappled with it inside the lock, working up a great unventilated perspiration. 'Is it the right key?' she asked. He checked each of his trouser and shirt pockets, fishing out coins and keys. 'Not this. Or this. Not this. Ah yes, I remember.' He pulled the door towards himself and juddered it a few times while turning the key. It came open.

It was steaming inside. He switched on the fan. It did not start. Of all the days – the electricity. Maybe this was what the old woman cursed, Miss Chitol thought.

The room was much as she recalled it, but she registered it in finer detail. The faded lavender on the walls brought to mind a failed honeymoon. Below the clothes-bearing nails lay a pallet of sorts. The stifled scent of cardboard reminded her of the loft in Kings & Queens. She opened the windows to let in air, and to protect their privacy drew the curtains, realising as she did that the curtains were lungis. She rid her hands of them instantly and wiped her fingers on her sari.

When she turned round she saw that J's shirt – the usual, plain white, ironed – now hung on a nail. He stood in his white vest, tucked into his pleated grey trousers, smiling like a hero. She was not prepared for the sight. As they walked to one another she acknowledged the waiting had run its course. She placed his hand on her beating breast, in signification to herself to have faith in the moment and the moment will reward you. She clasped his fingers with hers, then, releasing her grip, spread them over his strong back, feeling all the while for faith. Even if not her heart, she felt her body respond. He pecked her all over the neck with rapid moustache kisses. As his excitement rose he began to suck air through his teeth, making a hissing sound, the first time he had ever done so in their dealings, as though he was eating something spicy, or commuting on the unpunctual Central suburban. She understood it was meant to be the sound of desire, and suspected he wished her to reciprocate in kind. But how unnatural – how very odd and unnatural indeed! And where were they to lie down? No, not on the pallet, who knows whose sweat it holds; better to lie here, right on the floor, but it is hard and gritty; best to press some of these flattened cartons into service, although these are dusty, and here comes a sneeze, and another.

When they brought proceedings back on track, lying on cardboard, his face, all of him, felt more intimate than she had bargained on. A hint of triumph veined his face, like he was winning and she was losing. She could not help but feel shameless. She sat up and blew, as vigorously as she could, her nose into her pallu. She coughed and rubbed her eyes and blew her nose again, saying, 'I can't, I can't.' J let out a laugh to convey that these circumstances would soon be overcome – which, definitely, they were not, since she sneezed and blew her nose over and over.

After some time, walking back engrossed in different textures of failure, he tried to keep their spirits up. 'It will happen, don't worry, it is meant to be,' he said, with an undercurrent of disappointment, to cut past which he hummed. For the first time she was acutely aware of their age difference, nearly six years. She wondered if this was a regular system of his – but he had fumbled with the lock, so maybe it was not? Miss Chitol felt very strange and quite alone.

Three days later she told P she was in a relationship with J, and that the relationship was over.

She said it with as much neutrality as she could muster. She did not want to be seen as suggesting a transfer of relationships. Nor did she mention the unpleasantness – how easily J's chivalry had come unmasked when she told him she liked somebody else, and that while it may even have been true that she had acted like one thing and turned out to be another, as he charged her with, she had not expected J to say, 'You think you're too smart, ah?', and certainly had not expected him to *spit* on the ground and walk away. If she did not show him it was because she was terrified that he could turn up any time at the divisional office and disgrace her – and perhaps it was because of disgrace as much as anything else that she mentioned none of this to P.

'Yaar,' said P, fluffing up his hair carefully. He looked wounded – she kept herself from pointing out *he* was the one with a 'girlfriend'. Something about the adjustment of his hair at this stage she found relatable, the keeping up of appearances when vulnerable, and it drew her heart closer to his. But then P revved his scooter and drove away with a nod – goodbye. As he went out of sight, Miss Chitol was convinced there was nothing in this world but insults. Is the trouble with the insulters or the insulted? she asked herself. Am I an idiot?

Some evenings later she returned to a sealed envelope at the hostel reception. The note inside electrified her.

If you are serious, meet me at suicide point tomorrow at 6:30.

It was unsigned but she knew exactly who, and although not a distinguished landmark like the hill station suicide points, she knew which.

She reached before time, while the light was still good, glimmering good-naturedly over the lake waters. The mosquitoes came out; dusk hastily spread; the digits on her watch blinked past the appointed hour and there was no P. She worried that she'd got the spot wrong. Or could it be that he would simply not show up? Was this some kind of cheap joke? She had no doubt he'd written the note in irony, yet briefly she entertained the thought – was he in fact unsteady?

Pacing between a pair of trees, she oscillated from one extreme outcome to another. A pair of hands suddenly closed around her eyes and she let out a shocked little scream. She could sense his body behind hers, the warm furrows of his palms against her eyelids. Never had they shared such intimacy. She turned round, casting her gaze downwards, and said in a quiet voice, 'You scared me.' Drumming his chest tenderly with her fingers, she said again: 'You *scared* me.'

P held her tight, standing five fingers taller. There passed between them a flurry of kisses. 'You scared me, never do that again.'

They walked towards his scooter, spent some time among the malarial mosquitoes, then rode off.

His flat was a one-room-kitchen seepage-stricken affair. The flatmate, a researcher in industrial psychology, was spread out on a bare mattress among heaps of papers like a beleaguered scholar. Above him the distempered wall bore memories of plays, marches and protests, an ironic 'If you sprinkle when you tinkle' poster positioned above an ironic tap protruding over the mattress, a sketch of Che Guevara looking somewhat like Raj Kapoor, handwritten syllabi, lists of books with two-tier titles and joint authorships. The setting reminded her that in this relationship she was the older one.

The flatmate quizzed Miss Chitol about her experiences with the railways, going – 'wow!' – all the way back to the great strike. She occupied, at length, an expert's role. The flatmate wished to keep her talking, but it was understood he should vacate. Once he did, making his excuses, she did not feel nervous. Her expertise, her experiences, had secured her confidence. She had once gone underground: she could see that she had P's admiration.

Miss Chitol felt, all of a sudden, deeply in love.

She laid P's head in her lap and played with his hair. She did not ask him about his 'girlfriend'. He did not ask her about J. For her part, she viewed J as a sordid but necessary mistake. Maybe it was because of J that she felt confident in enlarging these kisses now, maybe it was because of J too that she could confidently withdraw, so that P felt the balance of power between them shift, which motivated him.

In the coming weeks, Miss Chitol and the psychology boy occupied a stupendous realm of love. His acuity thrilled her. Estranged from his family, who lived in the city – a family of reasonable means, she sensed – to follow his intellectual pursuits, he was constantly insightful, about the Shah Bano case, for instance, true modernity and true secularism, regressive clerics and the impact of giving in to maulvis in the long run. She liked how he tempered his Maggi with chopped green chillies; she liked his choffee.

When they talked about her childhood, it was as if for the first time her life *really* made sense: her need for self-reliance, her resistance to relationships, even her running away. If she did not find these assessments shaming, it was because he spoke with similar analytical candour about his own youth, losing his own mother in his teens, his inability to accept her replacement.

In the ultimate act she felt neither denuded nor strange. The complete possession of one another could only be expressed through complete utter reciprocation. Miraculous was this symbiosis! Private jokes developed between them, also tics and habits that were not tics and habits by themselves, when they were not together. When together, they could create a cocoon pure, uncontaminated. Sometimes an ecstatic feeling overcame her – write it on the winds, throw it to the stars, *ell-oh-vee-ee!* At work, she felt undiligent simply for the euphoria within, full of waiting. She did not need to ask, 'Is this what love is?' What use a question whose answer cannot be words?

One afternoon at work, she noticed J at the door of the ministerial room. He stood under the transom window and stared, and stood, and stared. She considered ushering him away. Then she noted the hostility in his posture, the thumbs tucked into his belt loops, his head tilted, his face set tight, the dull eyes. Let him be, she thought, I'll keep working. If he wants to come in and say something, let him come. If he wants to disgrace me, hmm … I don't think he has the guts. And still he kept standing there in a cloud of reproach. Hundreds of clerks in the room seemed to be staring at her along with him. She held her nerve. Eventually he was gone.

She remained ill at ease. She wondered if she should have gone over to him and extended the hand of friendship. It was, however, when she had expressed her desire to revert to friendship that he had become so provoked as to spit. No, he had not come in friendship. Preoccupied, she got late completing her task and missed the trains and buses she had planned on catching.

When she arrived, P was in a sour mood. Opening the door he said: 'You are late again.' She was struck once more by the alignment of the two men. 'Is he firing me?' she asked herself. It was true that this had become something of an issue between them, but she was surprised to have been spoken to that way. A few days later when she was delayed again, P said: 'If you are going to be this late, better not to come.' Yes, indeed, he was firing her.

How could she help it? Did she not have a job? Did she have a two-wheeler like him? Did he think it was very nice, instead of being late, to not show up at all, as he had often done? All right, not often she conceded in the subsequent argument, but at least twice. Fine, not at least, exactly twice. No, she was not trying to say that her reasons were reasons while his reasons were excuses. Could he not see that she wanted to be with him, despite her work hours and the hostel hours and all the hours in getting from one place to the other? She spoke with such passion that the psychology boy felt very stimulated.

This repeated itself on a few occasions, for insubstantial causes. The firing, the recriminating, the conquering. It was the sensation of being fired that stayed on her.

She noted a kind of intellectual's hauteur enter his manner. He felt the weight of his reading material piling up, the span of his education growing long. If she asked in greater than casual detail about his movements, he might serve up a lecture on being 'possessive'. He suggested that, if one were to look at things from a psychological point of view, the people who got 'attached' were those who tended to manipulate others to satisfy their attachments. He often pretended, in a brooding smoker's way, that he was not talking about her, but stating a general point, a *funda*, which not only hurt her but made her think he considered her a provincial fool. She wondered whether he was bored of her, whether he was perhaps plain superior to her, the way she had felt, she had to admit, superior to J. Or was it that she was someone who simply went about feeling insulted? How very sad it would be if such a trait, because of her ignorance of it, was constantly lowering her in his eyes.

At last Miss Chitol decided to swallow her pride and call Vimla.

To reach Vimla you had to ring her neighbours, who may or may not agree to fetch Vimla, and then Vimla, not permitted to talk long on the neighbours' phone, may or may not walk down to the public call office, to a phone which may or may not be in working order.

'If he is firing you, just tell him to get lost,' Vimla said when they were able to speak.

'Tell him to get lost?'

'In the end he will go back to that one.'

Miss Chitol fell briefly silent.

'The one who is like a memsahib?'

'That one,' said Vimla.

'Why do you say that?'

'He always does. She gets him back, spoils him, then she sits on him and squashes him. Poor guy. He's a genuine guy actually. But that doesn't mean you waste your time.'

'I will tell him to get lost,' said Miss Chitol.

'You are not his wife.'

'I am not his wife.'

'Let memsahib look after him.'

'If you saw the letters I wrote to him,' said Miss Chitol in a small voice.

'Did he write to you?'

'A one-line note one time. A two-line note another time.'

'Throw them away,' said Vimla.

'Memsahib can take care of him. They will both have something to do.'

She noted the impatient queue behind her. She put the phone down. Attempting to walk away she found herself, in a manner, blocked. Blocked, as though there was not enough air coming into her. She was shrinking, her heart was shrivelling up, all of her – crumpling before her very eyes, like plastic in a fire, melting into nothing.

To kill a fire you must cut the oxygen and so she did. She ceased meeting, phoning, writing, waiting.

She entered a period of convalescence. She became sloppy at work and in order to cover up told the same unconvincing lies as the lazy and the dishonest. In her room she lay around tiredly devastated, exhausted by her rebellion against dependence. She went hungry from lack of interest. She lost weight, her posture suffered, the puffs under her eyes grew dark. She read without immersion. The lines she tried to conjure as an amateur poet were so desultory she could barely reach their ends.

When the psychology boy tried to contact her she hadn't the inclination to reciprocate. His one note lay unopened. When they met outside the hostel gate, she was so plain and flat towards him he could see the spirit was gone forever.

Nine months on from that gorgeous, impostrous day she emerged both an ingenue and an aficionado. With the conviction of one hardened in the furnace of love – but was not glass, too, like iron, forged in fire? – she supplied advice to her new room-mate, from Digboi in Assam, across the country at the far end of the railway lines out east, which fact always gladdened her heart.

'If someone uses the word suicide with you, just remember to stop meeting them,' she said, shoddily stitching a fall on her sari. 'And don't feel empty because you think there is something lacking in you. Because that is not necessarily the case.'

Bornali, who was coy and culturally rooted, who knew to dance the bihu and how to make pitha for the occasion, replied with a coy and culturally rooted laugh, 'Commitment problems, *na ki*, Charu di?' And for a moment Miss Chitol was not sure which of the people in her story it referred to.

5

Booked speed

Vacancies arose; posts were to be filled. 'You do your work, that is what you do,' she had been reminding herself morning, noon and night, for life was larger than the vagaries of the heart and the body. Five posts to be filled, through the departmental quota in the selection ratio 1:3, meaning she would have to compete with fourteen of the most senior junior clerks in the P branch. She was determined to move ahead.

Writing the exam, she found her relationship with the Establishment volumes was sweeter than she had known. She ascertained with ease, for instance, whether a Himalayan Wood Badge Holder was eligible for recruitment in a Group C post through the Scouts and Guides Quota, distinguished with similar ease between Continuous and Essentially Intermittent categories of worker. When she reached the short note on the Family Planning Incentive Increment, she slowed. Her mind went back to the Family Planning stall, and from there to the one time she had not been careful. It can happen that our past actions only appear preposterous in the torchlight of the present. She had not adequately panicked then and compensated by doing so now, retrospectively hypothesising about her fate.

Perspiring hard, she dabbed herself with her handkerchief and returned to the note: 'also known as the Sterilisation Increment', she put down, and listed the eligibility criteria – reproductive age groups, not already a parent to three living children, an accompanying sterilisation certificate. Here she was sidetracked once more, into the size of the population. The last census figure, for which the amiable Fatima Memon had enumerated her the morning after her final day at Kings & Queens, was 685 million, she was sure. And the one before that, when the neat man had come to their quarters the day her grandmother died, what was the figure then – around 550 million, if she remembered correctly. So if the population grew by 135 million between '71 and '81, today, nearly five years later ... She covered her rough paper with hectic calculations and concluded that 750 million, at the very minimum, must be the figure. As always, the number left her impressed: all it represented.

It was an odd thing, she mused, to pay people a little to refrain from having children. Those who produced children for economic reasons, say farmers, would probably not be deterred by an incentive, while those who did for other reasons surely would not. Perhaps the idea was to remove the stigma from contraceptive procedures. It was a better idea, certainly, than the horrors seen during the Emergency. She was not required to express or indeed hold opinions on this matter. Nevertheless she ended her note by commending the sterilisation increment as a 'worthier endeavour than forced sterilisation measures we have seen in the past'. As she handed in her paper she wondered whether her comment might land her in trouble. After all, the prime minister's younger brother, who would have surely been prime minister had he not died, had enforced those measures. But she felt satisfied for having made the point. Besides, she had overcome her retrospection – she always felt a little triumphant when she did that. Such accumulated minutes and hours were reconstituting her. She felt it at a cellular level.

Her sentence was not held against her.

Miss Chitol became one of the five selected. She ascended to the post of senior clerk, and into the Rs 330–560 pay scale. She took Mrs Ghorpade and Krunalini for an ice-cream treat – double scoops, double laughs.

Not until the word 'junior' was gone did she realise what a stymieing word it had been to carry around. She got a fixed desk to herself. All of a sudden her present and future seemed very bright.

Assigned to the loco section, she enjoyed her chats with the loco men whenever they came in. The electric men told her of their fatigue from the high-voltage traction, the diesel men of their creeping deafness from the noise; they told her of back pains, the fear of paralysis from all the sitting, and of cardiac arrest from the pressure. She heard stories about landslides, cave-ins, derailments, pantograph entanglements. These conversations brought her a taste of life in the great railways outside.

Not that a clerk's life was without adventure, of the low intrigue kind. To manage its tediums and treacheries she cultivated a fixation with paperweights. The office-issued glass ones were smooth and roundish, like river stones, enclosing in them what always seemed to her coloured ferns; she continually wondered how they had got in there. To those she added a number of objects that doubled as weights: a conch shell she had picked up from the beach the day her father died; the terracotta locomotive that Dhrubo had gifted her; a transparent pen-holder that was also the world's most cumbersome magnifying glass; a wooden cube crafted like a die, with painted dots on each side, resembling not so much an enlarged die but the die-styled bathroom stools hawked around Crawford Market. Sitting before her flock, she thought back to young B in Bhombalpur flicking his handkerchief against his paperweight. Having earned herself a desk she became sensitive to it, the need to develop an intimacy with one's tools. If Digambar Bharti spun registers on his ring finger, would sometimes begin doing so mid-sentence, she now understood why. Not that Digambar Bharti was always at his desk, perfected as he had the clerical art of stepping out into the corridor to dig his bum. The wanton digging of male bums had become such a familiar workplace sight to Miss Chitol that, were you to pluck her out of that office and plant her elsewhere, say Japan or West Germany, the two most diligent nations in the world, she would at once marvel, 'Do people not dig their bums here?'

She often stared at the glass paperweights to see if the ferns might move. From the other weights she did not expect anything extraordinary. They stimulated a variety of emotions nonetheless. They kept her grounded. Papers will not fly. They will be ironed out into resolution. They imprisoned her, told her daydreaming mind: this is me forever. Yet they reminded her that on these desks, by these files and staplers and paperweights, did the railways and the country run as much as by the sheds and yards and stations and locomotives.

From Digambar Bharti's quip about her paperweights she learned that the word *wajan*, weight, was a term for bribe. Although this was merely the divisional personnel branch, through which no huge tenders flowed, whose role even in recruitment was limited, there were ways and means. Rulemaster Chitnis said: 'This is the maximum low department because there is no outside agency, all the corruption is against one's own people.' He proceeded to tell her how in the absence of favour-mongering, office superintendent Kulkarni might write the words 'Not Approved' on a simple leave application. When circumstances had amended themselves, he would transform the words into 'Note: Approved'. This was the power Miss Chitol now inhabited: the power to obstruct, the power to put up or not put up. Life and File, two spellings of the same word, as Rulemaster Chitnis had it, it depended on your side of the table – for one person the file is his life, for the other a life is just a file.

She instructed herself not to turn into a negative person. She could do little about the petty pocket-lining. But she could keep her head down in honest work. She believed there were those who performed their jobs without *wajan*, or wanton bum-digging, and in itself that was saying something, doing something. Indeed, even her greater exposure to these matters was evidence of her new standing. Where earlier she might have been privy to workplace politics because of her invisibility, now Rulemaster Chitnis was seeking her out and taking her into his confidence. Junior clerks were coming to her to learn and she was reliably teaching them.

Then came the windfall – the fourth pay commission, effective from the first day of the first month of the year 1986. Miss Chitol's pay scale vaulted up to Rs 1200–2040 – along with that, nine months of arrears! As she drew her money from the cashier she imperceptibly rolled her fingers into a fist. Afterwards she recalled, with some emotion, the booklet she had seen her father with: *Railwaymen and the Third Pay Commission: Will the Commission do Away with the Starvation Wages of Railway Employees?*

Over the coming months Miss Chitol bought two new nighties (but did not throw out the comfortable torn ones), experimented with a face pack and a Bridal Form bra. At the big handloom expo in Cross Maidan, which Krunalini took her to, she viewed the dotted and dyed contrast chungidi prints from Madurai, not so dissimilar to the tie-and-dye bandhej from Jamnagar, absorbed the Sanganeri block prints and the wavy leheriyas of Rajasthan, the earthy ikats of Pochampalli, the clean clean Mangalgiri checks, the eye-popping red-white-blacks of the Oriya Bichitrapuri. Never mind that she could not at this point afford more than two: there was so much a little money allowed you to understand!

Running out of space on her shelves and in her trunk, Miss Chitol passed on a few older clothes to Bornali, as Rajashree had to her. For her bags and dupattas she pounded in a couple of extra nails into the cupboard door – if only she had a clothes horse. When a vacancy arose at long last, she put in an application for a single-seater room, available at a premium, ten per cent of the working woman's salary rather than seven and a half. A few months later, updating her passbook to take stock, she drew her breath and decided to go for it. She retired digital time for an HMT analogue – so analogue it was free of a militant second hand altogether. The shine of the stainless-steel strap offset the dial of beautiful burgundy, which had become a favourite colour and a favourite word. For days afterwards she checked the time incessantly, smiling at whatever it was. There was no doubt about it: rising was a lovely feeling.

She acquired glasses. Watching herself in the mirror one day, wearing a new sari, spectacles and watch, she was shocked by the thought that she was growing old. She had indeed become senior. Never before had she understood why people had trouble with the idea of growing old – after all, they had their entire life to acclimatise. To think it had happened to her while she was not looking. As the days passed, ageing outlasted her patience for it, and she stopped paying attention. Yet despite her advances, there remained to her something unrealised about her life, like a spring that had not regained its natural bounce, waiting perhaps for the right kind of pressure to fall upon it.

When news came out that assistant personnel officer Geetanjali Rao had been promoted to divisional personnel officer, Miss Chitol felt that some of her professional gains had been undone. Krunalini, who had identified Miss Chitol's competitiveness with Geetanjali Rao, found it amusing, and Miss Chitol, aware of it, sometimes fed the amusement on purpose. But Krunalini was engaged and would likely leave her job after marriage. In that sense, their trajectories seemed more divergent than Miss Chitol's with Gitanjali Rao's. This is not something she could disclose to Krunalini.

There were days when a clerical inertia bordering on self-loathing crept over her.

Reading *Madame Bovary*, drawn from her father's collection of European novels, she was not frightened by Madame Bovary's fate. Borrowing did not fascinate her, that life seemed very rich, and in spite of her recent spends, she was in no danger of debts. As for love affairs, she had survived those too. The line that personally accosted her, rather, was about a lover who grew tired of the heroine: *Every notary bears within him the debris of a poet*. He was, like her, a clerk.

One day on the desk of Rulemaster Chitnis, she noticed a new parliamentary document on Central Railway suburban. It was an Action Taken Report about the problem she had discussed with J that fine, impostrous day. For a while she twisted her hair around her fingers and ran her mind over him and that relationship. She proceeded to read all forty-five pages of the report.

The parliamentary committee had asked: the motor coaches were so old and overloaded they had developed reverse camber, the Research Designs and Standards Organisation had therefore recommended that the booked speed of the trains be reduced from 72 kmh to 65 kmh, so why was this advisory ignored for four years?

The Central Railway had replied: the coaches were in poor condition partly due to public agitations, the public agitations were due to delays and cancellations, hence lowering the booked speed of trains would create further delays and reduce further the number of services, which would lead to further public agitation and cause further damage to the coaches. The advisory, therefore, was delayed to the extent possible.

It made sense to Miss Chitol. There was a momentum to recklessness that was its own logic, which derived from its own circumstances. Not always possible to dial down a booked speed. Life lurched along, moving always.

But, amazing, why did the ferns never move?

6

A short vacation

Dhrubajit, Charulata and Anandajyoti Chitol, who had acquired short names but never pet names, embarked on a vacation, just the three and nobody else, and the air was charged with unrequited childhood. All morning they bantered on the train and kept at it on the journey up the winding roads alive with spring growth till the company guest house, Dhrubo's new perquisite.

He was allowed three nights a year in a room of lower denomination. The room was dank and mossy and looked on to a wall. As soon as they put their bags in the Chitols went out into the back garden.

Dhrubo, in 1987, was dressed like a man who had hauled himself into the seventies. Corduroy trousers a shade between green and brown that could absorb any misfortunes the world might throw at them, flared as though bell-bottoms were just invented; tucked into them a patterned silk shirt of similar shade.

'Mama used to dress like this,' observed Miss Chitol.

'Intolerable,' muttered Dhrubo, unclear whether about his sister or his uncle.

They sat facing the valley. Small birds free-fell from the sky, beaks down, wings spread, leaving behind trails of this is my memory for you to keep.

With the passing minutes the remark affected Dhrubo's self-esteem. He considered showing pride.

Anando might have held his stomach and laughed. But he had gone off to buy cherries.

Equally, Anando may not have held his belly and laughed, since he had become 'moody'. The English word and condition was in vogue in several Indian languages, the contraction of moods. Many of Anando's actions were studied through this aspect: his declining to enrol at Chittaranjan, where he was given the option of transferring after the apprentice institute in Bhombalpur wound up; his becoming a journalist instead, which had taken him to Delhi; perhaps even his precocious decision to wed, which had occasioned this holiday.

Dhrubo did not mind Anando jumping him in the queue. He thought Charu ought to have been the first, but finding himself at the receiving end of what he saw as her idiotic fury during Pishi's attempts, he had withdrawn from the project. As for himself, he was sure he could use a wife, although to endure a marriage for that felt unfair. Besides, better to obtain a wife after obtaining a company flat and a company car, and access to the superior room in the company guest house. He may have to wait a while. But he would have status. The expectation of status in others created great problems, he had seen. He did not wish to bear a single taunt on that matter. Neither did he wish to obtain a bride without status.

Anando returned with cherries wrapped in newspaper. A beige dog who had taken him as master trotted alongside him.

The cherries were a shock of sour. The juice wet Miss Chitol's lips. She liked tart, its mischief.

'*Eesh!*' said Dhrubo, dropping a pit into his palm. 'Are these cherries or limes?'

He slid lower on the bench. The sun was a fading shade of warm. He gathered his arms around himself and declared: 'I'm not sleeping.' His eyes began to droop; he fell into a sleep of mingled thought.

Anando's stray sniffed the discarded cherry seeds and moved away. At a safe distance he spread his long belly against the earth, smoothed his eyes and lay content.

Miss Chitol dimmed her eyes but did not sleep.

She did not mind about Anando jumping her in the queue either. She would have to field more comments, yes, but it took the pressure off, the urgency.

'Dada is sleeping,' said Anando.

'I'm not,' said Dhrubo after fifteen seconds.

'You are,' said Miss Chitol.

That was the afternoon.

At night Dhrubo organised a bucket of hot water and went in for a bath. Miss Chitol spoke to Anando about his bride-to-be. She knew only the bare details.

Her grandparents had moved from Lahore at Partition, she now learned. They lived in what Anando described as one of Delhi's typical middle-class refugee colonies. From what Miss Chitol could gather, the girl's parents did not put up roadblocks. Neither were they thrilled. For Anando said quite plainly that they would have preferred somebody propertied. Wild things happened in the clan every day, he added with relish – dramatic fights, freak accidents, sudden disownings and disinheritances, one of which, as a matter of fact, she had learned of from a notice while proofreading a page in the office the other day.

Miss Chitol expressed her concern that he, too, would get sucked into these conflicts. They had considered the point, said Anando. It was on their minds to look for jobs in another city. That was one of the exciting things about journalism, the opportunities were growing, one could domesticate in parts of the country as far-flung as Shillong and Trivandrum. She was struck by how confidently he spoke in the plural, like the long-married.

Dhrubo stepped into the conversation in his towel. 'He is continuing the tradition of love marriage that Baba started.'

'Ma started,' said Miss Chitol.

'It was Ma who gave the name Chitol,' she added.

Maybe the brothers heard, maybe they didn't.

Dhrubo went back into the bathroom to comb his hair. She decided against pursuing it.

When she saw Anando she saw a delicate survivor and she knew love was a rough game.

'Are you *sure* about it?' she asked.

Anando said: 'She likes me and I like her.'

Instantly she felt she had been small-hearted. She had only been trying to look out for him.

'Yes, of course, fool, I know that,' she said, recovering. 'Now, when are we meeting her?'

In the morning, starting well before tea and continuing well after breakfast, the Chitols debated the lunch menu. If they were to eat in and wanted non-veg, the cook would have to be sent right away with money to buy the meat, with a little extra to keep it quiet, since the guest house was vegetarian. As the summit ran on, Dhrubo huffed out of the living area and into the garden.

'Do you think he went off because you made fun of the guest house?' Anando asked his sister.

'What did I say wrong?' she retorted. 'There *is* moss on the walls.'

'But, Didi, you said we can eat our lunch off the wall.'

'Those *are* mushrooms growing near the moss, aren't they? People do eat mushrooms. Anyway, he likes licking walls.'

'But he wants non-veg,' said Anando.

'And he won't get any if he doesn't come back and decide soon.'

Just then Dhrubo raced in towards the washbasin and furiously spun the tap the twenty-odd rotations it took to draw water. Too late. Cigarette ash had burned a hole in his silk shirt.

'Why didn't you use spit!' she cried, astounded.

All afternoon they wandered through the market. They paused a moment before they entered the Original Imperial Bakery. The painted menu on the polished wooden board was straight out of an Enid Blyton picnic and Miss Chitol found herself rehearsing Pearl Flanger: *scon, mirang* ... The prices were extraordinary.

The siblings held another summit, this one in whispers.

'We shall like to have a slice of Black Forest,' Dhrubo announced to the lady behind the counter at last.

The lady was part white, in a sleeveless dress, which was entirely white. A few white people lounged comfortably in the bakery, in vests and shorts and skirts, as though it were summer in the plains.

Having placed their order at one counter, paid for it at another, and taken possession of it from a third, employing wooden tokens to do so, the Chitols felt they had earned admission into the club of the deserving.

Their slice of cake sat on round matted paper, filigreed at the edges, itself resting on a porcelain quarter plate with a moulded floral border. On it lay a single gleaming fork with an embossed handle.

'Should we ask for more forks?' said Miss Chitol.

Anando cast a furtive glance around. '*Oi je!* They have some on the tables.'

They settled down near a window, lined with young money plants in bottles and fresh flowers in jam jars. Black-and-white photographs hung on the walls; they sat below a porcine Winston Churchill.

They ate without speaking a word, undemonstratively, rapaciously. Their cutlery clashed in the heart of the cake. The final sugary cherry Dhrubo plopped into his mouth and remarked to Anando, 'This is better than what you got.'

As they left the bakery, they noticed candy-striped boxes of jujubes, dusted with fine white sugar, sharing with their eyes their astonishment at the price.

Outside, everything seemed so reasonable they became rash.

Miss Chitol bargained her way to a shawl at the Tibetan stalls. Dhrubo bought two packets of jujubes, minus the fine sugar and the candy-striped box, and called out the price differential to his siblings. They registered it only cursorily, for they were engrossed in piles of second-hand books. Anando, more susceptible to Maradona than to any other human being, purchased an illustrated volume called *Argentina!* Miss Chitol bought him Vijay Tendulkar's *Sakharam Binder: An Explosive Play that Defied Censorship and Won Unprecedented Acclaim*. Compensating by virtue, she got herself a slim volume on the teachings of Vivekananda.

'Where is Dada?' she asked Anando some thirty minutes later.

Had they ignored him? Had he returned to the guest house? Was he showing pride? They strode up and down the mall looking for him.

They found him, at last, in a video-game parlour, packets of colourful jujubes sticking out of his windcheater pockets, a steering wheel in his hands, heartfelt ejaculations of *shala* and *beta* escaping his mouth. In short time the three were lined up before the giant car-racing machines, swivelling their rectangular blot this way and that. Glee bounced off their eyes, their teeth, off the token upon metallic token slid into the slot for another round.

Afterwards, walking back dissolute and repentant, they were held up by a noble sunset. They watched the great fire scatter into emberic ashes over the ancient mountain tops. Then they carried on, purified.

That was the afternoon.

At night Dhrubo proposed rum and poured out two glasses.

'What about me?' Miss Chitol said, incredulous. To cover her indignation, lest it look like pride (since she wished to distinguish her conduct from his), she added: 'Come on, Dada, our brother is getting married, we have to celebrate.'

Dhrubo did not object. He approved that he had been asked, and approved that he had approved.

'A cigarette also, Didi?' Anando winked behind Dhrubo's back. She threw him a 'very funny' non-smile.

Soon they were drinking at a good clip, establishing their grown-up personalities, their gleanings from the world – which was exactly the wrong time to talk about the Indian Railways. Dhrubo, in a managerial position at his conglomerate, assumed his let's-identify-the-problem mode, switching to half English, embarking on his sentences with you-sees.

'You see, the Railways is a *behemoth*,' said he. 'It can never attain efficiency in its current form.'

'The problem is not inefficiency,' said Anando. 'The problem is corruption. Didn't I see that even in the apprentice institute?'

'You should write an article about that,' said Dhrubo, placing a pink jujube in his mouth.

'I'm a sub-editor, Dada, I don't get to write.'

'You should write a play about it,' said Miss Chitol, encouraging of her brother's talents.

Anando had, in fact, long contemplated such a play.

'Inefficiency *is* the cause of corruption, therefore privatisation is the need of the hour,' Dhrubo came in, sounding like an op-ed piece that appeared nowadays in the papers.

'Your private sector will not run any unprofitable lines, Dada, they will just stop them,' Miss Chitol countered.

'And they *should*. To save the rest of the Railways.'

'And who was talking about the "romance of the branch line" as we were coming here? For you it may be only romance, Dada, but for many it is a necessity. How will people or things get anywhere?'

'You are mixing issues,' said Dhrubo, flustered already. 'You see, wherever there is demand, the lines can be made profitable by the private sector. Where there isn't, it will find another way. That is efficiency.'

'The Indian Railways *does* make a profit,' responded Miss Chitol, herself a little flustered. 'The passenger fares are subsidised by the Railways. Grains, sugar, dal, fruit, coal – the transport of many essential items are subsidised. For your kind information, the government does not subsidise anything. The Railways bears everything.'

'And everything suffers. Even the wagons are outdated – when it is clear that the need of the hour for coal is bottom-discharge wagons.'

'No more outdated than the rest of the country. Probably less outdated.'

'Have you seen the figures? One of the lowest staff efficiencies in the world! The wage bill is half the expenses.'

The note of callous triumph in his voice surprised Miss Chitol. He spoke of the Railways as though it had nothing do with him, as though his father had not put in decades of service in its cause, as though his sister was not now an employee inflating the wage bill – as though his own education had not been supported by that wage bill.

'You see,' he continued, 'if you try to do everything, you cannot do anything properly. Printing, manufacturing, schools, hospitals.'

'And what is wrong with that?' she said, raising her voice to meet his challenge. 'The hospitals help the staff, and help outsiders too.'

'And where was the hospital when we needed it most?'

Dhrubo's face was flushed.

A silence fell. She felt it necessary to break it.

'And the schools are better than many government schools. I think you have forgotten that we went to railway schools. Just because you left doesn't mean you forget.'

'I left?' Dhrubo said, dropping his voice. 'Or was I sent away? What about you? Did you leave or were you sent away?'

Miss Chitol felt the heat of liquor rising up in her.

'I can't remember, Anando, can you? Did I leave or was I sent away? Did anybody ask if I wanted to go?'

'And who stayed?' said Anando in a flat tone, as if to keep his voice from cracking. 'Neither of you knows what those years were like.'

He stood up, poured himself half a glass of neat rum.

'I thought this was supposed to be a celebration,' he said and walked out of the door.

'Stop drinking now,' Miss Chitol shouted after him, fearing an onset of mood.

'See what you made him do,' she said to Dhrubo, who went off to pee, slamming the door behind him. Struggling to extricate his sacred thread to loop it over his right ear before commencing the impure activity, he gave up with a half-grunt and sat down on the pot.

Left alone, Miss Chitol quietly downed her drink and tossed a yellow jujube into her mouth as chaser.

She opened the door to check on Anando.

'You are both selfish and *shala akebare* hypocrite,' she heard him say from somewhere.

She stood in the doorway, listening to footsteps.

'And my job was to stick around my whole life and look after whoever needs looking after?' she said with a mix of hurt and anger that she wanted everybody to hear for all times and nobody to ever hear.

The caretaker did. She caught him watching, and averted her eyes, which had welled up.

She wished she had her own room.

Early next morning she wrapped herself in her new shawl and set out on a walk. Sunlight had barely broken through the dewy air. She felt a vivifying leakiness in her nose. Turning off the main road, she went into a gentle uphill path bordered by dark elongated trees astir with birds. She strode away to wherever the path and its forks took her, occasionally passing women with loads on their heads. The mornings belonged to women and work and birds who kept them company. After a while she arrived at a big grassy clearing spattered with wild blue flowers. Walking through them she felt a creeping elation and although she wanted to slow down and savour them elation took her faster. Her breath became heavy and purposeful; her muscles were alive to their ache. On the far side she came upon a cluster of rocks. Beyond them the mountain dropped off into a cliff. She stood there orienting herself to the topological shock. Clouds floated down in the valley. In the distance she could see the mirage of the waking range. When she lowered her gaze she noticed the soft glint off the permanent way.

She sat down among the rocks, watching the wild flowers and the contented trees. Gradually the birds made themselves available to her. Magpies and treepies with fabulous tails and harsh calls, smartly dressed busy birds she suspected were thrushes. Her body cooled off; the exertion of her walk spread through her. She closed her eyes and began to cry in long streams. She didn't realise she had these many tears in her. They struck up a conversation with that deep part of her that alas remained always in touching distance, the part that could be prodded like a nerve ending, the part that needed absolution. She suddenly felt grateful to P. He had allowed her to consider that her instincts, her life, were the result of causes, like physics, as if her role in them had nothing to do with her per se. Even if she held it false, it was comforting, it was kind. In the end what becomes our truth is a negotiation.

When she finished crying she got up and prepared to return. She heard people coming, and noticed a handwritten signboard near the rocks. Suicide Point.

On the way back she stopped to buy cherries.

Her brothers were in bleary-eyed repose in the garden, waiting for the caretaker to produce tea.

None of them could read the other's mood properly. Each seemed a touch offended that the others too harboured hidden feelings.

'*Eesh!*' said Dhrubo, pulsing a pit out of his mouth. 'These cherries are like gooseberries.'

Anando held his stomach and laughed. It didn't come out perfectly.

Late that morning they were to journey back out to the railway station, from there to the junction, thence to different parts of the country.

The mongrel sensed departure. He hung helplessly about Anando's heels. 'Ei Vibhishana, will you come to my wedding?' he asked the dog, who responded with a morose blink of the eyes.

Otherwise the air felt light and the trip perhaps even a success. The three engaged in an involved conversation about how many layers of clothes to wear and how much water to carry. They discussed, at equal length, how much tip to leave the caretaker and how much the cook; in each instance they erred on the side of the conservative.

Miss Chitol prepared an envelope with a little money that she would slip to Anando. Three pieces of jujube they had saved for the journey and she triple-looped a rubber band on the mouth of the packet.

'Oh ho, we will miss the train!' shouted Dhrubo, racing past her into the taxi.

That was the tail end of spring.

In peak summer the Chitols met again, in Calcutta. Notun Dida had died.

She expired of old age in a relative's house. Her age was estimated at ninety. She had seen a lot, everybody said, as a neutral observation and as tribute – she had seen a lot.

Miss Chitol last saw her two years ago, while she was still in the old-age home. Despite its respectable reputation, the air held the damp weight of river, illness and cumulative age. Dida's teeth had left her entirely. By then she had given up paan. She only ate boiled rice with salt and oil, sometimes mashing into them lightly fried neem leaves or neem flowers. She drank the juice of neem leaves. It was neem that kept her alive, she told Charu; bitter things were good for one, that was the truth of life. Did she know that Rabindranath Tagore drank a cup of neem juice every day? That is why his mind shone like the sun! She asked Miss Chitol if she had ever met Tagore, why didn't she try to see him now, overlooking the fact that he had died half a century ago. She referred to Dhrubo, Anando and their father all by their father's name. But when she asked how her father was keeping, Miss Chitol was certain it was her father she was referring to, and she did not have the heart to remind her. She spoke about the little garden in their railway quarters, the time the police had come and trampled over her plants like demons.

Miss Chitol gifted her a sari, and money, which had become sporadic from them to her after the end of the family pension.

Following the visit, she told Dhrubo to see Dida more often, since he lived in the same city. 'Very convenient,' he had replied.

Now there is nobody left to die but us, each of the Chitol siblings thought to themselves at different stages after Dida's passing.

The death haunted Miss Chitol. It left her with the suspicion that a long life could be worse than a short one. Or was it so? Was it her limited imagination that relegated Dida thus?

For a long time afterwards Notun Dida appeared before her, professing to like certain things. They were simple things, oranges and lichu, bakul and joba flowers, the sound of children playing, a short nap in the afternoon, I like them very much she confessed, after which she laughed guiltily and wholeheartedly, baring her soaked red mouth.

7

By the haemoglobin of the atmospheric pressure

The television rose from a plinth and had its own gates, as a good temple should. After their morning bath, the most pious of the working women lit incenses and anointed the wooden shutters with vermilion. It was their appeals to the management committee that yielded the donated set, and at the first sighting of the divine couple they closed their eyes and brought their palms together. Not all the working women were pious. Many were rank entertainees, some were scoffers. But none could stay away. By the start of the telecast the recreation room was packed.

It was an episode heavy on husband worship. In Ayodhya, a weeping Kaushalya appraised her daughter-in-law Sita as one whose name shall always be foremost in the annals of husband worship, moving to tears Sita's mother, Sunayana, who instructed her wordless daughters and nieces to establish their own milestones of husband worship by devoting themselves to their mothers-in-law. For the husbands were not around. One brother had devotedly followed Ram and Sita into exile, another had retreated to ascetic life from shame, the fourth rarely got airtime; their father had died of grief after setting in motion the chain of dharma.

And in the forests of Chitrakoot, Sati Anasuya, wife of Sage Atri, so great a tapasvini that she had diverted a stream of the Ganga to this drought-ridden land by the ferocity of her meditations, taught Sita that it was all but the fruit of her single-minded service of her husband – for to the woman of supreme character the husband was the supreme lord.

Whether touched by the nobility of the women, saddened, inspired, galled or outraged by their plight, whether scarred by experience or yearning for it, at some point or another each working woman had a tear in her eye.

As soon as it was finished Miss Chitol walked out into the sun-sozzled drizzle, the better to take advantage of the roads wide open after Sunday *Ramayan*.

Jackals getting married, she thought to herself in Bengali. *Shiyaler biye*. That was what her grandmother said when it rained in the sun. *Nagda paus*, naked rain, smiled Vatsala Tai at her in Marathi.

She made her purchases from Hulyalkar snacks mart and waited for the bus. When she got to Juna Tanki, the clouds were back in place. She attempted to climb the four storeys of Jhunjhunwala Building at the pace of her memory. She no longer had the fleetness of that time, and when she rang the bell her face was a grinning huff of self-acknowledgement.

Bhagmati Prasad wore a harried grin of her own. She was in her nightie.

'Look at me. Took bath before *Ramayan* but did I get the chance to wear my sari? Arre oh,' she called out to her husband, 'Charu has come. Who gets time to breathe in the morning – oh ho, what is that in your hand, there is no formality. But now that you have got it, let us see – sabudana vada.'

Miss Chitol knew her aunt, who observed the Shravan abstinences, would appreciate compatible fare.

'Sabudana vada?' Her mama walked in clad in a sleeveless white vest and pyjamas. 'Let us have it now with tea while it is raining.'

'And who will make the tea?' said Bhagmati Prasad. 'Who has been doing this and that since morning so that even changing out of this maxi has not been possible? Why don't you put on something before you start sneezing on everyone.'

'*I* will make it, Mami,' said Miss Chitol.

'The problem is neither of you ladies knows how to make a rain special,' said her uncle. 'I will make it.'

'All for show. Are you listening, Charu? If it was just me he would have never offered. All for show.'

They watched him go into the kitchen.

'He has improved,' she added, dropping her voice. 'Last week he even pressed my feet.'

They heard and smelled him pound ginger and every whole spice going. They drank the tea, as planned, with the sabudana vada, while it rained, and it went down so well they decided to have another round.

'So, have you found anyone?' Bhagmati Prasad raised the subject with a nonchalant laugh over the second cup.

'Maybe he can help you.' She turned towards her husband, who did not respond.

'Tell her about it,' she urged him.

'I told you that won't be suitable,' he replied.

'*Offo*, there is nothing that can't be overcome.'

'Oh ho, how many times do I tell you?'

'At least, *tell* her about it. Is there any harm in that? Am I telling you to call the pandit and set up the *havan*?'

Miss Chitol did not discourage her aunt; at the same time she glanced at her uncle with a knowing half-smile, as though she was only humouring her.

'A very good family, I can tell you that much,' Bhagmati Prasad continued. 'I know them personally. What's more, he is a doctor.'

'A doctor for animals,' Jagdish Chandra Prasad corrected her.

'What is wrong with that? People who cure the sick are doctors. Aren't they? Are we any different from animals? Am I wrong, Charu?'

'Hardly any different.'

'Exactly. They want a Bihari girl, yes. But you are also after all a daughter of Bihar. That part you leave to me. And now can I tell you something? Keep this to yourself so other girls don't get to know.'

'Won't tell a soul.'

'*Lovely*-looking boy.'

'Let us see the photos, Mami.'

'That I don't have yet. Trust me, he could get a part in *Ramayan*.'

'As Jatayu maybe,' remarked Jagdish Chandra Prasad.

'*Offo*, what is your problem? Are you her uncle or her enemy? The girl is interested and you just pour water on everything.'

'You are not ready to understand,' he replied. 'How many times do I tell you, they don't want anyone independent.'

'Oh,' Miss Chitol said, grasping the implications. 'Maybe Mama is right.'

'Oh, Charu, *independent* and all that is all fine. There is more to life than a job. In the end everyone needs someone to fight with.'

'Fight?' said Jadgish Chandra Prasad. 'I knew you weren't watching properly. What about *pativrata*?'

'To devote herself to a husband also she will first need a husband!' Bhagmati Prasad exclaimed.

'But, Mami, Sita really comes into her own once she is free of one,' said Miss Chitol, and they all laughed.

Nobody pressed her further. And she wondered if they ought to have, whether she ought to have been the type they ought to have pressed. It was to do with her departure. Leaving, she had learned, sent messages that were all too clear. At any rate, the forfeiture of independence was a lousy expectation so what use wishing to be pressed?

Suddenly the day seemed to yawn out before Miss Chitol. Fifty minutes past twelve and nowhere to go.

When she got back to the hostel, passing her former room, she saw Bornali quietly doing her embroidery. 'Why don't you teach me?' she asked.

The following Sunday she went out to see her old friend Nalini. It was a different house from the one she had briefly sheltered in, since Nalini was now married, and in fact they were to have met not at the marital home, but at the cinema.

Nalini's bland as a boiled pea husband was on his way out as she arrived. He gave Miss Chitol the impression, once more, that he regarded her with a hint of judgement, a part of his wife's disreputable past as a smart girl. A shade of relief on his face indicated he was getting out at the right time. Inside, an attritional battle over the baby's congestion was in progress. Nalini's in-laws wished to cure it with onion juice, which she believed upset his stomach; besides Nalini had already put him on homeopathic pills that would do the job.

The baby's cheeks quivered each time he coughed; his large absorptive eyes had a dull glaze to them. In Nalini's eyes, too, Miss Chitol could detect the strain over the line of treatment. She tried to feed her child roti, tenderly puckering her own mouth as she did, then lightly working her jaw as he reluctantly accepted it. The in-laws retreated into another room for their delayed naps. The baby fell asleep, exhausted.

'I feel bad about today,' said Nalini, in the outbreak of quiet. 'You should have gone with someone else.'

'Arre, Nalli, what's the big deal in a movie?'

'It is a big thing for me! I have not gone to one in over a year. Sold the tickets?'

'Of course.'

'Profit or cost price?'

'Am I a professional blacker?'

Nalini shook her head in admonition.

'I have not slept in the last I don't know how long,' she sighed, stretching out. 'When everyone else is asleep, that is the only time I can sleep. But when they sleep' – she shot her eyes towards the room her in-laws lay in – 'that is the only time I really want to be awake. I can at least think without being watched.'

She tossed her head back and reminisced about their days representing shoes, their sessions at New Deluxe: how free we were, Charu, we were like birds!

The baby stirred beside them. Miss Chitol placed her hand on his chest, the way she used to with Anando and then with Biru, feeling the little ribcage waning and waxing against her palm.

The baby was still asleep when she left. Before going, she left a wooden toy beside him, kissed her finger and lightly touched it to his.

The evening was muggy. She felt tired. She considered a taxi, but the five-rupee loss on the movie tickets weighed on her. And yet these complications have their own comforts, she reflected in the bus on the way back. She thought of the Bangla word *shongshar*. The world, the earth, family, domestic life. She thought of the word often, a word with a large meaning.

Vacancies had arisen. Miss Chitol was thinking hard about how to live her life; indeed, how life should be lived. *Interests* were a part of this. Embroidery did not take; but it did make her more efficient at attaching her sari falls. To the cinema she was reluctant to go alone for fear of being touched or *pchewed-pchewed*. She fared better with music. She did not expect misbehaviour at recitals; indeed, by going solo she could embrace her inexperience.

This interest Miss Chitol approached with commitment. Recalling the Juna Tanki mornings, she tried to catch Vividh Bharati's Sangeet

Sarita capsule on her father's transistor radio. If she learned of a free show, she made sure to collect a pass. In the newspapers she read features on the artistes; in queues she kept an ear pricked for useful chatter. At first, the audience at these events seemed full of connoisseurs, who were intimate with the gharanas, knew the words to thumris, how to count the tala with their hands. When an artiste announced a raga, they extended appreciative murmurs or outright applause. The intimidation quickly left her. She noticed among the connoisseurs pretenders, also dilettantes, group-goers, and neophytes like her. Then she learned how to stop looking at others, and eventually herself. On occasion she felt so entirely possessed of all that the musicians intended and more, she said to herself, yes, yes, *this* is what we live for.

This, each time, is what she aimed for, and this, certainly, was the hope with which she set out one evening for the open-air theatre Rang Bhavan, a short walk from her office, draped in a deep blue bandhani, one of her 'going out' saris.

She reached while the sound-check was still on, at the hour the parakeets flew above in formations to wherever it was they went before dusk. The arena was only half full when the opening Dhrupad performance began. The second act, a pyrotechnical percussion fusion – mridangam, ghatam, tabla – made an atmosphere of wild virtuoso mischief, of come one, come all, and people did keep coming, so that by the time the crescent moon climbed into the sky, flapped out of sight now and then by large bats, even the VIPs had assumed their sofa seats up front, and the great sitar ustad and the great shehnai ustad took the stage to rousing applause from a packed theatre.

Despite her slight elevation, wriggling her chair this way and that, Miss Chitol could barely see their faces through the dot matrix of heads. But the dignity of their bearing, their shining spotlit silks, wet already, she marvelled at that.

'What happened?' one ustad asked the other, who tuned his instrument; the spectators laughed and clapped. 'It must be said, this a very large-hearted audience,' remarked the other. 'We haven't so much as started playing yet.' The ustads continued bantering, the assembly laughed and applauded, each person personally honoured by the exchange. The maestros let the banter taper off to announce Nand Kalyan, to further applause.

In the first plucks of the strings that emerged from silence like consciousness, in the first blows into the shehnai that expressed the inexpressible, it was clear even to the amateur that these sounds, the very sounds before they reached melody, were like nobody else's. She was aware that Nand was meant to be a restless raga. But how carefully the ustads waited on it, pulling here, dwelling there, cueing here, teasing there, carefully exploring each facet of its restlessness. Waiting and releasing, they becalmed the restless heart and yet, paradoxical, restless was this construction of the wait. Why, felt Miss Chitol, as the notes bore her along, without the wait everything is hollow, without meaning – oh why must I resist the waiting? These journeys we navigate every day, failing to recognise in them the exquisite. My heart, one pulling the strings of my heart, the other blowing into my soul bellows – the sadness, the richness, the pleasure of the waiting and the wandering, we forfeit all for the mundane. Now the tabla picked up, bringing tempo, improvisation and *taans*, and the thundershowers of notes and emotions soaked her, and the play of the maestros soared and soared, intricacy begetting intricacy, expertise expertise, crescendo crescendo and she wondered whether this was the condition they called divinity.

When they finished, and the applause subsided, the ustads bantered a moment. Then a great silence prevailed. They did not announce the next raga. With extreme gentleness and reverence the sitar plucked, awakening now a deeper sublime. To some aficionados the early notes revealed enough for a *wah!*, and halfway through the alap, as the melody began to surface and gesture at its grandeur, Miss Chitol too intuited, this being the finale, that it was Raga Bhairavi. A quiet shudder ran through her. *Was* it, in fact, divinity she experienced in the music? Was it not like the shivers of fearlessness she could feel while looking into Ma Durga's eyes? She felt the devotion to the notes the way she sensed devotion in her grandmother's cold baths before dawn. It was the cultivation of surrender, of total faith and immersion in the rules and traditions of one's life. But, no, worry not about restrictions, expand as the ustads are, enlargen to infinity, go beyond, far beyond, glorious Bhairavi. The mellower the maestros played, the more majestic the emanation. From the depths of her she felt her own power drawn out by the miraculous notes. Her closed eyes shed shy tears. The restrained culmination brought the performance to a finish, and as the tremendous standing ovation reverberated in the open arena and coursed through them all, she wished she could rush on to the stage and touch the ustads' feet.

It was in this state of ecstasy that Miss Chitol saw N again. For, yes, she did see N again. She felt no hope-he-doesn't-see-me anxiety, no desire to turn away. He too saw her – for he had left his companion, and was coming round towards her. To cut out awkwardness, he bowed obsequiously and pretended to greet a VIP. Both smiled. He looked much as he used to, more substantial. He had filled out, perhaps worked on posture. Same hair.

'This was … ' Miss Chitol's moist eyes completed the sentence.

'What heaven must be like,' N finished it nevertheless.

By the way he looked at her she could tell her tears had left a mess on her face. N's companion came along. As they shuffled out together with the crowd she dropped back, fished out a handkerchief, deftly applied saliva to it and rubbed her undereyes.

Outside, after a quick exchange in Gujarati, the friend took his leave.

'He's going to the airport,' said N.

'Aren't you? You were always ready to go to the airport.'

'Times have changed,' N smiled.

He added after a moment: 'In the old days when people used to travel by ship, do you know what they used to do? The person on the ship used to hold one end of a streamer and the person on land used to hold another. As the ship left the dock they used to move it up and down together to say bye.'

She found this lovely.

'Which way are you going?' he asked.

'To the station.' She pointed in the direction of the Western line.

'We have met after so long, should we walk?'

'Why not?' she said, surprised at her welcomingness, as though his disappearance had been nothing.

They came clear of the concert crowd, but the music continued to resound inside them.

'My hair is still on end,' she said, rubbing her forearm. 'I have been going to concerts but this was something.'

'I wanted it to never end,' said N. 'I can still feel it in me.'

'It was as though Ma Bhairavi was right before me. She's there, she exists!'

'Was there any doubt?'

'Why do you say that?' she asked, he couldn't tell whether in sincerity or provocation. So he walked on with a nonplussed smile, as though some things did not yield well to questioning.

'When we need it most who do we go to?' he took it on regardless. 'When Arjun needs help, it is Krishna he turns to. When you are in trouble, where do you go?'

She considered the point seriously.

'I do have prayers. When we were small, our grandmother used to make us pray. As I grew older I started to wonder who I was praying to. It seemed like cheating. Now I think the important thing is not who or what you pray to but who and what you pray for.'

He appeared to admire this.

'Without a supreme power there is nothing for us to reach for and touch,' he proposed. 'Nothing to hold on to.'

'Ya, it is an inspiring idea,' she conceded.

'When musicians talk about the divine and the oneness of God you believe them. If there remains any doubt they remove it when they play.'

'Correct!'

They had started at a saunter but worked up an energetic pace, as on the very first time they had met. At Queen's Road they turned not towards Marine Lines, but Churchgate, the farther station.

'I thought I would eat at Satkar before taking the train,' she said. Neutrally stated, but he registered, of course, that it was where they had once gone for fried idli.

'Me too.'

This drew a smile from her.

'I haven't seen you in a sari before,' he said. 'It's nice.'

'Because it's from your state?'

'That, naturally. Also because there is a dot under your eye that matches the design.'

'Oh!'

She stopped to reach for her kerchief. She was grateful it retained the salivary moisture, saving her from repeating the inelegant act.

She angled her face away and pressed the hanky into her skin.
'Gone?'
'Not really. Let it be, na. They call these beauty spots.'
It broke their brief eye contact.
'So what do you do nowadays?' he asked as they hit their stride again.
'I work in the Railways. I'm a clerk in the personnel branch.' She paused. 'Senior clerk.'
'You! Clerk? I thought you would have become a writer of some kind.'
She felt more complimented than she could reveal. It gave her the impetus to remark: 'I did not realise you thought about me.'
Her delivery was not sharp, or needy; there was an underlying wistfulness, which found an echo in his reply.
'There was a lot of time to think.'
'And you?' she asked, livening up. 'You are a ... share broker?'
'Just look at that. I think you would have become a writer and you think I would have become a broker?'
'Are *you* a writer then?'
He paused a second.
'I'm in business. It's not so bad. Saw the new *India Today*? The socialist ways are changing. Ordinary people are making themselves millionaires now. But there is one problem in the business world.'
'And what is that?'
'My heart is not in it.'
Miss Chitol considered the having of one's heart in something a terribly redeeming trait. She wondered: had his disappearance meant that his heart had not been in it? She did not voice this thought.
'And what is your heart in?' she enquired.
'My heart, what to say, is ... waiting.'
'The waiting is very long,' she sighed. 'But I was thinking about this during Nand. We underrate the wait. Without the wait everything would feel hollow.'
He nodded in recognition, and was now humming, at very low volume, 'Mera Saaya', set to Nand. She caught it. She did not comment on it, but hummed just as softly; they were barely audible to each other as they got to the station sounds, and the scents and sizzles of burji pao on the pavement.

'Actually, I write lyrics,' he confessed as they climbed up the short flight of stairs to cross through. 'Just for myself.'

'Serious lyrics or … '

'Both.'

'Can you still do it?' she asked. The bright in her eyes was on.

'Of course.'

At the top of the station steps on the far side, N stopped, stood tall and declaimed: 'Wait, wait, WAIT!'

He plopped down, crossed his legs and shook his long fingers about.

'You see, the coefficient of the *linea-ah*. Is juxtaposition. By the haemoglobin of the atmospheric pressure in the *country*!'

Then he bounced up right there among the chuckling night commuters, into the zu-zu-zu-zu-zu-zu-zu-zu-zu dance, kicking out his long legs with a comic flair equal to the hero's own.

8

Jackals

So he shows up after nine years and they fall in step as though there was never a break. The longer they walk the greater she feels the outrage of his disappearance. She wants to raise it but, protective of her feelings, she cannot bring herself to – and then he himself does.

It was the day she visited him at the godown in Chinchbunder. Not the stone warehouses over the tracks, reminders of imperial times, this more a tall garage, narrow and deep, fitted with a mezzanine. His father had built up the business at a time the flow of material in and out of the docks was strong. Nimish sat at the mouth of the building like a man craving transience. Thus the foldable chair, thus its position beside and not behind the desk, his legs drawn in to avoid the run of commodity-bearing handcarts. If not for the stroke, his father would still be here, managing transitional boxes in the lifestream of commerce, while he would be out trying something. Now he was here every day, keeping things ticking over.

His heart was not in the business, but Nimish was in his element. He relished the streets, the bustle of goods and people, things and where you got them. He walked her around the old commercial heartland: dyes and chemicals on Samuel Street, adhesives on Dariyasthan, in Katha Bazaar coir and ropes, in Dongri-Umerkhadi, where Muslim–Hindu were face to face, the trouble spots. At Imamwada near the Shia Kabristan, they looked at kites – his favourite festival, Makar Sankranti, was coming – caressing the smooth paper from Ahmedabad, running their fingers over the glass-enforced strings from Bareilly, debating with old Yusufbhai Patangwalla the merits of No. 30 vs No. 27, listening to him proclaim that there was nothing so good for the constitution as flying kites, fresh air flowing into the open mouth of the flyer looking upwards was how the Chinese treated tuberculosis.

There he was outwardly fine but coiled tight within and here she came along and by dint of nothing, by just being who she is, made him feel like his old self, *bindaas*.

Walking towards the stop for a bus to Grant Road station he told her.

'There was a reason I stopped coming.'

'Oh. What was that?'

'I had feelings for you. I did not know what to do.'

It seemed insincere – a shortcut, blowing hair out of his eyes. Yet a part of her resisted it in the way you only resist what you wish to be true. Her face turned a little hot, and her pleasure was not without vanity.

'How can that be?'

'It was.'

'You did not know what to do?'

'My parents. They were trying to arrange … '

This surprised her.

'At *that* time? With?'

'Just someone … But I did not have feelings for her.'

'Then?'

'I was very young then.'

'Not *so* young. But ya, quite young.'

'Ya, only now I realise how young I was.'

'Then?'

'I had feelings.'

'But … what *kind* of feelings?'

'Feelings I had not felt before.'

'About *me*?'

'Yes.'

'But … *what* about me?'

'You are making me shy.'

'Okay. But that was not a good way of showing it. Because … let it be, let it be.'

'What?'

'Let it be.'

'What, what?'

'Nothing, nothing.'
'What? What? Please, what?'
'Nothing, nothing. Nothing.'
'It was a mistake, na.'
'Let it be.'

She was transported back to her nights of unaccountable heartbreak, upsetting her balance. The bus was coming.

'Tomorrow I am leaving for the wedding,' she said, taking purposeful steps to greet it.

'I know,' he said.

'Don't come to the station,' she said, climbing on to the bus.

Miss Chitol had wanted to travel to the wedding in style. The Rajdhani Express was well above her Privilege Pass entitlements. So she had saved up and booked a full-fare berth, in the second-class air-conditioned sleeper, which cost her nearly three hundred rupees more than a seat in the chair car.

'*Chal*, bye,' said Nimish, seeing her off at Bombay Central, a cricket bag slung morosely over his shoulder.

'Okay, bye,' she said, and went inside.

She was escorted in style to her seat by an attendant. She looked out of the window to see if he was there to wave her goodbye. He was not.

But style continued non-stop. A uniformed bearer came by and asked whether she would like vegetarian or non-vegetarian for dinner, Indian or continental; another placed pillows and bedlinen in her berth; newspapers were at her disposal; over the speakers crackled a santoor composition, which she duly misidentified as Raga Hamsadhwani.

Her co-passengers seemed to be Rajdhani habitués. In a family of three, the man, a quiet bald Mr Chadha, head shape identical to belly shape, was an excise officer, Miss Chitol was informed by his wife, plump in a different, spreading way, who perhaps informed her only so that she could proceed to ask in northern Hindi: 'And where is your husband posted?' The questions mounted: 'Achha, you're in Railways? Very good, you can help us if we need anything!' 'Brother's marriage? How much older?' 'Younger? Oye hoye! How did that happen?' 'I saw your name on the chart, which side are you from?' – until she got busy ferrying food into the mouth of a son too old to be so fed, engrossed in a video game that opened up like an audio-cassette cover into two screens, which Miss Chitol could not help but deem misappropriated goods.

Two other passengers were a chartered accountant and a professional in the corporate sector. The men calmly perused work material, pausing to raise their eyes over the line of their glasses when conversing, as though that made them hear better. Occasionally they passed laboured jokes, punning for example on *safar* and suffer (in the days before the Rajdhani), or made stringent observations that showed their familiarity with the service: 'Looks like Surat will come seven minutes late.' And it was true, noted Miss Chitol, that the Rajdhani did not go places, places came to it. Places came and retreated and did not interfere while the Rajdhani proceeded unimpeded past the country silent beyond its double glazing.

When a rather wonderful dinner was served on thoroughly sound steel plates, one of the seasoned passengers remarked crisply that the crockery and cutlery were much finer in first class, to which the other pithily added that the food there was fresher too since cooked in the pantry car rather than uploaded from a base station, slightly puncturing her satisfaction. Thereafter the former observed that the number of coaches in second air-conditioned just kept growing and he had heard that three-tier air-conditioned coaches were in the works and who knew what would become of the Rajdhani in the days to come. This restored Miss Chitol's enthusiasm – perhaps she had caught her experience in the nick of time.

But it was going too fast. She had imagined she would read a book, perhaps write a letter, all these things that she thought she could accomplish in style. Rajdhani life was busier than she had bargained on: tea with hot snacks; soup with soup sticks and butter; dinner; ice cream; all the paraphernalia, trays, thermoses. And it was time for bed.

She arranged the bedlinen on her side upper berth. Drawing up the blanket she chided herself for not getting the most out of her journey. Far from reading or writing, she had not even eaten her chicken cutlet with French fries and boiled vegetables with sufficient relish, or appreciated enough the clean toilets, and here she was, preoccupied still.

In fact, in her heart of hearts Miss Chitol was downright disappointed. Why couldn't he have said a proper goodbye? Had she shown too much pride? He *had* come to see her off, after all. Yet what was that compared to the disappearance! she thought huffily. The other day Krunalini had told her, 'You're looking happy.' She was not being expressly joyous at the time, so Krunalini must have noticed something within, something wholesome. Why couldn't this guy be a little clearer? I *had* feelings, means what? What am I to think about *now*?

The night rolled away, veering between too cold and too warm, the air conditioning doubtless responding to the demands of seasoned passengers, one of whom was heard remarking on how temperate the Rajdhani climate used to be, and in no time the liveried bearer had appeared with morning tea and confirmed her breakfast choice of omelette, which arrived a short while later.

Afterwards, masticating on Rajdhani mouth freshener, the first seasoned passenger looked at his wristwatch and commented: 'Looks like NDLS will come five minutes late.'

'Even though fog was mild,' said the second, judiciously pouting at his own watch.

'All because of these damn outer Delhi signals,' returned the first, referring to the signals as though they were malign human beings.

It turned out he was wrong: NDLS came four minutes late.

Miss Chitol stepped outside into a sunless morning and a vivid January chill.

And there he was, N, to receive her. N? What! Was she hallucinating? What was this? A grand appearance to make up for the disappearance?

Further down the platform, she saw Anando, making his way towards her. Ablaze in blushes, she told her brother: 'This is my friend.'

'Hi! How are you!' said Nimish, proffering his right hand in his customary cheer. 'I have come for a wedding.'

'Oh, mine?' asked Anando.

'Uff, no!' laughed Miss Chitol, ushering them all along in the wrong direction. That, and the crowd of a big railway station, successfully kept them from a coherent conversation. Before she went off, he slipped her a note.

Anando's wedding was a shivering, heartfelt affair. Some of the elders were fantastically old, with wintered, pre-Partition faces of incalculable histories. Their Hindi was so far removed from the Hindis Miss

Chitol knew she thought at first it was Punjabi they spoke to her in. But their weathered glaucomal eyes and robust voices conveyed meanings clearly, and at the mehendi ceremony – to which she was invited, being a single girl on the boy's side – the women sang wedding songs to the accompaniment of a small dhol and handclaps in a way that brought tears to the eye whether or not one understood.

Naturally, there was controversy. A section of the girl's family had boycotted the wedding, not clear whether to do with internal feuds or the choice of the match. As far as Miss Chitol could tell, the bride was unruffled. Neither did facing the family she was marrying into seem to faze her. Was that their plainness, their inability to bring pomp and show to the occasion? She wondered whether the girl's composure was a mask, or indifference, or straight-up self-belief. Whatever it was, it was impressive, and in the usual dissection sessions Miss Chitol spoke up in her favour.

In the middle of things she met him in a park.

The sun had come out at last, casting brilliant rays on the grass. Dogs lay around like drying mats, men much the same. Women undid buttons on their cardigans and opened out their hair; the older ones propped themselves up on their sides and bellies and had a younger one press them, groaning with relief. Everywhere you could hear people thaw to life. Groups cracked open warm groundnuts, and the very sounds transmitted warmth. The park appeared to be intuitively segregated. A place for the working class; a place for the cricket boys; a place for elder middle-class men volubly agreeing to line them all up and shoot them in broad daylight, possibly about Khalistanis; another place for their spouses, their bhajans accompanied by fingerless, palms-only claps, turning them as mournful as grievers; a place for middle-class children and their ayahs; a place, among the trees, for couples.

They made a radiant, well-dressed pair, he in a muffler and a double-breasted blazer, the warmest clothing he had, she in a Garad silk, draped in the Bengali style, the Tibetan lady's shawl hung off her forearm, her lush yard-long hair worn open. They were in that late flush of youth where maturity has manifest itself, where the present moment is the very perfect ripening of the past and the future is long. Jokes and smiles trembled on their lips, attraction danced in their eyes, and when she threw her head back and laughed the delicate groove in the cartilage between her nostrils looked lovely; they seemed to bask not so much in the sun as the togetherness of their company.

'No, baba, I did not come by plane,' he reiterated.

'But there is no faster train than the Rajdhani. So how could you reach before me?'

'Arre,' he confessed at last. 'I came on the Rajdhani.'

'I thought about that! But how did you manage a ticket? You didn't book in advance.'

'A man can do anything when he wants to. And your railway employees are as "adjusting" as anyone else in the country.'

'I see. Let me speak to Vigilance when I return. Which coach were you? Chair?'

'I was somewhere or the other.'

'Why didn't you come to mine?'

'Because I wanted to see your expression when you saw me on the platform. That would have told the story.'

She could not bear for her expression now to tell the story. But it did. It lit up her dark eyes, her low, strong cheekbones, her full mouth. They were both of them players of a practical joke on the world.

'I thought just because you had disappeared you decided to suddenly appear,' she said after a few moments, unable to repress her smile. 'Like some hero.'

'Ya, but you disappeared too,' he said. 'That part we never discussed.'

'What do you mean?'

'I went back to look for you.'

'Where?'

'The reading room, where else?'

'Oh. When?'

'A few weeks later. Came many times.'

'And then?'

'Then I thought ... Let it be.'

'Arre, tell!'

'Let it be, let it be,' he continued, in imitation of her. She slapped his forearm.

'You knew where I worked.'

'I did not think you would like it if I came there.'

Miss Chitol felt this was perhaps the most respectful thing anybody had ever said to her. She had misjudged, at a level she had never quite admitted to herself, his character. She was filled with pride, in him, in herself.

She had forgotten to put on her watch while getting out, and turned his towards herself, holding his wrist as she did.

'Dada is acting very suspicious, asking many questions. Anando told him about you.'

'Arre wah! Maybe I should come and meet them.'

He had such an easy way with people, she could have even taken him, but for the scandal, the expectation.

'What I'm saying is I have to leave soon. They will be looking all over for the fiancy's sister, as everyone is calling me.'

They giggled.

'How is it going? Is he happy?' he asked.

'I think so. They already seem married in a way. He still feels so young to me.'

'Among the Vanias he would be past the normal age. In ours if you are not married by twenty-five, people think you are a defective piece.'

'So what happened to you?'

'They tried and tried. When I got to thirty, they gave up.'

She absorbed the information. These efforts in his past somehow diminished her. But why should they? At any rate, she too was approaching thirty and the point of no return.

'That is also my trump card,' he said, running his hand through his silky hair. 'Marriage will be such a bonus, they will not put up any objections.'

'I see,' she said. 'Objections are something I find very demeaning.'

She felt embarrassed all of a sudden.

'I mean,' she added in a clarificatory tone, 'when my parents got married, my father's sister was not allowed by her husband to attend the wedding. They had never even met my mother.'

They sat quietly in the crisp sunshine a few moments.

'There may be difficulties in a love marriage,' said Nimish with an adroit twinkle. 'But if we cannot overcome difficulties such as these what is the use of being in love?'

In the middle of the year Miss Chitol was herself married. There being nothing like a girl's home town or even a girl's home, the wedding was held in Bombay, before the commencement of Chaturmas, the four months during which the Gujaratis believed Lord Vishnu to be asleep under the hood of the serpent Sheshanag and unavailable to bless. It was an inter-community, inter-caste affair, like her mother and father's and her brother's, but in this case since she, the girl, was marrying down in varna, a *pratiloma* union, carrying the idea of a fallen woman degrading her caste. That was perhaps why she could not quite generate the enthusiasm she thought would have been appropriate from Kolkata Pishi, who had tried to matchmake for her as far as a decade ago. There was also the matter of language and culture, and that their side were not a people in thrall of business communities, even if Dhrubo was employed by one and liked espousing the ideals of capitalism. He was not disappointed, however, on hearing that there were no demands from the boy's side, that the expenses would not be significant, and that she intended to put to use the savings of their father's time.

They married like jackals on a day of chaotic pre-monsoon sunshowers. The wedding took the form of a simple ceremony and reception on the same evening at Kanji Khetsi Wadi near Victoria Terminus. That felt appropriate to her. A terminus where old things ended and new things began, where she had begun in the city half a life ago, near where she had first become a working woman at the Kings & Queens Shoe Emporium, and again as a clerk in the personnel department of the Central Railway. The venue allowed her colleagues to easily attend and it was their arrival, wet and laughing, that triggered her first tears of the evening.

The conventions and protocols were mixed and matched in a manner that could not have satisfied traditionalists on either side. For the ceremony she wore a red-and-white Gujarati Panetar gifted by the boy's side; but it was a Bengali priest who conducted the rituals, commandeered from the sidelines by Kolkata Pishi; and Dhrubo and Anando and their cousin Pablu huffed and cursed and puffed and swore in Bangla amid ululating tongues while bearing her aloft on a stool around the groom. For the reception, she changed into her mother's wedding-red Banarasi brocade, which had frayed and browned along a crease that was tucked into the pleats. The meal was strictly vegetarian; nevertheless the fajeto was an especial hit, and recipes were discussed.

For much of the evening, Miss Chitol, who had taught herself never to take things for granted, remained unsure about the day's outcome; yet she emerged from it fully wedded and almost in awe of this thing she was perpetrating upon her life.

She wasted little time in updating her nominee forms, and the Family Declaration Form for the pass section. She did not make a name-change application; her own had come to mean a lot to her. In any case, she believed his last name, Chitalia, from the village of Chital, was too close to hers to warrant substitution.

In the course of her submissions, a fellow clerk, herself recently wed, laughingly offered her a choice of Mrs or Smt for title. Trying them on, saying them aloud a few times – Missis, Shrimati, Missis, Shrimati – writing them out in abbreviation before her name, assessing the aesthetic consonance of each, she made her choice, and in this way into the files and the next stage of her life stepped Smt Chitol.

9

The Chitalias

Stepped into a plate of vermilion placed outside the door on the wedding night and carried her footprints inside. That signified Lakshmi had come into the house. The following week the couple set out to honeymoon in the southern monsoon, by the link express, there being no materialisation of the much-proposed coastal line, where thunderous rains lashed the ardent swaying coconut trees.

When they returned Smt Chitol's footprints had barely lightened.

'Do you have flat feet?' her mother-in-law enquired.

The women were bent over the red stains, set into the grey Shahbad stone tiles, two feet by two feet, the loose strands of hair on their heads almost touching.

'It's my fault,' the mother-in-law said. 'Everything happened in such a rush. I should have laid out a white sheet. That way we could have kept the prints and the floor would have been saved.'

'I will take off the marks,' Smt Chitol assured her. She hoped nail-polish remover would do the job.

'Instead of kumkum some families keep a vessel filled with grain at the threshold,' her mother-in-law continued. 'The bride kicks it over so the rice spills into the house.'

'I would have found it difficult to strike food with my feet,' Smt Chitol responded, tagging on half a laugh. 'I will remove the marks somehow.'

Her face turned the same shade as her footprints.

If there had been a girl's home, if they had wedded the proper Bengali way, that is where she would have spent the wedding night. Among the Gujaratis it was not so. The bride went with the groom.

This point of order, raised by Pishi before the wedding, had not exercised her then.

As the days passed Smt Chitol wanted a girl's home, she wanted back the extra night, she wanted to enter the marital home holding a wriggling fish like her aunts had.

Memories of her cousin Pulki di's *bidai* in Jhansi came to her, the parents and elders and younger sisters and nieces weeping, Pulki di herself weeping, tossing rice grain over her shoulder and bravely not looking back. It is not a kind idea. When Sunayana told Kaushalya before her dutiful daughters and nieces that her relationship with them ended on the day of their wedding, Smt Chitol had felt offended on their behalf. Yet, maybe the *bidai* helps, she now thought. Without a departure an arrival felt counterfeit. She had not prepared for being turned into Lakshmi, and from there into a floor-stainer.

Sensations of adjustment accompanied her every moment, anxiety hummed under her breath. She had disrupted the settings. Upon the Gujarati-speaking house her presence had foisted Hindi, and she could feel their relief when they slipped back into Gujarati. She attempted gamely to speak the language.

Bringing in the milk packets inside one morning, she asked her mother-in-law for the '*kachi*' to cut it open, reaching in her linguistic confusion for not the Hindi but the Bangla word. '*Katar*,' her mother-in-law said with a correcting smile. 'We call that *katar*.' The Gujarati word '*katar*' put her in mind of the Bangla word '*kator*', sorrowful, and she knew its power came from the Tagore poem she had memorised as a girl for the Bengali Literary Society, in which there was no sadness in the world like that of the penniless boy with the *kator* eyes who cannot buy the lathi he covets. She thought of the phenomenal rain over the haat in the poem; in her mind's eye she saw the haat in Bhombalpur, and a moment later that seemed to dislocate her entire life, she became again the daughter-in-law who had just uttered the word for scissors in the wrong language.

She resolved to put down word lists in her diary so her brain failed her less. A river develops an ease with all the terrain it traverses, that is what the wise say. And it was true that Smt Chitol's familiarity was rising.

When she turned into the building, the first of three wings in the housing society, she exchanged greetings with Ojasbhai, tucked in beneath the staircase with a pencil behind one ear, a stub of coloured chalk behind the other, a master of repair and alteration, able to stretch garments not just across siblings but generations, just as Eknath the cobbler outside the main entrance did with shoes. She grew acquainted with the warps on the wooden steps, edged with metal strips which performed, like the tailor and the cobbler, the life-extending function. As she came on to the landings, she was familiar to the pigeons in the courtyard congregating around the abandoned stone mill, once used to crush wheat, now a receptacle for pigeon grain, so that the more acerbic residents called the society 'Kabutar Chawl'. A middle-class chawl, however, whose inhabitants had never laboured in the cloth mills. Babubhai Terraces was the name, and Babubhai's son Lalubhai lived like an ageing dynast, facing west, atop one of the terraces of the three buildings.

The nameplates on the doors, she learned, bore a variety of caste names, albeit heavy on Vania. The caste mix, like the RCC construction – the Terraces claimed to be the first chawl in south Bombay built from reinforced concrete, half a century ago – was once a marker of modernity. All but two homes were Gujarati. A few had seen inter-caste Arya Samaj weddings, resulting from building romances. All, except the odd Jain, were Hindu. All were vegetarian. Some, not just the Jains, eschewed onion and garlic. Some tested the limit with eggs. Alcohol did pervade certain homes. A few took in non-Gujarati brides.

Walking past the doors and windows, past the heaps or neat rows of footwear, she shot a quick glance into each home, capturing through a frame or an overheard sentence a sense of its life and language, until she arrived, with an almost similar curiosity, at her own.

From the door of each flat you could see the entire house, and maybe that is why the flats were called rooms. The living-cum-bed, beyond it the kitchen-cum-dining, beyond that a *mori* or washing area, which over time the majority of residents had built up into a tiny bathroom with a tiny overhead tank and a tiny latrine, releasing them from use of the common toilet, and in this respect the Terraces had nearly ceased to be a chawl.

In these 325 square feet the four dwelled: Kantibhai Rasikbhai Chitalia, Rakshaben Kantibhai Chitalia, Nimish Kantibhai Chitalia and Charulata Chitol.

Coming out from her first meeting with the family, Nimish had remarked, 'You must be thinking you won't have privacy.' She could tell at once he did not want her to set a condition about the living arrangements – and given the physical condition of his father with the gleaming eyes and cheerful jokes, she too felt that would not have been the ideal thing to do. Not right at the start, anyway. Besides, there was much to be said for the downtown location. She could reach VT in twenty minutes by bus, saving at least ninety minutes of daily commute. They were in walking distance of Charni Road station. Marine Drive was twenty minutes away on foot. People would do anything for a location like this.

Nimish proceeded to tell her with a rehearsed brightness, touching in its own way, about an amendment that had proved successful in these flats. Thus came up the plywood partition in the front room, fitted with a sliding door, laminated in 'Burma Teak'; she helped pick the shade.

The marital bedroom so created measured six and a half feet by ten feet. In a corner stood a slim steel almirah with mirror that her mama had gifted her to begin a new life. Wedged beside it was a mini clothes horse from Calcutta, identical in design to the one in Bhombalpur, which she had chosen as Dhrubo's gift for her. In the mornings she rolled up the night mattress (seventy-six inches long and fifty-two inches wide, meant to flatten out with use to fifty-four inches) and placed it on the almirah; from the base of the clothes horse she removed the day *chatai* and rolled it out. The window gave on to the corridor and funnelled in breeze that wended its way over the foot and a half above the partition, left free for precisely that reason. The gap leaked their privacies; on the other side of the partition her in-laws slept on perpendicular divans used for seating in the day. The small fan fitted into the ceiling was thankfully noisy, the grilled kind found in trains, and in fact their bedroom reminded her of nothing so much as a train compartment.

When she came home from work, Smt Chitol briefly collected herself in the compartment. If she returned a little after her usual time, her mother-in-law asked: 'Got late today?'

What subtle phrasing! Was it a question at all? Was it concern? A pleasantry? Why should she feel monitored? In any case, she had lived under some form of monitoring all her life. Having adjusted into her uncle's home, and thereafter out of it, then from one paying-guest room to another with each of its rules, to the working women's hostel and its rules, she knew adjustments were ahead.

Whenever she fielded the query she thought back to the meeting, as if to reconfirm that she hadn't misunderstood. That, too, was something modern – a *meeting*, as if among equals, not a viewing, not an audition. She had asked Kantibhai, in formal Hindi, 'How are you?' He responded in English with a twinkling smile: 'I am suffering very happily, thank you.' He clenched and unclenched his fingers to show his progress. 'If you put a flute in my hand, I would be just like a young Krishna.' She would come to see that these were stock lines; nevertheless, they had settled her nerves. Rakshaben mentioned how, before the stroke, she turned out khakras and fafras and whatnot from this kitchen for a neighbourhood store; it seemed several women in the society did that. That assured her that Rakshaben was not averse to working women.

Nimish was right, his parents had put up no objections. They had only one condition: no non-veg. She did not challenge it. Her hostel, too, was vegetarian. Even if women were subjected to higher standards of purity, she knew they were aware of Nimish's fondness for chicken, so it was unlikely she would be restricted outside. Instead, she took the chance to confirm: 'I will continue to work.' 'Done,' he smiled. A slightest moment's hesitation and the very word *done* led her to suspect that the issue might have been discussed. Earning from home was a different proposition: was that the true meaning of the loaded question/non-question?

Meanwhile her shortcomings were coming to light. Although not essential, it would have been ideal had she the enthusiasm for Krishna seva: changing his clothes, washing his little silver cows. In the afternoon she was not around to rock Bal Krishna to sleep in his cradle and close the altar doors for the gods to rest. Her rotis were a joke. Manhole covers, Nimish joked, Bihari rotis, against the exquisite muslin of Gujarati rotlis. Eat rice, she bantered, it is the better staple and easier on the cook. She strove towards the house style for vegetables, the right consistency for the sweet dals; she perfected the family tea.

She was, of course, not to be involved in kitchen or godly activities if she was committing menstruation. An allied problem was her use of disposables. She had been careful enough to ask the protocol.

Mu*mm*y, as Smt Chitol called her mother-in-law, in the same intonation as her husband, suggested she use cloth, which could be washed clean, keeping the house unpolluted, and was cheaper besides. Each time she wished to dispose, she took the newspaper-wrapped parcel down to the communal garbage receptacle.

Sometimes Smt Chitol marvelled at the fact that, living in this housing society where the people all spoke the same language and had the same food habits and followed the same religion, her in-laws accepted her. It must have been a big modern step on their part. She intuited the stroke had a role to play. A great many things were 'before the stroke' and 'after the stroke'. There was no drama to the formulation, as there might have been with her Bengalis. They did not wallow. The stroke had destabilised their life and she supposed Nimish marrying was stability.

The stroke had strained income and increased expenses, and she was keen to contribute. Nimish did not like to accept money from her hands. She began placing two hundred rupees from her salary towards household expenses in the money drawer. She wondered whether that had even been noticed. One day her mother-in-law sent her to buy two single bedsheets from Narayandas Cloth House and Matching Centre in Angrewadi. On the way there it occurred to her that she had forgotten to place her contribution in the drawer. It had been noticed. She thought she liked that.

Slowly she moulted her old routine. This new one became her. Returning at a similar time every day so as to avert the deadly inoffensive question, she did not lie down and read. She prepared tea, had it alongside farsan, since she could no longer dine at the hostel time. Her father-in-law took an early dinner, but she could not possibly join him while the others had not eaten; after dinner she sometimes walked with him around the corridor and down to the streets he so missed, where he produced toffees for children, and people told her about how he would take the kids to Sunday-morning cartoons at the cinema or to feed the cows at Madhavbaug. When Nimish came back he was ready for dinner – yet she did not join him either, for Mummy liked him to have his rotlis fresh off the stove, and she could not very well sit to eat while the mother-in-law served.

Here a magic trick. Nimish, slowly, subtly shorn of N'ness, coming together as a different person before her very eyes. Nimish of the house had everything done for him. His mother forever asked him not to push himself too hard, and in return received minor shows of resistance that, Smt Chitol believed, could only be the result of such enforced dependency. He did his best to maintain the equilibria in the house, tolerating infantilisation. She watched his hair sometimes patted when he ate as though he were a child emerging from the depths of illness. She did not realise he was supposed to have so many likes and dislikes and that it was important to cater to them. She despaired for her husband's helplessness. No wonder he likes to be out of the house, free and capable.

Every night they slept close together and every day awoke close together on the cotton mattress creeping its way towards four and a half feet. Yet their time together dwindled. She left the house before him and returned before him. At home they were never alone, and outside likelier to be in groups than before marriage. They attended silver anniversaries, diamond birthdays, convened in hospital lobbies, where extended family seemed to gather every day for the duration of an admission. But the thing she could not bring herself towards doing was to suggest to him who had always lived in his parents' home that let us find our own.

Perhaps she was primed by a story Mummy told her. It was an old incident from the village.

A boy, she said, flattening out the dough to ultimate thinness with her slender rolling pin – a lesson in artistry – decided to marry a girl not known to the family. The family conducted their research. They learned the girl's grandmother had jumped into a well and killed herself. The boy stubbornly paid no heed to the warning. The girl was such that because of her they even moved out of the family house! A time came when the cotton crop failed and the family needed to sell off the women's jewellery. Two daughters-in-law of the house agreed at once. But this one, said Mummy, in her voice that hurt the ear just a little, this girl fought and fought. In the end she jumped into a well and killed herself.

Smt Chitol wished to be knowing about the story, but she gasped.

There were times in her years of adjustments she had thought of herself, in biological terms, as entering a foreign body. She was coming to understand this was not the case. She was the foreign object.

10

A very important matter

In the halcyon days the Chitalia home was always teeming. They took in kin trying to find their feet in the city, relatives on long visits, their children who came for studies. Prominent among the last was Bansi from Bhavnagar, who had stayed on so long she became a daughter of the house, a little like Smt Chitol in the house of the Prasads. A crucial difference was that Bansi had not run away to it, nor away from it in a sense, in order to secretly work. Bansi had duly married; yet so much her home did this remain that it was here, until her son became a schoolgoer, that she retreated to for her monthlies.

She was the energetically virtuous kind, quick to show emotion, to laugh, exclaim, comment on herself, to swiftly and insistently apologise for inane things, frantic in conversation, conversant in mind games – for example, always suggesting to Smt Chitol that only she, Bansi, knew the *real* Nimish. She was, in short, the kind who wished others to remark, whatever you say, she's a gem, totally open, very pure, cannot keep anything inside.

It was Bansi now shouting 'Ting Tong!' and bursting through the open door, holding her son Shlok's hand.

Behind them was her father-in-law, Purushottambhai. He was a tall man, heavy around the waist; his deep tan skin had a sheen to it, against which a pair of dull moles near one ear drew attention to themselves. Smt Chitol had heard he was a *kattar* Hindu, which is to say he believed Hindus endangered, and as a result was an active member of associations, including the Hindu Council. This was his principal aspect, what people spoke to him about and about him to others, her in-laws in a tone that suggested admiration; Nimish seemed to treat him as a bit of a joke.

'Say Jai Shri Krishna!' Bansi poked her son.

'Jai Shri Krishna,' Shlok greeted everyone.

Then, as if part of a performance, he raised his arms and chanted: 'Jai Shri Ram!'

Rakshaben laughed and clapped.

'He has got all the video cassettes of *Ramayan*!' Purushottambhai informed them through a wheeze.

'*Bas, bas, deekra*, there is no need,' he said to Smt Chitol, arresting her descent to his feet.

The guests settled on the divans. Smt Chitol brought out glasses of water.

'Purushottambhai's father and my father moved to Bombay in the same year,' her father-in-law addressed her as she served the guests. 'There was a drought in Kathiawar. Those days we cannot imagine today. Five days it took. By foot, bullock cart, train, steamer.'

He extended his arms for a hand-clutch, palms up, and Purushottambhai completed the clasp, smiling.

'*Cha peeso*, Kaka?' Smt Chitol ventured in Gujarati.

He looked pleased to hear her speak the language.

'*Jaroor*,' he replied. 'I have never had tea made by your hands.'

'When do we get to have it also?' said Rakshaben. 'She is on office duty all day.'

Smt Chitol got up with a sporting smile. She was barely out of view when her frown lines showed. 'Arre, she only meant to say you work so hard,' Nimish would have said. 'It was in your defence.' But there was little doubt to her. She began counting how many rounds of tea she made in the day, in the household style that she was not particularly fond of, with lemongrass and a little too much milk.

She put the milk and water on the stove and snipped the *lilicha* over the pot. I could have said something, she thought, nothing too combative, something charming to correct the misimpression.

Bansi clumped into the kitchen and hoisted herself on to the counter.

'I used to *love* sitting here, Charms. I think I'll call you Charms! And stop calling me Bansi ya, don't have to be so formal! Call me Buns. Call me Bonsai. I like Bon Bons. That's the one I gave myself.'

She fiddled with the cups and utensils on the counter.

'So, how's you?'

Charms did not get a chance to answer, for Bon Bons had turned her attention to the altar.

'How nicely Mummy makes these *pavitras*, na?' Rakshaben being one of three people Bansi called Mummy. 'I can never make them so nicely. Where does she get the *resha* from? I know from where, actually. But I'll tell you, it's not about the material actually. It's about the devotion. When I do it with all my feeling, it always comes out well. We have become too distracted. You don't do puja, na? Mummy told me.'

Smt Chitol's frown lines resurfaced.

Bansi poured a teaspoon of sugar into her palm and flicked it into her mouth, crunching away.

'How much sugar I can eat, I'm mad! Really. Shlok calls me Madoo. I used to call him Madoo when he was small. I still call him that sometimes. Should I go in for dieting? You are a lucky bug.'

Indeed I am, Smt Chitol thought. Then she brought herself to laugh. The full-house feeling was nice.

She turned towards Bansi and found a little finger stuck up between her eyes. She leaned back to view it clearly.

'Like this. Before Shlok, I used to be like this.' Bansi wiggled the finger. 'Oh take this sugar away from me! Oh ho, sorry, it's falling, I'm creating a mess. Sorry, haan. You'll sing today, na, Charms? Only once you have sung for us. Why so shy! Bengalis are so talented. People with no talent bray away like donkeys. Have you heard me? Sing one of Nims' songs, na. He's also too shy. Doesn't show his songs to anyone. He has shown me. Right from the start he used to show me. But I don't know if we'll get a chance to sing today. Pappa has to talk about a very important matter.' Pappa being Purushottambhai, also one of three people she called that. 'They are really working hard.'

'For what?'

'The Ram temple, what else?'

'What else,' said Smt Chitol.

'Really, that's the main. One sec I'll help you.'

The two went out carrying trays of tea and chivda and Rakshaben's golpapdi.

'They have started,' Bansi apprised Smt Chitol with a quick glance over her shoulder.

'Why did Somnath fall?' Purushottambhai was saying. 'Kulapati has written the reason ... '

This Smt Chitol could work out. Kulapati was K. M. Munshi. Her father-in-law only referred to him as Kulapati, chancellor, in the way that he only referred to Gandhi as Bapu, father. Bapu may have won freedom, but he was naive on the Hindu–Muslim question, believed Pappa, whereas Kulapati had helped keep the Nizam of Hyderabad from walking off with the middle of India, and it was Kulapati who had rebuilt the ancient temple at Somnath destroyed by Mahmud of Ghazni a thousand years ago.

'... We could not unite, that is why.'

'Those people have so much unity,' concurred Rakshaben. 'When they pray together in the middle of the road that is what they are showing.'

'Exactly!' chorused Bansi. 'They show their unity and we have to suffer in traffic jams.'

'Muslim traffic jams are worse than Hindu traffic jams,' remarked Smt Chitol, she hoped with friendly sarcasm.

'Really, they are too bad!' said Bansi.

Kantibhai turned to his daughter-in-law.

'Some of our people are such hardcore Vaishnavs, like our Hareshbhai on the second floor – if he goes to the tailor, he will not say *kapda shivdava che*. He does not want to use the word Shiv!'

'But it is changing,' wheezed Purushottambhai. 'Whether you are Vaishnav or Shaiv, Kapol or Modh, Gujarati or Marathi, everyone is coming together.'

Kantibhai raised himself off the divan and walked to the cabinet to extract a book, stacked horizontal for optimum space utilisation. He thumbed through the leaves until he found what he was looking for.

'I am reading from Kulapati's *Jaya Somanath*.' He settled back on the divan.

He had a tremulous reading style. Although it was not a function of emotion, one felt the power of an old man touched by the words before him. Where Smt Chitol couldn't follow the language, she relied on the tremble.

The passage featured a noble camel Padamdi and her master Sajjan, who sacrificed themselves by leading a section of Ghazni's invading army into an inescapable sandstorm. Death scenes in books moved

Smt Chitol easily, and she was indeed moved hearing about the Rajput's camel, her valour and intelligence, and their end, buried in sand with the enemy troops.

'So nicely he reads, na?' whispered Bansi to Smt Chitol. 'I think there are tears in my eyes. Look at me. In yours also I think!'

'Everyone cannot be a warrior,' said Kantibhai, closing the book. 'But we can all be Padamdi.'

'*Bas, bas,*' said Purushottambhai. 'You have explained it beautifully, so beautifully. What do you say, Charuben?'

He was assessing her, she felt certain. Her reputation preceded her – Bansi's comment in the kitchen left no doubt.

To her relief, Nimish arrived right then, flopping hair and wide smile. He'd been coming home late. From the godown in Chinchbunder he went to Parag's office in Khetwadi, where they were exploring a business selling computer hardware.

'Hi, Nims!'

'Hi, Bons!'

'Loafing around again after work, na, *rakdhu* number one. I know you!'

'*Chal, chal,* your husband must be a loafer.'

'Nims!' cried Bon Bons raucously. 'His son is here! His father also!'

She made as if to throw a cushion but burst out laughing. 'Total gonecase, Charms, your husband. Just tell him, ya. So much fun we used to have. Idiot.'

Shlok raced over for a high ten.

Nimish went to Purushottambhai and placed a hand between his. No touching of feet, observed Smt Chitol, a traditionalist in this matter.

'How is everything, *deekra?*' asked Purushottambhai. '*Tabiyat-pani?*'

'First class, Kaka.'

'Business?'

'Getting along, Kaka.'

'I heard they are making it difficult for everyone in that area.'

'Total mafia,' agreed Nimish companionably.

'This is what happens when you bow before them because of vote-bank,' Purushottambhai said. 'Have some patience, everything will change.'

The exchange surprised Smt Chitol. Who had not heard about the dons in the Dongri area – yet, as far as she knew, it was the municipality or the police Nimish usually had to pay off. Not many Muslims there.

'Good you have come, I was just telling everyone.' Purushottambhai looked around radiantly. 'I had gone to Somnath when the temple was rebuilt. I was a young boy then but that feeling from forty years ago is still inside me. Believe me, the mood in the country today is even more special. Every person wants the Ram temple. The poorest of the poor are approaching us with whatever coins they have, fifty paise, one rupee, saying please take this. They are coming to us with one brick with Shri Ram's name written on it, saying please take it to Ayodhya, that is all I want before I die. We are planning a grand brochure. It will give the *real* history of Ayodhya. Every single person who donates, their name will be there. I have brought this list of rates, I will leave it with you. Single line, box item, quarter page, half page, full page. Promise you will support.'

'Hundred per cent,' said Kantibhai.

'We have to spread the message, and spread it in a way that people will respond. I have come up with a simple motto. Do you want to hear?'

Everyone looked at him in anticipation.

'A A A,' Purushottambhai enunciated slowly, moving an empty space between his thumb and forefinger along an imaginary line.

'Awareness. Affort. Aggression.' He took a pause. 'Aggression, when needed. Those people can be very aggressive. This is what Bapu did not –'

'Effort is with E, Pappa!' said Bansi, shaking her head to convey exasperation.

'She is being an Angrez again,' Purushottambhai laughed. 'I tell her in ours we spell it how we say it. We are concerned with the message, not the spelling. What do you say, Charuben?'

'When I hear AAA,' she responded with a determined smile, 'I think of *Amar Akbar Anthony*. Nimish too.'

Bansi cackled.

'Wait, wait, tell them that one, na, Pappa.'

'Should I?'

'Say it, say it!'

'Hear this,' Purushottambhai said.

Everyone trained their eyes on him.

'U P U P.'

He ran the finger-thumb-space along the imaginary line.

'United Progress. Useful Purpose. UP. UP. Up Up. Where is Ayodhya? In UP. Where is Ram?' He pointed towards the heavens. 'Up.'

'This one is too good, na, Charms!'

Afterwards, stick-flicking clothes off the high line in the corridor, Smt Chitol said to her husband with calibrated liveliness: 'Can you believe he wanted a donation for that?'

Drawing no response, she added: 'And he thinks he will get it!'

'He isn't wrong,' laughed Nimish.

She stopped, deliberately, to look at him.

'I thought Pappa said yes for the sake of it,' she said. 'Otherwise that man would never stop.'

'No, no, I think they will give it. They were discussing the rates just now.'

'And you won't try to stop them?'

'*Stop* them?' said Nimish.

This made her feel like some kind of a family tyrant, hence badly misunderstood.

'I mean, you can say something.' She softened her tone to friendly.

'Arre, what can I say?' he responded in kind. 'They have their beliefs, they have their ways, it isn't a big deal.'

Noting that she had stopped to look at him again, he continued, somewhat disingenuously: 'Don't we put money in the box when we go to a temple? We contribute to the Navratri celebrations here. Didn't we offer something at the Durga pandal at Tejpal?'

'There is a mosque standing there for five hundred years,' she put to him. 'They want to contribute to a desecration? Why would anybody want to do that in the name of their own faith?'

'Arre, mosque, temple, it's all for God. This is India, a compromise is always found. That is the beauty. Demand, demand, meet in the middle.'

She considered this opinion silently, sifting through the clothes.

'Who really knows the exact spot where Ram was born,' he added vaguely.

'All this *they* and *those people*, that is what it is about,' she said. 'This Purushottam Kaka, I don't know … '

'Character he is.'

He imitated his wheezing delivery: 'If we don't build a Ram temple in Ayodhya, where should we build it, in Mecca?'

This drew a smile from her.

'Why did you tell him that about the collections?'

'Which?'

'You don't have to pay any hafta to any gangsters, do you?'

'I didn't say *I* have to pay. But many do. That is the reality on the ground. What has happened?' He went up to her with a smile, broke into street Bambaiya. '*Fokat mein kaiko* so much tension?'

'I don't want my name on any donation fonation,' she said, getting it off her chest.

'Okay, fine. Just tell them.'

'*You* tell them,' she said.

Your parents, he could almost hear her add. It pierced him. But he hadn't the confrontational instinct.

'Arre,' he replied. 'Just tell them if you feel so strongly.'

'Okay,' she said, clear that she would not.

'Okay,' he said, nearly certain of it himself.

She returned to the clothes, folding them into each one's piles with excessive briskness.

Once he went inside she stood looking into the courtyard, lost in thought. And is it only when Akbar gives blood to Ma Bharati and when the Muslim ustads play Bhairavi that they are to be embraced?

She turned round, resting against the banisters. Through the double-hinged ivory-coloured door, one half bearing a wooden nameplate for Chitalia, the other half an iron slot for Letters, her dwelling, her life, presented itself at an angle, lit up like a set, as if for review. She was here. Of course she was. What was it inside her that connected her to it? She thought this and for an instant floundered.

To have put herself in this position after the long quest for independence felt to her at moments the highest folly.

11

The perfect day of marriage

Day upon day of marriage piles up and exerts its weight. The perfect day of marriage is weightless. On the train they sat with arms touching. They were quiet. She was at ease. No tension about time. She had cut the carrots by the household rules, endangered nobody with their bilious cores. She felt light. She forgot about the carrots. They held hands. Kites wheeled and keened, you could hear them keening above the great hum of the electric multiple units.

They sat holding hands right through their stop, and only smiled when they realised their mistake. Smiled, then giggled. He called her Charuwati and Charumati, called himself Charupati, husband of Charu. He sang her a few lines from a song he had composed in honour of her laugh, 'Charu Hasee'. She linked her arm with his. Breeze blew over the seafront maidans and flittered through their hair. Last night they had made deep matrimonial love. She watched his profile.

They carried on till the end of the line. They were facing the wrong direction coming in. Now they could face forwards without having to shift, the way expert commuters doubling back at rush hour did. They did not know how long the wait. They did not check. Did not care. They revelled in the waiting.

One thing of note occurred, an exposed nail caught the tip of his index finger and drew blood. She sucked on it, and received from him a look of pure adoration, of utter indivisible companionship. She felt entirely his. The fugitive love of last night filled her senses.

The coach grew full. The train kicked off with a jerk. They talked a little, unrememberable, irretrievable talk that was everything. The heat did not bother them. The sweat on touching skin only enhanced the feeling of proximity. The novelty of their up-down run faded and it did not matter. Nothing mattered. No flexing of personality, no restraining. No masquerade.

The awful thought very briefly raised its head. Was he, under his equanimity and his imitations, a man of common prejudice, of ordinary capacity? What did that say about her? No, no, he is not, perish the thought, banish it at once! And it was banished, beautifully it perished. The world was an extraordinary, crowded place and they were tight, *close*, they had their seats, their touching arms, their marriage.

Afterwards Smt Chitol thought if somebody were to ask her again about a happy outing, this was what she would write. Happiness was so implied it could not be uttered. Pleasure was so fine it could not endure.

IV

Welfare Inspection

I
Beat

A little before she retired, Mohini Fonseca said to Smt Chitol: 'Come, dear, let us make one trip, the matter will become clear.' Ordinarily Mrs Fonseca, a welfare inspector, would not have put this request to a clerk, but in her assessment Smt Chitol was not the ordinary kind. For her part, Smt Chitol felt as though somebody was doing *her* a favour taking her out of the office.

The women set out in the afternoon. It was the time of the year the exhaustion with the rains turned towards regret at their passing. Smt Chitol still had her monsoon sandals on.

'So have you seen the notification?' Mrs Fonseca asked her on the train.

'Which one?'

'For welfare inspector posts.'

'Oh yes,' said Smt Chitol. 'It has been there for some time.'

'I hope you will apply. You have more than three years as senior clerk, no?'

'Almost four.'

'And in settlements how long?'

'About one.'

'That will help in preparation, definitely. And what about your record? It is good?'

'Very good,' replied Smt Chitol, with some pride.

From Currey Road station they carried the conversation all the way to the Parel Loco Workshop. So mentor-like was Mrs Fonseca that Smt Chitol judged her reputation for severity was merely a means by which the lazy persecuted the diligent. It could also be that she needed to put up a severe front: she was, at present, the only woman welfare inspector out of seventeen in the Bombay Division.

'How did you get into it?' Smt Chitol asked.

'Oh, I decided a long time ago,' smiled Mrs Fonseca. 'My father was in the Railways. When I was a young girl, I heard a man from welfare say he will help him in some matter if he lets his daughter warm his bed. That daughter is me. I made up my mind then and there. That is why we need more women welfare inspectors. In the zone out of ninety welfare inspectors one dozen might be women.'

'Frankly, I sometimes wish I could come out of that ministerial room,' admitted Smt Chitol.

'You can be in that room for ten, twenty, thirty years. But trust me, you will learn more in the field in one year.'

At the workshop, under the expansive roof, among the resounding machines and the great underframes, Smt Chitol was transported powerfully back to Bhombalpur. She relived the time she had breached protocol and gone to her father on the shop floor, the childhood recollection short on detail and strong on sensation. She watched workers come up to Mrs Fonseca to thank her and wish her good luck, touching their hands to their hearts.

By the time they had pieced together what they needed from the mounds of registers in the matter of medically disabled khalasi Babu Dongre, the one last case Mrs Fonseca wanted to clear before retirement, Smt Chitol felt immensely optimistic about the work and its nobleness.

Back in the office she did not find encouragement.

'You know what they say,' remarked Digambar Bharti when he heard. 'Welfare inspectors have three works. *Banana, bigadna, dabana*. Make a case, spoil a case, quash a case. If you can be smart in that, you can thrive.'

'Have you heard about protocol duty?' he asked her in his knowing way. He looked around, laughing. 'She has not heard about protocol duty.'

Mrs Ghorpade advised her against it. 'You have to be on the field. You have to be available twenty-four hours in case of emergency. You have to travel around the country for all this certificate verification. Means, it is not suitable for women. Especially married women. How long have you been married for?'

'Fifteen months.'

'Oh ho, I know that, who wished you first on your anniversary? Means, long enough for you to understand.'

It was not only the four walls of the ministerial room Smt Chitol sought reprieve from.

'I do understand,' she said.

A week later, as they were about to go to sleep, Smt Chitol said to Nimish: 'A promotion opportunity has come up.'

'But you are not looking very happy.'

'It will be difficult to get it.'

He yawned and propped himself on his elbow. 'How difficult?'

She began to apply cream to her legs, working up from her toes.

'The exam is tough. There will be applicants from all over the zone. And from other departments.'

'So what? That is no reason to look so dejected. You can do it.'

'You think I should try?'

'What is the harm?'

'Nothing ... The job will be slightly different. I will still be in personnel. But in the welfare section. Welfare inspector.'

'What is wrong with that?'

'Nothing. There will be some fieldwork, some travel.'

'Oh. Hmmm,' said Nimish. 'Sometimes these promotions are just a way to squeeze an employee. All other things in life go for a sixer.'

'But it is a good opportunity. There is a lot to learn. And about two hundred rupees per month difference.'

'How much travel and all that?'

'Hopefully not too much. Mainly fieldwork in the city.'

She paused to look at him, putting on the bright in her eyes. 'Remember I told you I went to the Parel workshop that day?'

'Mrs – what? Alphonso?'

She smiled, creaming up her calves.

'Mrs Fonseca said I should try. So you think I should try too?'

'If Mrs Alphonso says so. Hmm ... I suppose no harm in trying.'

She put away the cream, switched off the lamp and came to his chest.

Having obtained a no-objection certificate of sorts, she started planning her preparations.

Circumstances saw to it that she did not have to discuss the matter in depth with her in-laws.

Her father-in-law was tracking bigger things: the upcoming general elections, the brick-collection campaign for the Ram temple. He attended a brick consecration ceremony at Purushottambhai's invitation, and returned with death figures from brick-procession riots around the country that were demographically rather different from Smt Chitol's understanding of the matter. His physical recovery, which had been visible, so that he had started to spend a few hours at work most days, people attributed to the blessings of Ram. To pit herself in opposition was not just against Hindu glory but his health.

Meanwhile she erupted into her period, which signalled once more that she was not about to fruit: the baby Krishna calendar her mother-in-law had hung up mid-year on the partition, Smt Chitol now felt certain, was a hint. As protest against the menstrual restrictions, she had opted out of all household participation during the offending days, sequestering herself in the compartment, quietly pushing up the domestic tensionmeter.

In this instance she needed the time. The exam was not like the one she had written for senior clerk. To know all she was supposed to, she would have to swallow Rulemaster Chitnis whole. Unfortunately, he had retired. Besides, weakened by stomach cramp, she did not want to swallow anything at all.

By the time exam day came around, all she wished was to keep her dignity intact. She went in blank and emerged blank.

She was shortlisted for the viva voce. The panel asked her three questions she had already answered in the paper; she surmised that was to make sure that it was she who had written it.

Deputy chief personnel officer Smt Premalatha Naicker put to her: 'What is the aim of a welfare inspector?'

'To meet the employees for their problems and guide them in their privileges and rights, ma'am,' replied Smt Chitol.

'And who is a welfare inspector?'

'A welfare inspector is the eyes and ears of the administration, ma'am,' she returned with military smartness.

As soon she answered she suspected she had committed a grammatical error. Should she have stayed in the singular throughout? But surely a welfare inspector could not be 'an eye and an ear' of the administration. Maybe a welfare inspector is a *pair* of eyes and ears of the administration? Or welfare inspectors *are* the eyes and ears of the administration? Yet the question was not put to her in the plural, so to proceed that way would have been taking liberties.

With siesta eyes, Smt Naicker indicated that she could leave.

Presently Smt Chitol was appointed to the post of welfare inspector III, the entry category. She received the news with a deep, exhalational *Durga, Durga.* Up she slid from the Rs 1200–2040 to the Rs 1400–2300 pay scale; her annual increment rose from Rs 30 to Rs 40.

Her in-laws were jubilant. The day she was elevated Hindu volunteers had laid a foundation stone for the temple in Ayodhya.

Upon taking up her new position, Smt Chitol relinquished her hard-won clerk's desk and chair. She was sent up to the second floor and given an unfixed position on a row of benches behind a row of tables, like canteen dining. On her first day there she inaugurated a case diary with scraps of advice from Mrs Fonseca. *Always go to the spot. Go without notice. Learn Marathi. Take tea.* She checked into the room most days but rarely spent the entire day there. The remaining time she was out on her beat. She liked the very sound of it. An inspector's beat, the beat of her feet, *her* beat.

Her beat ran from Masjid to Chunabhatti, through Sandhurst Road, there branching off the Central main to the Harbour line, through Dockyard Road, Reay Road, Cotton Green, Sewri, Wadala, Guru Teg Bahadur. These nine stations were hers. To the east of Sandhurst Road sprawled Wadi Bunder yard with its ten thousand employees across fourteen storage sheds, a container workshop, a carriage & wagon depot, a permanent way inspector's depot, a health inspector's depot, a dispensary, and parcelling depots, and canteens, and the three residential chawls, Mahalakshmi, Master and Breakdown. Wadi Bunder was hers. Not entirely, that would be 'inhumanly possible', as retired a.p.o. (l&w) Pereira used to joke. Routine matters were handled from VT. Non-routine matters, Other than Normal Retirement matters, were hers.

Ravli Junction Cabin near Wadala, from where the Harbour line connected to the Western, was hers. The gangman *tapris* by the tracks between her stations were hers.

Her beat did not carry the glamour of the faraway or the difficult. Difficulty, she noticed, was a parameter welfare inspectors discussed competitively. Look at Vithalwadi to Lonavala, spanning seventy kilometres into the hills – say there is a midnight derailment between Monkey Hill and Nagnath Cabin. What do you do? Look at the workshops – say you are gheraoed by three hundred angry workers. What do you do?

She heard she had landed this beat because it was close enough to the headquarters for the superiors to manage her. On the other hand, Mrs Ghorpade reckoned she was given it because she lived close enough to be available to it at all hours. Smt Chitol considered the beat neither as something she was gifted nor saddled with. It was her beat and she just liked it.

She liked how the train rose to the upper level of Sandhurst Road to become the Harbour line, even if one could not sense the harbour except by the odd towering crane or a signboard for maritime services, glimpsed from the slight, curling elevation of the tracks. She liked the mood of the mill warehouses, the old basalt buildings, their corner balconies. The fruit trees of Wadi Bunder pleased her. She liked that if she timed it right – after her father-in-law had left and before Nimish had gone off to the Khetwadi office – she could walk down the ramp at Sandhurst Road station between the chawls to the godown in Chinchbunder and meet him away from the claustrophobia of home. On these surprise visits, she felt her promotion had aided the welfare of nothing so much as her own marriage.

Several of her stations were two-platform affairs staffed across shifts by one stationmaster, three assistant stationmasters, six pointsmen, five sanitation workers, fifteen booking clerks, a parcel porter, three announcers, five ticket checkers. She enjoyed talking to them, and she found people liked talking to her. Stationmasters sat her down amid the bustle of the day to tea as thick as mud and harked back, inevitably, to their first days of duty out in some godforsaken block station.

On his very first day at work, recalls stationmaster Das, who is especially happy to chat with her for he can do so in Bangla, he hears a scream like the world is ending. He rushes out. His heart is beating, the round blood-red sun is sinking and he sees a young man trudging towards him carrying something. Must be a vendor. The vendors here are notorious for riding the coupling between the bogies. He races towards the man. What is the man holding? It is his arm. 'Don't tell my family, they will be angry with me,' the man says, drops his severed limb and passes out. What do you do?

In his first week of work, what must stationmaster Intezar find outside his cabin up in a lonely ghat section but an abandoned baby. The baby has small eyes and a swollen face, a tiny, scrawny baby so confused and weak she can barely summon the strength to cry and when she does she cannot stop. He thinks, I have gone through each page of my manual before joining but there is nothing about how to stem the tears of a baby whose mother has left her. What do you do?

Whenever Smt Chitol set out on her beat it was with an intimation of discovery. Everything that happened in India happened also on the Indian Railways. Uncynical thoughts sustained her out on her beat, the idea of adding welfare to lives.

She ditched her handbag for a backpack. The combination with a sari was not the most elegant, she knew, but it saved her back, and it made her feel youthful. The bag was stuffed with forms and documents and their copies, responsible as she was for their filling and conveyance. She held weekly open sessions at designated depots across her beat, she gathered complaints from the grievances registers, although she learned that people preferred to tell rather than write that one Murugan had sublet his room in Breakdown Chawl to a pimp-prostitute brother-sister and at this rate they would turn the entire place into a brothel. They preferred to tell not write what parts of Wadi Bunder the pilfer artistes set up in the evenings and which employees they might be in cahoots with. Sanitation women got down on their haunches, mixing tobacco and lime on their palms, telling her that their man took their money again and burned it in alcohol; they laughed uproariously at her enforced vegetarianism and said, yes, come to my house, I will make you *gavthi* mutton and bhakri. Construction mukaddams became oblivious enough to use raw language in her presence. Pointsmen told her about the worst part of their job, clearing bodies off the tracks.

In her first month she encountered a death.

She was at a *tapri* at the time, noting the gangmen's complaints about the tin shack where they rested and sometimes spent nights. The roof was like a shower in moderate rain and a waterfall in heavy, the light connections were gone, the stagnant water outside bred mosquitoes and stank. And what about this smell of alcohol here? asked Smt Chitol in her rudimentary Marathi, attempting the taunting tone native speakers employed so well. That is when the news of the gangwoman came.

The gangwomen were an experiment. When the backlog of compassionate cases grew too large, those women who were illiterate and could not be fitted elsewhere were formed into a gang and trained. The sight of them at work always lifted Smt Chitol.

When she got to Gangubai Waghmare, the blood had not ceased spilling, flies had not still alighted on the festival, and the delusion hung in the air that lifelessness might be temporary even if parts of the body were paste. She was so young it was astonishing, the shock and the sadness of a life so young. Smt Chitol froze. In the chaos of call this one and call that one she stood around, in the words of old sheth from Kings & Queens, words whose sting had never quite left her, 'like a guest in her own house'.

Afterwards, running around morning, noon and night, it was she who obtained the police panchnama, the serial number in the accidental-death register, the post-mortem report, the death certificate, the dependants' information, the rough sketch of the accident site. She put together the Workmen's Compensation Act claim. She had the body placed in a coffin provided by Edward Jones Special Contractor & Undertaker of Clare Road, Byculla, obtained a certificate from the coroner stating that the coffin has been properly sealed and the corpse would not decompose on the way, and another one stating that this was done in the presence of a municipal doctor (she was not sure this had been the case). It was she who obtained permission letters from the police commissioner and the municipality to transfer the body from one district to another, and from the stationmaster to load the coffin on the train. She reserved, through the commercial manager, space for the coffin in the brake van, and handed copies of the receipt to the booking office, the guard and the accompanying teenage brother who would become eligible for a compassionate appointment at a concessional age the following year – and thus set Gangubai Waghmare on her journey home.

There were times during these days Smt Chitol wondered what she, until recently a blameless clerk, had got herself into. Mrs Fonseca had dropped her into a bad dream. The gruesome sight remained with her.

The harrowing vortex of procedures depleted her so much she sometimes lost her patience with the grieving, irate family. The mother, first widowed, now bereft of a daughter, was distraught above all by the speculation that the girl had taken her own life. That had not just a bearing on the workmen's compensation claim, it destroyed the very idea of her daughter, who had started to provide for the family at twenty. *Nahi, atmahatya nahi keli,* she said over and over. It is not suicide, Ai, Smt Chitol reassured her.

All the while she tried to keep from her own family the toll the incident, and the new post, was taking on her. When she called from the morgue and told her husband, 'I don't know what time,' she sensed something shift. On returning home late that night she found him away on a restless walk, her father-in-law asleep and her mother-in-law waiting up. In the manner Rakshaben told her, 'Go straight away for a bath,' once more as if she was a much younger wife than she was, it was clear she was responsible for springing on the house not merely unpredictable hours but unwarranted pollution. Pouring mugs of water on her body, scrubbing herself clean, she suddenly stopped and stood a long time leaning with her head against the bathroom wall, too empty for tears, watching water dribble its way through the hair stuck in the drain cover. She wished she could fall asleep like this.

To some degree she was able to overcome her helplessness at the moment of death. By her subsequent actions, she believed she had defended herself from the chatter of 'this is why we should not have female welfare inspectors'. Against the talk of 'this is why we should not have gangwomen', she was able to point out that on average one gangman in the division died every month and not for them was suicide conjectured, it was only remarked that a train is like an elephant, faster than it looks.

She used to think death indicated that there were no good outcomes to living. It occurred to her that perhaps no absurdity fitted so well the absurdity of life and its termination as paperwork. Could in that absurdity lie its honour, its redemption, making a little durable that which is ephemeral? If that was the case, she thought, perhaps she had in the end honourably committed gangwoman Gangubai Waghmare to ink and paper. She believed Gangubai Waghmare's family could see it, even if her own could not.

2

Eyes and ears

In his last year of service Shri I Am Chaturvedi fulfilled a long-held ambition and rose to senior divisional personnel officer, the highest post in the divisional personnel office. The powers that be were said to have favoured him. Fortune certainly had. It was thought that Geetanjali Rao IRPS would occupy the position. But, having married an Indian Economic Service officer who was posted in New Delhi, she had obtained a transfer straight to Rail Bhawan. It would now be hard, Smt Chitol accepted, to catch up with her.

The moment he took charge there was a perceptible change in s.d.p.o. Chaturvedi. He no longer carried about his openly conspiratorial manner. He had the air of a government that knew its time was short. He walked with exaggerated speed, emitting 'okay' or 'hmm' to whomever was on his heels, even if that was empty space. One could not simply knock and enter his office. He had gained a secretary, instructed to keep every visitor waiting at least two minutes.

When Smt Chitol responded to the summons and presented herself, therefore, she was told by the secretary to wait. After one minute he dialled the phone that connected this side of the wall to that, and one minute later signalled her in, as though any verbal exertion on his part was above her station.

Like in the old days, two others were already inside. Her immediate boss a.p.o. (labour & welfare) Patil, beside him welfare inspector Kshitij Deshmukh, looking smug and insincere even by his standards. Neither acknowledged her.

'Mrs Charu,' said s.d.p.o. Chaturvedi, addressing her in the Mrs-first-name format he favoured for female colleagues, regardless of their marital status. But she herself had risen enough for the s.d.p.o.

to address her by name. 'A complaint has come. Please verify this certificate in person. Do it immediately.'

That was all he said, for he was no longer loquacious, he was all command.

'Sir,' she said, not wishing to be the type who needed to be explained things. She took the papers off the desk and left.

The certificate under scrutiny belonged to signal & telecom technician Gautam Nikale, issued by one Brights Devnani Technical Institute in Kanshe.

Two mornings later, thus, in her role as the eyes and ears of the administration, Smt Chitol set out on the Prabhat Express.

It was not still light when she left the house. Nimish dropped her off at the station in a taxi. Being chaperoned made her keenly aware that she was being less than the ideal wife; it was the husband who was meant to go on tour. At departure they had a not-quite-argument about whether he was going to pick her up in the evening. 'As if you've ever picked me up from the station before,' she said, dissuading him with the good humour of the Rajdhani time. But there lingered in him a fidgetiness, the kind that had taken him out for a walk the night she had come home late.

Never mind, she told herself. She took in the cool air, bore the morning smells along the tracks in good cheer. They were travelling north-east; she spotted the whole sun atop a short thin building, like a lollipop. The suburbs grew further apart; the stretches of mangrove and farmland separating them grew longer. Oddly shaped hills went invitingly by. Soon they were climbing the Western Ghats, riding the precipitous viaducts and threading tunnels from the pioneering railway days. The hillsides were straw, but closer to her the vegetation looked freshly wet; the rain had turned the browns to scented red and drawn from the greens a tinge of brightness. She got a cup of tea and a fresh vada pao. What a pleasure to be able to do a job like this, she smiled to herself.

Disembarking in the late morning, she made towards the station gates, for 'Near Kanshe Station' was all the address.

She cased the area as well as she could, one side of the tracks and then another. Piles, fissures and fistula specialists were in abundance, inviting passers-by from the door of their operations with a brandished proctoscope; there were vegetable and fruit sellers and travel agents; there were temples, mosques, toy shops; she was encouraged to find coaching and tutorial institutes and English institutes, but none called Brights Devnani. Nobody had heard of it, and if they spoke about it they did in terms so vague as to be of no value.

She returned to the station.

'No place like that here,' said stationmaster Sankara with disconcerting confidence. He had an elongated, expressionless face that gave the distinct impression that he did not suffer fools, a philosophy enforced by a strict rationing of words.

'It says near the station, sir.'

'Is that a proper address?'

'No.'

She felt chastened.

'How are you sure, sir?' she nevertheless ventured to ask.

'There are no institutes here.'

'Institutes are there, sir.'

She listed the ones she had seen.

'Those are not institutes.'

'Then?'

'Those are moneymaking scams.'

'Right, sir.'

He did not appear to mind Smt Chitol sitting in his cabin, so she remained, cooling off after her ramble in the sun. Every visitor he dealt with a similar laconism, making them each a little nervous. As she grew used to him, so he seemed to grow used to her, at one stage employing a buzzer underneath his desk to order her tea. Over tea, loosening up, she praised the cleanliness in the station. If only one could describe the brief twinkle that passed over stationmaster Sankara!

'I'm happy you noticed that,' he remarked, as though she had passed a test. 'These vagrant children were making a mess. I handed over one or two to the police daily.'

She found this chilling, but managed an approving smile.

The stationmaster pulled open the drawer and placed a photograph on the table.

'That looks like you, sir. And that's the general manager? You got a g.m. award. Wow!'

'What is he telling me?'

'He is congratulating you?'

'He is saying, "Sankara, in you I see the very embodiment of dedication."'

'Wonderful tribute, sir.'

'I do not like to boast, otherwise I could have hung this up. The people here know about my contributions. Actually, my native place is Hombal. How about yours?'

'Bhombal!' said Smt Chitol, startled.

'Hombal,' repeated the stationmaster, sternly. 'How about yours?'

'Actually, I grew up in Bhombalpur, that is why I was so surprised.'

'I see. But native place?'

Whatever the right answer was, she knew that Bhombalpur, to the stationmaster's mind, was not it.

'Sir, what must I do about this certificate?'

He took it and turned it over, felt it between his fingers, as if appraising cloth.

'Look at this paper quality. No proper address, nothing. Your work is done.'

He tossed the certificate on the table.

Smt Chitol picked it up. In fact, the paper looked of reasonable quality to her. She studied it closely.

'May I use this magnifying glass, sir?'

She lifted an industrial-age-looking instrument, nearly spraining her wrist as she ran it forensically along the edges of the certificate.

'Do you know this Sai Printers, sir?'

'Printers.' Here, once more saving himself the tedium of speech, the stationmaster embarked on an intricate series of hand gestures, interjecting only to mention key landmarks, 'peepal tree', 'jalebi wala', 'Sai temple'.

'But you need not bother,' he concluded. 'It is an open-and-shut case.'

As Smt Chitol made her way out of the station, following the turns of stationmaster Sankara's hands, the sun higher and hotter than before, she was inclined to accept his verdict.

She did, however, reach a building in whose recesses was indeed a hive of photocopiers, cyclostylists, offsetters, specialist printers, none of them, unfortunately, called Sai.

At one counter sat a bored young woman, made up with luminescent cherry lipstick and evening-purple eyeshadow.

Smt Chitol began to explain who she was, Brights Devnani, and so on.

The young woman appeared to become oppressed by the sheer boredom Smt Chitol was adding to her life. On hearing the word certificate, she pointed a relieved, slender, beringed middle finger towards a flight of stairs, lowered her head on the counter and passed out from boredom.

Underneath the stairs stood the kind of notarising stalls one saw in the compounds of small courts. A man seated on a wooden plinth inside was thoroughly engrossed in sawing off a piece of toenail. He glanced at her and paid her no mind, angling his implement this way and that; his expression indicated displeasure at being intruded upon at a delicate moment. As she waited she noted the spread of papers and forms and certificates. On finishing, he dusted his hands together and gazed at Smt Chitol.

'Haan, yes, Brights Devnani, what course?' he said. But the conversation soon careened to a close. 'Arre, what do you mean how am I selling it?' 'Did I say I am selling anything?' 'How do I know if there is a campus or not?' 'If there is no phone number what can I do?' 'You may be from railway-shilway but can't you see I have a health problem?'

Announcing that he was closing for lunch, he stepped out of his box, pulled two short weathered wooden doors together and locked up the stall. He walked away gingerly without acknowledging further queries, and finding her walking alongside him, his health problem vanished and so did he.

By the time Smt Chitol returned home, she had made copious notes in her case diary, putting down not only the significant details but describing for her own pleasure the entire journey. She regaled her family with the narration: the stationmaster, her tip-top detective work, the young woman with the purple eyeshadow, the man at the stall, complete with imitations, and this way massaging the case for domestic entertainment she hoped she had made amends for her outstation visit.

The next morning she reported to a.p.o. Patil. He heard the account with quiet interest, then took her along to s.d.p.o. Chaturvedi, who did with visible satisfaction.

'Mrs Charu,' he said, 'you have gone a good job. Better than what I thought.'

'Thank you, sir,' said Smt Chitol, slightly offended.

'Have you made a verification report before?'

'I have made reports before, sir.'

'A prima facie investigation report.'

'No, sir.'

'I will guide you.'

The s.d.p.o. dictated.

To: Divisional Office, Personnel Branch, Victoria Terminus

Sub: Education certificate of Shri Gautam Nikale – employee details...

I have been nominated by the competent authority to conduct prima facie inquiry into ...

I have visited the given address on the spot and upon investigation found that said institution is non-existent ...

Further, I have found on site that said certificate is available for sale ...

In conclusion, hence it is noted that tendered certificate by employee is fake, false and fabricated ...

But her hand had long slowed to a halt.

'Sir,' she said. 'I have not come to that conclusion, frankly.'

'That is why I am telling you,' said s.d.p.o. Chaturvedi, not missing a beat.

'I would prefer not to have a conclusion, sir.'

A moment of astonishment descended on the room.

'What do you prefer, Mrs Charu? That we let these charlies make a tamasha of Railways?'

'The investigation is not complete, sir. What if there *was* an institute? This certificate is from years ago. Would it not have been verified at the time?'

'You have exposed the whole scam and now you have lost confidence.'

'Sir, the scam is the man selling these certificates. But that doesn't mean the employee got his from there. I will meet him and get his side. This was only the start.'

'The person we are investigating you will go ask him what to write? If someone commits a crime, do you punish them or ask them what should be done?'

'Just on the basis of this much can we be sure there is a crime?' She added: 'Sir.'

The s.d.p.o. glared at her with provoked, divergent eyes.

'How much experience do you have?'

'Two months as welfare inspector, sir. But I was a personnel clerk for seven and a half years.'

'Clerk,' he snorted. 'Put up the report to the a.p.o. He will add his notes.'

A.p.o. Patil nodded, comprehensively.

Smt Chitol was dismissed. She could almost hear him say the word.

The feedback reached her over the coming days.

She heard that Gautam Nikale had been suspended pending a full inquiry.

She heard the Scheduled Castes and Scheduled Tribes Association was angry with her. She heard Gautam Nikale was a rising man in it.

She heard s.d.p.o. Chaturvedi was out to get the association leaders because of 'all their politics'.

She was congratulated on showing those nuisance-makers their place, hailed for her courage.

She heard that Gautam Nikale was active also in the larger of the unions, and it was upset with her too.

She heard that the divisional signal & telecom engineer who had initiated the inquiry against Nikale was out to get him, and that welfare inspector Kshitij Deshmukh had a hand in the affair. It was he who had a complaint about Nikale's certificate filed by a member of the All India Exploited Workers' Organisation (Railways).

The Exploited Workers' Organisation, she knew, fought cases challenging reservations and relaxations. Every now and then it burned or blackened photographs of Dr Ambedkar.

She heard s.d.p.o. Chaturvedi was like an unofficial adviser to the organisation.

She heard she takes s.d.p.o. Chaturvedi's dictation, heard that he was on her interview panel and got her the post.

She heard she, like Chaturvedi, was Brahmin.

She heard she was Chaturvedi's *khas*, his special one.

Mrs Ghorpade called her aside and said, 'Some people are talking. S.d.p.o. will soon go, where does she think she will go?'

'What are they talking!' said Smt Chitol. 'He was not on my interview panel. He was not even s.d.p.o at that time.'

'Arre, baba, I am not saying anything. I am only saying you have to take care of your reputation. Everyone remembers that one from general admin.'

This shocked Smt Chitol. 'Everyone' remembers J whereas she had made herself forget – when she had convinced herself nobody knew in the first place?

She tried to remind herself that reputation was not solid like fact, it was shape-changing, like rumour. She had done her duty.

Then why did she feel ill, at war within?

As the idiotic innocence of Smt Chitol's privilege unravelled she wished to be cloaked in her virtues.

To safeguard her reputation she became more diligent about signifying marriage. She began clasping the black-and-gold mangalsutra around her neck. Some days, rather than stick on a bindi, she pressed a vermilion *chandlo* into her forehead. At home she tried not to leak out stress, lest she get advised to revert to her clerical position. At work she adopted a bearing of integrity – not so stiff, however, that her egalitarianism was in doubt. But all of these felt cosmetic to her. What she wanted was a clean chit, an authentic certificate.

So when she spotted old Ishwar Kamble in the canteen, whose settlements she had processed as a clerk, she seized the opportunity. Ishwar Kamble, whom everyone called Tatya, had served in the SC/ST Association a long time and still visited its office, and as a strategic bonus would be in a position to convey the excellence of her character.

She engaged him in a conversation about his years in the association. He spoke about the days venturing out into the districts and the employment exchanges to tell people their constitutional rights, so accustomed were they to not having any. He recounted the victory that was the free train pass for the recruitment exams. The victory that was the waiver for the form fee, since there were aspirants who could not afford even that. The victory that was the first publication of the 'Brochure on Reservation for Scheduled Castes and Scheduled Tribes'. And despite all these measures, how reserved posts were unfilled so long that they were de-reserved by officers he diplomatically described as 'orthodox'.

'Sugar Charlie Tango the officers say for SCT. They think we don't know or understand. They think we do not have eyes and ears.'

Sugar Charlie Tango. Of course. That was why the s.d.p.o. had used 'charlies' instead of his usual 'johnnies'.

'There was one case some years ago, this s.d.p.o., he was d.p.o. then, he did a purification ceremony after taking over Sonawane Sir's cabin. Then he tried to destroy a Babasaheb Ambedkar calendar. Maybe before you joined.'

'Yes, I was there,' said Smt Chitol. 'I was there. I remember.'

She remembered. Why had it left no mark? Was it because she was new and clueless? Because of her own unexamined entitlements? But in standing by her parents' disavowal of the caste name, had she not taken a position, done the needful? After all, she did not 'believe in caste'. She had married out of caste. But in her Hindu Stree Samaj Working Women's Hostel, although open to every caste, wasn't it that certain girls would room together and certain not? Had she noticed it was the privileged castes who could name their association the Exploited Workers' Organisation! Because how could you take Sugar Charlie Tango seriously?

Ishwar Kamble himself brought up Gautam Nikale.

'I was told to do only the spot visit, Tatya,' she said, coming quickly to her defence. 'That is all I did. I did not have any background.'

'He is being victimised. He is good at his work. In internal trainings he did well. I know, I was also in signal & telecom.'

'But, Tatya, that education certificate. Let us see what comes out of the inquiry. I hope they find nothing.'

'The boy has a full technical diploma. There is no shortcoming in his education.'

He trailed off into a smile. Had she heard of the Marathi people's poet Vamandada Kardak? He proceeded to sing, to a light tune, verses with the refrain *majhya pendyala salant ghala*.

Send my boy to school, Lord and Master, the wife petitions her husband, *send my boy to school*. Our clothes may be torn, and what use to me a jewel, she presses him, send my boy to school.

'Babasaheb gave us the slogan Educate, Agitate, Organise. We would sing this poem when we were young.'

Smt Chitol nodded, burning up.

Eventually Gautam Nikale was able to clear himself. If it was a fly-by-night institute, he submitted, that could not be held against him, and in any event that particular course was not his qualification for the job. His witnesses bore him out.

Tatya Kamble's recitation visited Smt Chitol now and then.

It was later, after the thought of being seen as Chaturvedi's special that did not let her sleep at night had passed, after some more life had passed, that the words interfered with her sleep.

3

Wives

K. Nagaiah, a senior khalasi in the inspector of works, died of liver-kidney, Smt Chitol was told on the phone. She set out for his house armed with forms, her case diary and five hundred rupees recoverable from settlement dues.

She knew Nagaiah. Tall, well built, stooped forward at the waist, head hair more pepper, face hair more salt, a chipped front tooth. He had a way with words. As a senior man, if the mukaddam was not around he could be found calling the attendance, threatening the post-lunch late-latifs and work-thieves with the mark of A or a kick up the backside. *Bole toh A for Ambernath, nai toh G for Gaand pe laat.* He had come to Bombay with enough in his pocket for two cups of tea and two rice plates, worked year on year as casual labour on this railway building or that roadway before he was confirmed, and he did not like slackers. Telugu kamathis had built Bombay, he told her; we built VT, we built High Court.

VT banaya apna log, High Court banaya apna log.

A for Ambernath, G for Gaand pe laat.

The two dialogues rang in her head as she made her way over.

She entered Dharavi from the wrong axis, off Sixty Feet Road rather than Ninety Feet Road.

Negotiating her way through that great city within the city, she cut through the scents of bakeries and masala units, through Chamda Bazaar, the heaped goatskins going from handcarts into low godowns where women sat salting them, the rat-a-tats of machines turning leather into belts, the explosive chemical stench of hide turning in drums, towards where the scripts on the shops and the temples turned South Indian. There residents directed her into the veins of Thiruwadi to the room in which a Railways man had gone 'off'.

The crowd had just returned from the cremation. Sulochana, the wife, sat in the doorway and received Smt Chitol with restrained courtesy. She was considerably younger than Nagaiah. There were three children. The smallest of them lay down by her, gauging a marble against the light, then turned herself over and buried her face in her mother's lap. In the course of the conversation Smt Chitol learned that the children were not Nagaiah's. They were from Sulochana's first husband. He too had died.

Nagaiah had his habits, his wife grumbled, as if he was around to take heed, habits that saw his money fly and his body suffer. There was something tender about the bare details, she a young widow with three children, he an ageing bachelor who, at last, had a family. He loved the children like his own, said Sulochana, stone-faced in her tears.

They were in debt. Expecting to be promoted to mukaddam, he had bought this place. The floor had been cemented even if the walls were still tin sheets. He had taken out advances from the office and loans from the Makadwalas, who would soon come round – whether a child is born or a man dies, it is all the same to them.

And so, said Sulochana, she would be grateful if the settlement money was delivered soon, as well as the job. She would find someone to keep the child or bring her along – the work would not suffer because of that.

Smt Chitol handed over the five hundred rupees of immediate relief.

Over the coming days the paperwork proceeded, was all but completed and, even if a permanent appointment might take some time, Sulochana was about to start lifting construction material as a casual worker in the inspector of works – when a young man showed up at her open session in Wadi Bunder.

'I am Nagaiah's son,' he said to Smt Chitol. He was tall and strong, similar in dimension to Nagaiah, with confident eyes.

'You are not Sulochana's son,' she said.

'I am Chandramma's son.'

'And who is Chandramma?'

'She is my father's original wife.'

'Then why is she not here?'

'She is dead,' responded the youth. 'But the job should be mine.'

A flutter of panic ran through Smt Chitol. Had she enquired about any previous wives? Maybe she had not. Certainly there had been no reason to think it. No neighbour had mentioned it during her information-gathering, nor anybody at the depot when she took Sulochana for wife-identification.

In life nobody much cared about a multiple wife, but in death she became a headache. The P branch had instinctive responses for each denomination. A first wife tended to be pitied ('Frankly, I think suicide is the only option for her'), a second thought evil ('If you see how many documents she had organised!'), a third merely mistrusted ('Just see how her eyes go from here to there'); a fourth was a walking gag, put on earth to seed havoc in a government personnel department.

On hearing the matter welfare inspectors plunged into reminiscences.

'Listen to this one. I call her to the depot for wife-identification at eleven o'clock, she's already there at ten-fifteen, so what do I say, you've come early, I called you at eleven, and what does she say, when did you call me, you did not even bother to contact me, so I say, who do you think came and met you in Titwala, madam, and she says, you might have gone to Titwala but I live in Diva, so I tell her, either a mad dog has bitten you or it has bitten me, and she says, you must have met my sister Jasima, I am the first wife Shamima. I take her to meet the supervisor, then after some time the first one lands up, the one I had met, and the peon calls me out, so what do I do, I go out and tell her why didn't you tell me about the other wife, I asked you till the time I strapped my sandals, *still* this one tells me, he doesn't have any other wife, so I say – go inside, your photocopy is waiting for you.'

'Sisters are the worst. I had a case, the mother of the employee was a torture-master. One after another two wives ran away. Now when the employee died, who came for the settlements? The mother. So I tracked down the first wife's village, found out there that she lives with her sister in Sewri. I reached there and asked for her. The sister tells me, she has run away with my husband!'

'I had a case, wife's name was Rani. Then a previous wife showed up. What is her name? Rani. Then I found out there was an original wife. Her name? Rani. Among some people, if the wife dies and the man marries again, the new wife is made to change her name to the name of the deceased wife.'

'Frankly, this is all CID *ka khel*. Oh I have climbed up to temples on top of hills, got records from the priest to check if such-and-such marriage occurred or not. That is what you have to do, you have to become CID.'

Sulochana's name was on the nominee forms, the medical cards and the travel passes, but she possessed no marriage certificate. The boy, on the other hand, had documents, but they had not been verified. He had no witnesses, no neighbour or colleague to vouch for him. Yet to the questions he had answers: he named villages and people, recounted life stories. And he had the advantage. If his claim held, he was first in line for the job.

For in cases like the one at hand, Smt Chitol understood from her seniors, convention had the second wife take the monetary settlement while the ward of the first took the appointment. If unacceptable to either party, they would need a succession order from the court. And while the boy was keen to settle for the job alone – in fact became desperate to – Sulochana would not hear of it.

'All my life I have slogged. I have salted hide, worked in waste, worked in bones, sorting the yellow stuff and the black stuff, the heavy stuff and the light stuff. One and a half rupees a day. Twice I was asked to come for government work by neighbours, such was the demand that time. But my mother-in-law did not allow it, she wanted me to work in the locality. Two husbands I have lost. Now I want such a job that if I die will go to my children. Who is this boy, where has he been all these years?'

Smt Chitol made her preparations, therefore, to dispatch herself across the Deccan to become CID.

It was the first time in her married life, indeed the thirty-two years of her life, that she was to spend the night alone in an unknown place. 'I have to take this trip, Pappa, what do you think I should do?' she asked her father-in-law.

Not only his eyes, his large forehead, pointy nose, his twitching lips over raked, cluttered teeth, his elegant wiggling earlobes, were each implicated when he experienced satisfaction. Smt Chitol could gauge that his being asked, as though her course of action rested entirely on his response, was half the job done. In fact, she had already made her reservations and did not intend to cancel.

Shortly after receiving his comments, she intercepted Nimish in the corridor and took him up to the terrace, from where she was to bring down the steel vessels of grated raw mango and sugar after their summer-sunning.

'Pappa thinks it may not be safe,' she told him, narrowing her father-in-law's misgivings, not entirely faithfully, into a security issue. 'The Russians and Americans are sending women into outer space, so it must be safe enough to go to the next state.' Here she segued into a rousing talk about the Indian civilisation and feminine power, reeling off names of powerful goddesses in various parts of the country such as she knew. Nimish liked when she talked like this. He responded well to leadership, and adventure, and he sensed, too, that he otherwise risked her showing pride; all of these things emboldened him to declare: 'Nobody will stand in your way.'

On the afternoon of her departure, however, that, literally, is what Rakshaben did. She stood before Smt Chitol at the main door and said: 'Just think of what you are doing, just *think*.'

From the moment she heard, Rakshaben had been wielding a belligerent silence, as though if she were to speak she could not be held responsible. The cunning with which this one had gone around working on the men! That had disturbed her more than the prospect of the trip, which was disturbing enough.

Smt Chitol stiffened.

'Sorry, I am missing some days, Mummy,' she said. 'When I come back I'll take the vessels up and down again.'

Rakshaben could scarcely believe the provocation.

'You can still change your mind, it's not too late,' she replied, to her own surprise. She had meant for her daughter-in-law to reconsider future trips, not this one. But it was not her who had escalated the situation.

'What can I do, Mummy, it is my duty.'

'Duty!'

Are the duties of home a lesser one? What if illness was to strike a family member? What happens after a baby, are you going to run around the country then? What is the effect of this on your husband, have you considered? It was all she could do to rein in her tongue.

'Did you know this when you started the job?' she said instead. 'Some labourer dies and you have to go to God knows where for God knows what? What if something happens to you?'

'Nothing will. If something is to happen, it can happen right here crossing the road.'

'At least we will be there to look after you. Do you know how upset your pappa is? He has not taken a drop of water today. His own son fighting with him.'

Not true, Smt Chitol thought. Certainly there had not been anything like a *fight*; she would have picked up on it, her husband was not so untransparent. Besides, she was certain she had seen her father-in-law consume fluids. As for food, he had been fasting lately. But this was not the time to debate. All of a sudden Smt Chitol believed she had been complacent in thinking she was through before she was out of the door. She had even entertained victor's guilt.

'Use this time well,' her mother-in-law was saying. 'Should I fold my hands before you?'

'Please, Mummy, please, *I* beg of *you*, I touch your feet,' Smt Chitol countered with equal drama. She proceeded indeed to dive into those feet. Her duffel bag swung over her shoulder into Rakshaben's thighs as she did, and she leveraged the clumsiness of the moment to position herself on the doorward side when she stood up.

'The train will leave, Mummy, please,' she said, manoeuvring her feet into her hardy Kings & Queens sandals she still employed for 'roughing out'. Without bothering to strap the backs on, she folded her hands once more and turned round to hasten down the corridor.

'What about *your* train leaving, have you thought about that?' Rakshaben called out after her. The words stumped Smt Chitol, but nerves being their own form of propulsion, she made her way dazed down the stairs and was presently aboard a three-tier second-class ordinary sleeper in the Summer Special overfull with vacationers. No sooner had the loco jerked them away, amid the bedlam of premature antakshari, than a tug in her own abdomen intimated that she was likely ovulating. Now it hit her. Her mother-in-law had been tracking her cycle; she had calculated these days as fertile. Bitch! How dare she insinuate herself into such intimacies, how dare – how dare, how dare! And it struck her she had forgotten to account for the spotting that might occur, and she would have to wash her underwear and keep the wet garment from the dry contents of her bag, all of which enraged her further. How dare she, let me see if I ever give her a grandchild, how dare! And if I tell my husband about this he'll act like I'm out of my mind.

She pushed back against her seat. The Rexine grabbed her flesh like hot tar.

Two mornings later she sat heatbombed in the station superintendent's office at Turadi Junction. Her scorched skin was peeling, her hair was infested with coal dust, everything about her was crumpled. Quite in contrast, stationmaster Srinivas was in a superior state of grooming. His shirt and trousers were very white and extremely well pressed. His face was fiercely talcummed. To his palmyra moustache he administered a wooden comblet, no larger than an infant's palm. He sometimes stroked the moustache, sometimes parted it, sometimes ruffled or assuaged it; at all times he was alert to its needs the way one is to a temperamental pet. His care was of such a calibre that Smt Chitol felt totally secure in his hands.

'Madam, did you have, what you call it, a vasovagal incident?'

'I hope not, sir. What is that?'

'Any fainting?'

'No, sir. Little vomit, mild fever. The heat, sir.'

'Should I send you to the clinic?'

'No need, sir.'

'Then you take this Glucon-D. There will be dehydration. I always keep it with me. People keep fainting and sometimes they are brought here. Then someone will say, bring tea. I say nothing doing, take this Glucon-D. Add one more teaspoon. One more. Stir it. Stir, stir. Drink it. Drink it. No, not so fast, take sips not gulps. Now kindly continue. You went to the government office to verify the certificate.'

'They did not have records, sir. They spoke mainly Telugu. But in the end I could understand. It seems when the old offices were broken down to make this new office, all the registers and files got taken away with the debris and dumped. They spoke about it like a divine occurrence. The happiness in their eyes I could understand. I was also a clerk.'

'He he.'

'Ha ha.'

'Kindly continue.'

'Then I thought I would try to go to the deceased wife Chandramma's village. The address was on the certificate. The boy had written it down for me too. That is where he said he grew up.'

'What was the problem?'

'Nobody knew this village.'

'Anh. Hmm.'

'Also it seemed there were no buses to go to this village which nobody knew was where.'

'Hmm. Anh. Then?'

'A schoolteacher was there for some work. Some Hindi-English she could speak. They had a long conversation. She had a Luna. She said she would give me a lift till somewhere they thought the village may be. I felt that it was my best chance.'

The women went bumping and hurtling over stones and dust. The heat was immaculate, gorgeous in its terror, tearing through the cotton pallus drawn over their heads. The driver's starched checked sari kept its shape and dignity, not so the pillion's batik. In the distance the astonishing rock formations, silvery gold, goldeny silver, with their precarious, self-accepting positions of repose, encouraged an eternal view of things. Yet when they came to a stop Smt Chitol's faith in geology as a guide to the case at hand was not so secure.

'She dropped me off at the place she was supposed to drop me off and went away. Her children were waiting at home.'

'What was the problem?'

'There really was no such village, sir.'

'Oh ho ho. Oh ho ho!'

'I roamed around a long time, trying to speak to old people. Some elderly people came to see me in one place. In another place I was taken to a man who owned a pharmacy, then to a postman. In the end it was decided there is no such village in the taluka.'

'Hmm.'

'So I thought I'll try and go to Nagaiah's village.'

'Who is Nagaiah?'

'Deceased employee, sir.'

'Why did you say Nagappa then?'

'Never said, sir.'

'Just now, five minutes ago.'

'Sir, actually you who were calling him Nagappa. So maybe by mistake I...'

'Kindly continue, madam. You went to Nagappa's village.'

'No, sir.'

'Anh?'

'His place of birth and permanent address in different documents in our records, and the village that his surviving wife gave me, all three were different. And all three of them were far away, in another district. People were not sure about buses. Also, I realised roaming around in the villages not knowing the language, it is not easy. I would not even have a place to stay for the night.'

'Yes. Good. What you did then?'

'I walked two kilometres in the sun to a bus stop. From there I took the bus to Emeeludupalli. Then from there I took the train.'

'Very nice. Caught the Mail?'

'It had gone, sir.'

'Passenger would have gone even before.'

'Yes, sir.'

'Then?'

'Took a lift from a goods train, sir. Welfare inspectors tell me sometimes to reach the spot that is what they have to do. It was quite exciting. I enjoy talking to the drivers. They tell lots of stories.'

'What did he tell?'

'A boy and girl stood before his train last year.'

'Double suicide?'

'No, sir. At the last moment, the boy got nervous and jumped out. But the clevis hook went right through the girl. The boy ran away.'

'Oh ho. Tch tch tch tch. Very unfortunate.'

'The guard could not bring himself to take her off it. So the driver did it himself. Said he had removed bodies before. He can do it because he has been taught that the body like a loco is a machine and a dead body is just one that has lost its function, that is his training. Painted a very lonely life for a driver. Living like a machine, without emotion, tunnel vision, point A to point B, far from family. Benefits like running-kilometrage allowance he called sweet poison.'

'Hmm. Sorry state of affairs.'

'Afterwards he heard they were husband and wife. They had eloped. Their families were after them.'

'Must be a religion or caste honour matter.'
'That is what he thought.'
'Finally, madam, you reached here.'
'Yes, sir, crossed the border and got here. And I had some good luck. The retiring room was available.'

Here the stationmaster opened a tiny canister and tipped a few drops of what smelled like rosewater into his palm and anointed his moustache.

'Madam, one thing is still not clear. Why did you come here?'
'You see, in Nagaiah's SR, his Casual Labour Service Card was there. It was in a terrible condition. Torn and dirty, ink totally smudged in parts. Parts of it you could not read. But I had seen he had worked in Turadi. More than that, I remember talking to him about coming to Bombay, and that time he had mentioned Turadi. So I thought I could get some information.'
'Which years?'
'Could not read, sir, that part was damaged.'
'Now what we will do?'
'The first number of the year was definitely 1. That means it was at least within the last one thousand years.'
'Not one thousand. Within last nine hundred and ninety years.'
'Ha ha.'
'He he.'
'Seriously, sir, it would have been at least twenty years ago. Twenty, twenty-five, twenty-seven, maybe something like that.'
'There will not be any labour registers from that period.'
'Sir.'
'Madam. You could have written to the government authorities asking for the information. Ninety-nine per cent they would not have anything. One letter you could have sent here also. Nicely you could have saved this trip.'
'That's what, sir. I would get no reply or a reply saying no information. The problem would not be solved.'
'Then what will you do?'
'I will try and find someone who worked with him, sir.'
'Madam, the general manager inspection is next week. Now when g.m. is coming – or he may not come, he has cancelled last-minute before – who will remember this fellow Nagappa? Especially

i.o.w. – last two weeks everybody is running about, breaking this, making that, recarpeting some road, relaying some tiles, who will have time? Anyway, so much labour they would have used over the years, who will remember this fellow Nagappa?'

'But over here he wasn't in inspector of works, sir. That part I could read.'

'Then?'

'Medical.'

'Madam. Half the workers may be dead, half may be retired. Half may be transferred, half will not remember anything.'

'Maybe I did not plan this well, sir. I am trying my best under the circumstances.'

'No, tch, do not become disappointed.'

'It is my first time, something like this. I should have been clearer in my approach.'

'Everything is difficult and nothing is impossible, okay. This is my motto. I am a fan of sports. It is also the motto of the Umpires and Referees Association, which I have founded.'

'That's what, sir. I took a chance and came here. Just the way he had mentioned it, it made me feel I should come to Turadi. Now I have to hope for the best.'

'Madam, then we will do one thing. You go meet the health inspector. A Bihari man. Lots of Biharis here. Go down the platform past the deputy s.m.'s cabin, cross the tracks, walk past the yardmaster's office, go past the p.w.i. office, before you reach the c&w sheds you will see the h.i. office. I am very much senior to him in age and I have helped him many times. Once I kept a train waiting full ninety seconds for his family. You say Srinivas has requested you to extend maximum cooperation.'

'Right, sir.'

'Now I will plan for the g.m. inspection, madam.'

'Sir, when I was small I used to think the g.m. inspection meant the g.m. is coming to get inspected by us. One by one we will all inspect him.'

'He he. Want more Glucon-D?'

'No, thank you, sir. I am feeling better.'

'Station food is hopeless. For lunch, you better go outside from this side, walk two minutes along the wall and eat at the Lingayat khanavali. Pure veg, clean and tasty and cheap.'

'Right, sir.'

'Take this cap of the Umpires and Referees Association. The visor is bigger than normally what you find. Maximum protection. People have started to become referees and umpires only to get this cap.'

'Ha ha.'

'You are looking smart in it. Or I can say, it is looking smart on you.'

Pulling it tighter on her head, Smt Chitol stepped out into the blinding light of Turadi Junction.

Jha, the health inspector, was built facially like a cauliflower, florety cheeks and clumpy hair baking away in the hot blast of a gargantuan straw-padded cooler. As she entered his office he cursed a peon that it had run dry again. 'Look how cunning he is!' he told her. 'I told him the divisional medical officer is coming and he should not see water collected anywhere. So what does the scoundrel do? He purposely does not refill my cooler.'

But Smt Chitol had an excellent effect on the h.i.'s mood. First, with her multiple-wife case, whereupon he gleefully volunteered that the divisional medical officer about to visit ahead of the g.m. inspection was reputed to acquire a wife in each of his postings. Next, by the fact that she grew up in Bihar and was in fact half Bihari. Through vigorous querying he determined that she was the product of Bihari Kayastha and Bengali Brahmin, now married to a Gujarati Baniya, and he found the whole thing comical, beyond rationale, and he thumped the desk and laughed. He further demonstrated his caste mastery by enumerating the communities under his command: Valmiki-Mehtar of UP-Haryana-Rajasthan original, in the Deccan for generations; then Matangi and Marathi Banjara or Lambada, whatever you want to call them, in fact several from Maharashtra and Karnataka, a number of them not traditionally cleaning castes, because of these compassionate appointments mainly, but most of them SC/ST *wale*; plus he had Muslims, he had the Jai Bhim *wale*, and in her Bombay Division was it not the Gujarati Rukhis in big numbers who were in sanitation?

At this stage the peon came by and put on the tap in the wall outside – which, it turned out, was all that was needed to refill the cooler – and to quell the thunderous shouting he received, informed the h.i. that the d.m.o. was expected in half an hour.

'Quickly bring tea for madam. And for me,' the h.i. ordered the peon.

'No, don't bring for me,' she overruled him.

'You won't have tea?'

'I just had Glucon D.'

'Stationmaster gave you?'

'Yes.'

The health inspector guffawed madly.

'Ey, Raju, bring tea.'

'No, Raju, don't bring it.'

'Why are you standing here? Go bring it.'

'Madam is saying no, don't bring it.'

'Just bring it, she will have it.'

'No, no, I won't have it.'

'Rest of the day I have to be around for the d.m.o.,' said the health inspector. 'So we might as well have tea now.'

'Where will I find the workers?' she asked him.

'Why should you find them? I will call someone to meet you. Right now, they will be on a break. No shortage of breaks for them. No wonder this colony is in this condition.'

'After the break?'

'The *dalel* work in the afternoon is at that end of the colony, near the porter *chali*, that's where they will be together. If they act smart, just tell them I have sent you. And if the mukaddam tells you any *ulta-seedha* nonsense tell me, we will sort her out. Raju, where's the tea! Wait, Charulataji, where are you going?'

In the dazzling white afternoon the chalk-clad quarters in the ageing railway colony shimmered like a maze of mirrors. She located the sanitation workers in a vacant lot, struggling against the brush over the open gutter that ran away farther than the eye could see. The women, dupattas wrapped around their heads and their faces, scythed the brambly vegetation along the borders of the gutter; the men, gamchhas on their heads, raked out garbage from it, releasing steam.

A welfare inspector all the way from Bombay led them to conclude that she must have come to assist in some systemic way and they began to list out their grievances. When they realised it was not so, that it was the health inspector who had sent her here, the women spoke with an edge, while the men went silent or intervened to counsel restraint, all in a vivid Dakhni that was the consensus tongue of this junction town near the border of three great linguistic states.

'Madam, if we sit and talk to you, somebody will see us. Then they will go tell the h.i. that all we do is sit and talk. If we stop to drink water, they think why aren't we working. If we sit two minutes in the shade, they think why aren't we working. When we sleep at night, they think why aren't we cleaning.'

'And if we sit and talk, who will clear all this along the length of this gutter? See how far it goes, two or three kilometres.'

'Then that other gutter up there, and then there, and behind there, and behind those quarters.'

'Madam, if we stop to talk to you, who will climb inside the gutter to remove the choke-up?'

'There are snakes in here. Scorpions and leeches. There is shit-piss, glass, nails, everything you can think of.'

'Do we get any tools, any protection? Even those rakes in the men's hands we have made ourselves, attaching the gangman's *panja* to bamboo.'

'Madam, we may not know to read but we know what the manuals have written – give them this, give them that, this should be done like this, that should be done like that. Manholes to be done like this. Big joke. I I.i. will come running and say what about the manholes, d.m.o. is coming in one hour. And he will send these men in just like that.'

'Look, madam, Jyothi here got bitten by a dog near that tank. She was reporting to work in the morning. She even got stitches – did they give her leave without cutting days? What did the h.i. say? Jyothi, tell her.'

'He said it happened before work hours, madam.'

'What else? Tell her properly.'

'Madam, he said what is wrong with your eyes and ears, can't you know when a dog is coming?'

'People are angry, madam, don't tell all this to the h.i.'

'Tell him, tell him, tell the h.i. everything. Somebody has to tell him.'

'Amma, calm down.'

'Why should I? Just because the g.m. is coming does it mean twenty people become two hundred? Madam, we wake up at four-thirty in the morning, cook lunch, report to work six-thirty. In the break we may have to wash clothes, take care of children, in-laws, whosoever, report for afternoon duty. *Marda log*, they don't have housework, they can say calm down.'

'At least listen to madam's problem, she has come from far away.'

'Okay, madam, sorry, tell your problem. You want to find out about that person who used to work here?'

'Oh.'

'Then?'

'Madam, who will remember, which *zamana* is all this from?'

'Show the photo, madam.'

'Never seen him.'

'Very difficult, madam.'

'Name again?'

'Which community?'

'Telugu – some were there, no? Oh Vasanti, talking to you.'

'How should I know? Send her to Kamlabai.'

'Where does Kamlabai live?'

'That you will have to ask Lakshmi amma.'

'Aahn, Jyothi, you take her to Lakshmi amma, she lives near you. Madam, first let her finish duty. Otherwise the h.i. will give me an earful. I'm the mukaddam. The way h.i. talks you would think he never sits down. He does not even get up to turn on a light.'

'Don't start again.'

'Then he will spit his paan masala on the floor and wonder why it is not clean.'

'Don't tell him all this, madam. She is angry but if you tell h.i. she'll get into more trouble.'

'Jyothi, tell her what we did last year.'

'We put locks on the quarters, madam.'

'Tell her what h.i. did then?'

'He wrote a complaint, madam.'

'She is not telling anything properly. I will tell you. They built new quarters. Never do they give us quarters in the colony, madam. They want us to clean the colony but not to live in it. How many huts I have tied myself! Tied one in Daund. One in Ahmednagar, but the water didn't suit me. Paid a worker here two thousand rupees for mutual transfer, and with that I told him, take the house I made there, and when I came I tied one here too. When they made these new quarters we found again all others workers would get them – track, engine, porter, whosoever it may be. We put locks on them.'

'We went and put locks on the new quarters, madam.'

'What does the h.i. do? He writes the complaint against us. Who is he in this? Does he have a problem if we live in the colony? I asked him – who are you in this?'

'Now he's after her, madam. She is our mukaddam.'

'I don't care.'

'Madam, everyone has become hot in the head. Look at this heat.'

'G.m. will come in a big white car. He will put on his sunglasses and ten people will fight to go hold an umbrella over his head. He will look around for two minutes and go back into the car. But we have to work under this sun.'

'Let us focus on helping madam. She has come from far.'

'Jyothi, you take her.'

'Madam, I will take you after work. I will meet you at the stairs on the platform near the ticket office. We will go from there.'

'Bye, madam.'

'Okay, bye, bye, bye, thank you, madam, bye.'

'Bye.'

'Bye. Bye.'

'When did you come here, madam?'

'How many days?'

'Who is looking after the children?'

'Where are you staying?'

'Rest in the retiring room, madam. This sun you will not be able to handle. We are used to it. You will faint. Already looking weak.'

'Madam, stationmaster gave you that cap?'

'Ha ha.'

'Ha ha ha ha.'

'Haha hahaha. Ha ha.'

'Okay, madam, bye.'

By evening the vaporising town speckled into form like a mirage. Along the edges of the road frantic pigs attacked the choked gutters. A herd of buffaloes with gleaming red scimitars on their heads made their way from the railway colony across the tracks, as if rested in their quarters and now ready for evening life in the nameless bars fluttering behind thin floral curtains. In the heat the animals, the bars, were like a dream. And who in this heat-dream could possibly tell her about Nagaiah?

Jyothi had flowers in her hair. The women walked into thin streets, between house walls made by roughly stacked grey stone slabs from the famous quarries in the region. Near a Mariamma temple Smt Chitol was asked to wait.

After a while Jyothi returned with Lakshmi amma, her spectacles thick, her back bent, her face cartographically lined, and in the fading light Smt Chitol put a photograph before her.

What's the use of showing me that, daughter? Oh so many years, how will I remember these people? Let me tell you how long ago it is, daughter. I started when I had four children, now they all have children. I joined when my husband went off. No, he was an engine cleaner. All the time he used to be coughing and falling sick. Someone told us, get a medical certificate, he will be able to change the department. One doctor asked for one thousand rupees for the unfit certificate. We gave him all that money, but still my husband he died. They were giving me waterwoman post, serve water to passengers when the train stops at the platform – summer months only, so I said *nakko*. Again and again I travelled to the d.s. office carrying a child on my waist, telling them, give me a letter for permanent work, I need a letter. They put me in sanitation, then I became permanent, so like that it was. Now I can't remember this person or see what you are showing me with my bad eyes. Acid has finished them.

Hau, acid. That is what they gave us to clean the bathrooms. Whenever any big officer would come we had to scrub the toilets, floors, tiles, make everything shine. Here, these marks on my skin. Acid. Acid would splash into the eyes. Tell me, daughter, you can cover your nose and mouth, how can you cover your eyes and work? So no use showing me anything. Acid has finished my eyes.

Kamlabai will be able to tell you. She is younger than me. You don't know where she lives? Oh, Jyothi, take her, ba. You can't? I will send my grandson with you. Jyothi, call him, ba, I can hear him.

You meet Kamlabai. Her mind is still sharp as a knife and her voice is like thunder.

Yes, I am Kamlabai. And who are you?

Hau. Hau. Hau.

Hau, hau.

Show. Show fast, I have dinner to make, don't I.

No, can't make out. Don't have a better picture? He has a beard in this. Did he have a beard that time? Don't know even that? This side of his face is totally shining with light, can't see anything.

Telugu, you said? Was it a couple? Yes, I remember a husband-wife. Hau, the wife was here too. I remember her. Why, I'll tell you? She always stood by us.

She was there when we showed the doctor. Don't know that story?

Now, listen. I was the first woman mukaddam we ever had, that is what they tell me. Once I saw the h.i. go into the doctor's chamber and heard them abusing. English abuses. Hau. I went inside and said – you abused us, no? They were taken aback. We may not speak English but we understand abuse. I told the doctor straight, you are a servant of Railways and I am a servant of Railways, what is the difference between me and you? Have they given you this chair to shout abuses? They refused to say sorry. The workers stood with me, some union people too, we lined up with flags outside his office. She was there. She was not permanent.

That h.i. If he would see us washed up after work he would say – did you work or not? Moment he saw us clean, he jumped on us. When we worked in the gutter he would come and stand like this on top, legs spread on either side of the gutter. Now we women have pulled up our *kasautas* above our knees and gone into the drain. We are bending and working, and he is standing above us with legs spread and shouting at us. One day my head became so hot, I decided he's going to have it. I scooped out the *chikkad* so hard it flew on him. Hau, shoes, pant, shirt, everything! He tried to take action against me. All the women stood together with me. She was there, yes, she stood with us.

Chandramma ... Chandramma ... hau, something like that. That could be her name. How am I to remember everything for you? Don't have her picture?

Whether his name is Nagaiah or Venkaiah or what I do not know. He left her, didn't he? Can't say if they had a son. Why don't you ask her?

Dead? When did she die? How could she be dead for many years when I saw her just a few months back?

Where, right here in Turadi, that's where. On the main road is where I saw her. I was in the bus, going to my son's house. He's lost his legs. His wife works in others' houses. Half the time I'm there. So I was in the bus, she was walking out of our Mahaveer bhaiya's lane. He was our old mukaddam. She may have gone there. Used to be close to him.

Hau, I can tell you where his house is. But he is dead, isn't he?

'So what you did?' The stationmaster touched his fingers to his eyes and brought them to the tips of his moustache, perhaps praying for its longevity.

'I went to Mahaveer bhaiya's house. It seems she had come to invite them to her daughter's wedding. She did not know he had died.'

'Hmm. So then?'

'She had left a card.'

'Anh!'

'It was in Telugu.'

'Oh ho!'

'Luckily the address was in English also.'

'Where is it?'

'A for Amberpet.'

'What do you mean, madam?'

'Just joking, sir. In Bombay for Absent they say Ambernath. A for Ambernath. The station code on the display is A.'

'He he. Amberpet, Hyderabad?'

'Sir.'

'Now what we will do?'

'I will go.'

'All the way you will go to Hyderabad?'

'Yes, sir. How else will I find out whether it is the same person or not?'

'Madam.'

'Sir?'

'Okay, then you better wait for some time and catch the Express. Passenger will come earlier but you will reach only by late evening.'

'I will have to take clearance from a.p.o., sir.'

'You call up from here. Call up your family also.'

'Okay, sir.'

'Then you will have to either spend the night there or catch a night train back. You study these timetables using this ruler. The centre strip is a magnifying glass. Slide it up and down as you read. I have seen so many stationmasters struggling with those old round magnifying glasses, making one mistake after another. Now they are taking this idea from me. If you go to Kacheguda, ask Naidu where he got the idea.'

'Definitely, sir.'

'If I get two minutes with the g.m. I will tell him to consider distributing these rulers to all the stationmasters in the zone. People will start becoming stationmasters just to get this ruler.'

'Ha ha.'

The stationmaster smiled, his moustache parenthesising his mouth.

'Now you kindly phone up, madam, I am very busy.'

The young man who showed her to the address, an Ambedkar pin badge on his shirt pocket, his hair quiffed at the front, curls running over his neck, was in a hurry for he had evening college to attend.

'Is there anyone called Chandramma there?' Smt Chitol asked him along the way.

'Chandramma? Oh yes, madam.'

'Means she is alive?'

'She is very much alive.'

'I was told she had died!'

'If she is dead then her ghost is here,' said the young man, 'but no ghost could talk so much!'

In a corner of the basti the woman looked up from her bundle of firewood to take in the mysterious arrival.

'*Kya hona?*'

She stared straight at Smt Chitol. A face of contours and dimensions, oiled black hair, elaborate nose jewellery, a red teeka, expressive eyes. A deep force emanated from her.

On hearing Smt Chitol's story, she let out a bemused chuckle, soaked in too many emotions to articulate.

'He had no such son,' she said. 'I do not know who came to you but I am Chandramma, original wife of Nagaiah, and I am alive.'

'Give me the full story, Amma,' Smt Chitol said.

Neighbouring women and children had started to gather around them.

'You are looking tired. Will you have a cold drink? There is a shop here. That man keeps an icebox.'

'I would prefer tea,' said Smt Chitol.

'Very good, I will make it.'

As she did the women and children made a semicircle on the cool mud floor, coming and going for chores, and when Chandramma began to speak, there were murmurs, prompts and questions, laughs and tears, and minor disputations and eggings-on that seemed to say: Tell us more, Chandramma.

What shall I tell you about Nagaiah? I had not met him till we got married. Father fixed it. He was friends with Nagaiah's uncle. We married. I went to his village to live. You never saw the village, did you?

Too bad, sister, you missed the magical wind of those villages. Always blows from west to east. Never the other way. Our Madiga wada was in the east, so the wind can only blow from them to us, you understand, never blow from us to them. If there is a storm, if the trees bend the other way, they are telling lies. If leaves fly this way and that, the leaves are telling lies. The Brahmins have made sacrifices, done all the pujas, instructed the sky, so how can it disobey? You are laughing, sister! The Brahmins have created the laws of nature, and you are laughing at such a serious matter?

Now one thing I can tell you about Nagaiah, it was always his dream to work in the Railways. He used to tell me when he was small he would go out to the railway lines and run with the trains. Actually, a lot of boys in the villages did that. They walked one–two hours to the railway lines just to run with the trains. Maybe they thought the trains would take them away to somewhere good, somewhere great, to a place they can have all they want. They believed in trains. So when we went to Turadi to work for Railways Nagaiah was happy.

Why did we go there? That is where my father worked when he died. They have the stone quarries around there, he used to catch work in those. Then he began to catch work in Railways as a substitute. When he died, Railways said we cannot give job to anyone in the family, we can only take as casual. My brothers, one had gone to Solapur to work in the mills, the wages were better, another one was in the village, working in the fields, off season he would come to Hyderabad and catch work. So I took the chance. In the village it was very difficult for us. Nagaiah had no land. First Railways said no, because I was a married daughter. In the end they said only place we can give work right now is health department casual. They took Nagaiah in sanitation also.

You have seen the colony, ah? We had to sweep the place, gather all the cooking ash, collect all the garbage, load it into the bullock cart, clean the gutters. Worst part was the shit. We did not know we would have to do that. No, sister, not septic tanks. Dry latrine. Some bungalows had septic tanks, rest all *kacha sandas*. Even now some are there, when I went I asked; in the track-side *chali* it is all raw latrine.

Pan system, if you really want to know. At the back of the quarters for each latrine there was a pan. We would pull the pan out, tilt it, drain out the liquid. We would scoop up the material with a *thikra*, they used to call it. It was a piece of metal. The part of the bicycle that goes over the wheel, that's what we used, Mahaveer bhaiya showed us how to make it. Scoop up all the material with the *thikra* and put it into a bucket. Not exactly a bucket. Sanitation used to have these phenyl boxes, twenty or thirty litres. After they became empty, that is what we used. Cut off the top on one side to put in the material, and that would give us a grip to hold it also. After we collected the material we would shout from outside, Amma, *pani maaro*, throw some water. We would wash the pans, let the water run into the gutter and put the pan back in place.

When our box filled up we loaded it on the shoulder and walked into the jungle to throw into a ditch. More than one round most days. It was usually the men who carried it away, but we did it too. People would hold their noses as we went past, as if it was not their shit we were taking away. Children would throw pebbles at us and run off laughing. It was difficult, sister. Sometimes if the load would become too much on one shoulder, you shifted it to the other shoulder or on to your head, and if the ground is up and down it could spill on you, even your face. I was not used to it. I would cry in the beginning, I would vomit, catch infections, get sick. The rains were the worst. But in the rains we could bathe like queens. In the hot weather we had to make every drop count.

Nagaiah hated that work. Who would not? And with that I think he started hating me too. Maybe he saw me every day and all he saw was shit.

Sister, in the village we never had to do this work. Our wada may be separate, at the tea shops our cups may be separate and we wash them ourselves and money they will not give or take directly from our hands, and the landlord – suppose that young man who brought you here, if he dared to wear a shirt-pant like that, with a nice hairstyle, wearing that Ambedkar badge, the landlord would make sure he was tied to a tree and got a good thrashing. In the village there were no latrines like this. Mostly people went out into the fields. In the towns the women swept and men sometimes did sewage work – that work is very dangerous, the gas can finish you, or you can get sucked inside and not be seen again. But we did not lift shit.

Madiga, we are leather workers. That is our tradition. We know how to make leather from hide, make *dappus*, make and repair shoes. Many of us worked in the fields. Some were *jeetagallu* – whatever the landlord wants, morning to night you do, get rice and two pairs of clothes and a blanket and some few rupees in a year. We made ropes. We made plates with leaves.

If our people did this work they did it far away from home and at home they hid it. I too did not speak about it. I remember one elder in our village saying, I would rather die than do such work. I felt so ashamed on hearing it. The reason I am telling you this, sister, is because I left it. I wish nobody has to ever do it, and that is another reason I am telling you.

In Turadi, I got to know some of the Mehtar community people. Hau, Valmiki. They did not like it when others came into this line. They would tell us, why are you trying to take our work, *pet pe laat kaiku maarri*? After some time people forget all this. The person who took most care of us there was Mahaveer bhaiya. If we needed money, whatever money he had in his pocket he would give us. Two rupees, three rupees, five rupees. If we needed rice, he would give. Any time of the night you could go to him for help. He would talk about his experiences in life, how his mother would go from house to house to pick up shit in a bucket, get four annas per house per month.

I wish he could have come for my daughter's wedding.

Hau, sister, forgive me for crying. Hardships don't make me cry. Life is hardships, isn't it? Sometimes there is so much love between people, that is what makes me cry.

Yes, everyone, I know she wants to know about Nagaiah. It is all part of the story.

Sister, we kept working in Turadi. Railways was too clever for us. After three months they would give us a break for three days. You have to do continuous ninety days or one-twenty days or whatsoever it was, if you break service you cannot become permanent. We tried for other departments. The mukaddams asked for a lot of money.

Sometimes Nagaiah used to be put on track cleaning. Women, even if we are given station duty, we were not put on the track. A train suddenly comes full speed, how will you climb on to the platform in a sari?

Have you heard of Ramanapuram, sister? These people are laughing. And look this Ellama is crying. Sometimes, sister, there is no difference between tears and laughter. They all know this one.

They say if you get married in the temple at Ramanapuram, you will be blessed with many healthy sons. They say the feast in the hall is like the food of heaven, everything cooked in pure ghee. The guests just cannot stop eating. They eat and eat and when they cannot eat any more they get on the train. By the time the train reaches Turadi they cannot keep the food inside them. Now you are not supposed to empty yourself when the train is stopped at the station. Does anyone listen? Everything comes out there on the tracks. Those people think, very good, we have done our job: we have gone for the wedding, we have blessed the couple, we have taken blessings from God, we have eaten so nicely the food cooked in pure ghee, and now we have taken it out also. Everything is perfect. We have completed our duties. Duty to clean it is someone else's.

Nagaiah's behaviour became very bad. Earlier he used to laugh and joke, bring things for the house. All that stopped. Yes, sister, drinking. In that line, all the men did. There was no family, no panchayat, he became free to act however. If he came home in a bad state I would refuse to serve his plate. That used to make him very angry. He would tell me I am such a person that no child will ever grow in my stomach.

How many children you have, sister? How many years since your marriage? You must have seen this, hau, if in the first two years of marriage you don't have a child people start looking at you differently. The whole family loses respect for you. But good, at least you are working, looking healthy, maybe it will happen. In the village the women in the big houses, they sit at home all day and get all kinds of health problems. I tried everything. Offered my hair in the temple. Took medicines. In the village my mother-in-law took me to someone who could remove the evil spirit. But the problem was not with me, sister.

When Nagaiah gave me too much trouble, I would go away to live with my mother. He would come and fetch me. It happened a few times.

He did not tell me when he went to Bombay.

I knew he might go one day. A lot of our people would leave the state to catch work: more than half would go to Bombay. There was always demand. Construction work. They say we built Bombay. The men would settle down, come back to marry or take the wife and children back with them. Not easy in the city. Rice as much as they could carry they would carry, twenty to thirty kilos, onions, dal, tamarind, haldi, chillies. The elders would go round to houses and say, my son's family is going to the expensive city, if you have any rice or tamarind to spare.

I knew he would not come back to take me.

Let it be, sister. Nagaiah story ends there.

You have come all the way from Bombay, gone here and there in the heat, that is why I have told you all this. Look at this Ellama laughing. She is saying that I love talking! In truth, I want to forget about that past life. Today you have told me Nagaiah has died. The way he was going I thought he would have died long ago. The boy, whosoever came to you, is right in one way. That Chandramma is dead too.

No, sister, what proof of marriage, proof of divorce will I have? My life is proof, more proof than I need.

I am a sweeper here in the municipality. I am permanent. Some of my relatives were settled here, that is how I came to this city. Two children. My husband, he is my mother's cousin's son. They were facing a problem with him. He is, what you call, *mooga*, can't speak properly. Look again, this Ellama, she is saying he has no choice but to stay quiet and keep listening to me! He is a cobbler. He will return when it is dark. Son is training to become a stuntman, here in the basti. Daughter has a job in a factory in Nacharam.

She can read and write, sister. I did not want her to suffer like me. Even taking a bus is difficult if you cannot read. She can read and write English too. We may not have any education, but let us send our girl to school, I told my husband, let us send her to a school.

See here. Give me your diary, sister. I can write my name. My girl taught me.

There, how do you like it?

Write your name, sister.

Hau, hau, I see.

Starting is same, ending is same, middle is different.

Hau, sister?

The entire journey across the flaming ghats, heat in her stomach, sunburn on her forehead, white glare in her eyes, she thought about the women.

About the boy there were several theories. He was an opportunist country cousin of Nagaiah, or a bold schemer from the neighbourhood, perhaps part of a conman gang. There was talk of welfare inspector you-know-whose 'placement agency', and all that was needed was another welfare inspector's compliance.

Nobody could find out. The chancer was never seen again. He was gone like smoke in the wind, gone like G, absent as A, as A for Ambernath.

4
Missing person

'Yes, tell me the case again,' said the new a.p.o. (l&w) to Smt Chitol, not for the first time.

'Missing employee, sir,' Smt Chitol complied, again.

'Yes, the pointsman. What happened you said, left home for an evening shift?'

'Left home for an evening shift, then was never seen again.'

'Yes. Hmm … right … tell me more …'

The a.p.o. dusted the globe on his desk with a feather as he listened. He kept a very orderly desk.

'Not seven years completed, is that correct? Cannot be presumed dead.'

'Yes, sir. But seven years not necessary for a "real hardship" case. She could have been appointed after three years with g.m. approval.'

'Hmm … and why was it rejected the first time?'

'Can't really say it was rejected. It did not proceed.'

'Must be a reason,' said the a.p.o.

'It is a very strange file, sir. Incomplete, disjointed. No notings where there should have been.'

'Very unusual.'

'Truly.'

'She is still young.'

'Yes, sir.'

'Six years gone,' mused the a.p.o. 'She can get permission to marry again.'

He allowed his thick bifocals to slide down the bridge of his nose so that the frames rested on his rosy leathery cheeks. He peered through them at the neat stack of papers on his immaculate desk.

'Did you get a chance to study it, sir?' she enquired a few days later.

'Achha, you have been in this department longer than me,' said the a.p.o., which was true, for the present assistant personnel officer (labour & welfare) was none other than stationmaster Intezar Ahmed, whom you may remember as one who had long ago discovered an abandoned infant in his first week at work. He had got to this position by an unusual route. A station superintendent by rank, he was transferred from Wadala, where Smt Chitol's path had briefly crossed his, to Dadar, where he ran into a public agitation and fielded a projectile on his head, which affected his vision and thereby his fitness for the post. Medically decategorised to the personnel ministerial room, he utilised his new day job and the experiences of his prior one to good effect, as well as the night hours between eight and two, so that when the a.p.o. examinations came round, for which he was deemed eligible, he aced them.

'You have been in the department longer than me, so you must know the priorities for compassionate appointment. On-duty death or permanently crippled, then in-harness death –'

'– then totally incapacitated, then medically decategorised. Yes, sir, I know. I was a compassionate appointee myself.'

'Now if the missing persons category is not in the list of priorities, we have to assume it is the lowest priority, don't we?'

'Actually, with regard to the priority there is a provision for special cases. We can get it sanctioned. And this is nothing if not a special case.'

'Is it so?'

'Yes, sir.'

'By definition all compassionate grounds appointments are special cases,' said the a.p.o. without argument. 'Yours was a compassionate appointment, you said?'

'Yes, sir.'

'What happened? ... Go on ... Oh Bhombalpur ... Hmm, I knew someone posted there ... What exactly happened? ... Most unfortunate ... Yes, you are right, life may have gone along a different track ... Life is a strange and unpredictable journey indeed ... Did I ever think I would have to come to a.p.o. because of some miscreants? ... I tell you, time changes everything ... And speaking of time, have a look, almost twelve o'clock, I should go see the d.p.o.'

'Right, sir.'

At the end of the Monday meeting in the a.p.o. (l&w)'s new plywood cabin up on the second floor, Smt Chitol chose to start, as Pearl Flanger had once suggested to the railway children, with an arresting detail.

'Sir, I found out about her limp.'

'What limp?'

'She has a limp.'

'Who has a limp?'

'The missing employee's wife, sir.'

'Well, what did you find out about her limp?'

'It's nothing serious. One is shorter than the other by one and a half inches, that's all, she says. Doesn't affect her in any way. Don't think the Medical will be an issue. She is prepared for any kind of job.'

'But, tell me,' said the a.p.o. with a frown that was not unpleasant. 'From what I know, the settlement is not done.'

'It is not.'

'How should we put up the application before the settlement is complete?'

'Actually, for missing employees the appointment is delinked from settlement. Board letter dated, one minute, sir, I have it, 27 December '83.'

'Two days after Christmas, 1983.'

'Sir.'

'Two hundred and thirty-six not out.'

'Sir?'

'When Gavaskar made his highest Test score.'

'Is it?'

'Madras. Once the cricket worm enters you, it doesn't leave.'

'I have anyway initiated the settlement, sir.'

'Have you? Why is she anxious about the job then? The settlement will give her ample relief.'

'That is the whole thing, it will be relief only. Nothing like a job for a woman to stand on her own feet.'

The a.p.o. had scar tissue on his temple, just beneath a centre-parted fringe. Perhaps it was left by the projectile that took him out of station superintendence. He inscribed circular motions upon it with his little finger.

'Came down to the middle order in that match,' he reminisced after a few moments. 'Pure concentration. Nothing could distract him from his objective. That is what a person should be like. Does your husband watch?'

'Yes, sir. And plays.'

'Once the cricket worm is inside you, it doesn't leave.'

'Should I put it together, sir?'

'Very well,' said the a.p.o., cordially.

'Do you remember retired stationmaster Das, sir?' Smt Chitol jauntily enquired the following week.

'Das? Why would I not know him? We used to play carrom. Can't say he was very good. Too emotional. His whole life went up or down after a shot.'

'I traced him. Have a nice character reference from him for the missing employee. In case anyone thinks he has gone underground for antisocial activities. I think the application is strong, sir.'

'But, tell me. If we give an out-of-turn appointment –'

'Not exactly out of turn, sir. Since there is a provision for it.'

'Yours is not the only case with us, Mrs Chitol,' said the a.p.o., with a polite smile given the interruption, which he did not appreciate at all. 'How many cases in front of me right now?'

'Yes, sir. Always a crush.'

'If someone comes in the front of the queue, everybody else goes back. You must have stood in lines. It is quite frustrating.'

'That is true, sir. The other way to think of it is she has already been in the queue for three years. Since the incident happened in '84, it means she became eligible three years ago.'

'When she has been managing for six years, what is one more?'

'She is at the mercy of her extended family. And she has to pay them rent.'

'How does she pay it?'

'Does piece-rate stitching.'

'Perfect. Doesn't even have to leave the home.'

'She wants to. It's not easy there, she tells me. She doesn't make very much income either. It is unreliable, as you can imagine. As you know, she has two minor sons.'

'That is why it is not bad that she is living with family, is it? At least they can make sure the younger one also doesn't end up in jail.'

'Not jail, sir. Observation home. He is an undertrial. But how does that matter?'

'What matters is that she hid it from you,' said the a.p.o., with a merest hint of belligerence.

'Didn't exactly *hide* it. She did not mention it. But I confronted her about that, sir.'

'And? What did she say?'

'She said she felt ashamed to talk about it.'

'Well, she should.'

'She said the place was such.'

'Which place?'

'The place they had to move to. SS Compound.'

'What was so special about it?'

'She said it was the kind of place you could not leave your slippers outside the door because they would be gone. A place where the butchers stitched testicles on to old she-goats to get a better rate.'

'That doesn't make any sense!'

'He fell in with a group of older boys who stole. She said that was his weakness since he was small – trying to impress older boys. He didn't do anything wrong, he just knew them, she maintains.'

'That's what all mothers say. Whose responsibility was he?'

'How does it make a difference, sir? Suppose there is a case against somebody's son in this office, can we hold that against the employee during promotion?'

The a.p.o. reclined his head in a deliberate manner and sighed at the ceiling fan.

'Can you imagine what she's saying about those butchers? What sense does that make?'

'Hello, sir, how are you doing? Any progress on the file?'

'Which one?'

She drew an audible breath.

'Missing employee.'

'Haan, good you reminded me. I wanted to ask you. This "real hardship" is subjective, isn't it?'

'Meaning?'

'The question is how do we decide what is a real hardship case. If she is with her family, she is engaged in work and she is managing for six years, is it justified to call it *real hardship*?'

'I would say so, sir. Consider how much she has lost. Her husband, her house, her possessions. The street she lived. Everything turned to ash.'

'All of which she hid from you.'

'Yes, sir. I didn't like that at all. Told her not to make me feel like a fool. I told her I had to learn from the police, and that is not helping her.'

'What did she say?'

'That she doesn't like to mention that it was a riots matter.'

'Why?'

'Doesn't like to think about it. Says she has nightmares about it. The dreams are worse, she says. She dreams there is a knock at the door and he has come with fruits and dates for the house and gifts for the children. Then she touches everything around her to remind herself she is where she is, nothing has changed.'

The a.p.o. ran his fingers over the scar tissue. As he did, his fringe lost its parting and it made him look unexpectedly vulnerable.

'If it is, it is,' he said at last. 'Why hide it? Is it possible to stop thinking about it by hiding it?'

'Totally wrong of her. I gave her a rocket. I think she got the message.'

'When you try to hide things, people become suspicious.'

'That is what I told her, sir. She said the moment she talks about it she is thought of as trouble. It works against her, especially now, with the atmosphere in the country. She definitely should not be hiding things from us. But I guess she is not totally wrong. Yesterday they announced this *rath yatra*.'

The a.p.o. excused himself, pleasantly enough, to visit the toilet.

A few days later the a.p.o. looked freshly unperturbed.

'Yes?' he looked at Smt Chitol, almost challenging her to say the words.

'Sir, missing employee application,' she squeezed them out of herself.

'Say, when did you say she first applied – three years ago?'

'Yes, sir.'

'Tell me again, why was the application rejected?'

'Did not proceed, sir,' said Smt Chitol, again. 'A very unusual file. Missing links. Incoherent. So no good reason maybe.'

'There must be a reason, we just don't know it.'

'Nothing seems wrong with the case, sir. Dependency of the family on the missing employee is established. Real hardship is established. The man is still missing, that is established from the police. In fact, when I visited the police made no adverse comments about him. Only about the community ...'

The last portion hung in the air, but she went no further. She did not mention the cut-foreskin slang which the policemen used among themselves, nor their definition of missing. 'You know missing means what? Missing means he must have gone to Kashmir to become a terrorist.' She did not divulge their looking-out-for-you advice as she departed: 'Be careful who you want to give a job to, railways is a matter of national security, it will come on *your* head,' and she did not mention how the visit was doubly disturbing as it had left her, too, wary of the applicant, enough to give her a rocket.

'Very strange,' remarked the a.p.o. 'Who did you say was the welfare inspector at the time?'

'Godbole, sir.'

'Who is no longer in service.'

'No longer in the world.'

'Hmm ... just her luck.'

'I don't know what all the police would have told him, sir,' said Smt Chitol.

'Hmm ...' said the a.p.o.

'She says she got tired following up with the welfare inspector. It seems he was very rude. I agree she can have an annoying manner, but still.'

'Hmm ... Didn't know the man.'

'He told her to go to court if she is in such a hurry. As if she has the money for that.'

'Strange indeed,' remarked the a.p.o. 'And the welfare inspector is no more. Just her luck.'

'She is relieved that the police haven't made her husband an accused in some case. It has happened to some missing persons she knows.'

The a.p.o. put his pinkie to his scar. It was a nice day, not so hot that he should be sweating in his plywood cabin.

'In less than a year she will become eligible without any special approvals,' he said. 'And who knows, maybe the husband will be found by then.'

'Some people are still being found, she says. They are beyond identification.'

The a.p.o. went silent. He turned his gaze to his lap. He scratched his scar tissue and spoke after a full minute.

'She is not old. Did you suggest to her that she marry again?'

'No, sir.'

The a.p.o. pouted lightly.

'How many thousands of things we are dealing with,' he remarked in a quiet voice, so it cannot be said that he snapped. 'Is this the most important matter in the department right now? Don't get stuck on one thing, Mrs Chitol.'

'What is it that is being held against her, sir?'

The a.p.o. took his fingers to the scar.

'What is being held against her?'

'Mrs Chitol.'

'What is, sir?'

'Mrs Chitol. Please.'

'Sir, if *you* won't help her, who will?'

'What are you trying to say?'

For the first time his face betrayed real aggravation.

'You have been after my life about this case. Look at the background, the riot, that boy in jail, the rejected application –'

'Not rejected, sir.'

'How many officers from our community do you see here? And I have only just started. How do you think it will look if I make a special push for this case?'

His voice did not rise but it had deepened and quickened. He was fairly crimson in the face. Perhaps she had already said too much. So she did not add what was on her lips: and would the application feel so dispensable if it was a Salim not a Salima?

'I don't mean a special push, sir,' she said instead. 'But she should not be made to suffer because of this.'

'This is what you do not realise,' said the a.p.o. 'I know that better than you.'

He stroked his scar, adjusted his bifocals and returned to the papers on his orderly desk.

Slowly, his crimson face subsided into its rose-leather complexion.

A little more time, she told Salima, who could have an annoying manner, who stood four feet eleven inches on her better leg. The settlement will give you relief. The a.p.o.'s very name is *intezar*, so of course there will be some waiting, and look how the months are passing, soon it will be seven years gone. The good thing is we have everything prepared.

'What happened to that case?' her father-in-law enquired one day.

'Boss put it on hold,' she replied.

'Actors!' he remarked approvingly. 'People with experience can tell. What is his name?'

5
Kamalpur

'Surprise!' Bansi stood at the door drumming her chubby fingers on Shlok's crown. She had persuaded the boy to forsake his friends in Borivali – there was 'no chance' she was going to let him miss Diwali downtown – yet nobody expected him to show up bearing a scarlet mouth, cloth tail and an aluminium mace; and upstairs Smt Chitol was a little surprised at the number of toddler Rams and Hanumans on show. The terraces had turned into a set of a children's *Ramayan*, or a cute montage cut from the *rath yatra*, the motorised chariot winding its way across the country, whipping up support for the Ram temple.

The children scrambled chaotically across the chinimati flooring to discharge their fireworks and the adults scurried about to reset them in battle formations. As the evening progressed, as the rockets went flying into the air, as the anars spouted fire, the chakras spun dervish light and the Lakshmi bombs resounded in the courtyards, it emerged that some of the mini heroes, Shlok a natural-born leader among them, were not just aware of the chants from the *rath yatra*, they were adept at teaching the uninitiated. The children waved their shining foil tridents and swords and broke out with gusto in their child voices.

Where Ram was born, That is where we will build the temple!
Every child is for Ram's cause, We'll work for the birthplace!

Verily, a child war! But with whom? She turned to ask the group.

These were Nimish's building and locality friends, and now their spouses, who had always gathered to watch the fireworks explode over the city from these well-located terraces, drinking from spiked soft-drink bottles, sometimes guessing which neighbourhood the spectacular firecrackers were sent up from.

'It's all in fun, Bhabhi!' Parag told her. 'Look how they are enjoying themselves.' So she took a glug and rectified her gaze.

'Watch your tail, *madoo*, it's going to catch fire!' screamed Bansi.

'He should fly to Mohammed Ali Road!' somebody exclaimed.

A jolly affair indeed, smoke and sparkle in so many eyes.

A knot of excitement developed in the part of the terrace overlooking the main road. A few young teenagers with keen eyes searched out skullcaps or burqas four storeys below, locked the target and released the arrow. 'Babur, Babur!' 'Dabur! Dabur!' The confused pedestrian may or may not have been able to discern over the festive din the words:

With the oil from Dabur, burn the name of Babur!

'Must be Lasarpatti!' someone cried.

Lasarpatti – that daredevil, who had gained the nickname when he slid head first down a slide and split his forehead, who lit rockets directly in his hand and released them in pairs.

'Ey, Lasarpatti, stop all that,' Nimish shouted, in a manner that only emboldened the guerrilla tactics against the sixteenth century.

Now came the Gandhians, for there were several staunch ones in the housing society. They watched the scenes in dismay. In response to the *rath yatra*, they wished to observe a quiet, prayerful Diwali for Hindu–Muslim unity. They had come upstairs with the proposal to the children and their young parents – it was what Gandhiji would have liked – and made no headway. As soon as their backs were turned, Bansi put a finger to her head and rotated it. 'How can you control and *dominate* kids and take away all their fun? Just wait, Charms, when you have children you'll know.'

Some tiny and tinier tots, too tiny for meaning, started going up and down the wooden stairs, stomping their feet to the chants of *Mandir vaheen banayenge!* We'll build the temple right there!

Smt Chitol went down to have a look, observing them with almost anthropological fascination, then continued past them. Reaching their floor, she saw that Pappa and Mummy had come out of the flat and were making for the staircase at the far end of the corridor. Neither enjoyed the pollution and wastefulness of crackers. All the excitement must have made them curious. She knew she ought to accompany them up.

She remained at the railing at the other end, watching them disappear. She hung her head down towards the courtyard and as her face fell forward felt the flush of C2, code word for the C_2H_5OH they secreted into the soft-drink bottles.

Below, the Gandhians and their kin were assembling. Their shapes converged near the stone mill. Old Sarikaben lit a diya and said a few words that did not travel up. Then they started to sing, 'Raghupati Raghav Raja Ram', and 'Vaishnav Jan Toh', which her mother-in-law could sing quite beautifully too, despite the voice that hurt the ear just a little. Through the great blasts and hisses of Diwali, and the stomps and chants reverberating in the stairwells, the words reached up intermittently, with a frail power.

She decided she would not go back upstairs.

'Coming for cards, na, Charms!' she heard a scream from somewhere.

Looking up, what does she see? Protruding from one of the portholes on the parapet, the bangled arms and triple-head of Bansi – triple, for she was shaking it about, making such an illusion – like a fantastic gargoyle in Victoria Terminus. It was perhaps the most fantastic sight Smt Chitol had seen in her life.

And here Bon Bons got stuck.

It would be impolite not to go up for this.

It took fifteen minutes to extract Bansi.

Shouts of Jai Shri Ram! went up when she came free.

Two nights later in the corridor, her flicking clothes off the line, him filling the bird bowl for the next day, beside him the black tea with lemon he had started taking after dinner.

'Did you speak to him?' she asked.

'Speak to who?'

'The broker. For a house. You said you would.'

She had been meaning to follow up, but had not planned on doing it right then.

'Oh,' Nimish said.

'Meaning?'

'What has happened now?'

She could hear the dread in his voice. He seemed to be forever feeling that he had just 'sorted things out'.

'Why should anything happen?'

Yet a part of her thought it wouldn't be a bad idea for something to happen. The tension of the past two days – Diwali night, her upcoming trip, the donation thing again, her father-in-law – it hung about the house like leftover firecracker smoke.

He looked up into the hazy sky, where the occasional rocket still exploded.

'I mean, where will we get a location like this?' he said.

'What about the room on sale in the other wing? It will be practically living in the same house.'

'That! Do you know how much our king on the terrace wants? Because of the location he thinks he can get any price he dreams up.' Since the flats were taken on a pagdi system, the tenant-owners were obliged to seek consent from the landlord-owner and share with him the proceeds of the sale.

'If you can manage the down payment, I can cover the instalments,' she persisted. 'Some of it at least. I can apply for an advance too.'

'No, that won't be needed,' Nimish was quick to clarify. 'I mean, we have to think carefully about where to put so much money. I need to put capital into the new business. We have to buy computers, hire more people, create more space in the office.'

He spoke in this way because he knew she knew.

Two mornings ago they had gone over to Parag's office for the *chopda pujan*, taking the silver coins they had bought on Dhanteras, and the priest had wrapped the old accounts books in red cloth and blessed the new. She'd been shown the work that had started on a mezzanine floor.

'There are other things we can use money for. We can get a car. Won't that be good? And I'm going to have the Western commode installed. One day we'll get a nice big house also,' he comforted her. She ignored it.

'Suppose I put in an application for railway quarters? It may take a long time. If we can get one at all. It means that we lose the House Rent Allowance, of course.'

'Didn't you say the quarters are in a terrible condition?'

'Yes.'

'It does not make sense, does it? Why would we do such a thing?'

She finished gathering the clothes in silence.

She could not tell where his convictions lay: whether he was persuaded of his practical arguments, or whether in his heart he did not wish to move at all – or whether it was simply that he did not want to upset his parents. If he were to propose so drastic a step as shifting out, he would be thought of as instigated by his wife, whom he had love-married. That prospect was not appetising to her either.

So she let it be. Perhaps he was protecting them? If they could not overcome difficulties such as these, after all, what was the use of being in love?

The next day she left for Kamalpur.

The case she was to inspect was of bungalow peon Ramkhiladi Kumar. Brought in by a senior officer for his domestic needs, he had served three continuous years in that home and was now getting screened for a reserved-quota vacancy in a Group D post that fell on her beat. Verify immediately and in person – the order had come straight from the chief personnel officer. A crackdown on 'backdoor entries'. A set of officers and their wives bringing youth into regular railway jobs via the bungalow-peon route, enjoying commission and bonded labour in the process.

Smt Chitol did not like to refuse or defer field trips. The moment she did people would say it was because she was a woman. And the truth was she could not wait to get away. Nimish could see that, and it was part of the reason that when they parted he did not quite look her in the eye.

Things started poorly and so they continued. A diesel generator caught fire on the platform, delaying her departure. Perspiring in the heat of the static coach, the steaming October heat of Bombay, she longed for air conditioning – although she was keenly acquainted with the provision in the Railway Servants (Pass) Rules by which she would be entitled to the privilege only upon reaching a basic pay of Rs 1680. At her current increment rate, assuming no promotions, that was six years away. Even if she wanted to, she could not delay her trip by quite that much.

The coach was sparsely occupied. The passengers in her compartment concurred that the rush was in the other direction, people returning from the villages after Diwali. The two discussants were men, as was the passenger on the side-lower berth. One's spectacles pincered a substantially deviated septum, which portended snoring. The second, in possession of a white stubble and somewhat orange eyes, had set up a steel glass and a bottle of water in a way that indicated eventual recourse to alcohol. The third man, across the aisle, already in a horizontal orientation with a thin sheet pulled over his head, appeared to be one of those remarkable passengers who slept all through a journey and yet knew exactly when to disembark.

She had not packed dinner; neither had her mother-in-law offered to. At Manmad she bought and ate an early biryani only because she had read the Nizam of Hyderabad's Guaranteed Railway once ran up till here. She repaired thereafter to her top-tier berth.

Travelling alone, that is where she felt secure. In her duffel bag she had her essentials: a bedsheet, a shawl, an inflatable pillow, chlorine drops, glucose biscuits, fruit, Odomos, a book. There came a moment after she had settled in, reading by whatever light available, when the rattle and lull of the train took over her body, like a massage, and she could feel herself drift towards sleep, in this private space, among strangers, and it filled her with a strange comfort. If the train stayed in motion she slept okay.

The coach went dark at the designated hour. The blue night-lights made an air of medical distress. It was a quiet train, the quietest she had been on, amplifying any available sound. She heard the tinkle of liquid, and the next moment the smell of prohibited alcohol rose up. From a few compartments away she received the acronyms of the English-speaking boys on a camping trip. 'Russia, Russia, tell him Russia!' one urged. 'Rape Until She Screams In Agony,' another obliged. They laughed and repeated. She did not wish to close her eyes thereafter.

The man who was going to snore did so in erratic thunderbursts. The orange-eyed drinker breathed with an anguished rasp. The train stop-started, over and over.

When deep in the night they were stalled a long time she climbed down and crossed the gangway to the adjoining coach. Sure enough, the travelling ticket examiner was awake.

What has happened? she asked him.

Near Itarsi, the t.t.e. had heard, protests against the prime minister's decision to expand reservations in government jobs to Other Backward Classes had turned violent. People had stormed the cabin, thrown out the cabinmen, taken over the signals. That had created chaos on the network. He seemed pessimistic about making up time. Rather, it was a matter of seeing how much more they would lose.

He was a few years older than her, the t.t.e., possessed of strong, raw features. They stood near the vestibule, speaking at a low volume, as if exchanging confidences. He tapped his shirt pocket and asked, a little apologetically, whether he had her permission. When she granted it, he opened the door. Travelling inland and upward, the weather had changed right under their noses. He exhaled out into the cold air, looking contented as he did, as if all worries could indeed be smoked away. Now she surprised him, and herself, by seeking his permission. He extended the box towards her, sliding up a cigarette as he did. She put it to her lips. He struck a match and held it to her mouth. She pulled on it until it glowed orange.

They chatted now with the freedom that accompanies small lawbreaking. The t.t.e. rued the state of the country. The chariot procession had passed through his home town, leaving behind clashes, fires, deaths, bad blood. 'I start my days with the Gayatri mantra, and when I am gone it will be to "Ram's name is the truth",' he said. 'That is exactly why I cannot bear this constant fuelling of religious enmity.' Here he quoted Kabir. '*Hindu kahat hai Ram hamara, Musalman Rahmana...*' She could not catch the rest, but inhaled with a knowing smile.

Outside, a patch of brilliant fireflies hovered about in the tar-dark country. She wondered whether they could discern the glow on the cigarette tips. She wished she could sit down with her mother and tell her about her whole life so far.

The travelling ticket examiner was right: it remained a stop-start night. By morning they were running six hours late. The air had the quality of ash, or maybe it was the trace of cigarette on her palate. The sun did come out, the day did come alive. Vendors and passengers climbed on at every halt.

An artist-vendor entranced everyone with his startling flip books. When the pages were turned at speed, the illustrations set into motion a group of men climbing up a dome, holding up a saffron flag. The final frames showed the men atop a dome, of the Babri mosque presumably, turning into monkeys, the tallest among them presumably Hanuman.

Nobody bought one, but everybody talked about it. Certain that there were no Muslims around, or that they were outnumbered so all the better that they heard, the snorer of the night advanced a diatribe, clearly not for the first time in his life.

Listening on, Smt Chitol felt grateful that her father-in-law was not this man. Not *exactly*. He did not revile Muslims; he was discreet in his passions. Unlike her mother-in-law, who had never really known a Muslim, he had cordial, even warm business relations with the 'Mohammedan transporters'. Yet she sensed her mother-in-law might just be tiring of the temple movement; it might be sufficient to simply dislike Muslims and kick them off the streets on Friday. To Kantibhai's mind there was nothing the chariot procession could not fix: history, geography, demography, polity, world-standing, Muslim traffic jams. He admired the charioteer and was possibly inspired by him. He was a temperate man discovering late the beauty of the uncompromising stand. It made him feel strong after a stroke. She found it hard to consider him unsarcastically any more.

Soon she had roused herself into a state of furious reflection. In such passages she sided with herself so wholeheartedly it dispelled any confusion engendered by the principles of even-handedness. She was reliving, in precise detail, the run-in with her father-in-law the morning after Diwali.

It was the Gujarati new year. Among the visitors to their home was the wheezing Purushottambhai, who made a new donation pitch in the old way. This time she mustered the courage to do what Nimish suggested.

Her father-in-law was seated on the cushioned bench in the corridor, as he liked to be at sunset.

'Pappa, I don't want my name on it.'

He looked up at her.

'On what?'

'The donation,' she spelt out.

She watched his expressions change, his face darken with the realisation that his wife may have been right all along. Her views could no longer surprise him; it was her defiance that did, she was sure. It was he who stood against her trip this time, couching his opposition in harshly tendered logic – her last trip had taken her to all kinds of places she wasn't meant to be in, and there was no way she could risk it with all that's going on in the country (meaning, she snorted to herself, his beloved *rath yatra*).

What is it that they want to control? she would sometimes ask herself. In those moments the answer seemed stark: everything, more or less. If you want to tie one limb, you must have to tie them all. They had her diet, they had her periods, they had her hours, they wanted her movements, most of all they wanted her mind. Until then the integration would remain incomplete. She could hardly be surprised that Nimish didn't see it, when she herself did not this plainly until now. Only when the knot tightens do the wrists chafe.

Vibrating his legs, meanwhile, the snorer looked around at the small congregation.

'Us four and our forty, that is their modus operandi,' he said, dropping the Latin words into Hindi. 'Even the census is hiding the truth. Come with me to these districts and see for yourself, *woh saale ...*'

She went off to stand by the door. When they suffered another long halt she crossed over to the t.t.e.

They were both a touch embarrassed after last night's cigarette.

A stampede at Manikpur Junction, he said to her. There were the usual crowds waiting to board for Allahabad and Kanpur. In addition, groups of young men and sadhus, whom he had seen had become very active in the movement since the previous year's Kumbh Mela in Allahabad, were making for Ayodhya for the chariot's arrival there.

Her plans of reaching in the morning for a full working day had long turned to mud. She supposed another hour or two did not matter.

At Manikpur, sadhus and young men with saffron bandanas did climb on, and the chants of *We will build the temple right there!* were with them.

By the time the train crossed the Yamuna the waters were dark. When she reached Kamalpur it was night.

The station was silent. The still stands and stalls were shuttered. The human figures were covered in light fog. It felt like a place in a novel where a crime had been committed or was about to be committed, and when she went to the stationmaster he looked as though he had seen a ghost not meant to be in the book.

'I am welfare inspector Charulata Chitol from Bombay,' she introduced herself and explained her purpose.

'How can you come here like this?' the stationmaster responded in agitation. 'Why did they send ladies? What do you think, this is Bombay? This is not Bombay, madamji, this is Kamalpur.'

'Calm down, Varmaji,' she was compelled to say. 'I tried to call but the number was engaged.'

'Why should it not be engaged? The lines have been down for three days.' He glared at her as though she were responsible. 'Only I know how I have managed.'

'I too have a job to do, Varmaji,' she stressed. 'I need a place to stay.'

'That is the trouble,' he replied. 'You have put me in a fix. Where am I to put you? You are now my responsibility. But where shall I put you? You tell me where. The two things famous in Kamalpur are mangoes and crime. The mango season has gone.'

'Varmaji, I am nobody's responsibility but my own. Are there no retiring rooms here?'

The stationmaster chuckled.

'There are two. For the last month an engineer from works and his family have taken them over. Their quarters are getting renovated.'

'Is there a subordinate rest house?'

'There is. But that place is in a bad way. I don't think it will be good for you. There may be men. They may be drinking. I cannot guarantee your safety.'

He turned agitated again.

'And actually, since you are a ladies, you will need clearance from the a.e.n to stay there. But look at the time. How can I disturb him at this hour for a matter like this? I just do not understand how –'

'Let it be, Varmaji,' she cut in. 'I will make my own arrangements. Just tell me how I can get to Godlan tomorrow.'

He appeared relieved.

'The buses leave from right outside the station, starting seven o'clock.'

She got up to leave.

'Wait, where are you going?' he said. 'I will send a pointsman with you. He will take you to the right place.'

The pointsman's name was Jawahar. She followed him out of the station. The streets were narrow and dirty. The dogs were thin and restless. Here and there men were huddled on their haunches, rubbing their hands together. Someone sang 'Oye Oye' at her, others laughed and said something she did not understand. Jawahar told her to ignore them – as if she didn't know.

In ten minutes they were at Adarsh Hindu Hotel – far from ideal. Nothing about the place gave her a good feeling: not the quarter-bottles of liquor in the rubbish strewn near the entrance, not the dim lighting in the reception, not the man sitting there she could see looking out towards them. Jawahar told her it was the only decent hotel in the area. The lilt in his Hindi, his vocabulary, reminded her just a little of the Bhombalpuriya style, and this familiarity was one reason she retained her confidence.

Once inside the room, that began to leak out. Everything was designed to raise doubt. The hollow-sounding door with the flimsy four-inch latch, the space at the bottom through which she could hear men and watch their shadows stride past, the blanket so heavy with dust it triggered sneezes that called attention to oneself, the rat tail swishing off behind the rat-bitten curtains hanging over a trail of rat or lizard shit, perhaps both.

She considered leaving the light on for the night but decided that would only attract more attention.

She washed and lay in the dark dread, listening to the rat's activities.

Khoos-khoos, chik-chik.

It would have been nice if Nimish was here. It would have been nice to embrace him, to touch his lips and look into his eyes before she left.

Khoos-khoos, chik-chik.

All night tiny rats overran her thoughts, scampering over her with their sharp feet and probing snouts, prising open her lids, flattening themselves against her eyes.

In the morning she saw it had bitten through her bag and nibbled its way into the biscuits.

But the night was finished. No harm came to her. It was dense and greenish grey outside, like phlegm. Yet it was indisputably morning. When she went downstairs, she found Jawahar waiting. He had not said he would come. She was touched.

They conversed enthusiastically on the way to the station. On learning that her visit was to do with school and caste certificates the conversation turned, naturally, to the new reservations. He belonged to a boatman community, and he hoped the court would uphold the prime minister's decision. After all, the Dalits and Adivasis had their quotas, while the Thakurs, Banias and Brahmins ruled the country no matter how few they were. Where did that leave the rest? The census was coming, so why only Scheduled Castes and Scheduled Tribes, count Other Backward Classes if you have the guts, then everyone will know how many we are and how little we have – count every caste, in fact, then everyone will know what is what, and she saw his point. The upper-caste students ought to think about this instead of going about setting themselves on fire, he continued, this entire *rath yatra* was a ploy to create division between Hindus and Muslims and divert from real issues like this one.

It was busy at the station. Men were chewing on neem sticks, drinking tea, bombing the ground indolently with spit, urinating over small heaps of garbage as if dousing little fires. Women lent dignity through abstinence. Jawahar pointed her to the kachori man's stall, showed her the bus she was to take, only then could she persuade him to carry on. Once the vendors hawking vials for potency and venereal disease were gone, and they were packed to double capacity, and there arrived among them a young goat, the bus grunted off.

The sun was up but its glow was diffuse, as though struggling to penetrate X-ray film. It was not beautiful. Clusters of unplastered brick structures, dusty in colour, in between them bare fields, some covered with low potato crop. The dry brown air stuck in the throat. A fly browsed her nape. She loosened her bun over it. She drifted in and out of sleep – she had barely slept the past few nights – and was shocked when she heard the conductor thump the side of the bus announcing her stop.

Nothing had quite prepared her for the sight of the tehsil office in Godlan. All that remained of the gates were the hinges. The weeds in the compound were so unseemly even the grazing cow chose to forage in the garbage heap instead. The only people around were a bunch of men at a tea stall and a typist stall across the office. She felt their eyes on her as she took the thin path through the weeds towards the building. The windowpanes were shards; a few windows had been pilfered whole, frames and all. Where the ceiling plaster had not come off, the paint gently flaked down, like dandruff.

Welfare Inspection

A bicycle on the veranda was the single sign of habitation. Climbing the two steps up towards it Smt Chitol heard unusual sounds emanate from a room. She peeped inside to find a shirt and a gamchha draped over registers on the desk; further in, a balding man in trousers, vest and sacred thread sitting cross-legged on the floor before a smoking claypot, staring at her. She had spoken barely two words before he interjected, in a very pure Hindi: 'This is extremely necessary. Wait outside, let what has commenced complete' – as though it were she who was asking to perform a ritual in a government office in the middle of a working day.

Waiting, she could feel once more the eyes of the men at the stalls. She walked over to another side of the veranda. Across the road stood a buffalo stable.

Now a boy, seven or eight years old, entered the compound. She watched in surprise as he bounded over the weeds, right up to her.

'I have brought a message for you,' he said, a little impudently.

'For me? From who?'

'Somebody is calling you to their house about the certificate. I will take you.'

She felt a shudder of unease.

'Who is this person?'

'Come with me,' he said.

'But who –'

The boy turned round and skipped away just as quickly as he had come.

He worried her. Perhaps, she told herself, he was playing a prank, a naughty village boy. What must people come here for but certificates? Or maybe he worked for a tout. She was sweating.

Presently the man emerged from the room in a bright tilak, sweater and muffler, which suggested abundant caution. Certainly he had never played in the rain.

He was L. N. Tripathi, the lekhpal.

And she was Charulata Chitol, welfare inspector, Central Railway, Bombay Division.

'Chitol, an unusual name. But Charulata will not be Muslim and you are not dressed like one either. The question arises, where is your sindoor? Maybe it came off on the journey – after all, women nowadays do not apply it properly. Some do not apply it at all. Nor can I see anything around your neck. That again could be because of the journey, who wants to risk theft, especially travelling in these parts. But perhaps you are not married. That could be the case, because who would allow you to come by yourself to Godlan of all places?'

He smiled, waiting for her to elaborate now that she had been regaled.

'Please let us start, Tripathiji,' she said. 'I have lost an entire day yesterday.'

'Our stars have aligned,' he responded with visible pleasure. 'For yesterday I was out on fieldwork. Two or three days a week am I here. Someone has to. They may be building a new office complex that will soon look worse than this, but people still show up here, just like you have. Now what is it that you need?'

'How should I verify this?' She handed him the caste certificate.

He took one look at it and declared: 'This is one hundred per cent fake.'

'How can you be so sure?'

'Look at the date – no certificate in the last many years has looked like this.'

He dispensed a sympathetic pause.

'A matter of great misfortune, if you ask me. What is a high-caste supposed to do? And with these new quotas, fake certificates will become a mania. *Stithi aisi aa gayi hai ki mor bhi murge ke kapde mein saj rahe hain.* The situation is such that peacocks have to dress themselves up as chicken.'

He nodded at her, agreeing with himself.

'If you ask me,' he went on, although she had not, 'these quotas are nothing but a ploy to divide the Hindus. A conspiracy to counter the Ayodhya struggle that is uniting Hindus.'

He was nodding at her again.

She handed him the school certificate.

'Where can I find this school?'

He pointed over towards the left.

'That looks like a buffalo stable.'

'Well, that is what it is. Anyway, it only ever produced donkeys. The school, that is.'

'So where is it now?'

'Exactly there. Except that is what it is now. Please understand.'

They returned to the caste certificate.

'Even the tehsildar stamp is wrong.' He flicked his finger on it. 'I can give in writing this is fake.'

'Then please do, Tripathiji,' she said. 'I will need that.'

'I do not have that authority,' he demurred. 'You will have to go to the new office.'

'Where is it?'

'Six kilometres by foot or cycle, seven kilometres by road. You will not be able to go by road.'

'Why not?'

'No buses are going that way. They have dug it up. All the new development is there, after all. Over here it is just me and a chaprasi, if the duffer remembers to come – he can barely remember his name. He remembers to sleep all right.'

Here she mentioned the boy who had brought her the message.

A convulsive terror lit up Tripathiji's face, splitting it into two.

'I request you, please leave from here as soon as you can, and please do not tell anyone a word of what I have told you. You must have heard the old saying. People come to Kamalpur to enjoy two things, mangoes and crime – and the season for mangoes is long gone. I will send the chaprasi with you, if I can find that good-for-nothing.'

He stepped out and shouted 'Chotte' in all directions.

A short, skinny youth appeared.

Turning a deaf ear to her, L. N. Tripathi wheeled his bicycle down from the veranda and pedalled off with his knees pointing outward.

Smt Chitol was left with the peon in the ghost office.

'What do we do now?' she addressed him. 'How do we get to this new office?'

She could draw no reply, not even a change in expression.

She walked out of the compound, Chotte trailing her – and those eyes from the stalls. She didn't trust those eyes, and decided against approaching their owners.

She contemplated the lekhpal's advice. But she did not want to return empty-handed.

Up ahead at the cement bus shelter she saw a pair of waiting buses. Further on, the road that led to the bazaar. She walked on, considering her next move.

They were not far from the bus stop when she noticed the men walking towards her. *At* her. Three of them, holding hands and strolling. Looking straight into her face. When she changed her path, they shifted theirs too. Then they were right before her, arranged in a loose C.

The man in the middle said: your name is Charulata Chitol, this is your date of birth, your husband's name is so-and-so, your address is this.

A chill went down her spine.

'I may be but who are you?' she said.

'Is your work done?' She had walked into a movie scene, a bad movie and a bad scene.

They closed around her. As they did, she felt it was something that had already happened and in another fraction she knew exactly what it was, it was the hooligans from the railway strike. She thought: I had not expected to be touched then, but I was.

Said the man in the middle: 'You did not find anything wrong, did you?'

She did not reply.

'All you have to say is that the report will be correct. Then everything will be okay. They can be very good, or things can be very bad for you. From top to bottom bad.'

He was looking her up and down.

She said nothing.

'Have you forgotten how to use your mouth? Say your name. I have just told you what it is.'

The sidekicks laughed.

Chotte was still lurking somewhere. At least he had not fled.

The man shuffled closer. He was tall, about the same height as her husband. To look into his eyes she would have to roll her head back and gaze up, as one would do in intimacy. So she did not. His tobacco breath fell over her, encasing her. A black pit grew in her stomach. She did not know whether to slap this man, or shout, or turn and run.

Sometimes the best way out of difficulty is through it. She used her bag to push herself between the men. A moment later she registered a sharp tug in her scalp and almost staggered backwards to the ground.

Everything went a little blurry now: the people who had gathered to watch as she climbed into the bus, the peon and the puny conductor getting slapped about, gesturing at her to come out, shouting that the bus will not move otherwise, she yelling back at the conductor saying she was from the central government and she would report him, then the large shape coming down the aisle, growing big on her, an arm reaching for her hair, she was sure, in order to drag her out – when a hand reached out and held it, veined, wrinkled, brown, with raisin moles, like her dida's. Another joined in, bangles over a green tattoo, stroking his forearm, begging for benevolence, 'Oh raja, forgive her. Let it be, son.' Other women shouted at the driver – give us our money back – we are going to miss our train. A choreography, someone cajoling, someone heckling.

At some point they began to move, and the man was not on board. The bus was full of questions but she barely spoke. Her heart hammered against her ribs, dryness settled on her lips, in her scalp lingered pricks of pain, and the particular disgrace of a woman pulled by her hair.

Slowly the banality of the journey established itself. Her nose streamed from the dust. They gained passengers with no knowledge of what had transpired. With every elapsing instant the incident was becoming the past.

Not till the end of the run was she able to take the women's hands in hers and thank them. They may have endured worse and they were giving her their strength, she felt it from their fingers to hers.

At the station all was pandemonium. Crowds, chants, news. The *rath yatra* had been stopped, they heard, the charioteer had been arrested. Or had he? She marched to the stationmaster's cabin. The evening shift had just begun and Pyarelal Varma was back on duty.

'This is Kamalpur, madamji!' the stationmaster cried when she apprised him of her intentions. 'You will go to the police, the police will instead deliver you to them. Take my advice, leave here as soon as you can. In fifteen minutes there is a Passenger towards Naklau.'

'My return booking is not from there,' she pointed out.

'You will work out what to do. If you stay here, I cannot guarantee your safety. All hell is breaking loose, and if something happens to you, you will create a big problem for me because –' she was his responsibility. Of course, she had forgotten.

She heard the great events roiling outside.

The Hindu whose blood isn't boiling, that's not blood, that's water!

We'll face bullets, we'll face sticks, but that's where we'll build our temple!

She could not tell whether they made leaving for the unknown less or more foolhardy. But they did make her want to get out of Kamalpur. She had notes to write up, a long report to contemplate. Her friend Krunalini had promised to take her shopping for polyester silks, and that thought was appealing. She would find her way back home.

As she pulled away from Kamalpur on the Passenger, she thought: it is true what Mrs Fonseca said, that in one year as welfare inspector I would learn much, I just did not know how much. She wondered: when I get home will anyone look me in the eye?

6

Census

Her gums did not bleed. She ate a besan ladoo first thing and hummed while cooking, parwal in the Bihari style, cut plump not fine, with potatoes and tomatoes, the way her mami used to. As she boiled tea, Nimish slipped his arms around her waist. 'Let's go somewhere,' he said into her ear. 'We can take Parag's car. I'll drive so slow you won't feel a thing.'

How silly to waste this freedom while it lasted. She did not voice the thought.

'You are mad,' she said instead. 'You're just a *madoo*, Nims.'

He giggled into her hair and spread his fingers on her belly.

'But how will you manage?'

'Do you know this is the first day in how long I haven't felt sick? Not even with this *lilicha* in your tea.'

'How much up-down will you do?'

'But what did the doctor say, exercise is good. And some buildings have lifts.'

After her bath she wandered about in a towel, another one wrapped around her head, like in films. If the profundity of such freedoms would never have occurred to her husband, in her happier moments she did not hold that as grudge or grievance, but as the fulcrum against which she could access a secret dimension of pleasure. He attacked the newspaper like a man scouting for absurd stories he might amuse a stranger with, should the need arise. She applied creams. Checked out the mirror: what glow, what nonsense! Patches and inflammations where there had been none. Even then, she felt happy, she felt glorious. A large, growing feeling. It was the February of a year ending in 1 and every person in India would be counted.

'Food is there,' she called out from the door. 'Buy vegetables for the night if you can.'

'Wait, where are you running off? I'll come down with you.'

In the corridor Nimish stayed a half-step behind and placed his hand on her elbow, ridiculously, as though she were in danger of losing her balance. 'Jai Jai Krishna,' he squawked at the caged parakeets – 'J. J. Kris!' they screeched back. '*Sambbhhlo chhoo!*' he whispered as they approached old Shantibhai scrutinising the *Bombay Samachar* on his bench; almost on cue, '*Sambbhhlo chhooo!* Are you listening!' yelled out Shantiben to her husband of sixty years, who smiled at them oblivious. Old folk smiled at Nimish as though they were each a repository of his imitations and jokes.

They linked arms on the way to the bus stop – the wakened streets crowding up, waiting to be netted on essential parameters, the weight on the balls of the feet, feel the weight, feel the spring! He helped her into the bus; when it caught the red light he waited alongside on the footpath. There he bought a morning paan, laughed as he popped it into his mouth and performed a little jig. She was sure he did not really want the paan, he did it just for her entertainment. For all the tension in the house, for all the turmoil in my heart, she thought, we must have done something right.

Her backpack was fat with enumeratory paraphernalia: maps and sketches, houselists, slips and schedules, her plentiful stationery, and she was too far out when she realised she had forgotten those post-graduate-degree-holder and technical-personnel forms. Bloody shit, she chided herself, where is my mind? Worth Rs 15 each completed form, if she was lucky enough to encounter the qualified – which in that fairly well-off set of buildings she ought to be – over and above the Rs 225 for the entire work. The fees were called 'honoraria', and even if the money was welcome, she did consider the task an honour.

To work through her block of approximately seven hundred and fifty residents she estimated half a dozen sessions. Thereafter, on the last night of the month, enumeration of the Houseless, which even in her block, she knew from her recce round, numbered in the double digits: the old lady who lived by the Sai Baba shrine under the banyan tree, the family who dwelled in a hume pipe at the end of the road,

Anna's assistant at the cigarettes and miscellany stall, unaccommodated servants who took the footpath in the shadows of their masters' buildings. Following on its heels, the revisional round to account for fresh births and deaths. Through the month they were to spread themselves across the country, to each nook and cranny, to every field and forest, mountain and island – seventeen lakh government servants, the same number, in fact, as in the Indian Railways, but going further, deeper, leaving out nobody.

The buildings were mixed, of diverse heights and vintage. The name boards in the lobbies showed Hindu, Parsi, Jain, Christian, Sikh, Muslim, of a stratum that did not necessarily share her enthusiasm for the general census. Twenty-three questions to be canvassed per individual slip and thirty-four columns per household schedule, to be tallied and transferred into twenty-nine columns in the enumerator's working sheet and fifteen rows in the enumerator's abstract. Some respondents instructed her to wait indefinitely or come back later, and although she could remind them that participation was compulsory, she could not very well force her way in. Some were hostile or guarded, and to extract information from them could take as long as from the loquacious, for whom each question was a personal history, which was part of the pleasure, the honour. The wear or shine on faces, the contour of wrinkles and moles, the variety of peeping eyes in children – no enumeration of those. What an astounding number of things indeed, thought Smt Chitol, went unrecorded in the census of India! Whether you were tolerated at the door or invited in, whether you were asked to take off your footwear or not, offered water or not, whether seepage attacked even these fairly well-off ceilings, whether such ceilings were false or true, or hung with three chandeliers above seating that was all marble as in the Marfatia house.

Complications abounded. The very question of who should be enumerated. Domestic Servants/Cooks, yes, but only if they 'commonly lived' there and took their meals from a common kitchen. Visitors, yes, but only those visiting for the entire duration of enumeration and thus not already enumerated or to be enumerated elsewhere. Definitions were critical; the success of the entire project rested on understanding and observing them. What is a Census House, a Household, a Head of Household, a Household Industry? What is

Work? What is Majority of the Year? Which crops do not come under Cultivation? Who is a Rentier? Who is a Beggar?

It fell to the enumerator to ask 'probing questions'. If rather than a specific Scheduled Caste or Tribe, said her instruction manual, 'a person is negligent and insists on calling himself/herself merely "Harijan" or "Achhut" or "Adivasi" or "Girijan", as the case may be', she must probe. Special efforts, in the form of probing questions, were required to capture women's work, delicate probes to net infant deaths and stillbirths. 'You might ask where the child has gone. The answer may be "dead" or that it has gone elsewhere. If dead, then you might ask when the child died and this will bring out the fact whether or not it was a stillbirth.' This she was not sure she could bring herself to probe, not in her current state.

Slowly the slips piled up. Smt Chitol enquired, noted, ticked and crossed, clarified to citizens, as Fatima Memon had done to her one decade ago, that the mother tongue is nothing but the language spoken in childhood by the person's mother to the person, that two other languages known should be given in order of proficiency. She recorded Konkani and Tamil and Sindhi, Telugu and Tulu, one Kodagu, one Dogri, an Arabic, a Nepali, one Kurukh, one Halabi. Of merchants, merchant-navy sailors, gastroenterologists, watchmen with living quarters, child servants and the wheelchair-bound, she recorded educational attainments, natures of work, places of last residence, reasons for migration, from ever-married women the number of children ever born alive. All these lives, their variety and volume, to become one number.

In her work as welfare inspector, she reflected, she went from names on the page into measureless lives. Here was the opposite. She pinned people to the page. This was something to think about.

You could not have two mother tongues, or none, and your complications in matters of proficiency were immaterial to her, the census enumerator. Outside of those Scheduled, there was none for caste, as if by the omission caste would cease to be. Eunuch or hermaphrodite, you were to be coded 1 for Male. You could not profess two religions, or half, and it was of no consequence to the enumerator if you upheld a common creator with destiny as his design and no other religious principle. The rigidities of the columns were not to be her concern.

This did not exactly deter Smt Chitol. In her instruction manual she had underlined the sentence 'You are privileged to be a census enumerator', as well as the next: 'At the same time, your responsibilities are great.' She did not disagree with the proposition that the exercise 'provides valuable information about the land and the people at a given point of time', nor could she contest that such information is 'very much needed by the public and government organisations for many aspects of economic and social planning and forms the very basis of electoral constituencies', and as such concurred that it was a 'great national task'. Seen in a certain way, it was a form of welfare inspection.

There remained something bothersome about the columns, however. Each within a column the same as the other, together different from those in another column. This was, after all, how a bigot's mind worked.

The heart of a person was not one thing or the other. Its grievances, its smartnesses, its vacancies and welfares were not one thing or the other. The heart cannot be columnised. There is no bigger mystery in the whole world, Notun Dida used to say, than the human heart.

Musing so, Smt Chitol, who had only just turned thirty-three we must remember, lest we judge her severely, neither a learned dissertator nor a professional scepticist, fascinated by Rules but literary in her sensibility, got to what she planned as her last floor of the day.

She felt stimulated and tired. Her aches were no longer intense, they were insidious. They made her doubt herself, as though her body had found a mind of its own, and so had her mind. It was the time before new nighties, the time after non-stop nausea, before swollen soles and swollen toes, a time of sore calves and heavy thighs, of simple calculations gone awry and written reminders never before needed misplaced, the time before the inside-outing of the navel and the sealed-with-a-candle line running through it.

She depressed the push-button bell, eliciting from it a famous Western classical composition.

Footsteps jogged frantically towards her. A thin young maidservant in an oversized salwar kameez opened the wooden door and remained behind the safety grille.

'Memsaab, somebody has come,' she called out diffidently into the passage. She trotted silently into the house and repeated herself.

But memsahib did not emerge, it was P who did. Smt Chitol was sure for a long moment that it was him, then sure for an endless one that it was not. Here he came up the passage, now clicking open the safety door. It was not her new mind playing tricks. It was P. Like animals in the jungle most alert to those they want to avoid, she was shocked and yet not, and could recognise this being the case even as it happened. She had run into N nine years later, so maybe not so absurd that P was here after what, five? Short hair, grey stubble – intellectual stasis? maturation? – a little slacker, all of which gave him a somewhat refined air, not exactly flaccid, although he was dressed in the flaccid clothing of a higher class.

She found herself gathering her sari over her belly, even though she was not showing.

'How did you know where I live?' he said, with the old intense-eyed smile.

Challenged by it from the very start, she was now astonished by his presumptuousness. The question, frankly, left her speechless.

'Why don't you call the head of the household?' she replied after a few moments, glancing at the name board, and watched to see if the cut drew blood.

Then she noted that the intensity in his eyes had the form of curiosity. He looked, above all, amiable and therefore surprised by her words.

From down the passage busy, huffy sounds fluffed up towards them.

'Who is it? Which person?'

Large and breezy, she had matured coherently into the memsahib she was destined to become. She had a robe on – silk or satin, something shiny that made her sweat.

'*Kya hai?*' she arrived uttering breathlessly. She took in the person at the door: seemed the educated type.

She switched to English.

'Yes, what do you want?'

'I have been deputed by the Registrar General and Census Commissioner's office,' answered Smt Chitol.

The woman fluttered her eyelids.

'For census enumeration,' Smt Chitol spelt out.

'You people just come whenever you feel like without telling us.'

'We are not required to inform you,' said Smt Chitol, keeping her calm at being called a people. 'There is no such provision in the Census Act 1948.'

'What? 1948? This is 1990!'

'It is not.'

'Excuse me?!' The memsahib's eyes and nostrils flew open.

'This is 1991.'

Her expressions hovered tantalisingly between rejecting and accepting the claim.

'What are all these marks on the wall? You all just come and make a mess.'

'I did not perform the house-listing operation,' replied Smt Chitol. 'Anyway, it is compulsory and standard for everyone.'

'You people have an answer for everything.'

Just then the telephone began ringing in loud trills; it further exercised the memsahib.

'Who is it!' she shouted into the passage, which appeared to be code for the maidservant to pick up, for how might the phone answer the question?

She turned again to Smt Chitol.

'Every day someone or the other comes. Are we just waiting for you? I can't answer your questions, okay?'

'You are not bound to state the name of your husband,' Smt Chitol informed her. 'Or any other person whose name is forbidden by custom for you to mention. That is in the Census Act.'

The memsahib broke into a new flutter, gobsmacked at this person's superciliousness.

'She is saying it's urgent,' the maidservant reported meekly.

'*Offo*, everybody just wants something,' the memsahib announced, flouncing down the passage.

'We are not at your disposal, okay,' she called out over her nose as she went into a room. 'Parvez, just tell her we are not at her disposal, okay.'

P looked like he had come back from the dead.

'You haven't changed much,' he said to Smt Chitol, working himself up again into a half-smile. 'Except for the specs.'

'Why would I change?'

'Why are you being so cold to me?' His voice again carried an amiable strain, which once more drew a recalibration from Smt Chitol. 'Where are you? How are you?' She even detected a concern in these enquiries.

The memsahib could be heard flouncing back up the corridor. The humiliation of being some woman at the door became intolerable to Smt Chitol.

Before she could be talked at, she handed over the forms.

'Here, you seem educated, you will be able to fill these. Fill them for any staff who live with you also. Whatever you don't understand, leave it blank. I'll collect them another day.'

The memsahib extended her hand for the papers but did not take them.

'Wait,' she said. 'I know you.'

'There are also post-graduate-degree-holder forms,' Smt Chitol continued. 'They may be applicable. I will bring them when I collect these.'

The memsahib pinched her eyes into a parsimonious stare.

'I have seen you somewhere.'

Smt Chitol pressed the papers into her hands, and looked up to meet her gaze.

'This is …' P began, but the memsahib shushed him with her hands.

'Are you the one who sits at the dispensary?' she asked.

'No, I am someone else,' replied Smt Chitol, keeping her gaze firm. When the memsahib broke off with blinks, she turned and left.

The building was equipped with a lift, but she could not bear to stand around. She took the stairs and stopped a few landings down. Descending fast was an irresponsible thing to be doing. Light-headed, she considered sitting on the steps but knew that standing back up she would be dizzy. Instead she rested against a wall. A tear washed the sting out of her. When she felt herself restoring she resumed down the stairs.

Was this the day of the fallen slips? It is how she would remember it afterwards. The day when coming out of the building into the rambunctious breeze she held her L-folder at a preoccupied angle and the slips tumbled out and took wing. Aruna Krishnan F 63 sliding under the wheel of a parked 118 NE, Zafar Khan Hosiery wrapping himself around a banyan tendril, Sukhi Ram 8th Std Pass skittering along the footpath, Shakuntala Chavan Age at Marriage 15, Captain Beri Pensioner Yes, wafting about needlessly, and 'Aila' said a driver and plucked Telugu and Maithili and Varhadi and Seraiki from the wind, while 'Thamba, Thamba' said the kind peanut-man, seizing Matang, Rohidas, Dongar Koli, Chalvadi from the air, though dashing into the compound wall were Sawantwadi, Madurai, Shikohabad, Bombay, flapping away towards the postbox were Natural Calamity like Flood, Children Surviving at Present 6, they were racing away from Smt Chitol, exceeding her grasp.

At home she ate two ladoos and toast-butter and fell fast asleep. When she woke up, in a disoriented haze, she forgave Nimish for not buying the supplies and went down to get them. She had nodded off again by the time he returned from work.

He lay down beside her on the divan.

'Guess who I met today?' he whispered to her.

She tightened.

'Who?'

'Sheetal Kedia. Sheets!'

She took his hands in hers and snuggled up against him. A few more days and they would be back, the home would no longer be his and hers.

When the provisional population was released, the number was near 844 million. The figure included a projection for Jammu and Kashmir, where the census could not be conducted because of the insurgency.

7

Incompetence

I had never been to Mrs Ghorpade's house. On the phone she discouraged me from coming. Said it was a long trip to make and her husband was not in the best of health. In any case, she planned to visit the office next month to sort out that pension matter so why did I want to take the trouble? She must have sensed something because she then said: 'Come, *baba*, come.'

The last time I saw Mrs Ghorpade was seven or eight months ago. That could be one reason I wanted to see her: no expectations. Another reason could be what P called 'mother figure'.

As I made my way over in the train I felt very dull. I could crumple myself over two seats and lie right there. The empty seats soon vanished and I became distracted by a newspaper somebody had left behind. It occurred to me to think of mine as a minor event. Another prime minister assassinated, a general election on pause. At one end of the country the Tamil Tigers. At the other end Kashmir. One could submit oneself to the accepted significance of things, the orders of priority. Could one not?

When Mrs Ghorpade opened the door we laughed a little, as if we had once been partners in something grand and mischievous, namely clerical service. Just a year into retirement she looked like she had aged five. She remarked on her ripened hair. All this staying at home did not suit her. She pointed to the room where her husband rested. 'Actually, he is fine now,' she said. 'I don't know how anyone can rest that much.'

Mrs Ghorpade asked whether I wanted cold water or plain and, as always, scolded me about taking cold water in the heat and reminded me of all those trips to the water cooler in the office after we got one and for a moment I was back in my twenties.

We went out to the balcony. It was entirely in the shade. She had arranged potted plants on the ledge and at the corner placed the first roti from the pan for the crows. It was a nice balcony, breezy, broad enough for a small swing. The moment she set it in motion I felt nauseous and I grazed my feet against the floor for friction.

It was just as well that we sat next to one another because I could not look Mrs Ghorpade in the eye. I felt I was confessing something that warranted disciplinary action. *'Arre baap re'* was her reaction when I told her and immediately I wanted her pardon.

She asked me the questions, I gave her the answers. I realised I wanted to go over the details because my own memory of what happened was so confused and reconfused. I wanted to speak it myself, hear it for myself, give it order. First this then that, before that this and after this that, and at the end of the narration I felt awash in blood.

'Incompetent cervix' the doctor said it was, 'probably'. I knew Mrs Ghorpade would understand the relevance of the term. In service, this is a severe insult. She knew I would have been ashamed to show my face if I was called incompetent. I was ashamed to show my face now. Unfit for the purpose. Under pressure just gave up and let go.

In the house I am not sure they believed the doctor. None of us had heard of such a thing. They did not think my cervix was incompetent: it was I who was. Nothing like that was ever said directly to me, of course. But I have eyes and ears, don't I?

My 'rakhi sister' Bansi began to come home frequently, I have no idea why. Maybe it was to lift the mood because Bansi is supposed to be bubbly. Or maybe as a successful mother she could shed light on what happened. And between my mother-in-law and her they did. Through bits of small detail and probing questions to one other, a full picture emerged. Did I eat properly, did I consume the right root vegetables for binding, did I take food outside? And what was to be done if I could not stand to have *suyo* for gas, or *ajwain* for digestion? Did I consider my age? I strained myself too much with work; I had chosen a strenuous line. Even volunteered for the census. There was no blame. Yet, since I did not do any of the right things and did so many of the wrong things, could this be a surprise? Little by little, through minor repetitions and implications, it seemed the case was quite straightforward after all: I had disobeyed my way out of giving birth.

Or had I indeed? Was I blind to my own incompetence?

How could Nimish allow this talk? And if he wasn't around, he ought to have been. I seethed inside.

I cannot forget the sight of him during the first days, sitting with his hands clasped behind his head. His soft, playful eyes had never looked so open and shell-shocked. I felt so angry seeing him like that, angry at him, at myself, the stupid world. He was the first person I ever met who gave me the feeling that things are fine, there is no need to keep fighting this thing that is life, you can laugh along. If I could not change my way of thinking I could put my trust in his. So why in this hour was he not what he was required to be?

Possibly because he had always wanted a child and I was never quite certain.

That is understandable, said P – because of your mother, how could you have the faith? But if it was to happen, he was sure my fears would prove unfounded and encouraged me to stay open to it. Talking to him has helped, that is all.

There were practical considerations too. I could not imagine space for another one of us in that house. I could not imagine mothering under that scrutiny. But the world seemed to shift a little bit. For the first time Nimish began to talk openly about the lack of space. My mother in-law sometimes patted my hair and stroked my forehead in the way she used to for Nimish when he ate.

As the baby grew within me, turned my body and mind inside out, I could not imagine not always wanting her. I knew her every move and she did mine. Think of the confidence she must have had in me, that despite the pain and discomfort she gave me, making my breasts and hands, feet, teeth, brain unrecognisable to myself, the confidence that I would make *her* hands and feet, toes, heart, spine. That I would take care of her no matter what. So why didn't I? Was I reluctant or was I complacent? Five-plus months and I thought she was already here. Five-plus months and there was no hiding, my incompetence was public, and it was she who paid the price.

How could I tell Nimish, sorry, you can't take responsibility even if you want to, she was not yours like she was mine? How could I tell him that the way the family said 'our' child, 'our' baby, I could not stand it?

I don't know how it happened, I told Mrs Ghorpade. I don't know how or why, and that is the truth.

If she had hugged me I would not have objected. After years in an office our body language was quite formal. She placed her hand on my head and patted it, while I looked into my useless lap and wet it.

'I cannot bear to live in that house any more,' I told her.

Mrs Ghorpade remained quiet for some time. Then she advised me to put away that kind of thinking.

'Charu, if a wife is to be happy, she has to be like sugar in milk.'

'Is that not old-fashioned thinking?' I said to her. 'We are in the nineties.'

'What I have told you I have learned in my own life,' she said. 'Peace I could find only after I accepted, yes, I must dissolve into the family.'

In fact, I had been indirectly recommended this before. My mother-in-law had said to me: 'Be not like chaff in wheat, be like sugar in milk.' That is what her own mother had advised her before her wedding.

'If the milk is cold,' I told Mrs Ghorpade, 'the sugar won't dissolve.'

'Keep it for long and it will. And the milk will be sweet.'

Here she herself smiled sweetly.

'Charu, what happened to you is one of the worst things that can happen to a mother.' She corrected herself. 'To a woman. Only time will tell you why it happened. The one upstairs will give you the reason.'

The one upstairs, his reasons, nonsense. But I wanted her to go on.

'The best thing you can do right now is put your mind into your work. Means, you have so many responsibilities: you are a wife, you are a daughter-in-law, you are an earning member, you are a railwaywoman.'

I felt proud when she used the word railwaywoman. People only say 'railwayman', and usually for those in operating. Mine too was fieldwork, perhaps that is why she said it.

'I have seen you. In thirty-five years' service I got three promotions. In less than one decade you have got two. After Kamalpur, you got Outstanding, no? You can become Group B officer one day, you can get to a.p.o., maybe d.p.o., who knows, more that that. You can sit in the historical building.'

My spirits rose as she spoke. Sometimes all it takes is for someone to say: I have seen you.

'You don't have to go via welfare inspector, you can go up from office superintendent,' she then added.

She meant that I return to the ministerial room and climb up the ranks of clerks – exactly as my family had wanted, had assumed is what I would do after the baby and, given what happened, were now more sure.

Why on earth would I do that? This is the most interesting thing I have ever done in my life. I had lived in a fool's world. They do not realise. I need the people whose welfare I am meant to inspect more than they need me.

'Mrs Fonseca said I would learn more in one year in the field than ten years in the ministerial room,' I told Mrs Ghorpade.

'Fonseca is bachelor,' she replied.

Mrs Fonseca, I pointed out.

'What is there in that? Means, any woman after a certain age people say Mrs. She is confirmed bachelor.'

My mind went back to the progression. I was not even a graduate. It was possible to become an officer without a graduation degree – or was it not? I was certain it was, right until this moment. But suppose that changes, then? What must I do to rectify it? The very thought was exhausting. I felt dull and tired again. I wanted life, wanted it to course through my veins and to tremble with its power, but I just could not find it.

'I am tired,' I said. 'I just feel tired and guilty all the time.'

'Guilt comes,' said Mrs Ghorpade. 'Go into service, guilt comes. Husband does not have his hot meal, guilt comes. Children are sick, guilt comes. Curtains unwashed, guilt comes. Go for a movie, guilt comes. Think of some other man,' she laughed, 'guilt comes. Guilt comes and you have to make it go.'

I put my head on her shoulder. She took my hand between hers and rubbed it. The swing creaked a little.

I supposed I should go home and dissolve like sugar in milk.

8

Into the rain

In unseasonal rain they met like lovers who in another time might have craved a single umbrella. Instead, each came separately without one. Smt Chitol arrived first and settled in the covered section outdoors. The floor was splattered with the chaos of shoe prints. It was beautiful. Under the trees students laughed in wet voices, the set of their faces very different from the commuters starting to pour into Churchgate station by the thousand.

She observed Nimish make his way in, shaking drops off his hair with a touch of pleasure, and she felt like she was seeing him after a very long time, such was the concentrated, detaching effect of the impending meeting. She saw a tall man in a full-sleeve checked shirt and pleated gaberdine trousers, material from Babubhai Jagjivandas, elegant in limbs and proportion, a former gallivanter who even visited the library in that spirit. His lively eyes were somewhat sunken from work, for he had begun to work very hard, handling two businesses, papering over his cracks, determined to make a success of it, a man who came home late in the evening while his wife left home early in the day.

He settled down busily; as we have just noted, he *was* busy, but more curious, and the mischievous weather encouraged him to anticipate a surprise that would float them clean over any life problems.

In this atmosphere of rainy glee, Smt Chitol said to her husband of three years, almost experimentally: 'I have found an opening in a hostel.'

'Christian-run hostel, for working women, Sion side,' she added, as though these details cast the matter in an entirely different light.

They sat face to face, not side by side, at the restaurant that was the site of their first meal together, and of their first meal on reunion nine years later. It was what he quipped about. 'Where you wanted to marry me, the same place you want to divorce me.' He had not totally registered the seriousness of things, or wished not to.

Smt Chitol was keen to avoid the word. Too drastic, with too many consequences to account for at just this moment. But here it landed when they had barely started.

'Who said *divorce*?' she said. 'Why do you say divorce?'

Nimish nearly smiled in relief. Unsure, he waited for her to go on.

'You know, I never expected to get married. Not that I didn't want to. I wanted to. But I was surprised that it happened.'

'If you had only said that in the beginning,' he replied, wryer than his usual humour. To tell the truth, he did not know what to make of these reflections, as if she were talking to herself and they did not involve him in the least. At the same time, the fact that she was expressing them meant something – there was little doubt about it. On the whole things sounded a lot worse than when she had started.

As ever, his first anxieties were to do with confrontation. Already his mind was hurtling towards how he might take this strange development to his family, to his mother – the awful subterranean way of women and their relationships, which had trapped him, the mother and the wife, by God, how long could one laugh off this cliché, which had cut him into half, left him spiritually exhausted. If there was anything he could do to make this exact moment go away.

But what does she mean, 'I have found a hostel'? Imagine being able to say 'I have found a hostel' and *bas*! How was one to compete with a person who kept leaving houses and had become a master of how to manage? His face tightened with resentment. He wished he could be young again like the wet laughers outside. But here he was, a more or less dry shirt tucked into his trousers that were held up by a belt, facing love divorce.

'You called me here to tell me this?' His tone was a touch 'masculine', which he had started to employ erratically, if she was to put a finger on it, from the time his new business began gathering momentum, and, she knew this too, when he felt ignored or outdone by her. It was a tone of being owed, which still felt alien to her from him, and she sometimes wondered whether it did to him too.

'Called me to our special place, and here I am leaving work when it is so busy because I think it must be for something special. You call me here to tell me you' – he lowered his voice – 'never wanted to marry me and actually want to divorce me?'

He considered standing up and walking away but lost purpose midway into the thought.

'Why do you keeping saying divorce, divorce, divorce?' she protested. '*I did not say anything about divorce.*'

She now asked herself whether the venue, chosen in good faith, was a mistake. She regretted having started the discussion with the hostel. But she was unsure that she would have been able to get to it later.

'I called you here because, yes, I did want to show I love you,' she said, surprising them both with the word. 'But it is too difficult for me in that house. I cannot dissolve like' – she cracked into a slight smile – 'like sugar in mil—' and they both giggled, inappropriately, for a second.

The sobering was stark.

'I cannot recognise you sometimes. I cannot even recognise myself. My mind fills up with petty thoughts. Sometimes I feel I cannot breathe. I need time. I need to keep working. Where should I go but a hostel?'

Feel I cannot breathe! So affronted was he by the severity of her feelings he wished to counter with comparable overstatement, but nothing at all could match it.

He looked very hurt.

She looked out into the rain.

Steeling himself, he brought himself to check: 'Is there someone else?'

The question embarrassed her. For although purely in the realm of friendship, yes she had been concealing.

'No, there isn't,' Smt Chitol replied, not lying.

He willingly overlooked her pause.

'Then what is it?' he asked softly.

She took a deep breath.

'The last six–eight months have been very difficult for me. How do you think I feel when I hear about how I didn't...' she could not bear to be more specific, 'how I didn't look after myself?'

He went quiet for a while.

'How do you think I feel that we even stopped trying?' he said at last, eyes of fragile pride barely concealing a splintering heart.

It is not that they were supposed to be trying or not. But it was the only form in which he could confess to the combination of humiliation and sorrow and desperation he felt after her physical withdrawal.

His grievance embarrassed her further. She returned to hers.

'How do you think I feel lying in that compartment when I have my periods? That I have to rush my sanitaries out of the house as if they'll explode.'

'I don't know why you do that. I've told you so many times. One time Mummy made a comment and you took it to an extreme.'

'You won't understand. You have always lived in your own house. You don't know what it is to feel blame in another.'

'Why do you say *another*? It is your home too.'

She was determined not to be defeated on the integration issue.

'Not in the same way. No matter what, I will never have the same independence as you. What is the point of working hard if I can't get this much freedom?'

'You don't *have* to work,' he said, perhaps from the momentum of retaliation, at any rate not unsympathetically. 'You are tired. You can take a break.'

Something about this statement dumbfounded Smt Chitol.

He moved on to the business of having to defend his parents. He resolved to do so without pointing fingers at her, at the quick pride, the flashes of superiority, even a certain gracelessness that she could sometimes wield, almost exclusively, upon them.

'They have their drawbacks, I don't deny. They are far from perfect. Think about the adjustments they have made too. Accepted a love marriage without any questions. Accepted someone from a different community, no objections. Allowed you to do whatever work –'

'Am I a child? Why should I be allowed or not allowed? Anyway, you weren't there when she stood in the door blocking my path, doesn't matter if she told you she was only worried about me. And if you know how many times she has suggested that I give up this position, especially after…' she trailed off again.

'They *do* think about your well-being. Whatever she did then was totally wrong. But whenever you get the chance, you also take the wrong meaning. If there's a good or bad way of looking, you will choose the bad.'

Listening to her husband she felt him a suitable candidate for arranged marriage. She wondered, not for the first time, why he had simply not gone along with one. Why take a shot at love? Whenever this had occurred to her in the past, however, she considered whether her mother might have conjectured similarly about her father. That made her take a more nuanced view.

Here the waiter inexplicably brought food and put it before them. Nimish stared at it in incomprehension: how had she managed to place an order in all this? The fried idli and ketchup sat there like a particularly tasteless joke. It occurred to him to do something dramatic with the food, push his plate towards her perhaps, or at the other end of the scale, do something exceptionally tender. But the thought merely dulled his outrage to great sadness. Steam rose from the sambar. Neither of them reached for the food. Its presence on the table lent the meeting an absurd semblance of normalcy.

'I told you we would look at the house issue, promise,' he entreated her. 'But don't hold it over my head like this.'

'For a long time I wanted us to find our home, our own way in the world,' she responded. These parts she had rehearsed. 'But to know that I would have taken you out from your environment, your home, your duties – not that we would ignore our duties to the family. In fact, just the opposite, we would make ourselves more capable of fulfilling them, live out of everyone's shadow and find our own ways of doing things. To know I have taken you away from all that and be seen as the cause, that would be the opposite of freedom.'

The rebuff, stated in these righteous terms, silenced him a long time.

'Your whole problem,' he commented frankly, 'is that you think of yourself as alone, one.'

'That is not true,' she said, biting back a tear.

Watching her made him feel terrible. And somewhere in the back of his mind he had always harboured a worry about the karmic repercussions of his disappearance all those years ago.

'I am sorry,' he said.

'Oh,' said Smt Chitol, unexpectedly flushed with affection.

When he resumed the defence it was with a nervous, uncertain energy. He listed instances, not outright accusatory, which nevertheless showed her voluntarily incomplete integration or her suboptimal behaviour, such as during *that* Diwali. She could scarcely accept that hers was supposed to have been the questionable conduct then, but to start a political discussion felt at once too pertinent and too superfluous. He carried on, making his case with hedging propulsion, now suggesting how little she was expected to do at home – when, in fact, she did not feel like pointing out, it was that she was not trusted with doing more, not in her own way anyhow. Briefly she felt her confidence dipping. What he told were not lies. It could be that her complaints were petty, her dissatisfactions unreasonable, her plan unnecessary, and she ought to be ready if not to bow her head in shame at least settle for an honourable stalemate. At the same time, what he spoke was designed to survive an argument and to her mind there was no argument any more. Once she had felt something deep within her, it was impossible for her to unfeel it. As she had done close to this spot a few years ago, Smt Chitol considered the not having of one's heart in something a most valuable instinct. She saw suddenly that she was very bored of all these things he had never said.

Equally, she could sense his panic, and the scenarios unravelling in his mind, and how far those concerns and ways to rectify them were from the heart of her alienation. She did not, at the moment, possess the capacity to reason out her true experience.

'I will not be able to do it,' she said. 'I will not be able to come home tonight.'

He was not entirely sure what happened next, because within moments his wife of three years had stood up, come across to kiss him on his head and gone off into the rain. Instantly the waiter was over with the bill and was annoyed to find the food untouched; all the same, he slapped it down on the table.

The rain had diminished to a drizzle. The wind bore along the light raindrops uncharacteristically, like paper planes, gliding them into the eyes and mouths of walkers where they burst deliciously. Here is a present for you. And you, and you and you.

To some, the facts that Smt Chitol had found herself a hostel, had readied a bag with her things, planned for all that went into these preparations, may indicate a calculating heart, but afterwards it was precisely these arrangements she was proud of. Going in to meet her husband she had been willing to change her mind and she came out of it in near disbelief. If she had not made preparations she would have had no opportunity to exercise her daring.

Through the commuter crossfire of Churchgate she pressed on, by the route she had once known as routine, via the urine-laced pedestrian street beside the Western Railway headquarters, cutting through the great maidans by way of Fashion Street, towards the distant dome, crested by Lady of Progress, of the Victoria Terminus, where her life always began again. All the while her thundering heart barely slowed, her disbelief barely ebbed.

The office had emptied out by the time she got there. The tubelights were switched off; in the gloom the odd punching machine sounded ghostly. She sat on a chair, tossed back her head and stared at the ceiling fan. It stirred to life intermittently, by dint of wind rather than electricity. Now at rest in damp clothes, she felt she might sneeze and when she did she startled herself.

Once she was completely alone, she walked across to a telephone. She dialled P and told him she would not see him or speak to him for a while. Clicking the receiver down on its cradle she felt liberated and honest.

She made further calculations, about the tapering off of rush hour versus her arrival time at the hostel. Having decided to wait longer, she found herself pulling out her duffel bag and backpack from the common cupboard and leaving well before the agreed time, by a train route also intimately familiar, since she boarded the Harbour, disembarking at Chunabhatti, and in this way felt at home even while going away from it. And still her disbelief, a tepid form of shock, stayed with her, and it persisted as she took possession of her room.

Smt Chitol's new living quarters were a single-seater laid with peach ceramic tiles, attached with a bathroom given to a different shade of peach tile. It was the first *en suite* bathroom of her life; the foreign words emphasised the decadence, and she went in and out of it with novel abandon, relieving herself on the Western commode with the door wide open. She opened up the windows, her bag, the cupboard, and began populating it with her things, as if arranging somebody else's life.

Halfway in she threw herself backwards on the bed and closed her eyes. Her husband's face at parting kept appearing before her, now him popping the morning paan into his mouth and performing the jig on the footpath. Tears leaked into her ears, tickling them.

What is wrong with me? she asked herself silently. I will be all right, she replied. I have myself, I have the railway lines and railway people, I have uncountable others, said she who was always aware of the power of latent ideas.

She lay a while in loneliness.

After some time she opened the door and peered out into the tungsten corridor, walled with lizard and prey. At its end the matron's helper leaned forward on a plastic chair, applying mirrorless lipstick. When Smt Chitol's eyes met hers she looked caught, and they laughed.

9
Chitol's census

Much of the year 1992 Smt Chitol spent out on the railway lines. She did nothing by correspondence that could be done in person. When the slightest doubt arose, she seized the chance to 'go to the spot without notice', never mind that said spot was two thousand kilometres away.

In the case of deceased parcel porter Jodu Basumatary, it was observed that the difference in age between the son applying for an appointment and his mother back home was a mere nine years. Was it clerical error? Impersonation? A multiplicity of wives? To find out she clambered across the country on the Lohit Mail, alighted north of the Brahmaputra, and in a green paddy field under horizonless blue skies found herself chasing Akasi Boro in her orange-yellow dokhona, telling her, no, she was not a police inspector but a *welfare* inspector, this had nothing to do with the statehood agitation or underground groups.

In the matter of Shambhu Bhagiwant, the discrepancy was that one certificate showed him not as Mahadeo Koli (Scheduled Tribe in his state of ordinary residence) but Koli (not a Scheduled Tribe in his state of ordinary residence). Into Ahmednagar district she travelled in pursuit, hitching a bullock-cart ride for the final stretch, to quiz the village panchayat and the family, who had for generations been jambul sellers until Shambhu secured a government job.

As for gonorrhoeally deceased booking clerk Brij Mohan, it was brought to the administration's notice, three years after he perished, that the older brother of the deceased had presented *his* wife as the wife of the deceased to avail of benefits. Off Smt Chitol went to Khandwa. There she met Lalita, who said she was the true wife and her brother-in-law was a tyrant, he did what he liked, forced her to do many things. He forced me. *Jabardasti* was the word she used, lingered on it with stony tears.

In the non-hermetic sealing of second-class ordinary sleeper, where she had developed the skill to write in locomotion while remaining legible to herself, she put down heartfelt accounts of her cases and carefully detailed every person in them. It might be said that it was on the strength of these that she did not wither and she did not wilt. She felt implicated in situations and lives, theirs illuminated hers, by contrast or concurrence; they expanded her mind and her spirit, her very heart. In her early days as a railway employee she had established that for the secure feeling you must stay within the boundaries of what you are required to know. She rebelled against this idea that kept one a fool. She recalled what retired dy.c.p.o. Sinha had posited all those years ago, that every person on average harboured five to seven grievances at any given point of time – so if you could understand the approximately hundred million grievances of all seventeen lakh railway employees, from chairman to cinderwoman, why, you could understand the life of the entire country! She felt close to the country, to life itself, and the nutrients of the physically resilient life, the life of emotional survival, of mental curiosity, seep into one another, feed the whole like the elements do a tree.

In the evenings she began to frequent AAA – for, yes, she discovered another such initialism, this one a seepage- and silverfish-ridden room at the back of a building off Gokhale Road. Despite the first A in its name, Smt Chitol had expected scholars at the Amateur Anthropologists Association (Bombay Chapter) (the only chapter), but most comers were indeed passionate amateurs, from entirely unrelated fields, among them a retired permanent-way inspector on Western Railway who remarked to her, as if compelled against his wishes to state the obvious, that it was 'but natural' a person from the Railways should be here.

Upon a mossy parapet the amateur anthropologists enthused, in fact rather like the railway enthusiasts who could identify a locomotive's home-shed and manufacture-year by 'her' livery and by her number list all the important services she had ever run. Where the rail amateurs planned rail-fanning trips, these amateurs thought up anthropological expeditions, say to the Andamans or the Lushai Hills; they contested with one another the number of ethnicities in the Northeast, or, here Smt Chitol contributed, whether the country had sixteen hundred or eighteen hundred languages as per the general census and how many of those would be for minor variations in spelling or dialect.

Inside, books, journals and cyclostyled sheaves lay heaped upon slotted-angle iron racks. She pored over the volumes, collecting communities like some gone-case colonial gazetteer. She acquainted herself with as wide a selection as she could, from the Brus of Mizoram to the Bakarwals of Kashmir. On the Asurs, who had sheltered her family in their hour of need, she came upon an article challenging the orthodox anthropologies written so far, which made no mention of Mahishasur, the noble Adivasi king and buffalo herd whom the tribe considered their ancestor, slain unfairly by Durga and depicted as a demon speared through the heart in the tableaux of Durga Puja, observed by some Asurs in mourning, pierced in their own hearts. This gave her much to think about. In a sociological tract about a predominantly Hindu village she studied the clinically delineated commensal relations – that is who could take what food in what form in what vessel from whom – between and among its sixteen castes striated into sixty-two sub-castes: the village was close to Bhombalpur, so great was her ignorance.

She concluded she knew nothing. Her head ached, overwhelmed by the inexhaustibility of the country. Hereabouts it occurred to Smt Chitol that had she shown such determination in college in these very subjects she might need not be here now. She decided she might find a way to finish that degree after all, start filling in dot by dot the canvas of her remarkable ignorance. This time the thought did not tire her. She could get to it – there were so many things to get to!

To be sure, many were the times Smt Chitol sank into despair and dreariness. It took her a whole lot of time and precious tears to overcome the loneliness of her en suite hostel room. She steeped herself in her guilts, her self-pities and indignations, all the mistakes she had made in her life and all the mistakes made by life to her. She was thirty-four years old and her actual life was a maelstrom, everything she did was an escape from that, and her inspection became tainted by self-involvement, tinged with cynicism, and what was the point, and she suspected that like Rulemaster Chitnis she was, due to the nature of life, becoming a negative person.

Dear N, Sometimes I feel so alone in this huge country ... she began a letter to her husband and did not send it. Her meetings and phone conversations with him and them had tended towards dreadful, so that she could not see any other way out but living her current life, and as a result of her actions it was a real possibility that she would be left 'high and dry'. She made sure, however, to recover the jewellery she had taken into the house (but not that which they had gifted her) and the most-important miniature clothes horse, which brightened up her room immensely.

As stillness is the greatest journey so motion felt the only stillness. Up and down her beat ranged Smt Chitol, Masjid through Chunabhatti. Every day some encounter or other lit up sparks in her misery, at least one situation challenged her capacity, concentrated her mind and her heart. Vicissitudes were everywhere, every single where. If she did not have a long-distance matter at hand, she was not averse to ferreting out a pending case, a forgotten case, a case in limbo, to hit the rails again.

One trip she shared a compartment with an itinerant Buddhist nun travelling to Bodh Gaya. The journey was shambolic for the common reasons – delays, overcrowding, the unreserved spreading into reserved coaches, cockroaches strewn about like litchi seeds, toilets running out of water, excreta showing up in unforgettable places. Through it all the delightful bhikkhuni maintained a disposition so equanimous it could have been role-playing. All who came to her with questions, harangues and appeals for guidance, she dealt with gentleness and generosity and just enough words. Asked about the renunciate life, she laughed that the most difficult renunciation of all is the barrier between oneself and others. On this point Smt Chitol reflected the entire time and long afterwards. The simplicity of the idea shocked her. Unattainably true. Of extraordinary beauty. It gave her impetus to keep on.

Everywhere around her people, people, people, people like raindrops. She used to think that lonelinesses lock into one another – how very teenage! (Even if she was twenty at the time.) She considered whether instead it was the opennesses that embraced one another. As another tended to plants, collected bus tickets or sang kirtans, so Smt Chitol wrote people. With styles she experimented. She could be telegrammatic, florid, prosaic, on occasion very parametric and censal; she wished to be crisp and feasible. Sometimes all she had was a name and a date. Sometimes a place and a community. At other times she made beautiful lengthy compositions, rich with dialogue and cultural discovery, unseen by us all. She dipped into past people, the Kachnars among whom she had spent seismic days and exchanged eternal friendship; the lady who had cared for her on the runaway train; the flaming moustache who supplied her the transformational advice *palti kar dene ka*; the bug-eyed girl who so nicely guided her through women's hostels; she recalled the fine people, the exemplars, the repulsive ones, the innocuous, the women of astonishing courage she had met on her case trails. If one was to look back there was no limit to the people in her life, and in turn to each of their lives. She marvelled at this phenomenon she had not attended to all these years. Sometimes she was touched by a strain of patriotic fervour. *The country linked by the permanent way,* she jotted down, *people holding one another by the hand, like flanges gripping the rail.* Long were Smt Chitol's hours of journeying, long were her hours of waiting, long were her nights in the hostel. She hummed the wanderer's song bittersweetly, *Strangers have become my own, My own have become the other!*

Late in the year she went to see her brothers. In Chandigarh Anando, who with his wife reared a tiny potbelly and two stray pups, also rearing tiny potbellies; in Calcutta Dhrubo, who as a prelude to acquiring a bride of status contemplated fashioning himself backwards into a Chatterjee, when she told him about their mother's letters and flung him into reconsideration. She informed them both in person what she had only hinted in correspondence, of her estrangement, which may or may not be permanent.

From Calcutta she travelled to Bhombalpur, on its last legs as a workshop town but on fresh legs as a junction town. The streets were plastered with Learn English and Lose Weight-Gain Height advertisements, and in the windows of Lalji's Gramophone & Recordings glowed a television set fitted with a cable connection that drew a spectating crowd.

The railway colony had acquired the decrepit charisma of a wartime facility peacetime forgot. She visited their old quarters which, though not officially condemned, lay abandoned. The garden was clouded with violet lantana, the pipes and discolouring brick walls were run over with climbing vines and strenuous young peepal. The chicken-wire gate had kept its form. Raising the rusted throw-over latch, she pushed the gate across the ground that Dhrubo used to paw in another age and proceeded inside. Slowly she cased the quarters, startling the lizards when she opened the lavatory door. The shed leaves and flowers of the madhumalati, closing down for the season, she lifted in her hands and brought to her face. She peered through the vertical iron bars into her childhood, much as she would have done as a girl during the time of the tragedy. Then she left, guiding the throw-latch back in place over the gate.

She went to the rocks; they were still there. She visited Salima's old quarters, occupied by the family of a fitter from Munger, with whom she drank a leisurely cup of tea (and afterwards reproduced paragraphs of conversation).

At the mission she asked for Pearl Flanger. After a while a bent old lady came out and asked her name. 'I see,' the frail voice told her. 'You must be Mr Chitol's daughter.' She nodded. 'Pearl passed on last year.' 'Oh. I'm sorry, I'm very sorry,' said Smt Chitol. 'I brought this for her. It is from the fence between our quarters.' 'Ah, she did always like the Rangoon creeper,' said the old lady, studying the flowers nestled in their leaves. 'Come on through that gate to the back, dear, you can offer them.'

At the Institute she returned a copy of *To Kill a Mockingbird* eighteen years, six months, one week and two days after the due date. Rather than a fine, she attracted a book of self-published Bangla poems from a charmed young librarian with shapely eyebrows.

She spent a happy night at the subordinate's rest house, smiling when she heard the jackals through her sleep. Early in the morning she took a long birdsung walk. The honest cold brightened into a fresh sunshot winter day she knew by heart. As she wandered about the township that at the time she ran away had felt so restrictive but she could now understand as something modern and sincere, she experienced the same intense homely attachment to the earth and shine her father had in his final days, as those before the railway colony must have had to the village pastures, and those before to the forests of sal and mahua and trees we may never know. She collected her bags and went to the railway station and waited, one more time, for a train to Bombay.

Additional platforms and an overbridge had come up at the recent junction, high on filth, busy beyond her childhood imagination; from her spot she could no longer view the siding that had carried away the grains to the township during the famine.

Down-platform a group waited for the same train as her, she was sure, since dressed in blue and white, and tomorrow was December the sixth – Babasaheb Ambedkar's death anniversary, for which lakhs converged every year in Bombay, frustrating the station superintendents at Victoria Terminus with nights on the concourse, the gorgeous rangolis that came and went with them, the praise songs of electrifying power boding equal days. And now they started to sing, rehearsing new compositions she conjectured, accompanied by tambourines that made the sounds shiver in the air. And here, such being the simultaneity of the country, went coachfuls of saffron chanting *One more push that's all, the Babri mosque will fall!* towards Ayodhya, as they had been for weeks, for the big volunteer service tomorrow, the sixth of December.

Waiting on the bench, she grew absorbed in the activities of the staff: a rather punctilious-looking pointsman with rectilinear hair and flags rolled up tight as batons under his armpit, the contemplative trackman with his tools, the platform sweeper with her broom against too much to do, the garrulous guard who climbed off to look at the brake pipe, scratching his head, the loco driver leaning out of his cabin to shout something to him, spit-bombing crimson midstream, the people of the Indian Railways, of whom she was, without whom, according to *how could I forget retd c.p.o. Harsharan Singh Bedi! – khatri Sikh, born Multan, present-day Pakistan, beard in net, toothaches addressed by cloves, legaches by midgets* – without whom there will be no India. There being no India was a comedic thought. Yet watching the trains pull in and out, the crissing and crossing, thousands of people making their way, their hearts in transit, their languages on the go, their origin stories, mythologies and migrations and conquests possibly in stark conflict with those of another, the gods and heroes of one the demons and villains of another, she became vividly sentimental and felt sensationally alive.

Over the past months she had lost some weight, and her cheekbones seemed to radiate a shadow upwards, as though lit from below. Her lumbar-long hair was coiled into a bun, her sari was crisp with leftover starch; her soles were worn with walk. The straps of her backpack impressed into her shoulders a great many written people, a disorderly bunch which only had in common that their lives had crossed hers, flickering upon each other the miracle of their journeys, like travellers on a train to who knows where, but somewhere, certainly somewhere; and pressing on her worn heel, into the song of the rail climbed Charulata Chitol, who had wanted to count people.

Acknowledgements

My debt to all in the Indian Railways and beyond who opened their doors, spent time with me, entertained esoteric queries, shared material, is profound and permanent.

Thank you to Bharatiya Vidya Bhavan for permission to quote, on page 153, from Kamala Subramaniam's *Mahabharata*; to Orient Longman for a line, on page 318, of Priya Adarkar's translation of a Vamandada Kardak poem published in *Poisoned Bread*, and to Arjun Dangle for sending me the Marathi original, *'Pendyala Salant Ghala'*. The epigraph is from Shantideva's *A Guide to the Bodhisattva's Way of Life*, translated by Stephen Batchelor, published by the Library of Tibetan Works and Archives. The Urdu line on page 42 is Ameer Minai's. The lines quoted on page 76 are in Robert Louis Stevenson's 'From a Railway Carriage'. The lyrics of a Bangla song that appear on page 69 are from Salil Chowdhury's *'Ami Jharer Kachhe Rekhe Gelam'* (translation mine). A line each on page 158 and page 399 are from the song *'Ami Ek Jajabar'*, Bhupen Hazarika/Shibdas Banerjee (translations mine). In other instances, the source of a quote is indicated in the text.

I'm immensely grateful to Srinath Perur and Nandini Mehta for reading the manuscript.

For their belief and their expertise, extreme gratitude to Paul Baggaley, Sivapriya R, Callie Garnett and Ragavendra Maripudi, as well as to Francisco Vilhena, Katherine Fry, Rahul Srivastava, Jaishree Ram Mohan and Amy Whitaker, and to everyone at Bloomsbury involved with the book.

Deep love and gratitude, as ever, to my mother and my sister, and my late father.

Unlimited and, frankly, inexpressible thanks to Shruti Debi, my primary reader and editor, literary agent and lighthouse, for shepherding *Railsong* through the stages even as she did, we do, our two young girls. Crazy about y'all.

A Note on the Author

Rahul Bhattacharya is a writer, journalist and editor. His first novel, *The Sly Company of People Who Care*, won the Royal Society of Literature Ondaatje Prize and was shortlisted for the Man Asian Literary Prize. *Pundits from Pakistan*, his first book, was a *Wisden Cricketer* top ten cricket book of all time. He was born in Bombay and lives in Delhi with his wife and two daughters.

A Note on the Type

The text of this book is set in Linotype Stempel Garamond, a version of Garamond adapted and first used by the Stempel foundry in 1924. It is one of several versions of Garamond based on the designs of Claude Garamond. It is thought that Garamond based his font on Bembo, cut in 1495 by Francesco Griffo in collaboration with the Italian printer Aldus Manutius. Garamond types were first used in books printed in Paris around 1532. Many of the present-day versions of this type are based on the *Typi Academiae* of Jean Jannon cut in Sedan in 1615.

Claude Garamond was born in Paris in 1480. He learned how to cut type from his father and by the age of fifteen he was able to fashion steel punches the size of a pica with great precision. At the age of sixty he was commissioned by King Francis I to design a Greek alphabet, and for this he was given the honourable title of royal type founder. He died in 1561.